The True History of
Jack the Ripper

The True History of

Jack the Ripper

The Forgotten 1905 Ripper Novel

GUY LOGAN

with additional material by Jan Bondeson

AMBERLEY

First published 2013

Amberley Publishing
The Hill, Stroud
Gloucestershire, GL5 4EP

www.amberley-books.com

British Library Cataloguing in Publication Data.
A catalogue record for this book is available from the British Library.

ISBN 978 1 4456 1388 8

Typesetting and Origination by Amberley Publishing.
Printed in the UK.

Contents

Preface

When looking through some bound volumes of *The Illustrated Police News* in late 2011, I was surprised to find, serialised in the volumes for 1905 and 1906, a previously unknown novel about Jack the Ripper, never published in book form. It was written by the journalist Guy Logan, of whose later career as a distinguished author of true crime books in the 1920s and 1930s I was already aware. What did Guy Logan know about Jack the Ripper, and what made him write this extraordinary novel, the earliest full-length English-language fictional treatment of the notorious Whitechapel Murders?

1

The Early Life & Opinions of Guy Logan

Guy Bertie Harris Logan was born in St Leonards-on-Sea, Sussex, in July 1869. He was the only son of Captain George Eugene Logan and his wife Louisa. Guy had a sister, one year older, named Eugenie May, and another one year younger, named Violet.[1] The Logan family was quite a distinguished one: Guy's great-grandfather was Walter Logan Esq., of Fingalton, Renfrewshire, a wealthy and influential squire and businessman. His grandfather was Major-General George Logan, of the old Indian Army, who had married Eugenia Emma Harris, the granddaughter of the distinguished soldier Lord Harris. At the time of the 1871 census, George Eugene and Louisa Logan, born in Madras and Gibraltar respectively, lived in Colchester with their three children and two servants.

George Eugene Logan had served in the Indian Mutiny, not without distinction. But he seems to have tired of Army life already in the 1870s, planning to retire on half-pay to pursue a civilian career. George Eugene left the 2nd Dragoon Guards and became a Brevet Major in the 12th Foot for a while, before retiring on half-pay in 1873. He never achieved much in his brief civilian career, however, since he died suddenly and unexpectedly, from an aortic aneurysm, when visiting his mother at Hampton Court in February 1875. Louisa Logan was now alone with three children, and although she had her husband's Army pension, her circumstances in life must have become seriously straitened after the untimely death of the family breadwinner. Although there had once been a good deal of money in the Logan family, little of it appears to have come the way of George Eugene and his family.

After George's untimely death, Louisa Logan moved to London with her children. Already as a schoolboy, Guy took a strong interest in London's criminal history. After school, he made excursions to look for houses where famous murders had taken place. Setting out from the Bloomsbury lodging house where the Logan family had secured a gloomy asylum, young Guy went to see No. 11 Montague Place, where old Mrs Jeffs had been murdered by a mystery assailant in 1828, and No. 12 Great Coram Street, site of the unsolved murder of Harriet Buswell on Christmas Eve 1872.

In 1879 there was sensation when an old lady in Richmond, Mrs Julia Thomas, was murdered by her servant Kate Webster. The horrid circumstances of the murder, with the harmless old woman being brutally done to death by her sturdy, muscular domestic, who then proceeded to dismember the body with a chopper and boil it in the kitchen copper, made a great impression on young Guy. He of course went to No. 2 Vine Cottages (today

No. 9 Park Road), Richmond, where the murder had taken place, to admire this famous murder house. When a friendly aunt took Guy to Madame Tussauds, he shocked her by demanding an immediate descent to the Chamber of Horrors, to which an effigy of Kate Webster had recently been added. As Guy himself later expressed it,

My depraved interest in the models of the notorious criminals was such, I have been told, that it was with difficulty I was persuaded to return to the 'central transept', where the waxen kings, queens, and other celebrities held court. I could not be induced to come away from Kate Webster, whose image I regarded with fascinated horror. There, in front of me and as large as life, was the waxen counterfeit of the dread woman whose crime had caused such a stir, and who looked capable, in my youthful imagination, of boiling half a dozen mistresses in as many choppers.[2]

'I well remember, being a lad at the time, the excitement occasioned by what was called "The Euston Square Mystery".' Thus wrote Guy Logan many years later, referring to the murder of Miss Matilda Hacker at No. 4 Euston Square, kept by a mysterious foreigner named Severin Bastendorff. Guy had himself seen the future murder victim, an eccentric old lady who 'was a conspicuous figure in her youthful finery, flaxen curls, and high-heeled shoes, and was, I am afraid, a constant source of enjoyment to the mischievous boys of the neighbourhood, who made her the butt of their misplaced humour'.[3] Guy left it unstated whether he wolf-whistled and exclaimed, 'Cor blimey! 'Ere's one of the chorus girls!' when he passed the hapless Miss Hacker, or if he merely enjoyed a quiet chuckle at her expense; given his genteel upbringing, one would expect the latter.

In 1877, Miss Hacker disappeared, and nobody appears to have missed her or instituted a search. Two years later, her remains were found in a disused coal cellar at No. 4 Euston Square. She had been stabbed and then strangled, and her former bedroom at the premises had a large bloodstain on the floorboards. Since it turned out that Hannah Dobbs, a former servant in the lodging house, had been selling Miss Hacker's belongings, she was tried for the murder, but acquitted. As Guy would later put it, the Bastendorff ménage was a very queer one indeed: Hannah had been seduced by Severin, before 'carrying on' with his younger brother Peter. Either of these two dodgy, bushy-bearded foreigners, both of them natives of Luxembourg, is likely to have been the accomplice of Hannah Dobbs. No. 4 Euston Square became one of London's most notorious murder houses. In 1880, the inhabitants of the southern part of this square successfully petitioned that their part should be renamed Endsleigh Gardens, as it still is today. This is one of just a few instances of a gruesome murder changing the name of a London street in Victorian times. The haunted murder house at No. 4 Euston Square kept its sinister reputation for many decades to come, until it became a victim of the rebuilding of Euston station in the early 1960s.

Another of young Guy's favourite crime-related outings was to visit the famous murder house of Denham, near Uxbridge in Buckinghamshire, where the tramp John Owen had wiped out the entire Marshall family, seven people in all, in a bloodbath. Some locals 'in the know' gave Guy a guided tour of the site, which he would never forget. The peaceful, rustic cottage looked nothing like a sinister murder house, but there was no denying its fearful history. The dismal murderer Owen was later captured in Reading, found guilty of murder and executed in Aylesbury in August 1870.

*

The 1881 census finds the thirty-two-year-old Louisa Logan at No. 3 Peak Hill Avenue, Lewisham (the house still stands). She no longer had any servant. The children, Eugenie, Guy and Violet, aged twelve, eleven and ten, are all listed as 'scholars'. There is no record of Guy attending a private school, but by some stratagem or other, his mother made sure that he received a good education. As an adult, Guy would write good English, read French without difficulty, and display excellent general knowledge. He was a keen student of the works of William Shakespeare and Charles Dickens, and of poets in the school of Thomas Hood and Richard Harris Barham. But there was not enough money for Louisa Logan to even consider sending Guy to university or allowing him to follow the example of his father and grandfather and become an Army officer. After leaving school, Guy was apprenticed to a clerk.

After a few years of clerking, Guy had enough. There must be something more interesting in life than such drudgery, he seems to have reasoned, and after some consideration, he decided to join the Army as a private soldier. Perhaps he hoped to go to war, rise in the ranks, and earn his spurs as an officer, thus joining his distinguished forebears. The Commanding Officer of the London recruiting centre thought him 'a very good lad, son of an officer formerly in the Buffs' and on 7 January 1891, Guy signed up for Short Service in the Royal Artillery, namely seven years with the Colours, and five years in the Reserves. According to Army records, he was 5 feet 8¼ inches tall and weighed 128 lbs. He had fair complexion, dark-brown hair and blue eyes.

Gunner Logan was sent to the Artillery Barracks at Portsmouth, where he must have received some serious square-bashing from the angry, red-faced sergeant-majors. He was assigned to No. 31 Battery of the Southern Division of the Royal Artillery, and taken for long and gruelling marches round the Portsmouth artillery grounds, carrying a full load of equipment. During one of these exercises, on 7 April 1891, Guy plumbed a novel low in his career by deserting from the Army, after just three months of service. He cunningly hid in some bushes, and the others did not notice that he was missing until it was too late. After the soldiers had been counted in by their superiors, a search was made, but the agile young Guy had successfully absconded from the artillery grounds. When Gunner Logan was court-martialled *in absentia* on 2 May, it was noted, with disapproval, that he had stolen his uniform, boots and equipment, and that he was still missing. The close description of the deserter, quoted above, was made use of to track him down, but the Army did not bother much about a few soldiers deserting in peacetime, and the hue and cry for Guy did not persist for very long.

One does not need to be a close student of male psychology to suspect that the reason for Guy's sudden decision to leave the Army, for good, must surely be wearing skirts. And indeed, our hero had barely dodged the search parties of the Royal Artillery when he married, on 11 June 1891, Miss Melville Stroud, the daughter of a Staines publican. On his marriage certificate, the twenty-two-year-old Guy rather grandly describes himself as being of independent means, and the son of a major in the 2nd Dragoon Guards. His oddly named wife was one year younger, and by profession a barmaid.

*

Although Guy's mother and grandmother may well have helped the young couple, Guy and Melville had very little in the way of independent means to command. They settled down at a cheap lodging house in Kingston-upon-Thames. The ever-optimistic Guy rather fancied himself as an actor, but he could only get miserably paid 'extra' parts. He also began dabbling in journalism, writing about celebrated crimes, and reporting on trials and horse races. A graduate of the Tom and Jerry school of journalism, he learnt his job as he went along. Already in the 1890s, he became associated with *The Illustrated Police News*, a sensationalist newspaper that mainly dealt with crime and criminals. It had existed since 1863, and was still going strong in the 1890s, when it expanded its number of pages and broadened its contents. When there was a scarcity of murders and other sanguinary outrages, *The Illustrated Police News* sometimes published features on celebrated historical crimes, written by Guy Logan and other impecunious penny-a-line journalists.

In March 1893, Guy was in Liverpool, representing a London morning newspaper. The celebrated murder house at No. 20 Leveson Street, where John Gleeson Wilson had dispatched Mrs Henrichson and her two children in a bloodbath back in 1849, had since been converted to a small hotel. Although the street had been renamed Upper Grenville Street after the murders, Guy found the hotel and booked a room there to have a poke around, and to study the landlord's scrapbook about the murders. When Guy went to see a friendly police inspector to have a chat about Liverpool's criminal history, he received a hint that if he went to Rainhill straight away, he 'might pick up something in the way of startling news'. And indeed, when Guy arrived on the scene, he found out that the bodies of a woman and four children had been found under the floorboards of a house called Dinham Villa. Guy literally had to fight his way through a wildly excited crowd of people outside the house. Producing the card of his friend the police inspector, he was allowed to see the house. He learnt from the police that the victims were suspected to be the wife and children of a man named Deeming, alias Brooks, who had absconded.[4]

Returning to his Kennington Road lodgings in triumph after his unexpected Liverpool scoop about Deeming the mass murderer, Guy was dismayed to find that his wife Melville had deserted him, for good, taking their infant son Eustace with her. Making inquiries, Guy found that she was living with an Australian named Harry Verner, as his 'wife'. If Guy had been the hero of one of his own future novels, he would have purchased a horsewhip, thrashed the Antipodean interloper within inches of his life, and frogmarched the errant Melville back to Kennington Road. But in real life, there is nothing to suggest that Guy even contemplated such rash heroics; although Melville was living openly with her Australian lover, poor Guy could do nothing about it.

The unexpected breakdown of his marriage must have been a serious blow to Guy and his self-esteem. But still, he remained a member of bohemian London's sub-literary and thespian circles, hobnobbing with his fellow journalists and actors. In the autumn of 1893, Guy was invited to a dinner party at the lodging house at No. 11 Montague Place, where one of his fellow thespians was living. As Guy well knew, this was one of London's most celebrated murder houses, where Elizabeth Jeffs had been murdered by an unknown assailant back in 1828. As Guy himself later expressed it,

> We had an excellent dinner, but at the sweets stage I completely ruined the harmony of the repast by more or less innocently remarking, 'Talking about past crimes' – no one had been talking about them but by the way! – 'I dare say no one present has knowledge of the fact that a brutal murder was once committed in the kitchen of this very house!' Grim silence, of the kind that can be felt, followed this auspicious preamble; but, regardless of the scared looks of the lady boarders, and the frigid frowns of the landlady, I plunged into a full account of the sensational murder of Mrs Jeffs, and unfolded, for the general edification, a truly harrowing tale. That dinner party broke up 'in most admired disorder'.

But when Guy next met his actor friend, this individual looked most gloomy, reproachfully exclaiming,

> 'A nice thing you did for me with your sanguinary tales! I was ordered to leave the very next day, which was deuced inconvenient, I can tell you, and Mrs B— hasn't got a boarder left. Why can't you leave your beastly murders to yourself?' Which was all the thanks I got for entertaining [?] the guests on that memorable night in a certain house in Montague Place, Bedford Square.[5]

Throughout 1893 and 1894, Guy Logan kept struggling as an actor and journalist. He hammed it out on stage in various minor parts, and attended criminal trials and racecourse meetings in search of copy. He made sure that from the early 1890s onwards, he did not miss any trial for murder at the Old Bailey. In 1895, Guy decided to try his hand as a playwright. He wrote a two-act comedy entitled *Up the River*, with music composed by a certain Dr Storer.[6] In the last minute, the title had to be changed to *An Actor's Frolic* since Guy had forgotten to check and discovered that there was already a comic opera called *Up the River*. Guy must have felt proud when his play was taken on a provincial tour by Mr Charles de Lacey's company, premièring at the Operetta House, Clacton-on Sea, on 30 September 1895. A critic from the *Era* newspaper found the plot decidedly thin: the Duchess of Spoofshire wants to arrange some society theatricals, and employs a musician named Professor Lutestring. When Lutestring falls ill, he is impersonated by the young actor Arthur Getabit. Still, the easily amused Essex theatregoers liked *An Actor's Frolic*, and they are recorded to have given it a hearty ovation.[7] In September 1896, when his comedy *A Society Scandal* premièred at South Shields, 'the young and clever author Guy Logan' was presented as the author of *His Agency*, *An Actor's Frolic* and *Sunny Sundown*. His most recent play had its plot fetched from closer to home: the diabolical villainess Nadine deserts and ruins the young London gentleman Arthur Dare, and then proceeds to blackmail a wealthy duke, armed with a bundle of compromising letters. But in Bath, a grumpy theatre critic thought Guy's new play most execrable; the most charitable criticism he could offer was that Mr Guy Logan and the composer Mr Arnold Cooke were both still young men, and that they might perchance do better in the future.[8]

Although Guy Logan does not appear to have acted in any of his own plays, one of the mainstays of his existence in the late 1890s was touring with various provincial theatrical companies. A jolly extrovert, he liked the bohemian existence of a travelling thespian. In November 1898, he hammed it out vigorously as the villain Captain Lebaudy in the seafaring drama *The Mariners of England* at the Theatre Royal, Edinburgh. A reviewer in the *Era* newspaper was much taken by this stirring patriotic play, and even noted that 'Mr Guy Logan made a vigorous villain, and threw plenty of vindictive force into his performance as Captain Lebaudy'. The year after, a reviewer in the same newspaper found Guy 'sufficiently impressive' as Sir Michael in *Lady Audley's Secret* at Her Majesty's Theatre in Aberdeen. In October 1899, he was acting manager of Mr Ernest R. Abbott's company, performing *The Mariners of England* at the Prince's Theatre in Portsmouth.[9] Guy is likely to have spent much of his time travelling between various provincial theatres. Being a second-rate actor may have been amusing for a while, but it does not make you rich: the 1901 census lists Guy as an actor, living at the Working Man's Temperance Hotel, Bevington Bush, Liverpool. The rooms at this hotel, opened in 1900 to cater for impoverished working men, cost just a penny a night, as long as you kept sober.

*

But even as poor Guy was languishing at this gloomy Liverpudlian temperance hotel, without even a chance of a drink to lift his spirits, his future had actually begun to look a little brighter. *The Illustrated Police News*, to which Guy had contributed an occasional article already in the 1890s, had changed its editorial policy; the number of pages had been increased from four to eight, and in order to bolster its contents, it began to publish sporting and boxing news, and even serialised fiction. An editorial commented that although the newspaper was now in its thirty-first year, it needed to adapt its contents to suit the modern world. In 1897, the number of pages was further increased to twelve, and regular columns like 'Doings in the Divorce Court', 'Saucy Songs' and 'Racing News' were added.

The outbreak of the Second Boer War provoked an orgy of jingoistic flag-waving in *The Illustrated Police News*. The Boers were depicted as subhuman brutes, given to strip-searching English ladies and trying out various unsporting and cowardly military ruses. *The Illustrated Police News* headlines about the Boers included gems like 'Another Wicked Boer Trick!', 'Mafeking as Plucky and Buoyant as Ever!', 'Her Majesty Graciously Receives the Wounded Boy Bugler!' and 'Another Dastardly Instance of Boer Trickery!' So why not publish a really patriotic novel about the Boer War, written by one of their staff journalists like the versatile Guy Logan? Realising that he had come on to a good thing, Guy did not mention that he had never been anywhere near South Africa, or that as a former Army deserter, he was singularly ill equipped to depict military heroism. Instead, he started writing with alacrity, since the editor of *The Illustrated Police News* wanted *Violet Kildare, A Romance of the South African War* to begin straight away. The canny Guy spent the first three weekly chapters describing the heroine's departure from her Lincolnshire home after her father's death, while he was thinking of a plot for the rest of the book.[10]

In *Violet Kildare*, the pretty and virtuous young heroine departs from home to visit her aunt in South Africa, no person objecting that this could be a trifle dangerous, since there might soon be a war on. On board ship, she meets the young gentleman Cecil Goldworthy, the son of a retired major-general who regrets his previous bohemian life, and wants to enlist in the Army as a private soldier. Violet also comes across a tall Boer named Paul Flaubert, who is a secret agent plotting to make sure war will break out. When the lustful Boer tries some hanky-panky with young Violet, Cecil comes to the rescue of the swooning heroine, manfully exclaiming, 'Release that lady! Are you man or brute?' The tall Boer replies, 'You verdoomed Englishman, I'd sjambok you if I had you across the Vaal! I'd …' But Cecil interrupts the sturdy, barrel-chested cad by striking him a tremendous blow on his glass jaw, knocking him out cold.

As Violet and her two rival admirers arrive in Cape Town, Guy provides a description straight from the guidebook:

> One beautiful morning the green Table Mountain, the Lion's Head and Rump, loomed out of the sea, and the Glenfallon Castle's voyage was over. There was Cape Town, the white villas glistening in the sun. There the lively docks, swarming with negroes, with Malays and long-limbed Englishmen. Here was South Africa at last.

But the demented Paul Flaubert is up to no good. He plots with anti-British Boers and other undesirable elements to make sure that war breaks out. He orders his henchmen to kidnap Cecil Goldworthy, and kicks him in the groin region when he is already down. But when he again attempts to molest the virtuous Violet, she is saved by the diminutive Irishman 'Patsy' Nolan, a loyal old retainer of the Kildare family. Patsy leaps over a hedge and saves the swooning heroine, but only to receive a thrashing from the Boer's sjambok (heavy leather whip).

Cecil manages to escape and joins forces with the funny 'stage Irishman' Patsy, who provides comic relief throughout the novel with his droll and earthy doings, and his frequent outcries of 'Bedad!' or 'Begorrah!' They join the Cape Mounted Rifles, and enjoy many adventures together. In Guy's version of South Africa, there are no black people, nor any African animals; the British and Boer armies are depicted as if they were out on manoeuvres near Aldershot. The British generals are wise and noble, and the soldiers honest and brave; although the Boers try various dastardly and unsporting ruses, they are slowly heading for defeat. The villain Flaubert lies and cheats, and makes use of his sjambok to discipline helpless prisoners. His aim is to abduct and ravish Violet, who works as a nurse at the military hospital, but the brave Cecil is always there to protect her, landing some powerful blows on the villain's glass jaw. Cecil also finds time to distinguish himself in the war, winning the Victoria Cross and a commission.

Guy believed that one plot was not enough for a proper novel: there had to be a second one. Abruptly, the reader is taken away from the South African veldt and back to London high society. Maud Harcourt, a former girlfriend of Cecil Goldworthy, is of course most upset when she sees his engagement to marry Violet Kildare announced in the newspapers. Unlike the chaste Violet, Maud is a 'modern woman', addicted to a 'fast' lifestyle. This wicked woman smokes cigarettes, wears revealing outfits, and flirts with various blokes. Intent on wrecking Cecil and Violet's romance, Maud persuades a penniless young journalist to insert a libellous notice in an obscure newspaper, to the effect that Violet had an affair with Paul Flaubert before seducing Cecil Goldworthy and persuading him to marry her. But Cecil's father, General Goldworthy, seeks out the skulking penny-a-liner and forces him to retract the libel.

In the meantime, one of Violet Kildare's patients at the field hospital, an old man dying of fever, gives her a bundle of documents proving that she is the rightful owner of the vast Kildare estates in Ireland, which her family had been cheated out of. She is now a wealthy woman, who can marry Cecil as an equal, as she expresses it. Plotting revenge against Cecil and Violet, the frantic Paul Flaubert tries one final roll of the dice, namely to lure her on board a ship full of explosives. But Cecil and Patsy keep the appointment instead, and thrash Paul and his henchmen. Paul tries to blow the ship up, but the clumsy Boer has miscalculated the length of the fuse, and is himself blown to smithereens. All ends well for young Cecil: he is welcomed back to London by his proud father, marries Violet the heiress, and lives happily ever after.

*

The serialisation of *Violet Kildare* in *The Illustrated Police News* was concluded on 16 March 1901, to general acclaim. Guy would remain one of the most trusted and regular contributors of that newspaper for a decade and a half to come. *The Illustrated Police News* did its best to advertise the activities of their star performer, pointing out that

> Mr Guy Logan, author of our popular serial story *Violet Kildare*, is the author also of a new musical-farcical play in three acts, entitled *When a Man's Married*, which is to be produced at the Theatre Royal, Dover, on Monday next. The music is by Colet Dare and Arnold Cooke ... Mr Logan is also engaged on a drama for the same management, and a new musical comedy on a very big scale for the well-known Mr Alexander Loftus, of *New Barmaid* fame.

In addition to articles on criminal history, famous trials, and the occasional serialised novel or short story, Guy also wrote occasional poems. An admirer of 'strong' poetry of the school of Barham and Hood, he had always rather fancied himself as a poet.

In one of Guy's earliest *Illustrated Police News* poems, 'A Christmas Hero', a train driver on duty in South Africa sacrifices his own life to save that of Lord Kitchener and his staff, when the dastardly Boers have dynamited the railway. In 'At Last', an embittered husband takes back the wife he had turned out of doors after wicked rumours had been circulated about her lack of marital fidelity.[11] In 'Waifs and Strays', for the plot of which he was indebted to one Mr Dickens, Guy pulled out all the stops, inspired further by George R. Sims' lugubrious masterpiece 'Christmas Day in the Workhouse'. Billy is a London street urchin, trained as a beggar and pickpocket by a Fagin-like gypsy. Billy has a heart of gold, however, and takes care of the pathetic waif Joey, an ailing child who has also been trained as a beggar by the gypsy:

> 'What's Christmas?' asked Joey, in whispering tones
> And drawing his rags round his poor little bones.
> And Billy replied in his sage little way,
> 'Oh, folks eats and drinks plenty, is merry that day –
> And fortunate kids – not like you, Joe, or me –
> Get things wot drop off a big Christmassy tree.
> You 'ang up a stocking aside of yer bed,
> And a jolly old cove takes it inter 'is 'ead
> To fill it wiv toys and wiv crackers and sweets' –
> Said Joey 'E'd never come down these 'ere streets.'

Driven desperate by hunger, Billy tries to pick the pocket of a passing gentleman:

> He failed. And the gentleman, catching the thief,
> Said, 'So young, too! This thing almost beggars belief:
> You wanted to rob me, I fear, little lad,
> What drove you to conduct so foolish, so bad?
> But you're not to blame; 'tis the life you have led –
> I ought to blame those who have taught you instead.'

As good as his word, the gentleman seeks out the gypsy and confronts him. But this brutal-looking, Fagin-like creature confesses that Billy is in fact the gentleman's own son, stolen by gypsies all those years ago. And indeed, once cleaned up, Billy looked very much like the gentleman's late wife. Offered a life of luxury and abundance, Billy refuses to stir unless the pathetic Joey is also taken care of by the gentleman.

One of the most sensational news stories of 1902 was that a jealous Parisian theatre hand had cut a rope supporting his unfaithful acrobat girlfriend, and sent her crashing down onto the stage, blood-spattered, maimed and crushed. This deplorable incident set Guy's poetic fantasy working, and he produced his masterpiece, 'The Centre Figure'. At Christmastime, an old gentleman seeks shelter from the elements in a dilapidated London theatre. An elderly stall-keeper entertains him with some anecdotes from the theatre's history, including the reason why the pantomime *Aladdin and His Magic Lamp* had to close rather abruptly several decades earlier. It had featured a scene with some pretty actresses dressed up as fairies:

> Amongst the girls who used to pose
> As fairies from the flies
> Was one, a lovely bit of goods,
> With pure and perfect eyes.

She was a favourite here with us,
I see her face now. Lord!
You've never seen a prettier girl
I think, Sir, than was Maud!

She was the Centre Figure in
The Transformation scene.
In flimsy gauze and silver wings
She looked a perfect Queen!
'As good as pretty,' we would say,
And so we all believed –
Which only goes to prove, Sir, that
All men can be deceived!

One of the stage hands, a likely lad named Jack, admired Maud very much, but although she 'led him along', she refused to tie the knot with him, preferring various wealthy admirers. Jack became gloomy and apprehensive, and sometimes came to work drunk, cursing the faithless Maud whom he had once loved so very dearly:

But whispers soon declared that she
Had found a wealthy friend
One of the sort, you know, Sir, who
Deserts them in the end!
And Jack would never talk of her,
We thought he must be blind,
We little knew what even then
Was fashioning in his mind!

There came a night – I mind it well –
A night like this, I know
You couldn't see before your face
For wind and driving snow!
There came a carriage to this door,
A coronetted one –
And then I knew the siege was o'er,
And that the girl was won!

The jilted Jack becomes quite desperate, and makes some very sanguinary plans for Maud, once the great love of his life. When she is dressed up as a fairy, and hoisted high up above the stage, Jack stands ready in the flies:

And soon about her lovely form
The coil of wire was placed.

The crowning scene was on, and she
The transformation graced!
The people clapped with lusty hand,
And shouted out 'Bravo!'
This scene, 'A Glimpse of Fairyland,'
Was prettiest in the show!

And then! Oh! God! from sixty feet
(The memory does appal!)
I saw her flying through the air,
I heard her frightful fall!
I saw her form upon the boards,
Blood-spattered, maimed, and crushed.
And then, with many others there,
Towards the flies I rushed!

Still in his hand he held the knife
That set her spirit free –
He laughed and muttered to himself,
A fearful sight to see!
And the he broke from us and fled
Leaving us over-awed –
Down to the stage where still there lay
The fairy form of Maud!

Poor Jack! Oh, no! He wasn't hung
He died some ten years past.
In Broadmoor, Sir, as well I know,
Who saw him at the last!
Quite mad! Quite harmless! There he lived
In those ensanguined walls –
And shrieking out at dead of night,
'The Centre Figure falls!'

But as the poetic Guy was amusing himself with this sanguinary fantasy, a friend and kindred spirit would soon employ him in a project that would result in some of his most valuable and original work.

*

Harold Furniss was born at Birkenhead in 1856. He began his career in Liverpool, as a journalist and illustrator, and started a satirical journal called the *Liverpool Wasp*. After a libel case in 1881, he had to close down the *Wasp*, and migrate south to London. Just like

Guy himself, Harold was an inhabitant of sub-literary London. He was a penny-a-liner specialising in crime and boxing, a police-court reporter and quick-sketch artist, and an illustrator of various risqué prints.[12] In 1883, there was scandal when Mr Joseph Biggar MP had lost a breach of promise case instigated by the barmaid Fanny Hyland. A former pork butcher, Biggar was known for his ugly looks and earthy mannerisms, and the mischievous Harold Furniss thought he could add insult to injury through writing a letter of condolence to this dismal legislator, expressing admiration for his political integrity, and enclosing a cheque for £400 as a testimony of his esteem and sympathy. The overjoyed Mr Biggar wrote him a heartfelt letter of thanks. The problem was that Harold's bank account did not even contain 400 pence; it was completely empty! A pro-Biggar newspaper wrote that this was one of the most diabolical and heartless practical jokes ever perpetuated, and that the conduct of Harold Furniss ought to be unanimously condemned.[13] After this deplorable caper, the well-known artist Harry Furniss found himself forced to write to the newspapers, in order to point out that he and Harold were two different persons.[14]

After some very lean years as a London penny-a-liner, things were looking up for Harold Furniss in 1893, when he became the editor of the cheap boulevard newspaper *Illustrated Police Budget*, a competitor to the better-known *Illustrated Police News*. Harold cheekily described it as 'the Leading Illustrated Police Journal in Britain', but initial sales were far from brilliant: the early issues of the *Budget* are not even kept by the British Library. In 1894, when a naughty illustration in the *Budget* caught the attention of a police inspector, Harold had to give evidence in court, claiming that the illustration was not indecent. Sir John Bridge, the Bow Street magistrate, sternly pointed at the offending image, showing a 'lady' with her dress up around her knees, and a 'gentleman' singing, 'I long to linger, linger long with you!' and asked, 'Is *this* not indecent?' 'I think it is a charming scene, and worth illustrating,' Harold replied, as cool as a cucumber. Mr Charles Schurey, the proprietor of *The Illustrated Police Budget*, testified that he was most careful what appeared in his paper, and that he regularly turned down advertisements for 'rubber goods' and other dubious merchandise. Nevertheless, he was fined £2 2s costs, and sternly admonished by the fierce Bow Street magistrate. Sir John Bridge added that the proper object of the press was to improve, instruct, and elevate the people; indecent publications like the *Budget* instead had the tendency to lower, to degrade and to demoralise.[15]

But in spite of the angry tirade from this forthright Bow Street magistrate, the circulation of *The Illustrated Police Budget* steadily increased. It managed to establish itself as Britain's second 'Illustrated Police' newspaper. As its very name suggests, the *Budget* did everything on the cheap. Whereas *The Illustrated Police News* prided itself on the quality and accuracy of its illustrations, the images of famous crimes and criminals executed by the *Budget*'s draughtsmen were often based on imagination alone. The *Budget* was strong on boxing, and also on stage and music-hall news. Drawings of lantern-jawed bruisers and scantily clad, buxom female performers abound in its pages. Images of women fighting or getting drunk appear with a frequency indicating a pathological appeal. *The Illustrated Police News* was well known for its lurid drawings of women in various stages of undress, but the *Budget*'s bawdy-minded draughtsmen did their best to outdo their rival newspaper. Thus the *Budget* had all the faults of *The Illustrated Police News*, but none of its merits: its crime reporting was low-quality, its illustrations shoddy and inaccurate, and its lurid sensationalism unbridled. It was printed on very brittle, low-quality paper, meaning that few intact copies have survived in private hands.

Nevertheless, *The Illustrated Police Budget* continued to flourish: it achieved its greatest circulation in early Edwardian times. In 1901, Harold Furniss added to his publishing empire by founding *Famous Fights Past and Present*, an illustrated weekly for the boxing fraternity. In early 1903, he introduced yet another twenty-four-page weekly journal, *Famous Crimes Past and Present*, for aficionados of criminal history. He recruited a team of journalists to write for it, Guy Logan prominent among them. Each issue contained a longer illustrated feature, about some famous case like Mrs Maybrick, the Ratcliffe Highway murders, or Charles Peace the burglar. Sometime, these lengthy features stretched over three, or even four, issues. Each issue of *Famous Crimes* also had a number of illustrated shorter articles and features, nearly all about (mainly British) historical crimes. The frontispiece of each issue, sometimes drawn by Harold Furniss himself, often had a graphic, penny-dreadful character: the mariticidal Catherine Hayes being burnt alive at Tyburn, James Blomfield Rush shooting Mr Jermy at Stanfield Hall, and the brutal-looking Kate Webster advancing on the terrified Mrs Thomas, chopper in hand.

Guy Logan was probably the most prolific contributor to *Famous Crimes Past and Present*, from its inauguration until its very end. He wrote many full-length features on famous crimes, like the unsolved Cannon Street and Hoxton murders, and the railway murder of Elizabeth Camp. Some of these features, like those on the Denham massacre and the Gleeson Wilson murders of 1849, have tell-tale resemblances to Guy's later published writings. Although the articles were all unsigned, Guy's elegant, rather prolix style of writing stands out compared with the laboured offerings from his fellow penny-a-liners. There were several other feature writers on the *Famous Crimes Past and Present*, however, and the full-length study of the Great Coram Street murder of 1872 is definitely written by an older journalist, who was an adult already at the time of this celebrated murder.

There has been speculation as to who wrote the four-part *Famous Crimes* serial feature about Jack the Ripper, in issues 15–18. The caption said that it was not by any of the regular contributors to *Famous Crimes,* but by 'a Journalist who was specially engaged to investigate the crimes at the time they were committed'. This would rule out Guy Logan, who was not active as a journalist until after deserting from the Army in 1891, and also Harold Furniss, whom no respectable newspaper would be likely to employ. George R. Sims may well have written the Great Coram Street feature, but the one about the Whitechapel Murders lacks his characteristic mantra about the doctor leaping into the Thames after the murder of Mary Jane Kelly, and is unlikely to emanate from the hand of that prolific scribbler. Informative and well illustrated, high on detail but low on interpretation of the data available, the 'Ripper' issues of *Famous Crimes* have of course been sought after by collectors. The first issue was reprinted by Dave Froggatt in 1999, and all four issues by Thomas Schachner in 2007; it is a pity that the latter high-quality production was limited to fifty copies. Another reprint would be most welcome, albeit not as welcome as a good-quality reissue of *Famous Crimes* in its entirety.

Famous Crimes Past and Present is a surprisingly high-quality production, given the resources available to Harold Furniss and his team, and this is largely due to the influence of Guy Logan. Guy wrote many shorter articles, and also an amusing 'Leaves from our Notebook' column. In imitation of George R. Sims' 'Mustard and Cress' column in the *Referee*, Guy also answered real or imagined queries from the readership, producing gems like:

PHILO – There is much difference between an executioner and an executor.
SANITAS – Yes, spitting is punished by a fine in New Zealand.
HIRSUTE – Bearded murderers are rare in England.
CONSTANT READER – If you had read Numbers 7, 8 and 9 of *Famous Crimes*, you would have there found the history of Eugene Aram.
PIOUS – It is a misdemeanour if a clergyman demands a fee for performing the Baptismal service.
QUID – You are liable to a fine of 40s if you bore a hole through a sovereign.

Guy was rarely stumped when the readers of *Famous Crimes* posted various uncouth questions:

NO NAME – Yes, several fools had their children baptised Charles Peace.
B.F. – We really cannot be expected to answer questions foreign to the paper. If you want a bulldog pup advertise in a 'doggy paper'.

He was fond of various in-jokes, including a pun on his estranged wife's name that gives away the true authorship of the column:

JUDEX – No Logan has been hanged – as yet!
MELVILLE (STROUD) – The scene of the murder by Mr and Mrs Manning was Miniver Place, Bermondsey. The name of the street was changed, since the houses would not let.

Another in-joke was supplied by one of the other journalists, who commented that Mr Guy Logan had once based a play in the case of Benwell and Birchall in Canada, which had, however, not met with the success its author no doubt felt it merited. One of the shorter features has the epigraph:

For many a soul to Hell is sold
For nought but a little lust for gold.
Guy Logan, *The Devil's Idol*

This particular production by our poetic hero (a poem, or a play?) is otherwise unrecorded, however.

The chronology of *Famous Crimes Past and Present* has puzzled the bibliographers of two continents, since the issues were all undated, and numbered only by issue and (quarterly) volume. There have been suggestions that it began in 1901, 1903 or 1905, and went on until 1912. But the start date for *Famous Crimes Past and Present* is not in doubt, since *The Illustrated Police Budget* of 10 January 1903 announced that the first issue of its new weekly *Famous Crimes Past and Present* would be published on 9 February that year. It featured that all-time favourite bogeyman, the burglar and murderer Charles Peace. Seven quarterly volumes followed, each with thirteen issues, but due to some mishap, the eighth volume had not less than nineteen issues and its pagination continued onto the ninth volume, which had only six issues. The tenth and final volume had eleven issues, making 125 in all, and *Famous Crimes Past and Present* ceased to exist at the end of June 1905. That leaves 47, 52 and 26 weekly issues, a total of 125, and the mystery has been solved.[16] The final issue of *Famous Crimes* contains a message from the editor that from this issue, it will cease to exist as a separate paper. A note in *The Illustrated Police Budget* of 1 July 1905 declared that *Famous Crimes* was 'now incorporated with this paper'. This rump of *Famous Crimes* would continue, with full-page spreads in most but not all issues of the *Budget*, many of them written by Guy Logan, until 23 May 1908, when it disappeared for good, being replaced by Major Arthur Griffiths' *All About Our Police*.

Both *The Illustrated Police Budget* and *Famous Crimes Past and Present* are rare publications, and if you can find issues for a reasonable price, you should purchase them, since they are little pieces of sub-journalistic history. Although the *Budget* is of less value to the crime historian due to its unreliability and inaccurate illustrations, *Famous Crimes* is a valuable and much-neglected source, and both amusing and instructive to read. I have secured several issues of *Famous Crimes* on eBay for less than a pound each, and later a disbound volume containing more than twenty issues for £90. The British Library has a complete run of *Famous Crimes*, as do the New York Public Library and the Yale University Library. The Albert Borowitz collection at Kent State University Library has two bound volumes and a number of loose issues, and the University of California Library and Ohio State Library also have incomplete runs. One of the finest collections in private hands was advertised and sold by Clifford Elmer Books in 2008, for £1,850. This may sound hefty, but there were three bound volumes and many loose issues of either *Famous Crimes* or *The Illustrated Police Budget*. Both Jonathan Goodman and Wilf Gregg owned bound volumes of *Famous Crimes*, and there may well be other substantial collections in private hands.[17]

*

Now the time has come for Guy Logan to provide some of the Leaves from his Notebook, as quoted from *Famous Crimes*:[18]

Murder Houses

May I ask if you have ever passed the night in a room where a notorious murder has been committed? I have, on three occasions. I rented an apartment in a house in Manor Place, Walworth, some six years ago. It was at No. 16, and I only took the place for a week, but I had the satisfaction – if there was any – of knowing that I had spent seven nights in the room in which William Godfrey Youngman murdered his young brother preparatory to butchering his sweetheart, his mother, and another brother for motives of petty gain. Two years later I had business in Liverpool, and I took occasion to pass a night at the Leicester Hotel, in Upper Grenville Street, the scene of the slaughter of Mrs Henrichson, her servant, and her children, by Manrich Gleeson, or Gleeson Wilson, in 1849. This vampire took rooms in this house, slept on the premises on night, and got up the next morning and murdered the entire household. I slept in the same room – the back bedroom on the second floor – as this miscreant had occupied, and my night's rest was disturbed by dreams of the frightful series of crimes. I have also stayed at the house in Burton Crescent – I am asked not to mention the number – which was the scene of the murder of a widow named Samuels, in the seventies, the perpetrator of which, if he be alive, is still at large.[19]

Many other murder houses in London are familiar to me. There is the little house in Priory Street, Kentish Town, where Mrs Pearcey murdered Phoebe Hogg because she was the wife of the man she loved. The premises have been occupied incessantly since the time of the crime, from which it may be inferred that we are less emotional and superstitious as a people that we were even a few years ago, since it used to be the custom to alter the name even of the road in which a great murder occurred, and in every way to purge the house of any identification with the tragedy enacted therein. How many people today could point out the little street once called Miniver Place – in Bermondsey – and show you the obscure dwelling in which Patrick O'Connor met his death at the hands of the Mannings? I have often passed the place, though the street is now known by a different name.[20] The same might be said of the house in Lambeth – close to the Hercules Tavern – where James Greenacre, together with his paramour, Sarah Gale, were arrested for the murder, accompanied by mutilation, of Sarah Brown. At No. 28 Montagu Place, Bedford Square, a singularly atrocious murder was enacted in 1828 – Corder's year. The housekeeper at the time was found in the basement with her throat cut and her head battered in. A well-connected young ne'er-do-well, named Jones, was tried for this murder, but acquitted, though he was probably guilty, and is said to have afterwards confessed. This house – a fine building – failed to let for many years after this tragic affair.[21]

Granard Lodge, Roehampton – the scene of an atrocious murder in 1842 – is still standing, and bears the same name as when Daniel Good was tried and convicted. It is a very fine mansion, standing in its own grounds, with stabling about a quarter of a mile away. These stables were the scene of the murder and the dismemberment of the corpse, and they are in no particular different to what they were when Good, the coachman, lived there. I have been shown the very corn-bin in which the first horrible discovery was made.

Murderers' Letters

Close to me lives a gentleman who has one of the oddest collections in the world. He has acquired at different times – and with much trouble and expense – an assortment of letters written by notorious criminals, the majority of whom have been hanged for murder. He has over two hundred of these interesting epistles, ranging from a note sent by Tawell, the Quaker, hanged for poisoning his paramour in 1845, to a postcard sent by Dougal from the Moat Farm asking a certain medical gentleman resident near to 'drop in and take pot luck with him!' I am not aware if Dr S. accepted this sinister invitation.

That faded letter he hands you – the writing is small and scratchy, though still legible – was written by George Frederick Manning, ex-railway guard, publican, broker, and murderer. 'Dear Charles,' it begins, 'I'm sorry to have failed you that day, but the missis was ill.' In this careless and irreverent way does he refer to that modern Lady Macbeth, Mrs Manning, as determined and unrepentant a murderess as our criminal history can show. My friend likewise possesses a confession signed by Manning, that criminal having a partiality for writing 'confessions' each of which masterpieces contradicted the other, and were only consistent in their endeavours to fix the guilt upon the woman. Cowardly person, Mr G. F. Manning!

Percy Lefroy Mapleton had a fancy for writing absurd love letters to actresses, and here is one to Miss Kate Santley: 'To admire you from afar is bliss divine, what would it be to merely call you mine?' He was a minor poet as well as a murderer was the poetic Percy, and wrote the book of the pantomime (1879–1880) for the Theatre Royal, Croydon.

Deeming's letter, like that of the Moat Farm miscreant, is couched in the hospitable terms of the '*bon garcon*,' the '*viveur*,' the '*bon soldat du plaisir!*' It is dated from a temperance hotel near Rainhill, and is written to 'Dear Mr Swann'. The murderer is anxious for Mr Swann to join him at dinner with a few particular friends at the — Hotel. 'You know,' he says, 'just a few of the best lads, and a song afterwards.' 'Order,' he writes thoughtfully, 'some headache powder for the next morning.' Kind, hospitable, ever friendly fellow this Deeming, or rather Williams, as he signed himself at that time!

A few lines, badly written and expressed, from William Godfrey Youngman, applying to a tailor in Camberwell for a job 'as cutter,' are not without interest – I think this young gentleman was a tailor, by the way – and particularly appeal to me, since I have always thought that callous young slaughterer of his mother, sweetheart, and brothers about the worst and bloodiest murderers this country has ever known. There is in this weird collection a postcard from Bennett, of Yarmouth Beach notoriety, and a letter-card sent to an estate-agent by Edgar Edwards, or Owen, the last being extremely well written and well worded.

My friend possesses not less than three letters written by the infamous Dr Palmer, in a small, but neat hand. Two of these productions refer to betting transactions, and one explains what, in the writer's opinion, caused Nettle's accident in the Epsom Oaks.

A letter, clumsily written, by Hannah Dobbs, in 1879, makes a reference to the charge against her of having murdered Miss Hacker, in Euston Square, and in this interesting and instructive communication the woman plainly states whom she believed the murderer to be. There is a long letter, mainly on religious subjects written by that strange character, Constance Kent, and, of course, the inevitable 'Ripper' letter, this being one of those numerous epistles which were addressed to the police during the scare in 1888.

'That one I retain,' said the collector, 'though I believe it is a clever forgery.' It purported to come from Henry Wainwright, and its contents need not be indicated here. Another letter recalled the Hampstead murder of 1845. This was written by a youth who addressed letters to Hocker when the latter lay under sentence of death, in which the writer confessed that he was really the murderer of Mr Delarue, and stated that he would give himself up before the day of his – Hocker's – execution. I may add that this young man was apprehended, and that it was conclusively established that he had nothing whatever to do with the murder in Belsize Lane, though it is probable that someone – never discovered – assisted Hocker in that fell enterprise.

A badly scrawled line from Mullins, ex-policeman and the murderer of Mrs Elmsley at Stepney, is the last I need refer to. It is addressed to his solicitor, and alludes to the line of defence, an alibi, but Mullins was undoubtedly guilty, and was hanged.

Taverns Associated with Famous Crimes

Few stories of crime are more extraordinary than that of Jonathan Bradford, for, though it has passed almost into a legend, it is perfectly true and has been already fully described in these columns. The public-house in which the murder of the rich old gentleman by his footman occurred was on the Oxford Road, and situated in a very lonely part of the highway between London and the university town. It was called the Ring o' Bells, and was distant some fourteen miles from the seat of learning. The house was an old one, and when coaching ceased and railways came into being, it was demolished – the year being 1841 – and not the oldest habitué of the road could today show a curious visitor the spot where it stood. 'The murder at the roadside inn' as this case was always talked of, became the subject of many dramas and ballads, and is played in booths and portables visiting country fairs even to this day.

There is an old tavern at Ludlow, in Shropshire, which was once the scene of a very famous crime, though I shall not give the appellation, for obvious reasons, of the hostelry to which I allude. In the thirties and forties of the last century it was the usual resort of commercial travellers visiting the town, and there arrived at this house, on one occasion, a certain Mr Mackreth, who arranged to stay till morning, and was given his customary apartment. He awoke in the middle of the night to find himself terribly wounded in the throat and covered with blood. He heard some person glide swiftly from the room and then, injured as he was and faint from loss of blood, he proceeded downstairs and gave the alarm. The unfortunate traveller was seen to be in a dreadful state indeed, and it was a marvel that he ever recovered from his wounds. It was clearly established that someone had been concealed beneath his bed, and that robbery was the motive for the bloodthirsty attack. A very young man, named Josiah Misters, was suspected of being the guilty intruder, and it was proved that he had followed Mackreth from the town he had visited previous to Ludlow, and engaged a bedroom at the latter place next to that of the man he had designed to kill. A blood-stained razor was found in the yard at the back of the inn, and this lay in a position suggesting that Misters had flung it out of his bedroom window after the attempted murder. He was tried, convicted, and hanged at Shrewsbury, though I believe he never actually admitted his guilt.[22]

The crime of the brothers M'Keand in 1826 has already been described in these pages. They murdered a Mrs Blears, the wife of the landlord of the Jolly Carters, at Winton, near Worsley, which is a few miles from Manchester. This roadside house was taken down a year or two afterwards, as it was found impossible to let it, even at a very low rental, but there is now a big modern tavern not very far from the spot.[23]

Also in the county of Lancashire there is the well-known hostelry called Bill o'Jacks, which is on the high road, not far from Oldham. The bodies of two men were discovered in an outhouse attached to this place many years ago, and they had been barbarously murdered. The criminal or criminals in this case were never discovered – the year was 1837, if I remember rightly – and the scene of the crime, which is quite one of the show-places in the neighbourhood, is not far from the lonely moor where two men were found shot, probably by poachers, a short time ago.[24]

Chapman's public-house, The Crown, in the Borough Road, will, we suppose, always be an object of interest to the morbidly inclined, as will the miserable little shop in Wyndham Road, Camberwell, where Edwards, or Owens, performed his murderous exploits. The stories of both tragedies have yet to feature in these pages.

At a village near Chester stood until recently a low, thatch-roofed alehouse, where a double murder was committed a few years back. The place was then conducted by an old man and his housekeeper, who, beside retailing beer to thirsty travellers, were in the habit of letting beds to the tired wayfarer. Both were found barbarously murdered one evening, and a tramp was arrested, charged, tried and ultimately hanged at Chester for this crime, which originated from motives of plunder.[25]

The Rising Sun, at the corner of Holywell Street – now demolished to make room for the Strand-to-Holborn improvements – was the scene of a crime of passion a few years ago, and in this case the landlord, having killed a woman in his employ, was judged to be insane. Many other public houses in London have been the scenes of atrocious crimes, and last year (1903) there was quite an epidemic of barmaid-killing.

At Liverpool there is a street running from Great George Square which is now called Grenville Street, and at the Leicester Hotel, in the farther end of this road, was committed a fearful series of murders in 1849, by Gleeson Wilson, a man who engaged apartments there, slept one night, and murdered the entire family the following morning. The house was transformed into a tavern almost immediately after the crime, and has met with many vicissitudes since then, though it is said to be prospering under the present management. Until comparatively recently a stain on the grate was always pointed out as the life-blood of one of the victims, a maid-servant named Mary Parr, and the proprietors – there have been many – have produced a sketch-book with some horrible pictures of the murders and their details which was prepared at the time, and which have been preserved at the house ever since.

Criminal Lunatics at Large

It would be difficult to compute the number of criminal lunatics who walk daily in our midst – lunatics who have been convicted of crime and released as cured. According to a statement by Mr G. R. Sims, who has made this subject a special study, 'Jack the Ripper' was confined on at least two occasions in an asylum, and, upon showing signs of complete recovery from his mental trouble, let loose upon society to gratify his hideous lust for the blood of immoral women. It is more than probable that if this demented demon had not in a moment of suicidal frenzy thrown himself into the Thames and perished in its waters, he might have gone on being detained and liberated in the intervals between his ghastly murders.

Among the medical acquaintances of the writer was a brilliant young surgeon, who, whilst performing a certain operation upon one of London's many fallen women, became inoculated, through a scratch on his finger, with the loathsome virus. He had been married only a year at the time of the mishap to a most beautiful woman. Hardly another year had elapsed before he developed into a raving lunatic. The curses which he heaped upon the sex and the oaths of revenge which he uttered were terrible to listen to. The closest watch was kept upon him at all times. Twice or thrice he appeared to have returned to sanity, and was restored to his relatives and friends, only to be taken back to the asylum where he was cared for, until one fateful day, when he leaped from a window incautiously left open, and ended a career which had been blasted so miserably on its very threshold. It is within the knowledge of the writer that when the earlier 'Ripper' murders were a-doing this brilliant young surgeon's friends were fearful as to the identity of the bloodthirsty culprit.

A 'Ripper' Anecdote

A very well-known journalist records a startling incident which occurred to him during the Reign of Terror in the East End of London, when the infamous 'Jack' was on the war-path. He was travelling with his wife on the underground railway, and the only other passenger in the carriage was a singular-looking man, who eyed them with great curiosity and suspicion. When this person alighted – at Mark Lane – he left behind him a copy of an evening paper which the journalist in an idle moment picked up and casually glanced at. It contained a full and lucid account of the latest Whitechapel atrocity. On the top of one of the pages in the paper was written the ominous words 'Look for me again in Mitre square'. A few days after the Mitre Square Ripper murder was committed. Who was the stranger?

Great Criminals at Large

A confession to the Jack the Ripper murders by a man named Hermann in New York some little time ago serves to remind the student of criminology how many there are rubbing shoulders with their fellows who, if justice had been done, should have suffered an ignominious death at the hands of the common hangman.[26]

Of late years, there have been an extraordinary number of undiscovered murderers and unavenged crimes. I do not particularly allude to such celebrated cases as the slaying of Miss Elizabeth Camp on the South-Western Railway and that of Mr Tower at Stoke Newington, but to more obscure tragedies, which, by the lapse of time, have been more readily forgotten. The Euston Square, Burton Crescent, Kentish Town, Great Coram Street and Harley Street mysteries are mysteries still, and the perpetrators of these atrocities have probably gone before their maker to answer for their crimes. No light is ever likely to be thrown upon them now. But many murderers are still abroad, as a complete list of crimes which have baffled the best detective faculty would only too plainly show. Such a catalogue of undiscovered crime would extend to great dimensions, and its perusal would not increase the feeling of personal security or of faith in the police.

Take the remarkable murder committed on a Sunday in 1900 at Birkenhead. Who killed the old caretaker at the post-office in that town, and decamped with a big haul of cash and postal orders? The inquiries of the police seemed to suggest that more than one was engaged in that bloodthirsty enterprise, and that the arrangements at the office and the customs of its custodian were well known to the malefactors. Yet no light has since been thrown on the affair, and the inhabitants of the Cheshire town, if not the authorities, have already well-nigh forgotten it. The murderers may now be living in the very neighbourhood, and may often pass the scene of their cowardly deed, or even be customers for stamps and postcards! The old man's blood still cries for vengeance, but God, we know, will atone.[27]

What of the murder of John Robert Wells on Barnes Common on 24 April 1894, of which there have been so many bogus confessions? That was, without doubt, a premeditated crime, accomplished by one who had a grudge against the unfortunate man, whom he waylaid and beat to death with most tenacious purpose. That murderer, if he is alive, walks abroad and mixes with his fellow-men, none guessing the hideous secret he keeps so closely and so well.[28]

What fiend in human guise deposited the gruesome remains of some unknown female, whom he had killed, at the rear of Doulton's pottery works at Lambeth on 11 June 1902? That was assuredly a case of murder, rivalling in transcendent horror the similar exploits of James Greenacre, Daniel Good, and Henry Wainwright. No one was ever suspected of this crime; the murderer must now feel himself secure, unless conscience finally, as in the cases of Sheward and Geydon, makes a coward of him – unless remorse fills his embittered soul and he confesses all.[29]

Why was the man Martin, night-watchman at the Café Royal, cruelly done to death on the night of 6 December 1894? He was not known to have any enemy, and robbery did not enter the mind of the miscreant who fired the pistol. What obscure, but none the less determining, motive had the murderer for this deed? He escaped from the scene of his fell crime, and breathes freely, perchance, in some foreign land, now that all chance of suspicion and all likelihood of capture are past and gone.

Nothing more has ever been heard of such notable cases of undiscovered crimes as the Cannon Street Mystery of 1866, the Eltham Murder of 1881, the Purton Tragedy of 1874, the Battersea Barbarity of 1873, and the double murder in Kentish Town in 1878.[30] What became, one wonders, of the murderer or murderers of Mrs Wakenell, who was found dead in the front room of her house in Water Lane, Brixton, on 13 May 1900? In this case the police thought that they had an important clue, and were confident of catching the guilty party; but it all came to nothing, and only the officers in charge of the case at the time now allow their thoughts to recur to the strange fate of this lonely woman.

Still more unaccountable, because of the difficulty of imagining any motive, was the murder of W. James Bassett, a mere child, whose body was found in Upton Park in the month of December 1897. This tragedy, which has never been explained, somewhat recalls two earlier cases, viz., that of the brutal murder of a young boy at Ruislip, near Uxbridge, in

1837, and the slaughter of a boy named James Gill at Manningham, near Bedford, in 1889. In neither case was the perpetrator ever brought to justice.[31]

Then the mind reverts to the murder of Mrs Tyler, in Kidbrook Park Road, Blackheath, on 15 August 1896. The poor lady was found suffocated in a manner which the murder of Donovan and Wade last year in the East End recalled.

A horrible crime, reminding one irresistibly of the unnatural deeds of Frederick Baker, John Coates, Harold Apted, George Pavey, Cross Duckworth, John Wakefield, Walter Lewis Turner, William Fish, and other murders of little girls for lustful purposes, occurred at Barking in the last week of 1898. A child named Mary Voller was found, murdered, in a ditch, and no light was ever thrown upon the mystery, though I believe the police made herculean efforts to discover her brutal assailant. A similar case occurred in 1890, when a fine girl of fourteen, or thereabouts, named Amelia Jeffs, was found to have been barbarously done to death in an empty house facing West Ham Park. The poor girl had struggled hard with her assailant, who had not accomplished his abominable purpose, but had slain her for her resistance. How and by whom was she lured into such a situation? The police believed that she would not have accompanied a stranger, and that the crime was the work of an acquaintance, but no one was ever suspected, and the case is well-nigh forgotten. In this connection it may be added that about twenty years ago there was an epidemic of such crimes in the neighbourhood of East and West Ham.[32]

A Visit to Elstree

Recently we paid a visit to Elstree to inspect what remains in the way of relics of the famous Thurtell-Weare murder of eighty years ago. The most careful inquiry and the most particular scrutiny could not reveal to us the whereabouts of Gill's Hill Lane, in which dark and dismal path the awful crime was consummated. Weare's grave, too, in Elstree churchyard – he was buried near the beautiful victim of the curate Hackman's jealousy – is nameless and cannot be pointed out with any degree of certainty. Probert's cottage was long since destroyed, and the pond by the roadside in which the body was immersed has been filled in; but the Artichoke, at which the inquest on Mr Weare's remains was held, is still the most important tavern in the place, and we had a small ginger-ale – ahem! –in the very room in which the coroner's investigation was conducted.

Great 'Crime' Houses

Houses wherein have been enacted notorious crimes must always be of interest to the student of criminology. It would be interesting to know, how many buildings with such a sinister history are still standing in England, but many of them the writer has himself inspected, and can, therefore, vouch for their continued existence.

No. 12, Wellington Terrace, Waterloo Road, is daily passed by thousands who have no idea that it was once the scene of a most mysterious murder. There Eliza Grimwood – fair and frail – was cruelly done to death by a male 'fiend' whom she had permitted to accompany her home from the Strand Theatre – that is, if William Hubbard, who lived with the girl and upon her shame, did not himself commit the deed. No serious evidence could be advanced against him, but the people in the neighbourhood believed in his guilt, and he was obliged to fly to America.[33]

The writer has actually stayed – for one night only – at No. 16, Manor Place, Walworth Road, where, in the 'sixties,' that unexampled young villain, Youngman, killed his mother, sweetheart, and two brothers in order to procure the pitiful sum of £100.[34] My rest was not disturbed by the memories of these ill deeds, nor was it when I passed a night some five years ago at the Leicester Hotel, in Upper Grenville Street, Liverpool, though the tavern alluded to was the house at which Gleeson Wilson murdered the Henrichson family in 1849. I have been over the house – in Priory Street, Kentish Town, at which the somewhat mysterious Mrs Pearcey slew her rival, Mrs Hogg, and the little house in Church Villas, Richmond, where Kate Webster killed and mutilated Mrs Thomas, is sufficiently familiar to me.[35] Houses in Montagu Street, Bedford Place, in Harley Street, in Euston Square, in Burton Crescent, all of which still stand, have the stain of unavenged blood upon them, as has Great Coram Street, not so very far away from those mentioned.

The warehouse in the Whitechapel Road, in which Henry Wainwright killed and buried his paramour, Harriett Lane, has not been done away with, and the dwelling in which the ruffian Seaman killed Mr Levi and his housekeeper – hard by the Commercial Road East – still frowns upon the passer-by.[36]

The house has been pointed out to me in which Greenacre was arrested. It was No. 1, St Alban's Street, Lambeth, and is near the Hercules Tavern. I have also discovered the residence – rather a pretty house it is – in which Corder was taken. It lies in a lane between Ealing and Brentford, nearer to the latter place, perhaps, than the former, and used at one time to be a school for girls.

*

In mid-1905, when Guy Logan was aware that *Famous Crimes* would not survive long as an independent paper, the editor of *The Illustrated Police News* approached him with a suggestion that must have gladdened his heart. The time had come to serialise another full-length novel in this newspaper, since there was not enough serious crime to fill its twelve weekly pages, and since he would not follow that disgraceful Harold Furniss in allowing drawings and photographs of brutal-looking pugilists and half-naked floozies to take over the contents of his venerable newspaper. No, instead there should be a really thrilling novel, written by the stalwart Guy Logan, about – Jack the Ripper!

Left: 1. The murder house at No. 12 Great Coram Street, from *Lloyd's News*, 20 October 1907.
Below: 2. Kate Webster, from *The Illustrated Police News*, 3 May 1879. The bottom-right panel depicts the attempt to steal Mrs Thomas's furniture from the murder house.
Bottom: 3. he main characters from the Euston Square mystery, from *The Illustrated Police News*, 12 July 1879.

Right: 4. The murder house at Euston Square, from an old engraving.
Below: 5. Denham village, from a postcard stamped and posted in 1914.
Bottom: 6. The murder house at Denham, from an old postcard.

Marshall's Cottage, Denham.

Taken at the time of the Murder 1870.

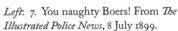

Left: 7. You naughty Boers! From *The Illustrated Police News*, 8 July 1899.

Below left: 8. A heroic bugler boy shoots some bearded, subhuman Boers. From *The Illustrated Police News*, 4 November 1899.

Below right: 9. 'Take that, you bounder!' Cecil Goldworthy knocks down the caddish Boer Paul Flaubert. From *The Illustrated Police News*, 9 June 1900.

Bottom left: 10. Violet Kildare defiantly cries out 'God save the Queen!' when threatened by Paul Flaubert, with the buffoon 'Patsy' Nolan coming to the rescue in the background. From *The Illustrated Police News*, 28 July 1900.

Bottom right: 11. The 'fast' Maud Harcourt plots against Cecil and Violet, from *The Illustrated Police News*, 24 November 1900.

Right: 12. Guy Logan's poem 'The Centre Figure', from *The Illustrated Police News*, 27 December 1902.
Below: 13. The first page of *Famous Crimes*, issue 35: Catherine Hayes and her two associates brutally murder Mr Hayes.
Below right: 14. The first page of *Famous Crimes*, issue 36: Catherine Hayes is burnt alive at Tyburn in 1726.

THE MURDER OF MR. HAYES.

THE BURNING OF CATHERINE HAYES.

Left: 15. The first page of *Famous Crimes*, issue 44: James Blomfield Rush shoots Mr Jermy at Stanfield Hall in 1849.
Below left: 16. The first page of *Famous Crimes*, issue 45: James Blomfield Rush awaiting execution.
Below: 17. The first page of *Famous Crimes*, issue 42: Kate Webster attacks Mrs Thomas.

Bradford, going to murder his Guest, finds the Deed already accomplished.

Above left: 20. The Angel Inn, from a postcard stamped and posted in 1910.
Above right: 21. The M'Keands are apprehended, from Camden Pelham's *Chronicles of Crime* (London, 1889), vol. 2.

22. Bill o'Jack's, from an old postcard.

23. Gill's Hill Farm, Elstree, site of the murder of Mr Weare by John Thurtell and his cohorts, from Guy Logan's *Masters of Crime*.

2

The True History of Jack the Ripper, by Guy Logan

1. The Escape

Half-way between the villages of Broxbourne and Hoddesdon in Herts, and standing in its own grounds, some little distance off the main road was, in the year 1887, the private lunatic asylum of one whom, for the purposes of this history, we will call Dr. Kent. Private asylums for the insane have not, since the revelations of the novels *Hard Cash* and *Valentine Vox* been in very good odour in this country; but the establishment of Dr Kent was exceptionally well favoured. To be a patient there was almost to be distinguished. None could be received at that model abode whose relatives were not prepared to pay highly for the privilege. Dr Kent's 'Home for the Mindless', as it was termed, in that gentleman's admirably drawn up prospectus, was only suitable as a resort to those with more money by a great deal than brains, and that is how Mr Mortemer Slade became an inmate.

It was the evening of a fine October day in 1887. Ordinarily speaking, summer had long since taken its departure, and the rigours of early autumn seemed close at hand; but this was the last warm day of the year, the last expiring effort of a genial and benevolent summer to maintain its supremacy. It had been an ideal day, and the inmates of Grange House, sane and insane, normal and abnormal, had been loath to abandon the grounds in which cricket, tennis, and even the old-fashioned croquet had for the last six hours been in full swing.

The gardens of this rural Bedlam were the admired of all the countryside. The house stood on a gentle eminence looking towards the north, and green lawns and verdant plantations stretched away for a mile and a half towards the main road to Sawbridgeworth and Bishop's Stortford. Great banks of rhododendron bushes intersected the various fields, and these were topped by oaks and chestnuts and limes that were universally pronounced to be the finest in the county. In this spot, nature was at her loveliest. In this same spot poor Humanity, staggering under a load of mental afflictions, was at her worst, for the men and women who gazed with lacklustre eyes upon the beauties of the surroundings were mad – some more, some less – but all indisputably, undeniably mad.

Two men were walking apart on the paths which skirted the boundary of the higher grounds. A high fence and then a higher hedge divided the garden at this point from the high road beyond. It was about half-past six in the evening, the sky was still clear and of a beautiful pale blue colour, while the air had all the peaceful balminess and charm of early summer. Away in the distance, beyond a belt of trees, the madhouse stood on its prominent hill. How little it seemed to have in common with the gay surroundings and the mild and pleasing air.

The two men – of a height, both tall and spare – slowly paced the well-trimmed paths in friendly arm-in-arm. They were Dr Crosbie, one of the assistant medicoes attached to the sanatorium and Mortemer Slade, an inmate of the asylum. On the former we need bestow only a brief description; of the latter, we shall have much to say. Dr Crosbie was one of the most treasured assistants to Dr Kent, the urbane and talented principal. He was admittedly an expert, a connoisseur in all matters that directly or indirectly concerned the insane. He had learning. He had theories. He had enthusiasm. He had the divine gift of sympathy. He believed from his heart that all men are mad, but that some are more mad than others. He did not scoff, even in his own mind, at the foibles of the mentally weak. He had a hobby for collecting the corks from champagne bottles. One of his most hopeless patients insisted on collecting old bootlaces, of which useful commodity he was the proud possessor of some seven hundred pairs. 'For the life of me,' said Dr Crosbie in an occasional burst of candour, 'I don't know which of us is the bigger idiot.'

Mortemer Slade had also qualified for the medical profession. Mad or sane, he was an intensely clever man. Both Dr Kent and Dr Crosbie, his ablest assistant, had often been surprised and even awed at the extent of his understanding. They reverenced him for his erudition, but they were equally convinced that Mortemer Slade was very mad indeed. Yet they considered him to be mad in a peculiar, unconventional way. Slade could be permitted to mix with any society with the certainty that he would not betray his want of mental equilibrium. He could be left at any time and anywhere. He might be trusted, under all circumstances, to behave like a gentleman; he would never betray himself to be the harmless, clever, pleasant, easy-going maniac his 'keepers' one and all pronounced him to be. They even had hopes of curing him some day; of restoring him to his wealthy relatives sane and healthy in mind and body. 'Mark you, Crosbie,' Dr Kent would often proclaim oracularly, 'If Slade recovers we shall give the world a great surgeon!'

Slade paused for a moment in his walk, unlinked his arm from that of the friendly doctor, and proceeded to light a cigarette. There was nothing in his aspect or demeanour to suggest the mental warp which had wrecked a promising career. Insanity and genius, we know, are closely allied. The soul of Mortemer Slade hovered over the borderland between the two.

'Even now, doctor,' he remarked in suave, even tones, 'though I am, unhappily, a patient under the care of a mental specialist, I feel that I am destined to become famous – or infamous. Which, I wonder?'

Dr Crosbie smiled. 'When you have undergone our treatment a little longer, Mr Slade,' he said, 'neither fame nor happiness should be beyond your grasp. You will be restored to your friends and fortune, and modern surgery will have cause to rejoice thereat.'

Mr Slade smiled grimly. He had not a nice smile. His lips were thin, his teeth rather sharp and discoloured, his eyes placed rather close together in his head. He had a fine, intellectual brow, and his face was pleasant in repose, but the smile was sinister, and he never laughed.

'The world shall yet hear of me,' he said calmly. 'I feel sometimes a moral elevation, doctor, which seems to place me beyond and above the common wants, the likes and dislikes, of conventional humanity. Let us take Alexander of the Great, St John the Divine of the very Good, and Nero of the very Bad. I could not hope to eclipse the first two. But I, even I, might surpass the deeds of the Roman Emperor whose name posterity abhors.'

Dr Crosbie glanced at him unobserved. Slade seemed calm, dignified, intelligent as ever, but something in his tone vaguely alarmed the doctor, and he determined to report this speech to his principal. The words had been said lightly enough, but the tone was significant of much. They returned to the house together, and Crosbie marked and called a game of one hundred up between Slade and a mad squire of considerable property, who, except when he was playing billiards, of which game he was passionately fond, imagined himself to be one of his own fox-hounds, and conducted himself in approved 'doggy' fashion.

After dinner, at which Dr Kent presided, and which was not taken till eight o'clock, Slade sat in the magnificent library reading the evening papers, which had just arrived. He had professed a mild sort of interest in a case of murder recently reported from the East-end. A woman had been found dead beneath the archway of a bridge with her throat cut. The assassin had not been found. He tossed the paper aside with an impatient movement. 'Some day,' he said aloud, 'I shall be credited with that, and it was only a bungling piece of work after all.'

The patients – 'guests' as Dr Kent preferred to call them – were not permitted to leave the building for any purpose after dinner; but certain privileges were granted to a very few, and Slade was one of them. He had the right, if he chose, to sit on the terrace and enjoy his evening or even to walk in the grounds, if the night was fine. At nine o'clock on this particular occasion he put on his hat and overcoat, for the night was chilly, and proceeded towards the garden. Four attendants, strong, active, muscular men, promenaded the grounds till all the inmates of the establishment were in bed; but these did not take much notice of Slade as he passed, for he was regarded as three-fourths sane and one fourth mad, and treated accordingly. Slade walked towards the great gates which separated the grounds of Grange House from the outside world. To the left of them were beautifully appointed stables. Several of the wealthier patients possessed carriages and horses, and Dr Kent, a famous whip, had his own drag, which was a familiar feature of the main London road. On either side of the great gates ran a hedge dividing the Grange House estate from the road.

At exactly twenty minutes past nine by his watch, Slade, looking cautiously around, gave a low whistle. This he repeated two or three times. Then he lightened intently, and from the other side of the hedge came a responsive whistle, somewhat shriller than his own. He approached closely to the hedge.

'Is that you, Dagenham?' he asked.

'Yes sir,' was the reply.

'No one stirring your side?'

'Not a soul, sir. It's a dark night, and just suited to your purpose. I'll hand you the ladder.'

As noiselessly as possible a small ladder of the telescopic kind was placed on the top of the thick hedge, and instantly secured by Slade. He placed it against the hedge, which was high and of dense thickness, and proceeded to ascend it. On the other side a similar ladder was in readiness. In less than a minute Slade was in the road standing by the side of Dagenham, a groom employed by Dr Kent, whom he had contrived to bribe to assist his escape.

'I've got the trap and horse ready, sir,' whispered that worthy. 'It's a-waitin' for us down at the Black Bull. You'll be in London inside an hour and three-quarters. Leave the turn-out at the place we appointed, and I'll look after it.'

Slade considered a little.

'I don't think it prudent to go to the inn,' he said. 'The landlord has often seen me, and my appearance there at this time would excite remark. He is one of those ignorant fools who think that every poor devil staying at Grange House is of necessity a dangerous lunatic. Go you and fetch the conveyance. I'll wait in the hollow of the hedge there. How long will you be?'

'Seven or eight minutes,' replied the groom.

'Hurry up, then,' said Slade, turning up his coat collar, slouching his hat over his eyes, and slinking back into a recess in the hedge. The man departed with light and hasty tread. Slade waited. With haste and restlessness, however, that characterises the actions of the morbid-minded, he presently ventured from the obscurity of his shelter, and approached the gates. Peering through, he was able to see the lights of the great house through the intervening trees. He chuckled at the thought of Dr Crosbie's face when he heard of the abrupt and unannounced departure of the model patient! An escape from the well-ordered establishment of Dr Kent! Unthinkable! Then his mood changed, and he threatened the distant mansion with his clenched hand.

'When yonder wise-acres pronounced me mad,' he muttered, 'I there and then determined, in a spirit of pure mischief, for I am saner than any of them, to justify their decision. The time is ripe. The moment has come! Let the madman live up to his reputation. The whole world shall ring with the dread name I shall assume. I will flout every protection which an effete civilisation has created for its own safe-guarding. The resources of all the forces of detection shall not avail themselves against me. I will strike terror to every heart, and plunge this great ugly London of ours – the home of vice, and filth, and crime – into a miasma of death and desolation. To the end of time, humanity shall shudder at the name of–' He stopped. Stealthy footsteps were rapidly nearing. He swung round and made for the sombre aperture in the hedge. Too late! A dark figure sprang forward and confronted him.

'Don't you think, Mr Slade,' said the voice of one he knew, 'you had better return to the house with me?'

Slade replied with an angry snarl like that of a wild beast. The newcomer, who had arrived so inopportunely, was a young medical man attached to the Grange House establishment.

Slade had disliked him vigorously. This young man had seemed to fathom the dark passions which animated the madman's mind. Others – experts in lunacy – had thought him nearly sane. Young Welman had never thought so, and Slade knew it.

'I do not propose to return to Dr Kent's,' said the latter. 'The farce has been played long enough. Stand aside, sir, and permit me to pass.'

'I have my duty to perform,' said the other firmly, 'and I shall not shrink from it. Come, sir,' he added, persuasively, 'you are too sensible to perform foolish little tricks like this. Let us return to the house.'

He made a movement towards the gates. If he could but reach them, ring the great bell and thus give an alarm! Slade understood. He remembered the bell. Its clings would arouse the two keepers in the lodge, the stable-helps, and the employees in the servants' hall. He strode past Welman and permitted that gentleman to get nearer to the gates. But the doctor knew too much to turn his back on the other, or to remove his eyes from his face. They continued to face each other. Suddenly the sound of wheels from behind Welman reached the ears of both. A vehicle was approaching. Involuntarily, Welman glanced behind him. With a spring like a tiger, Slade was upon him. He had contrived to secure, unseen, a heavy, jagged stone and with this implement he struck the other a tremendous blow, cracking the back part of his skull like an egg-shell. Without a groan, blood and particles of bone pouring from his fractured head, Welman fell to the earth as a horse and trap driven by Dagenham reached the spot.

'My god!' said the groom, springing from the box. 'You've killed him.' He stooped and examined the prostrate man. 'Sir – sir –' he stammered, 'you're a murderer.'

'I commence well,' said Slade, tossing the blood-stained stone into the hedge. 'That was not bad for a beginner. Help me to hide the body in the hedge.'

Dagenham hesitated. He had 100 pounds of Slade's in his breast-pocket, but he looked round as if seeking the means to fly.

'Help me, you fool,' hissed the murderer, and threatened him with upraised arm.

Dagenham seized the legs of the dead man, averting his eyes from the poor, battered head, and Slade lifted the body by the shoulders. They placed it in the dark recess of the hedge, and Slade covered it as best he could with dead leaves and decayed branches.

'Not a word to a living soul,' he said to his unwilling accomplice, 'as you value your life. When that corpse is found, let them assume what they please. Remember this, however. I will never murder another man.'

He sprang into the trap, seized the reins, and turned the horse's head towards London.

'Free!' he said. 'Free to pursue the course I have mapped out.' He plied the whip with vigour, and was soon swallowed up in the darkness.

This was the beginning of a series of crimes without parallel in the history of the civilised world.

2. The Old Love and the New

The honourable Phyllis Penrose was the youngest daughter of Lord Caversham, of Caversham Castle, County Cornwall. That peer had been blessed with four daughters, and for each, though he had no wife to assist him, the good lady having long been gathered to her fathers, he had secured an advantageous and happy marriage, except for Phyllis, who was nineteen. The Honourable Editha, learned and proud, had married the Earl of Sutcliffe. The Honourable Pamela had wed Mr Silas B. Betts, a wealthy American. She was frivolous and devoted to sport. The Honourable Gladys had bestowed herself upon Mr Lestrange, a prominent politician on the Liberal side, who was pretty certain to attain office. She had ambitions, and made an ideal hostess, with passion for entertaining Cabinet Ministers. The Honourable Phyllis was very popular in society. She was a typical English girl of great charm, and as a débutante, had been unanimously voted the beauty of that season. Tall, slight, fair, with glorious blue eyes, and the complexion of a peach, this young lady was a delicious mortal whose hours were mostly spent in declining offers of marriage. She had rather vague, old-fashioned notions of love and the sanctity of wedded life, ideas which, to do him justice, her father had done his utmost to eradicate. But they remained, and Phyllis held to her resolution not to bestow her hand where she was unable to give her heart.

Two years before, and when she had only just come out, an acknowledged beauty, the Honourable Miss Penrose had made a very great impression upon the mind of a certain Mr Mortemer Slade. That gentleman came of an ancient Yorkshire family, and was extremely proud of his lineage. His ancestors had served the kings as soldiers or Ministers of State when the forefathers of Lord Caversham were but homely yeomen un-honoured and unsung. In respect to race, therefore, Mr Mortemer Slade was a worthy suitor, even to the beautiful and patrician Miss Penrose. In the mere matter of money he was equally eligible. Lord Caversham was almost a poor man as peers go. He had led rather a riotous youth – the record of the Turf spoke for that – and the family possessions had suffered. His marriage, moreover, had been an improvident one. Now, at sixty-five years of age, his lordship was constantly alive to the value of money.

Mortemer Slade had £7,000 a year and expectations of more. Furthermore, he had a profession, and, if reports were to be credited, he was likely to rise in it. He was one of the coming surgeons of the day. He had a handsome town house, and a fine place – the pictures were quite famous – near Richmond, in the Yorkshire wolds. True, he was thirty-eight years of age, and Phyllis was but seventeen. But marriages in which there is a considerable disparity of age between the high-contracting parties are fashionable nowadays, and often prove the most successful. Phyllis felt that the age of Mr Slade was not against him. She liked and admired him, too. How was it, then, that she could not prevail upon herself to utter the one word which Mr Slade declared would make him the happiest of men? The fact was that, though she could hardly describe it to herself even, there was something repellent in this gentleman. She could not put her repugnance into words, but it existed, and the sentiment could not be subdued. She praised him when others praised him. She admired his courtly manners, his brilliant conversational powers, his evidences of extreme intelligence. He compared favourably in nearly every way with the vapid noodles who paid court to the peer's daughter. And yet she often caught herself shuddering, as before her mental vision arose the sombre figure – he always dressed in black – and somewhat cadaverous face of her persistent wooer. Those penetrating eyes placed a shade too near together – those thin, colourless lips – that sleek, black hair – those finely pencilled eyebrows – the sallow skin

– what was there in these to cause her a feeling almost of mental and physical discomfort? No, she would never marry Mortemer Slade.

That gentleman smiled a little wistfully as she declined, as kindly as she could, the honour of his hand. He was enigmatic as usual as he rose to take his leave. 'You might have saved me,' he said, 'but it is not to be. Each one of us has his or her predestined end. You will marry a title, and, I hope, be happy. I shall never forget you. I love you. Remember that, if ever people come to shudder at my name.'

Some six months later rumours as to the want of mental balance of Mortemer Slade began to reach the gossip-loving ears of Lord Caversham. He verified them. The eminent surgeon was declared to be rapidly going what the peer called 'dotty'. He told his daughter bluntly. 'That Slade who used to hang round after you,' he said – his lordship was not gifted with extreme delicacy – 'is as mad a a hatter. I suppose your refusal drove the poor chap out of his mind. His people are making arrangements to have him put away. A pity I call it. He was a clever fellow.'

Phyllis sighed, and looked her astonishment. She could not easily realise that so learned a gentleman could go mad, and least of all, for the love of a young girl. Slade was pronounced in due time to be insane, though perfectly rational at all times and seemingly harmless – his uncle had drowned himself in 1879 – and retired into oblivion and Grange House.

Shortly after, Phyllis really fell in love. Mr Lestrange, the prominent Radical member, whom her sister had married, had a private secretary, a very good-looking and entertaining young fellow named Darrell, Stephen Grant Darrell, to be precise. He was of a good family, had no vices to speak of, and a few hundred a year of his own. He was intended for the diplomatic service, and Phyllis was convinced that a very few months at the outside would see him installed at the head of one of our Embassies – at Paris, Berlin, Vienna or St Petersburg. She hoped, fondly to herself, that it would be Paris.

'With my salary and that, Phyllis,' he had said, 'we shall have about £1,200 a year to start housekeepin' with. It's beastly little, I admit; but I'm not without prospects, and if we're not extravagant, we shall hold our own. Naturally, your father won't much fancy me as a husband for the last and nicest of his nest of birds, so we'll contrive to manage without going to him for the usual cheque now and again.'

So it was arranged that they should be married when Stephen got his diplomatic appointment. Lord Caversham grumbled, but his pretty daughter had a knack of getting her own way, and he at length reluctantly gave his consent.

'I can give 'em five hundred a year,' he ruminated, 'and Darrell's just the sort of young man to get on.'

News of the brutal and apparently unprovoked murder of a young doctor near Grange House Asylum rather perturbed London society, but by no one was it connected with the name of Mortemer Slade. The secret of the escape of that person was zealously guarded. Dr Kent had, of course, communicated with his relatives, cousins for the most part, who coveted his worldly goods; with his solicitors, who had control of his affairs, and with the police. Every effort to trace the missing man failed, however. The groom Dagenham carefully destroyed the two ladders with which the escape over the hedge had been made, and did not come forward when the body of poor Welman was found. An open verdict was returned at the inquest. Dr Crosbie, for one, indignantly refused to believe that his model patient could have been guilty of so foul an assassination. Dr Kent agreed with him. The police took a different view, but they could not find the escaped man, and soon abandoned the search in disgust. Tragic events in the district of Whitechapel were soon to claim all their attention and all their care. They asserted that Mortemer Slade had committed suicide. It transpired that his solicitors had, at his urgent request, forwarded him £500 in gold – a clerk had brought down the money to Grange House – some fortnight or so before his escape. How and where he had secreted this cash was never known. We know that Dagenham, the groom, had £100 of it.

On the night of 6 August 1888, Phyllis Penrose was present at a ball given by her sister Editha, Countess of Shincliffe, in Eaton Square. With her was her fiancé, Stephen Darrell, who had been much disturbed throughout the evening by the air of gloom and depression which had settled upon the fair young brow of his sweetheart. After taking a listless part in several dances, she complained of the heart of the rooms, and Stephen persuaded her to put on a cloak and to come into one of the cool conservatories which were level with the garden at the rear of the mansion. Here, beside a towering palm, they were alone and likely to be undisturbed.

'You are pale and trembling, dearest,' said the anxious young man; 'Are you ill? What is troubling you?'

'I am quite well, Steenie,' Phyllis replied. 'But I have had something on my mind all day, and now that we are alone, I feel that I ought to tell you.'

'Indeed you ought,' he said, 'how can I be indifferent to anything, the mere trifle, that concerns my dearest love? Tell me all, Phyllis. Your future husband, and your devoted slave, has the right to know.'

Phyllis replied with a question. 'You have heard people speak of a Mr Mortemer Slade, Steenie?' she asked, placing her hand confidently in his own.

He laughed. 'Oh, yes!' he said. 'Who has not? A wealthy eccentric, a doctor, I think, who went mad, and is now capering around a private asylum, believing himself to be a bicycle or something. By Jove! Wasn't he a great admirer of yours, Phyllis?'

'He proposed to me,' she said, simply.

'The devil he did! I beg your pardon, dear, but it was a consummate bit of cheek on his part. He must have been mad then.'

'Thank you!' she said; 'you're very complimentary.' Stephen laughed and squeezed her hand. 'I hadn't seen you then,' she went on, 'and anyway, I refused him.'

'Is he involved in this precious little secret of yours?' asked Stephen.

'He has written me a most extraordinary letter.'

'The communications of gentlemen under the care of Dr Kent at Grange House, Herts, could hardly fail to be somewhat peculiar,' remarked Stephen, airily. 'May I see the maniac's missive?'

The girl produced a crumpled envelope from the bosom of her dress, and straightened it out on his knee. 'There,' she said, 'read it for yourself, and confess to me that it was sufficiently alarming to spoil one evening at least.'

The letter had been delivered by hand – a mysterious stranger had brought it to Park Lane, where Lord Caversham's house was situated, early that afternoon – and was addressed in an obviously disguised hand, to 'The Honble. Miss Penrose, Caversham House, Park Lane, West.' Instructions had been given that the letter was to be delivered only to Miss Penrose's maid. Stephen Darrell read aloud as follows:

Freedom!
   Aug. 6 1888
   On the eve of every great event in my life, I shall appear to you. Whenever I am about to strike a blow at this rotten civilisation of ours, which is pure savagery veneered, I shall appear to you, to remind you that you might have saved me from myself. Remember that, if ever you, and society, should come to shudder at my name. Read, meanwhile, the evening papers of August 7, and the dailies of August 8. You will hear of me therein. Blow number one will be struck tomorrow. Look at the sky tonight! The sun shall go down in a bath of blood. The heavens shall be red as in a glow of fire. Madmen must justify themselves. Fame and infamy are but names. If I cannot secure the one phantom, the other shall be mine. Remember, above all, that you are safe from me. It is not from the ranks of those who have never sinned, because the necessity has been spared them, that I shall select my victims. I shall find my prey in the mud and slime of this ghastly city. I shall destroy only those who have no joy in life and no purpose to serve. Look at the blood-red sky tonight.
   Mortemer Slade.

After reading this extraordinary epistle, Stephen and Phyllis gazed blankly at each other. He would have wished to laugh away her fears and to explain to her that the letter was the work of a maniac, and had no significance, but somehow the words would not come. The note, disconnected, vague, indefinite, exaggerated as it seemed, had not failed to make an extraordinary impression upon his mind. With an effort, he shook off the feeling.

'Let me keep this letter, dear,' he said a little gravely, in spite of himself. 'Try to forget it came. I must take steps to prevent a similar one from reaching you. Let me see your maid. Say nothing to anyone and dismiss the matter from your mind. Remember, this poor man is insane. His rambling inconsequences are not worth a moment's thought from you.'

'I know,' she said. 'I am safe. I fear not! I have you. But – Steenie, did you notice the peculiar sunset this evening, only three hours ago? The sky was blood-red.' She shuddered, and rose to go. 'Let us go back to the ball,' she said, 'we shall be missed.'

He gave her his arm. As they passed some of the conservatory windows, which opened out into the grounds of the house, Phyllis suddenly stood still. A look of the most awful fear passed over her usually serene face. She became white to the very lips. She gave a stifled scream and clutched his arm. Her eyes, wide open with awful, paralysing fear in their depths, were fixed intently upon the window.

'Look!' she cried. 'Look! He appears as he said! 'Tis the face of Mortemer Slade. My God! My God! Hide his visage from my sight.'

She sank to the floor and hid her face in her hands. Stephen, appalled, dashed to open the glass door of the conservatory and sprang out into the darkness of the night. Behold! There was no one there!

3. The First Murder

The evening papers of 7 August 1888, announced the perpetration of a very horrible crime in the East-end of London. The morning papers of the day following supplied other and fuller details and greatly augmented the interest taken in the murder, which promised to be exciting to the last degree. It was a mysterious case, and your average Londoner – or his provincial brother, for that matter – is a lover of mystery. Here was a sensational crime after his own heart, and he revelled in the gruesome details. The facts were as follows:

At five o'clock in the morning of that day, a labourer employed on the waterside, named 'Jack' Reeves, having a lodging at 37, George Yard Buildings, left his abode for daily work. A dark stone staircase led from the landing on which his room was situated to the ground beneath and, as he descended this staircase, he thought he observed a drunken woman – which would have been no unusual sight – lying on the landing of the first floor. He gingerly approached the prostrate figure. He had interviewed 'ladies' in a similar condition before on that same landing, and knew well their powers of vituperation. But abuse of any kind was denied to this female, whoever she might be, for she was dead. She was lying prone on her back in a deep pool of blood and with her clothes wantonly thrown upwards. No case of suicide this, thought the horrified discoverer; this was clearly murder, and nothing less. Reeves sent first for a doctor and then the police. The former could do nothing, except pronounce the victim to be dead; the police could only theorise and speculate for the time being. The woman was dead, and her decease had occurred at least three hours before the medical man examined the remains. The wounds upon the body were of a most frightful character. Dr Kelane, who conducted the post-mortem examination, declared at the coroner's inquest that there were no less than thirty-eight wounds upon the body and the legs. The left lung was penetrated in five places, and the right in two. The heart had been cut through, the liver had five punctures, and the spleen had two, the stomach also had been cut in five places, and there was a deep wound in the left breast which must have been caused by a long, sharp instrument, suggestive more of the surgeon's knife than of any other weapon. The woman had been, the doctor thought, comparatively healthy, and he attributed the death to shock and the loss of blood. He scouted the notion that any of the injuries could have been self-inflicted. It was murder; cruel, brutal, relentless murder. Of that, there could be no doubt from the first.

The news of this painful discovery in the East-end street spread like wildfire, and created almost a panic in this and surrounding districts. At the early hour at which the remains were found, an awestruck crowd of affrighted sightseers collected themselves at the bottom of the staircase, while others swarmed down from the rooms above. The duties of the police were likely to be interfered with, and orders were given that the body should be removed to the mortuary without delay. The first thing it was necessary for the police to establish was the identity of the victim of this barbarity. It was discovered that the body was that of Martha Turner, a single woman aged thirty-five, who had been recently living at No. 4, Star Place, Commercial Road, E. At the close of the inquest the jury returned a verdict, customary in the circumstances, of 'Wilful Murder by some person or persons unknown'.

On the morning of the discovery as to the identity of the victim of this barbarity, two men were seated at breakfast in furnished apartments in Gower Street. The one – the fair, languid, indifferent, smartly attired one – was Edmund Blake, the private inquiry agent. He was only thirty years of age, and was, by his enemies, declared to be 'assuming, cheeky, fat-headed, aggressive, over-rated' – there were other epithets which may, with advantage, be forgotten – while his friends delivered themselves of the theory that he was a 'coming man, a Sherlock Holmes, keen, inscrutable, analytical, an improvement upon any of the great French detectives of the past.'

Edmund Blake was assuredly a very clever man. He was a poseur, and his 'pose' took the form of satire and absolute indifference to all that interested ordinary specimens of mankind; but behind this cloak of carelessness lurked an intensely keen mind, and a genius for analysis which might be backed, sportively speaking, to unravel the most intricate of mysteries. A problem in which his fellow men and women were concerned delighted him. He loved to preside over a chessboard on which the pawns were living men and women, to be moved at will. The more inscrutable the mystery, the more dark and disheartening the surroundings of a cause célébre, the more involved and apparently difficult its features, the keener was the zest which Edmund Blake brought to bear in its investigation. He was an artist in detection. It was a labour of love.

Young as he was, Blake had already scored some notable triumphs. He it was who had recovered certain incriminating letters in which a prominent member of a foreign Royal House had been involved. Blake it was who had run to earth the murderer of Mr Woods at Carnarvon. To that same analytical mind could be attributed the evasion of a great scandal in the peculiar case of Lady Balmoral. It was Edmund Blake who discovered why a certain popular sprig of nobility disappeared about the time of the Cleveland Street discoveries, and it was Blake who fastened the rope around the throat of the Great Weevil murderer. At something over thirty, even the authorities at Scotland Yard, who were jealous of his skill and influence, envied and respected, in silent admiration, talents which they knew themselves to lack. Edmund Blake occupied a little suite of four rooms in Gower Street. He was passing rich, and could have rejoiced in a commodious flat, with all its conveniences, if he had cared to do so. But the Gower Street rooms were good enough for him and answered all purposes. He had the telephone in his sitting-room and at his bedside; his housekeeper was an admirable cook – he would not trust his culinary arrangement to the tender mercies of the landlady – and his cigars and wines were equal to those provided by the well-to-do City men with large residences in Bedford, Russell, and Tavistock Squares. Edmund Blake, the 'last word', as an American patron called him, in the gentle art of detection, had many acquaintances, but few friends. One of the latter was Ralph Thorpe, a young and, at present,

very briefless barrister. The latter spent most of his spare time in Blake's apartments, and his faith and admiration for his senior were unbounded.

On the morning when the discovery of the identity of the body found in George Yard Buildings had been announced in the columns of the daily press, Mr Blake and his friend, Mr Thorpe, sat together at breakfast, which was quite an elaborate meal in Gower Street. The time was eleven o'clock and the principal features of the Bohemian meal were a goodly portion of salmon which had been swimming about in the Tay forty-eight hours previously, a dish of devilled kidneys and green bacon, a pot of caviare, a Yorkshire ham, boiled eggs, coffee, and toast. Mr Blake rejoiced in the good things of his life, though he drank – and made love – very sparingly. They sat, the two young men, vis-à-vis with a pile of daily papers near them.

'Just a nip of curacos to make all right inside,' remarked the detective, 'and then to business. I have a little matter here' – touching his breast pocket – 'which I should like to discuss with you, you budding KC. But first, let me tell you that the identity of the poor woman found murdered in the East-end has been established.'

'Any clue?' asked Thorpe. He was somewhat of a gourmand and, I am afraid, spoke with his mouth full.'

'Apparently none. Or, if one exists, the police are not going to make me a present of it.'

'A sordid enough affair, I expect, hardly worthy of your deductive prowess, Blake,' observed his friend.

'Humph! I don't know about that,' said the other. 'There are circumstances connected with this crime which appear to me to lift it out of the ordinary. What was the motive?'

'Robbery,' suggested the young barrister.

'Nonsense,' was the unambiguous reply. 'The poor creature was a waif and stray of the streets to whom a threepenny bit was a fortune. Try again.'

'Committed in a fit of jealous passion,' Thorne again hazarded. 'Or in a drunken frenzy.'

'Hardly. Murderers of that class would be satisfied with the mere taking of life. This man ran the risk of capture in order to savagely mutilate the lifeless clay. There were some forty wounds, remember.'

'With what weapon had they been done?'

'I can't say,' Blake replied. 'The police theory inclines to a sword-bayonet and a pocket-knife. For my part, I doubt the sword-bayonet, and I question the pocket-knife; but I have not yet seen the body. I may ask to today.'

'Had any man been noticed with the deceased just prior to the murder?' inquired Thorpe, who knew his friend's methods, and felt certain that Blake had even now formed some theory.

'I think not,' was the answer. 'A soldier had been loitering in the neighbourhood of George Yard, and a constable advised him to get back to the barracks. A woman named

Mary Connolly declares that she and the murdered female, whom she knew as Martha Turner, were drinking with two soldiers for some hours the night before the discovery. At 11.45, she says she left the deceased in or close to George Yard with one of the soldiers. A cabman who lived at 35, George Yard Buildings, returned home at half-past three that morning and observed a woman lying on the landing, but the sight does not appear to have been an uncommon one, and as he thought the woman was merely drunk, he gave no alarm. The murder was actually discovered, you will remember, at five o'clock.'

'No screams had been heard I suppose?'

'Not a sound,' replied Blake, as he rolled himself a cigarette of fine Larrakia. 'In fact, the woman could not have screamed. The man was an artist. He put his arm round her neck as though in a clumsy, vulgar embrace – there was a slash across the throat with a fine knife, and silence. The mutilation was pure wanton savagery.'

'An afterthought, perhaps,' Thorpe suggested.

Blake pushed away his plate, and deposited on the table an ash-tray and a lens.

'No, planned and premeditated I should say. A cool hand this murderer, and I think we shall hear of him again. In the meanwhile, let me call your attention to this.'

'This' was a dirty and crumpled sheet of common note-paper which the detective had extracted from an even dirtier envelope. Applying the powerful lens to his eye, Blake looked long and carefully at the few sentences scrawled thereon in ink of a peculiar colour. At length he tossed envelope and paper over to his companion.

'Try the glass,' he said, 'and then oblige me with your opinion of that document.'

'Thorpe examined it with care. The envelope was addressed to 'Mr Ed. Blake at 38, Gower Street, London,' and had been posted in the S.E. District the previous evening. On the paper that had been enclosed were written these words.

> Freedom. August 12 1888. You are a bit above the police, and they may come to you for help. But even you, though you think yourself so clever, will fail to find this murderer. Try! I defy you all! – Jack the Ripper.

That was all. There were two or three smudges and blots on the letter, but these appeared to have come by design rather than accident, and the handwriting had been obviously disguised.

Blake called his friend's attention to the inside of the envelope.

'What do you make of this?' he said.

On the reverse side of the address had been drawn a rough picture which a half crown piece might have covered.

'What does it represent?' Blake asked again.

Thorpe looked at it through the lens.

'It's meant for a heart with a stiletto through it,' he said, 'and beneath is the motto, "All for Love." A strange device, truly.'

'It might be a crest, don't you think?' Blake said.

'Possibly.'

The detective took down a volume from his well-lined shelves. 'That's Deat's *Armorial Bearings*,' he said, 'and here's *Burke's Peerage*, and a treatise on heraldry.'

He rapidly turned the gilt-edged pages of *Burke*.

'Let me see,' he said. 'Cadegan – Cairns – Cawdor – Clancarty – Cowley – Caversham. Ah! Here we have a Baron Caversham, of Caversham Castle, Trelawney, Cornall, and of Park Lane, London, West, JP for two counties, member of Boodles', Turf Club, Raleigh, etc., motto; "All for Love." A curious coincidence, my dear Thorpe.'

Thorpe looked at his host with increasing interest.

'Is it a coincidence only?' he said. 'But the whole affair is very strange. Is this letter signed "Jack the Ripper" an attempt to hoax you?'

Blake smiled. 'Faith!' he said, 'I take it to be the real genuine article.'

'But why should the murderer write to you?'

'My good Thorpe, murderers are not usually rational, reasoning beings like you and myself. They do strange and bizarre things because their temperaments and dispositions are unusual and grotesque. I take it that the man who wrote that letter to me, or who caused it to be written, murdered poor Martha Turner. He got clear away this time, but if he goes in so largely for the additional luxury or mutilation, he may not be so fortunate again. Heigho! I wish I had a little more to go on. My mind hankers after activity. By the way, has not Lord Caversham a pretty daughter recently engaged to be married?'

'Yes, to young Stephen Darrell,' was the reply. 'I know him slightly. Why do you ask?'

'I may want you to introduce me soon, that's all. What is our programme for the day? You've no brief to worry you, I suppose?'

Ralph Thorpe laughed a little bitterly. 'Divil a one,' he said. 'If it were not for my earnings as a journalist, I could not keep afloat at all. Do with me what you will. There's a matinee of the new piece at the Hilarity. Pretty girls, capital music. There's a day's racing at Windsor, I believe. I'm told The Scorpion is good for the Handicap. There's a polo match at Roehampton, and there's the trial of Dawson and Higgins at the Old Bailey. Which is it to be?'

'A medley of entertainments, indeed,' said Blake, laughing. 'The trial is a walk-over; guilty, without leaving the box. It's too hot for a theatre. Let's drive down to Richmond and dine at the Star and Garter. I'll stand Sam. I feel like Heidsic and Truffles aux Perigord. Are you on?'

'It's a deal,' said Thorpe. 'Here! Take back your precious letter. It's an uncanny thing, and I confess I don't like the look of it.'

'He tossed the paper and envelope over to his friend, who deposited them carefully in a secret drawer in his roll-top desk.

'I shall want them again,' he explained, 'before long.' Excuse me a moment while I inform my excellent Mrs Saunders that I shall not be home to lunch or dinner. I won't be long.'

He was gone exactly seven minutes, and returned attired in a smart lounge suit which did infinite credit to his tailor. He filled his cigar case, brushed his hat, and made a final survey of his tie at the glass. Then he added a pink carnation to his buttonhole and prepared to depart.

'By the way, Thorpe,' he said, slyly. 'I suppose you noticed nothing else that was peculiar about that letter?'

'Hang the letter!' returned his friend. 'Come along!'

'The ink, for instance?' queried Blake, with his hand on the door.

'It was rotten ink,' said the barrister.

'It wasn't ink at all,' said Blake, a trifle gravely. 'That letter was written in liquid human blood!'

4. At Work

It was early in the October of 1887 when Mortemer Slade escaped from Dr Kent's establishment near Broxbourne, but it was not till the last day of July in the following year that he took up his abode in London. What became of him in the intervening time has never become known. It has been suggested that he went abroad for a time, and this seems the most plausible theory; but no one, not even his solicitors, knew of his whereabouts, and it was commonly assumed that he was dead. All we know for certain is that on 31 July in the eventful year referred to a man calling himself John Maidment took a modest lodging on the second floor of a home in Stamford Street, Blackfriars, and that 'John Maidment' effectually disguised the identity of Mortemer Slade. He had assumed for the purpose of concealment a false beard and moustache so artistically contrived that the great Clarkson himself might have taken them for natural hirsute adornments. He wore a black Inverness cape, a dark slouch hat, and shabby boots. He had the appearance of a foreigner and he had cultivated an accent to induce people to believe that he came from abroad. Terrible passions seared their way through his heart, and worked havoc in his mind, but he permitted no sign of these to be revealed to his fellow man. He was calm, urbane, dignified and posed most successfully as a gentleman in reduced circumstances. Not one who daily and nightly came in contact with Mr Maidment knew him for the awful thing he was.

It was half-past six on the morning of 7 August about an hour and a half after the discovery of the murder in George Yard Buildings, when Mortemer Slade, walking rapidly and with long and even strides, crossed Blackfriars Bridge and turned into Stamford Street, a thoroughfare not then notorious by reason of the exploits of the almost equally infamous Neil Cream. He glanced behind him two or three times as he walked, as though he contemplated the bare possibility of his being followed, but, satisfied apparently on that point, he crossed over and entered the saloon bar of the Brunswick Arms, calling for a brandy, which he drank neat with a perfectly steady hand. His nerves, he told himself, were in good order, in spite of what he had passed through during the last few hours. He sat for a while and sipped at a second glass of the ardent spirit. The morning was bright and warm but he felt a little chilly, and had shivered once or twice as he crossed the bridge. The barman was polishing glasses and whistling a popular tune. Slade asked him for the morning paper, and glanced indifferently at the news. Soon he returned it to the barman.

'Nothing in it?' asked that youth with an eye on the sporting intelligence.

'Nothing much,' was the reply. 'Perhaps there'll be more in tomorrow.'

This reflection did not appear to afford vast consolation to the youth behind the bar. 'For my part,' he said, 'I likes a good spicy divorce case as much as anything; plenty of blue love-letters and servants' evidence, and so on. Ain't there no murder in today's paper even, sir?'

This last was said with quite an air of injury. Slade gave him one of his electric glances. The bright eyes, placed a shade too near together in the head, shone fiercely.

'Perhaps,' he remarked, with a ghastly smile, 'you'll get a murder in tomorrow's issue. I'm not sure about the spicy divorce case, but I think I can promise you a fine murder in tomorrow's. Good morning.'

The barman stared at his ominous customer, and Slade, with a careless shrug of the shoulders, passed out into the street. His apartment, called by courtesy a 'combined room', was situated at the Waterloo end of the street. Thither he betook himself. Not many people were about. The workmen's trains had not yet delivered their loads from suburbia, though the rush would begin in a few minutes. A newspaper boy was delivering papers at some of the better-class houses. Slatternly-looking girls, in various stages of deshabille, were taking in the matutinal milk.

From one or two of the houses emerged gentlemen accompanied by ladies. These looked a little ashamed of themselves, and apt to resent the curious glances cast at them by the passers-by. A street Arab exchanged badinage with another of his species on the subject.

'Look at Bertie and Flossie,' he said. 'Fair old night-birds, ain't they? Met at a music-'all, supper at restyrong, night at a 'otel – for self and wife. We knows! Wonder what his missis will say when he gets 'ome.' A policeman meandered up the street in solitary grandeur. A few miserable-looking figures emerged, blinking at the sunlight, from the unsavoury side-streets.

'This is life,' said Slade, as he gazed about. 'I like this better than Belgravian halls. I feel alive here.'

He produced a latchkey and entered one of the houses on the left-hand side coming from Blackfriars. Softly he crept up to his room, unlocked the door, entered, bolted it again, and sat down upon the wretched bed.

'Monarch of all I survey here,' he muttered, gleefully rubbing his hands. 'Here I can be as mad as I please.'

He got up and removed his cloak, spreading it on the bed and examining it with the utmost care, turning it over half a dozen times, peering into corners of it with keen intensity. Apparently satisfied with his scrutiny, he turned his attention to his boots, which he took off, and the legs, particularly the lower part, of his trousers. 'Not a stain,' he said, 'the size of a pin-prick. Not a mark to suggest the little game of last night. And yet what seas and oceans of blood seemed to pour from every gash I inflicted. How the knife cut through and through the juicy flesh. Oh! The ecstasy of killing, the joy of it, the beauty of it! 'Twere well to have lived for this.'

He took from a leather case concealed in an inner pocket a long, thin knife – a surgical instrument, in fact – with a blade six inches long, keener than most razors. He then wiped the blade carefully upon a sheet of white paper. It left a deep red stain, still wet, upon the surface. He put the paper in the empty grate, set fire to it, and watched it burn away.

'I'll take a scalpel as well with me next time,' Slade muttered, replacing the knife in its case. 'And now for my letter to the smartest detective, private or official, in London. Bah! He'll have to be that to cope with me.'

From another pocket came a little phial containing a dark liquid. He dipped a pen carefully into this and wrote a few sentences. 'I won't post it till the inquest,' he remarked.

'It will give this Blake something to try his ingenuity upon. And now for a couple of hours' sleep. I shall go out on the prowl again tonight and mark down a suitable victim. If I get a few moments more spare time with the body I'll make their blood run cold, policemen and detectives all. They shall see what sight a genius can produce, a genius in crime such as Victor Hugo might have painted, De Quincey have imagined, and Poe conceived. Fame is coming to you fast, Mortemer Slade, fame is coming fast.' Gradually he sank into an easy and dreamless sleep like the sleep of a little child.

On their return from the gaieties of Richmond, where Edmund Blake had been the life and soul of a joyous party, that gentleman abandoned his friend Thorpe at Waterloo, and, hailing a hansom, drove to the mortuary where rested the remains of the unfortunate woman barbarously done to death in George Yard. He had official permission to view the body, and also an appointment for later in the evening with Mr Wallace, the deputy coroner for S.E. Middlesex, who had just brought the inquest to a conclusion. The murdered woman was to be buried the following morning. Her identity had been clearly established, and nothing more was to be gained for justice by retaining the poor remains above the ground. Relatives or friends this Martha appeared to have none. She was a derelict on life's ocean, and had gone down in a storm.

Reverently did the clever young detective view the corpses. He made copious notes of the situation of every wound, and drew a sketch of the victim as she lay. The position in which the body had been found, rigid on its back, with the hands so tightly clenched that the nails were driven into the flesh, was carefully explained to him by the inspector in charge of the case. He interviewed PC Barrett 266 H, who had seen a soldier enter and had warned him that it was time for him to be back in the barracks. Two Coldstream Guardsmen were, indeed, even now under arrest at the Tower, but the witness Connolly, who had seen Martha Turner, quite failed to identify either of them, and they were soon released. Dr Kellune, who had been called in when the body was first discovered, explained the precise nature of the injuries inflicted, and was pleased to express surprise at the extent of Blake's surgical knowledge.

With Mr Wallace Blake remained nearly an hour. 'Everything possible has been done,' the deputy-coroner assured him, 'but I fear, I greatly fear, that this sad affair will be added to the catalogue of crimes that have never been discovered. You cannot assist us in any way, Mr Blake, I suppose?'

'I have not been officially consulted,' was the guarded reply. 'I am afraid the C.I.D. Authorities regard me as a bit of a charlatan, don't you know. I am quite the last court of appeal. I have, however, taken it upon myself to suggest that a strong body of police and private-clothes men should be drafted into this district without delay.'

Mr Wallace stared. 'The murderer, as likely as not, lives in quite another neighbourhood,' he suggested.

'Most probably,' said Blake. 'I was alluding to the likelihood of him paying the East-end another visit.'

'What!' cried the official, aghast. 'You contemplate that he will commit another murder?'

'I regard it as almost certain. Steps should be taken without delay. The streets, and more particularly the alleys, should be closely watched and patrolled. This crime, Sir, is not an ordinary murder actuated by sudden anger, jealousy, or revenge. You have to deal with a madman, or, at least, with an epileptic, and one possessed of cunning only equal to his ferocity. We are men of the world, Sir, and need not mince matters. With what purpose did this woman take the man who killed her to that landing in the dead at night?'

'The soldier?' exclaimed the coroner.

'No soldier. A man who picked the woman up in the street, treated her to liquor, and bargained with her for a purpose that shall be nameless. She knew the vicinity. He did not. They reach the dark landing, and the man, who has drawn a scalpel, or a similar instrument, without being observed, puts his arm around her neck and presses her chin upward so that she cannot give forth a cry. He draws the long thin knife across the throat, and then noiselessly lowers the body to the ground. Then he kneels by it and plunges the weapon again and again, violently in his blood-lust, into the quivering flesh. The murderer is, I think, left-handed. As likely as not he left the scene without a mark upon him, and went home quietly to bed.'

'I can see no motive if they were strangers,' remarked the bewildered gentleman, who, like the police, had clung to the soldier theory with a great tenacity.

'Nor I. As yet. But that I have reconstructed the crime to you currently, I am convinced. *Qui vivra verra!*'

Mr Wallace rose. 'Your theory may be right, Mr Blake,' he said, 'but pray Heaven I may not have to hold an inquest over another victim to this savage's ferocity.'

'I hope not, indeed,' replied Blake. 'But baleful shadows darken our paths at times and we can only shudder at them as they pass us by. Good-night, Sir, and thank you.'

He drove towards Gower Street in a thoughtful mood. When half-way there, he put his hand through the trapdoor and bade his man drive him to his club.

'A rubber of whist, or a game of pool, won't hurt me,' he said. 'I'm interested in this "sordid murder", as Thorpe calls it, and I may want to get the plaguey thing out of my head.'

He alighted at the handsome and imposing entrance to the club and paid the cabman from a handful of loose change. As he turned away, a tall, spare man passed him, who was wearing an Inverness cap and a slouch hat. The 'baleful shadow' had momentarily darkened the path of Edmund Blake, who little knew whom or what he had thus encountered.

Inside Thorpe, Adams, Cousens and half a dozen others hailed him, and he was made to partake of a whisky and soda, which went down well after his recent exertions.

'That fellow you spoke of this morning is here,' said Thorpe, 'a guest of John Tresham's. They've been supping together. He seems a good sort.'

'I haven't the least idea to whom you refer, Ralph,' remarked Blake rather wearily. Thorpe he found a little trying at times.

'Deuce take it! To Stephen Darrell, of course. Didn't I say so? Shall I introduce you?'

'Oh! The lucky young dog who is going to marry Lord Caversham's youngest and prettiest. Yes, I'd like to know him. I'll come with you and you can make us known to each other.'

Darrell seemed to take to Blake intuitively, and the liking was reciprocal. The two young men retired to a corner of the smoking-room, and Blake took the opportunity of congratulating the other upon his engagement to Miss Penrose. In a burst of candour, and aware that he was speaking to one eminent in the art of detection, Stephen confided to Blake the circumstances attending the strange appearance of his fiancée on the night of the ball.

'I make light of it to Phyllis,' he explained, 'and have half-persuaded her that she imagined she saw his face pressed against the glass of the conservatory, but for the life of me I can't get over the letter which he sent, and in which he threatened to appear to her in just such a mysterious way on the eve of every great crisis in his life. Of course, the man is mad, but I have learnt that he escaped from Grange House some months since, and he may cause Miss Penrose serious alarm and annoyance. Do you consider I should warn the police?'

'Publicity,' said Blake, 'would hardly be be pleasant for your future wife or yourself. I think, in your position, I should wait awhile. If Mortemer Slade is really mad he is pretty sure to betray himself sooner or later, and you will soon hear that he is safely back amongst the "luneys". I confess I should like to see his letter.'

'I have it here,' said Stephen, and he handed the envelope and its contents to the detective.

'Did Miss Penrose recognise this as the handwriting of Mr Slade?' the latter inquired.

'No. As a matter of fact, she had only once or twice seen his calligraphy. He forwarded her a parcel of books occasionally, I believe, and had written notes of acceptance to dinner, and so forth, but, naturally, his writing had left no impression upon her mind.'

Blake's eyes were riveted upon the word 'Freedom' at the top of the letter. He had only that morning received a note similarly commenced, and that note lay, ready for comparison, in his bureau at home. What did it mean? Upon what hellish mystery was he blindly stumbling? 'I hope that you won't think me impertinent, or actuated by mere vulgar curiosity,' he said, in serious tones, 'but if you will kindly consent to leave this letter in my hands for twenty-four hours I may be able to relieve Miss Penrose's mind, for the future, of all apprehensions as regards this – this Mr Mortemer Slade. I assure you I have good reasons for asking this.'

'Keep the letter as long as you please, so far as Miss Penrose and I are concerned,' Stephen rejoined. 'We don't want to see it again, or hear more of poor, mad Slade.'

The two men shook hands, and Blake rose to go. 'Come and dine with me one night,' he said, 'if you don't think Gower Street too far afield. There's my card. My housekeeper is a tolerable cook, and the wines won't poison you. Do come.'

Stephen promised to avail himself of the invitation, and went off in search of his friend Tresham, after bidding a cordial goodbye to his new acquaintance. Blake went home post-haste in a hansom.

'It may be nothing more than a coincidence,' he muttered, as he turned on the electric light in his silent den, 'but the peculiar use of the word "Freedom" as though it were an address, and the writer was staying there, is extremely curious, to say the least.'

He went to his desk and removed the letter which had been written in human blood from the secret drawer. He compared it with that Mortemer Slade had sent to Phyllis Penrose. Rather to his dismay, he saw that the writings were totally dissimilar. Was his theory, already half-formed, at fault then?

5. Slade Appears Again

On 28 August 1888 – by which time the brutal murder of Martha Turner was already well-nigh forgotten, except by those whose duties or interests compelled them to keep it in memory – Mortemer Slade, alias Mr Maidment, left his Lambeth lodging at about nine o'clock at night. He had slept heavily throughout the best part of the long summer day, and his landlady had hesitated to disturb him. Her lodger paid liberally for his meagre accommodation, made no complaints, and gave no trouble, so that the worthy woman felt that he was entitled to sleep as long as he pleased, though she could not altogether approve of his habit of being abroad at night and remaining in bed all day. Her sentiments in this respect she confided to Mrs Dawkins, her neighbour.

'He's got,' said the worthy soul, 'a piercin' look with him, that at first I owns I found a little disconcertin'. But his voice is soft and low, his 'ands are as white as mine after a washin' day, and he says "thank 'ee" fair and civil-like, if you takes him a cup o' tea. In my belief, Mrs Dawkins, ma'am, he's one of them there refugee noblemen from Roosia or them parts, who's got 'imself into 'ot water through a-blowin' up of the 'Ouses of Parliament, or somethin'. You know them furriners are always a-blowin' up somebody or somethin'. But live and let live, I say! His 'abits may not be the most respectable, but 'e's plainly a gent, born and bred, and it ain't for me to inquire too closely into the dark shadders of his past.'

Mrs Dawkins agreed, and remarked that he could sleep all day and night if she had him, so long as he woke up at nine o'clock every Saturday morning to pay his rent.

Attired in the everlasting Inverness cape, bewigged and bearded, Slade proceeded westwards, and did not halt until he had reached a certain little hostelry between Soho and Fitzroy Square. At this tavern, the resort of German, Swiss, French and Italian waiters, he expected to meet an acquaintance to whom he had once confided the untruth that he himself had at one time been a waiter in New York. Slade had made this statement rather with a view of ingratiating himself with the Frenchman at this time, for that gentleman had the lively Gallic temperament and kept the morose lunatic amused. Now, however, his acquaintance was likely to prove of use to him.

At a quarter to ten this individual entered the private bar of the house in question and called for the absinthe beloved of his countrymen. Slade spoke to him in French.

'And how,' he said, 'does M. Brat find himself this morning?'

M. Brat – Jean, as he was known to the customers at many a swell restaurant at home and abroad – received him, though he had only met him four days previously, with enthusiasm.

'Ma Foi,' he said, 'the very man. Sare, this is a coincidence of the most agreeable. This is a rencontre of the most delightful. My gratification it is, Sare, profound.'

'Well?' said Slade, smiling at the exuberance of the little Frenchman, who was considered quite an artist in at least seven capitals of Europe, and was known to and approved of by all the patrons of Delmonico's.

'You have been, you tell me, a waitare yourself, you also. *N'est-ce-pas?*'

'For a brief period in a not uneventful career,' returned Slade. 'Why do you refer to it again, *mon cher* M. Brat?'

Heavens! To think that he had once tipped the little Frenchman a sovereign after a successful dinner with a *chere amie* in a *cabinet-particulier* at the Cafe de l'Europe in Vienna!

'Ze hand of ze waitare does not lose its cunning. You have not served for some time? Eh *bien! N'importe.* If you cared – there is a – what you call? – a leetle job at the Hotel Oriental – oh! Quite ze first-class! – tomorrow evening.'

'You mean I could come as an assistant waiter on your recommendation?' said Slade, laughing. 'Well, it would distract my thoughts. I might even find amusement' – he paused. Some of the visitors might be intimate friends of his own. There was humour in the idea. He wished his cousins might be there. 'I'd add a little prussic acid to their *potage-a-la-reine*,' he thought grimly. 'And the pay?' he added aloud.

'Ze pay?'

'The remuneration – the wage.'

'*Soyez tranquille!* M. Maidment will leave that to me. The guests are of the tip-top. They will treat the artists who serve them with a generosity the most princely. Monsieur's dress suit? It was quite – ze thing?'

'Oh! I shouldn't disgrace the Ancient and Honourable Order of Waiters as regards my dress,' said Slade, with his cutting smile. 'You have your own particular table, I suppose?'

'*Mais oui*,' returned the Frenchman. 'Ladies and gentlemen of the most distinguished. *Voila!* Zare will be ze Earl of Shincliffe, Milor Caversham, Madame ze Countess, ze Viscount Hardcastle, the Honourable Miss Penrose – I kiss my hand to ze Honourable Miss Penrose – and –'

'Enough!' said Slade, briskly. 'You can count upon me. The time?'

'At the seven and half a clock?'

'I ask for you?'

'For me; for M. Brat. I will keep ze eye upon you. You shall make no what you call a error. You shall be as ze right hand of M. Brat. *Quel honneur!*'

Slade shook hands on the promise, called for two more glasses of the pernicious green liquid, bought cigars, and chatted to the Frenchman of gay doings in his beloved capital. Other members of the fraternity – they also serve who only stand and wait! – joined them, and it was nearly eleven when Slade, shaking off the voluble Frenchman, left the tavern. From Soho he walked towards the east, into

the Commercial Road and back into the Whitechapel Road, accustoming himself with a painstaking diligence to the alleys and courts of that densely populated district. 'In a couple of weeks,' he reflected, 'I shall know them all.'

A quarter of an hour before midnight he was in Church Row, Whitechapel, and was hailed by a woman as he passed a brilliantly lighted tavern.

'Thought you were never comin', dearie,' she hiccoughed, and laid a detaining hand upon his arm.

'Not here,' he exclaimed, impatiently. 'Walk ahead of me towards Essex Wharf. I'll speak to you there.'

The woman, aged about thirty-five, and coarse and bloated, was three-parts intoxicated and she stumbled up against him as she turned reluctantly towards the direction he had indicated.

'Ain't you goin' to stand your lovin' Mary Ann a drop o' gin first?' she said in hoarse tones. 'Not a leetle drop o' the real white satin, lovey? Lor' luv yer, there's plenty o' time. Gord! Couldn't I do a big drink of it.'

'Go on before me,' he said, sternly. 'I've some spirits in my pocket – a flask. Better stuff than you'll get in there.'

'Now, you are talkin' ducky-bird. You're a real gent you are, as knows 'ow to treat a lady 'andsome. I'll walk to Essex Wharf and you'll follow me close behind, case some of these nasty, rough men may get insultin' to me, wot's been a domestic servant in 'er time, and come down in the world through drink and the men, devil take 'em – all save you, ducky, all save you.'

Muttering to herself in incoherent vein, she preceded Slade along the street and did not pause or look round again till she neared a stable-yard used in connection with Essex Wharf. Then she stopped, and, leaning against the wall, awaited the approach of Slade. The place was silent and deserted. She knew how long it would be before the constable on the beat would be round again.

'We're safe for twenty blessed minutes, darlin',' she said. 'In what pocket 'ave you got that there gin, I wonders?'

'You'll have none of it till I've made you understand what I have to say. Then you can take the stuff to your den and drink away all thought or care for the morrow. Laugh and be merry, for tomorrow you die, and all that sort of thing.' He gave a harsh laugh, and the woman made a ludicrous attempt to embrace him.

'Blime!' she said, 'I don't likes you, gov'nor, 'streuth I don't, when you looks like that. Look amiable, cawn't yer. Ay! That's better! What's your name, lovey? You ain't never told your pore dear Mary Ann your name.'

'Call me – Jack,' he said, with his wolfish grin.

'Jack?' she repeated. 'Jack what?'

'Jack is enough for you to know for the present. What's your name?'

'Mary Ann Nicholls, a respectable married woman, a-separated from her lawful 'usband. Oh! I ain't too particular, gov'nor. My old man 'opped it with another girl, and I ain't above lookin' at another bloke now and again. Especially when – like you, lovey – he's got money. I 'eard it rattle – and a bottle of hell-fire.'

'Listen,' Slade said, impressively. 'Meet me here at this very spot – not tomorrow, but the next night at one o'clock. The next night to tomorrow, remember. Keep the appointment, and I'll treat you generously enough.'

'Cawn't you stay tonight, ducky?'

'No. You can keep till Thursday. I shall be ready for you then. Remember, at one o'clock; here, by this stable, near this wharf.'

'You can depend on me, gov'nor. I ain't goin' to miss a chance like this. Blessed if I knows what you can see in me, but I'm yours, gov'nor, strike me, body and soul.'

'You are, indeed,' said Slade, with the usual cruel contraction of the lips.

'Mayn't I 'ave a taster of that 'ere gin you're stickin' to so tight?'

'Here, take it,' said Slade, 'and there's half a crown. That's an earnest of what you'll get if you're up to time on Thursday. If you fail me—'

'There you go again with that there look of yours,' said Mrs Nicholls, piteously. 'Don't I tells yer I'll be 'ere. I give yer my dyin' word if Gord was to—'

'Enough! I trust you.'

She took his hand. 'A kiss,' she said, with a leer – she had been a pretty woman once – 'a kiss just to show there ain't no ill-feelin on either side.'

His lips met hers. 'Off with you,' he cried, and the poor creature lurched towards the Whitechapel Road again, with many a backward glance, and a drunken kiss of the hand.

'Phaugh!, he said, rubbing at his lips with the back of his hand. 'That such a pestilential harridan should breathe the same atmosphere, should exist in the same world, as Phyllis Penrose. I'll wipe out the stain of that kiss, my lady. Never fear! Never fear!'

The constable attached to that beat came along with silent tread, and flashed his bull's-eye upon Slade's averted face.

'Good-night,' he said. 'Good-night,' muttered Slade, and walking slowly away. 'That's the very spot for it,' he said. 'Look at your papers this weekend again, noble sirs and noble dames. I'll give you blood enough and to spare.'

He spent another hour or so exploring the darksome labyrinths of Whitechapel. These mean streets, these squalid courts, these noisome alleys, seemed to have a peculiar fascination for the blood-stained monster, who, under a smiling and almost benignant exterior, concealed the worst of frenzied passions. It may be wondered that his appearance in these densely populated and poverty-stricken districts did not attract a certain degree of attention, but it must be remembered that he rarely passed through them except at night, and that aliens, even fairly well-dressed aliens, whom, in outward aspect and demeanour, he most resembled, were as legions in the close and stuffy thoroughfares of the East-end.

Night-bird as he was, he had no desire as yet to return to his lodging on the other side of the water. Time enough for that, he thought, at the first break of dawn. He went towards the twinkling light of one of those caravanserai of poor streets, a coffee-stall, and stood there idly for a time drinking the weak and mysterious liquid which, at a penny a cup, had the one merit of being hot. A couple of roughs, fair types of the Hooligan tribe, were talking and laughing together as he approached. They took no notice of Slade beyond one casual glance, which satisfied their well-trained eyes that he was neither a 'slop' in plain clothes, nor a 'copper's nark', out on the prowl, nor a ''tec' searching for some much-coveted offender.

'Four more eggs,' one said to the proprietor of the gutter hotel, 'and a couple of slices. Blime, Snookey, your pure Devonshire butter, like cream, one and eight a pound, gets worser and worser, strike me if it don't.'

'Make grand grease for cartwheels,' said the other, with an unsavoury adjective which can be omitted with advantage.

'Yer seems to thrive on it, anyways,' grumbled the often abused Snookey. 'This ain't the Servoy 'otel, Blinder, nor yet a Lockhart's neither, Mr Bleater! Some of you blokes is more particular nor a barge-load of dooks and dookesses!'

Blinder tuned, Bleater whistled. They went on eating. A seedy-looking man in frock-coat and silk hat, the glories of which had long since departed, approached the stall, and had 'a slice', for which he paid one halfpenny. Somehow or other, Slade believed the coin to be his last. He ate it hungrily, casting every now and then a sidelong glance at Slade. But that gentleman was suddenly interested in the conversation of the two young ruffians. 'I tells yer I knew her well,' said the one who answered to the comprehensive name of Blinder. 'I ought ter because–'; a coarse expression followed, and the coffee-stall keeper laughed.

'Was 'er moniker really Mawtha Turner?' asked the latter, as he spread some villainous-looking margarine on a slice of brown bread. 'I 'eard different.'

'That was 'er name right enough,' said the Hooligan, with an oath. 'Swivel-eyed Martha, they called her down our way. Couldn't she lower 'er gargles. Oh! No, not 'alf!'

'Wonder who did it,' said his friend, rather envious of the honour attaching to intimacy with a lady who had been so barbarously done to death.

'Dunno. But I'd put 'im away if I did know. Many a pint she stood me when she'd got the ready; she was one of yer good-natured sorts.'

'Seems strange, when you come to think of it,' said the seedy gentleman in the frock-coat, with a hungry eye on the slabs of cake, 'that the murderer is abroad now, and may at any moment rub shoulders with you or me. He might, for anything we know, be standing here now.'

The two youths were prompt to resent this interruption. They looked him up and down with an expression of great disgust.

'And who the hell was a-speakin' to you, Baron Rothschild?' inquired one. 'Ain't you got no manners a-breakin' in on the conversation of two gents to whom you've never been introdoosed?'

'What do yer bloomin' well mean by it?' said the other more savagely. 'What are yer, a split? Come now, out with it, yer pryin', interferin', ferretin', ugly, rotten–'

There followed the usual string of expletives.

The seedy man looked embarrassed. He muttered something about not wishing to intrude or to thrust his conversation upon them, hoped there was no offence, and made as if to go away.

'You ain't worth punchin',' said Mr Bleater, 'but I'll revive that precious cady of yours.' He made a sudden movement and the seedy gentleman's already battered silk hat rolled into the gutter, where he surveyed it ruefully. 'Take it to Lincoln and Bennett when they opens, and get it ironed, old Bank of England,' said Blinder with a laugh, in which the coffee-stall keeper joined.

Some remnant of the instinct of a gentleman was suddenly revived in the twisted mind of Mortemer Slade. He faced the two blackguards, youths of the hobbledehoy calibre, eighteen or nineteen years old, but well-built and powerful. 'Pick up the gentleman's hat and hand it to him,' he said to the one who had rolled the seedy man's head-gear into the dust.

'Go to —! I ain't no — lacquey! Pick his hat up your blasted self.'

'I don't propose to. I tell you to do it,' Slade remarked, with incisive coolness.

The one addressed as Blinder seemed amazed at his audacity.

'Well, you are a-askin for it,' he remarked, almost with an admiring look at Slade. 'Why, the Bleater can make mincemeat of yer, gov'nor. 'Ere, Bleater, do it on 'im, just to show the bloomin' furriner 'e can't bring his orders and commands 'ere.'

Slade had been an athlete in his youth, had even now muscles of steel, and had learnt what the French call 'le boxe' in an admirable school. He had forgotten nothing.

'Pick up the hat,' he said, slowly.

The Bleater struck out viciously. Slade easily warded off the clumsy blow. His long, sinuous left shot out like a propeller – and Blackguard Number One bit the dust. A nasty cut over one of his eyes spoke to the power of Slade's arm. Blackguard Number Two approached Slade and made a feint, and then struck out heavily. Slade put in a clever piece of head-work, and then got both hands in; lifting the astonished Blinder clean off his legs with a crashing blow on the jaw, and administering a beautiful body-punch at the same time, which accelerated his fall. The two roughs gazed up at their conqueror in ludicrous fashion.

'I'd rather be kicked by a 'orse, I would,' remarked the crestfallen Bleater when, with some difficulty, he had recovered his footing.

Blinder took longer to rise.

'A man with a arm like the 'ind leg of an elephant ain't got no right to use it on a unoffending young chap like me,' he said gravely.

The seedy gentleman and the keeper of the stall gazed at Slade in silent admiration. That gentleman was pointing at the hat.

'Oblige me by picking it up,' he said politely.

The Bleater advanced awkwardly, raised the unfortunate 'topper', and handed it to Slade.

'It belongs to that gentleman,' said the latter, and, without further parley, the rough turned to its seedy owner and gave him the hat.

Bleater and Blinder slunk off.

'Never knew a furriner could 'it like that,' quoth the first-named worthy.

'Never want another like it,' said his friend. 'Let's go to the Markit 'Ouse and get a gargle.'

They went.

'I have to thank you, sir, for a very kindly act,' said the seedy gentleman, endeavouring to smooth his silk hat into a more-or-less reputable state again. 'Will you accept my card?' He handed him a soiled atom of pasteboard. 'I was a gentleman once, I was indeed. I feel somehow that we shall meet again; that I may, excuse me, sir, even be of a little use to you. Good morning, sir; good morning.'

He was hurrying away. Slade put his hand in his pocket and produced five shillings.

'No,' he said, softly, replacing the money. 'He was a gentleman once. So was I. I should have resented charity; so would he. Am I – am I – I wonder! I wonder! – mad or sane?'

Half an hour later he had reached his 'home'.

6. The Dinner at the Oriental

A beautifully appointed room, long and lofty. The ceiling richly enamelled. The walls hung with some soft, dark, heavy material, and the floor covered with a carpet so thick and yielding that no foot tread upon it could be heard. A magnificent crystal candelabra reflecting a thousand gleaming lights. Statuary – all works of art – in odd corners; rare porcelain on odd shelves; fine bronzes on odd brackets; paintings, suggestive for the most part, of women, wine, and song, in odd niches of the wall. Round tables in every alcove, covered with snowy table-linen, costly glass, expensive fruits, silver plate, and exotic flowers. Handsome lamps throwing, by means of their crimson shades, a red glow over the luxuriant splendour of each snow-white table. Glorious upholstery and furniture which had once adorned a king's palace. Deft-handed waiters, in faultless evening dress, moving noiselessly about. A gentle hum of subdued conversation. An occasional ripple of silvery laughter, or rustle of silken skirts. Deep manly tones and the tender treble of women. Above all, M. Brat – the Prince of Waiters, as the King of Portugal had once called him – superintending the operations of his small army, but without fuss and without noise. And a cook below stairs who had reigned two years over the cuisine of Napoleon III! The room was known by habitués of the Hotel Oriental as the Golden Chamber. There was a legend that twenty-five American millionaires had once dined there, and that the bill, paid by one of them, amounted in all to £1,250. The Prince of Monaco, on a brief visit to London, had entertained his friends to a dinner there, of which feast M. Brat talked to this day. The Plunger of the year 1887 had retained the Golden Chamber on one occasion, and gloriously dined the chorus ladies of the Gaiety and Avenue Theatres. Not to have dined at the Golden Chamber at the Hotel Oriental was never to have dined at all.

At every table on this occasion were well-known members of the higher circles. At one an eminent foreign banker entertained a select party of guests, which included a near relative to the Khedive of Egypt. At another, an Indian Maharajah, of fabulous wealth and great influence, was the leading figure. At a fourth, a prominent member of the late Lord Salisbury's Government sat with a party of friends. A dissolute young Marquis, since deceased, the in-and-out running of whose racehorses was the subject of remark at that time, was at a fifth. A well-known baronet, of cosmopolitan reputation – a reckless rider, a splendid athlete, and the assistant, on one occasion, of the common hangman – entertained a party of the *jeunesse d'oree* at yet another.

At the further end of the room a large and splendidly appointed table accommodated the party of the Earl and Countess of Shincliffe. The members of it may be briefly described.

Lord Shincliffe himself was a reserved and discreet young man, somewhat taciturn, and of an unduly serious bent. He cultivated an austere manner, talked gravely of the duties of wealth and the rights of landowners, dressed plainly, and was really industrious and painstaking in his own way. In the House of Lords he was regarded as steady and plodding and a great master of statistics.

The countess was of the marble type of beauty. She was clever, well-read, and seriously inclined. She treated her pretty sister Phyllis as a child, and lectured her father, Lord Caversham, when he won, with one of his last remaining thoroughbreds, the Chesterfield Cup at Goodwood with John Lackland.

Viscount Hardcastle was the elder son of the Earl of Dewsbury. He represented a Northern constituency in the Tory interests, and was regarded as somewhat of a political firebrand. 'A clever young man,' the Premier had pronounced him, 'but there is a little too much venom in his speeches.'

Lord Caversham was there – a handsome, portly gentleman with white hair and an iron-grey moustache. He had lines, suggestive of a dissipated youth, about the mouth, and a somewhat blunt, abrupt manner.

There was Stephen Darrell, and next to him – they were dining, as it were, *en famille* – his beautiful fiancée, Phyllis Penrose. She had quite recovered from the shock of Mortemer Slade's strange appearance, and was in excellent spirits. Stephen had been appointed to our Embassy in Paris, and the marriage was to take place in three months' time. Lastly, to complete the part of seven, was Lady Marion Minting, a pretty girl, decidedly 'smart', and the particular friend of all Lord Caversham's daughters.

M. Brat hovered unceasingly near this table. The dinner had been arranged and ordered some days before, and every luxury in or out of season had been requisitioned to do honour to the occasion. The chef was famous for his soups, and Lord Caversham condescended to praise the perfections to the ubiquitous M. Brat.

'A capital soup,' he said. 'What do you call it, Brat?'

'Milor must christen it,' was the response, 'since it has met with Milor's approval.' This with a bow.

'Not a bad idea,' cried Viscount Hardcastle. 'I suggest, though, "potage à la Penrose".'

'Call it anything you like, said Caversham; 'it's capital tack. Is the wine iced, Brat?'

'To the moment, assuredly, Milor.'

A magnum was opened, and Hardcastle and Caversham, who thoroughly enjoyed the luxuries of the table, settled down to an excellent meal, washed down with generous draughts of Pommery Sec, 1882. The Earl of Shincliffe preferred Roederer. Stephen Darrell did not like champagne, but the claret he drank at dinner cost eighteen shillings the bottle.

Meanwhile, Mortemer Slade awaited the appearance of M. Brat in an ante-room, plainly but comfortably furnished. He felt tired and listless, and sank into a deep arm-chair, and mused while he awaited the coming of his little French acquaintance. His tall and spare figure was seen to advantage in his rather too fashionably cut evening clothes, but he was clever at disguises, and a few touches here and there had given his physiognomy all the look of a foreign waiter of the best class.

'Not one of these fools with whom I used to mix will know me,' he thought, 'but I must contrive to meet the eyes of Phyllis. She will know me. At every crisis in my life I vowed I would appear to her. Tomorrow – another victim, and lo! Here I am.'

His reflections were interrupted by the appearance of M. Brat, who bustled into the room, all life and action, a vivid contrast to the subdued little mortal in the splendour of the Golden Chamber. He took in Slade's appearance at a glance.

'*Bon garçon!*' he exclaimed, in pleased tones. 'You look – ah! – quite ze nobleman. You make me quite ze proud man. I am enchanted.'

He kissed his hand to Slade, and brushed off an invisible speck of dust from his own immaculate coat. In his heart he believed Slade's appearance to be correct, but immeasurably inferior to his own.

'*Vous etes pret?*' he asked. 'You are to accompany me ready?'

'Look here, Brat,' said Slade, rising; 'it's some years since I was a member of your ever-to-be-esteemed calling. I confess to feeling a little doubt, at the last moment, of my abilities. I am perfectly willing to forego the remuneration with which my services would have been rewarded, but should be grateful if you could oblige me in another way.'

The Frenchman raised his eyebrows, but was too well bred to express any surprise at this change of front. These Englishmen, he thought, are so what you call eccentric. They must not be regarded as rational beings. '*Mais certainement,*' he said. 'What can I do?'

'My failure to fulfil my duties at the tables will not, I hope, put you to any anxiety or inconvenience?' said Slade. 'I should regret that after your kindness in engaging me.'

The waiter gave a superior smile. '*Pour moi,*' he said, 'I am nevare anxious over one of my dinners. They go on what you call right as a house on fire.' The services of Monsieur will not be missed.'

'Then my request to you is that I may be permitted to view the scene as a sort of passive assistant. I can pass as one of your underlings' – he bowed, and the Frenchman, delighted at the phrase, but his hand upon his heart – 'without being called upon to actually assist. Is that in your power, my dear M. Brat?'

'*C'est un fait accompli,*' said the vivacious Frenchman. 'Monsieur, it is done. Come with me.'

He led the way through a long passage with a glass roof and palms on either side. On the left of this, at the end, was a cloak-room. 'Leave your hat and coat here – on this peg,' he said. 'A sip of cognac before I take you in? Monsieur will find it of ze best.' They drank to each other, clinking the little liqueur glasses together, and Slade followed the Parisian into the Golden Chamber.

At the lower end of the room stood, observing but unobserved, some six or seven men whom Brat had pressed into his service. They were the rearguard, as it were, of the waiting army. They performed small and menial duties when the superior waiters were out of the room or elsewhere engaged.

M. Brat motioned Slade to join the ranks of them, and he did so. One of the men handed him a serviette, and he placed it over his arm in the approved fashion adopted by the others. Then he took his stand against the wall and surveyed the room with an air of interest. Many of the faces there were familiar to him.

There was Jack Gregory, a handsome ne'er-do-well, who had borrowed a hundred from him four years before at Mentone. Jack was too addicted to baccarat and ladies of questionable morals. He watched him flirting with the somewhat notorious Lady Charterhouse, and smiled to himself a little bitterly. Yonder, whispering a good story into a friend's ear, was Major Dewhurst, VC. Slade found himself vaguely wondering if he remembered how he, Slade, had beaten him in 1882 for the Grand Prix de Nice. Yet Dewhurst was a good shot, too.

There was little Mrs Warlingham, a widow who had conveyed to him in the plainest terms that she would have no objection to becoming Mrs Mortemer Slade. He had been a coming man then, rich and prosperous. What was he now?

He thought how these dainty dames would turn sick with horror if they could see into his heart and know him for what he really was. He thought how these men, fine gentlemen though they were, would gladly seize and rend him if they could but know what manner of man looked upon them with such cool disdain. 'This,' he thought, 'is power. This is real power. To be what I am, and for none – none to know it.'

He turned his eyes towards the table presided over by the young Countess of Shincliffe. There was Phyllis, with her back towards him, and that gentleman next to her, he presumed, was the lucky Mr Stephen Darrell to whom she was engaged. 'He was with her that night – the night before the murder – when I looked through upon them in Eaton Square,' he thought, and paid special attention to the young man's form and features. Once or twice Lord Caversham looked up over his wine and caught his eye. No sign of recognition appeared in his lordship's face. Would the gaze of the beautiful Phyllis be more penetrating, he wondered. Once she dropped her fan. Anticipating her lover, Slade sprang forward and recovered the costly trifle and handed it to her with a slight bow. She thanked him carelessly and continued her conversation with Marion Minting. She had not recognised him, then. The fact was that she had not seen his eyes.

'Did anyone of you notice,' began Viscount Hardcastle, playing with his glass,' the very peculiar sunset of today?'

'I did, for one,' said Shincliffe, 'it was most unusual and uncommon.' His lordship spoke ponderously, and at times was inclined to be tautological. It had even been said, with bated breath, that the earl was a bore.

'There was a sunset like it a few days ago, I remember,' remarked Lady Marion Minting. 'A sky as crimson as that lamp shade. It really, excuse me, Phyllis, dear, for mentioning the fact, but it really reminded me of blood.'

'Blue blood, I hope, Lady Marion,' said Hardcastle, with a smile.

Lady Marion affected to shudder. 'I can imagine,' she said, 'a sky like that on the eve of an eruption, a great battle, or an earthquake. It seems to promise a catastrophe.' There was a pause.

'Phyllis, I declare you are quite pale, love,' exclaimed the countess. 'Is the room too warm for you? Would you like the windows opened?'

'It's nothing,' Phyllis replied. 'Don't mind me, Editha. Perhaps the room is a little hot.' She took a sip from a glass of champagne handed to her by the anxious Darrell. 'There! I feel better even now; nay, quite well. Have you seen Arthur Roberts in the new burlesque at the Avenue, Lord Hardcastle?' Stephen glanced at her anxiously. The mention of the curious sunset had brought back to both their minds an active recollection of the ball in Eaton Square. Phyllis had plainly not forgotten the ominous letter from that man Slade. On the subject, Stephen had heard nothing from Edmund Blake, who had merely said that he was 'prosecuting inquiries'.

'Confound it,' thought Stephen, 'I wish this Slade was safely back, in a nice strait-waistcoat, in Dr Kent's asylum!'

Gradually the company thinned. Most of the diners went off to one or other of the theatres. Many of the gentlemen betook themselves to their clubs. Others went to seek a partner for a rubber of whist. The Caversham party was ready to depart. The Earl of Shincliffe had paid the bill, and handed a generous tribute to M. Brat, in which that functionary's assistants would participate. The gentlemen had finished their coffee and liqueurs. The ladies rose to seek their opera-cloaks in a room adjoining. This gave Slade the opportunity he was seeking.

Heavy curtains hung before the folding doors to which the ladies would have to pass. As the latter, headed by Lady Shincliffe, approached, he sprang forward and drew back the curtains and threw open the doors. He bowed as the party passed through. Lady Shincliffe honoured him with a nod, and Lady Marion murmured her thanks in a well-bred and indifferent undertone. Phyllis came last. Slade fastened his eyes upon her face, and by sheer force of will, compelled her to involuntarily meet his ardent gaze. She turned an ashen hue, gave a momentary start, and looked back at Stephen Darrell, whom a waiter was helping on with his overcoat. Then she recovered her presence of mind, bowed coldly, and passed on. But – she knew him!

Early in the afternoon of 31 August, the day following the dinner at the Hotel Oriental, Phyllis Penrose was out driving in her brougham alone. Passing through the Strand, on her way to pick up her father at the club, the raucous cries of a newsboy attracted her attention. She let down the window and gazed out on the crowded street. The boy was carrying a flaring bill, which said, in bold and brazen headlines:

AWFUL MURDER IN WHITECHAPEL!
GHASTLY MUTILATION!
NO ARREST!
SPECIAL!

7. A Monstrous Deed

Mary Ann Nicholls, the woman with whom Mortemer Slade had made the midnight appointment near Essex Wharf for the Night of 31 August/1 September – as recorded in the previous chapter – was a married woman, who had long been separated from her husband. She was thirty-five or thirty-six years of age; but, though of drunken, dissolute habits, she had not altogether lost the good looks which had been her portion in earlier and happier days. She had been for nearly seven years, at intervals, an inmate of Lambeth workhouse, into which institution she had first been admitted as a lying-in patient. Early in the year 1888 she had left the workhouse to go into domestic service at Rosehill Road, Wandsworth, but she had left her situation under discreditable circumstances, and had then drifted into Whitechapel, that emporium of vice and crime. Such was the woman whom Mortemer Slade, at one time a petted darling of London society, rich, honoured and distinguished, had arranged to meet at night in an East-end slum.

She made no elaborate preparations in order to win favour in the sight of her 'admirer'. She did not spend hours, or even seconds, in the nice adjustment of her hair, or much care and thought in the choice of her costume for the occasion. As a matter of fact, she held the corner of her coarse and not over-clean apron under the tap in a crony's backyard and 'swilled' her red and bloated face therewith until she considered that she had made sufficient exertions in the cause of that which is credited with being next to godliness! She borrowed, from another 'lady' acquaintance, a silk handkerchief of gandy pattern and startling colours, and adorned her neck with this piece of incongruous finery. Her hair she placed on her head in a rather more dignified angle than usual, and her worn and dilapidated boots she dusted with another corner of the apron aforesaid. Her toilette was then complete. Behold, Martha Ann Nicholls, ready for conquest! It was difficult to discover where Mrs Nicholls, unhappy daughter of Rahab, lived. She had, indeed, so far as could afterwards be learnt, no fixed abode. She drifted, it would seem, from lodging-house to lodging-house, and roamed the streets throughout the night when money was scarce and her matured charms had failed to attract the not-too-particular sailor or the unsavoury Jew pedlar who throned the alleys and courts off the Whitechapel Road. She was a human derelict, drifting idly and indifferently on the troubled ocean of life, and no human endeavour could ever get her back once more into port. She was, in a word, beyond redemption.

At about an hour before midnight Mrs Nicholls, who, reserving herself for the evening's debauch, was at that time unusually sober, betook herself to a certain public house much frequented by her male and female acquaintances in Thomas Street, Whitechapel. Arrived there, she was received with a shout of acclamation. She was always good-natured even in her cups, was generous when in funds, and gave herself no airs, although she had once been in domestic service! For these and other reasons, Mrs Nicholls was a rather popular personage in the circle in which she radiated.

She was immediately invited to drink. 'You look dry, Mary Ann,' said a stout lady, who was at that moment administering to the infantile needs of a most consumptive-looking baby and freely disclosing a matronly bosom in the maternal process; ''ave what yer fancy, my gell.' In response to this invitation, Mrs Nicholls confessed to having spent an abstemious day. 'I've 'ad no more than a couple o' pints of stout and mild all the blessed day,' she explained, 'and I'm beginning to know what my old man meant when he said his throat was as dry as a bloomin' limekiln. 'Ere's 'ealth, Missis Robbins, and may the kids be a comfort to yer in yer declinin' days.' Mrs Robbins was understood to express an opinion that, whatever the infant might achieve in that line in the years to come, it was anything but a comfort at the present time, and Mrs Nicholls, declining to press the point, buried her face in a quart-pot filled with a liquor which her friend assured her was 'four-'alf, and wouldn't 'urt a lamb!'

A man known in the habitués of the place as 'Slogger' remarked at this juncture that he had not previously been aware that Mrs Nicholls included dukes and earls in her circle of acquaintance. 'Lor, lumme,' he said, as he applied a lighted spill about a foot long to a quarter of an inch of cigarette. 'Mary Ann don't know a lot of aristocratics, I don't think. Why, it's a wonder to me, strike me if it ain't, that she consents, in a manner of speakin', to mix 'erself with such as us.'

'Wot yer mean?' asked that lady, regarding him darkly.

'Oh! I don't mean nuffin', I don't; never did,' returned the Slogger; 'but I'd give a quid to know who that bloke is wot I sees you with night afore yesterday. A toff, he was – a real, live toff, a tryin' to look shabby. When is the weddin' to be, Mrs Nicholls, ma'am? Send us a bit o' the cake and we'll drink yer very good 'ealth and that of yer old pot-and-pan, the Dook of Limehouse, KG.' A general laugh followed this sally. Mrs Nicholls, in order to describe her embarrassment, ordered a pot and whispered to the villainous-looking barman that she'd 'bring it in tomorrow, lovey. I've got a 'alf-quid cove to meet tonight, good as gold he is.' 'Mind yer don't forget it, or I'll remind yer of it with the toe of my boot,' said the servitor, politely. Mrs Nicholls was not a bad customer, and he knew that the four-pence would be forthcoming. The woman joined Mrs Robbins and one or two other ladies, whose condition in at least two cases spoke to their affection for their lords, in a corner of the bar, and the men spoke in whispers, their conversation being for the most part of a nature which rendered it prudent not to speak too loudly.

Lounging against the bar, apparently alone and engrossed in cutting up tobacco for his pipe – evil-looking tobacco it was too – stood a foreign sailor, a Portuguese perhaps, though rather taller than the average man of that race. He was spare of frame, but athletic, and though 'his demeanour had something suggestive of the lazy and languorous South, his eyes were keen and watchful. He had been reading a newspaper issued in Lisbon, but had glanced up and taken stock of the personality of the woman Nicholls when her unknown gentleman-admirer was spoken of. After that he continued, without himself being noticed, to observe her closely.

Mrs Nicholls remained at the Friend of Man until that hostelry closed for the night. She stood outside for some few minutes after 'Time!' had been called conversing with her

friends. The Portuguese seaman strolled over to the other side of the road and continued to read his newspaper beneath a friendly lamp. When Mrs Nicholls metaphorically gathered up her skirts and departed, after bidding many 'good-nights' to her friends, he methodically folded up his paper, put it in the breast pocket of his pea-jacket, crushed down his sou'wester upon his head, and walked after her. Unfortunately for Mrs Nicholls, and unfortunately for humanity at large, this Portuguese missed her in one of the alleys off the Whitechapel Road, and was unable, in spite of his utmost efforts, to alight upon her again. She had vanished, completely swallowed up in the narrow, tortuous courts with which the main artery from Aldgate to Stratford abounds. Mrs Nicholls, for better or for worse, was lost to him. Nevertheless, the sailor remained in the vicinity.

Meanwhile, Mrs Nicholls hurried along and speedily found herself in Buck's Row. There was a stable-yard there, used in connection with Essex Wharf, a dark, lonesome spot, well-known to the woman and those of her class. It was here, in this remote, solitary, and ill-lighted spot, that Mortemer Slade, closely muffled up and inscrutable as ever, awaited her. He stood in a dark recess near the stable. It was a sombre sort of night, great banks of clouds obscuring a pale and watery moon. The wind blew freshly from the river, and it was chilly for the time of year. He grasped her by the arm as she, not seeing him in the shadow of the wall, was about to hurry by.

'Whither away?' he said quietly. 'Do you fly on the wings of fear, or of love, or of what? Would you flee from the ardent wooing of your impatient and devoted lover? Have you another more profitable assignation? What is it, my fairy of the midnight hour? Have I arrival? Whither away?'

The woman had shrunk back almost with a movement of fear. 'S'elp me,' she whimpered, 'how you startled me. It's early yet, and I didn't think you'd be here.' She recovered her composure with an effort. 'I thought I'd get here first and give yer a pleasant surprise, lovey,' she said with a ghastly attempt at a familiar jocularity.

'Thoughtful and considerate beauty,' said Slade, with his sardonic smile. 'It is enchantment to know I have so devoted a lady-love. We shall not be disturbed here?'

Mrs Nicholls shook her head. 'The slop avoids this place like the devil would a church,' she said. 'He only comes round once or twice throughout the night. Them coppers ain't popular in these parts, gov'nor.'

'So I should imagine,' Slade returned. 'Well, we shall have plenty of time to talk. May I ask, madam, if you can conjecture with what purpose I plan these little encounters of ours?'

Mrs Nicholls grinned. 'I'm afraid I've forgotten the meanin' of them long words,' she replied.

'Why do you suppose I come here to meet you?' he said, leaning back against the wall and leisurely surveying her.

'My fatal beauty, I s'pose.'

'Your attractions, Queen of the Night, are undeniable, but, great as they manifestly are, they would hardly draw me to Whitechapel at this hour,' said Slade. 'Yet I have my reasons too. Tell me what you have already said again. You have no friends, no home, no hopes, no money, no beliefs, no fears?'

'Devil a thing, guv'nor. I ain't got a relative as would own me, or a friend I can respect, or a home I can go to.

'Then,' said Slade, 'you have no purpose in life at all?'

'Devil a one,' returned the wretched woman. God! If she had but known! If she had admitted just one hope in life, one single interest in continuing to live, one little wish that even for her there might, in some distant future, be pardon and grace! He would have stayed his hand. But she had no hope, no faith, no hold on life, and it was from the ranks of such as these pitiful outcasts the victims were to come.

'If I 'ave a 'ope in this world,' she went on, little knowing what was passing in his mind, 'it is that I can get a bed at night and drink always.'

'Nothing more? Nothing more?' he asked, almost wistfully.

'And I'd like not to be buried by the parish when I die.'

'When you die?' said Slade. 'You may have years before you yet.'

She shrugged her shoulders. 'Come soon, come late,' she replied recklessly, 'who knows? Who cares? There's a churchyard I know down in a country village, I played there as a nipper. Sometimes I think as 'ow it would be nice to be lyin' there, for the grass looked always cool, the breezes blowing from the great Orne were so fresh, the flowers so sweet, and the sea so deep and blue. Ugh!' She shivered. 'Give us a drop o' somethin', guv'nor. I've got the bloomin' shudders. Someone's a-walkin' over my grave, maybe! Who knows? Who cares?'

He handed her a flask of spirits. 'There! Drink your fill,' he said. 'We never know when the end is to come.' She drank deeply. The clocks struck one. 'Come this way a little into the shadows,' said the woman. 'The slop will be round in a few minutes.' She tightened the handkerchief at her throat, and the gesture caught Slade's attention. 'Take that off,' he demanded. 'Why?' she asked curiously. 'My fancy is your law,' he said, 'take it off.' She removed the gaudy trifle and stuffed it in the pocket of her gown. Her throat was bare. Slade smiled.

An hour later he was bending over her body. She was dead and warm. A sickening odour of hot blood permeated the atmosphere about him. A thin red streak ran from the pavement on which she was lying, and congealed into a ghastly pool of blood in the gutter. Her eyes were open, directed heavenwards, in an awful unseeing stare. The hands were clenched tightly in the death-agony. Her murderer stood above her, and deftly, silently plied his knife. He had cut her throat with a left-handed slash to deceive the medical authorities. Now he wreaked upon the stiffening remains unnameable horrors. Hack the dead flesh, thou man of blood! Tear at the quivering limbs, thou monstrous fiend. Glut thy leprous self with the yet-warm blood! Time flies, madman, and murderer! Even now, those who are to discover this deed of savagery are hastening to the scene! There are those who would tear thee to pieces and scatter thy shattered remains to the winds of heaven if they could seize thee now, who to the end is destined to escape them! It is three o'clock. Soon it will be dawn. Stab, slash and cut! Thou art safe from aught, but the vengeance of the Most High!

About a quarter to four on the morning of 1 September 1888, Police-constable Neil, being on his beat in Buck's Row, while passing by a stable yard used in connection with the Essex Wharf, observed the body of a woman on the pavement. By the aid of his bull's-eye, he saw that a most brutal murder had been committed. The throat had been cut from ear to ear, the stomach ripped open, the bowels had been slashed and cut, and there were more stabs about the body than at first it was possible to count. The resident manager of the wharf was aroused and Dr Llewellyn, living close at hand, was sent for. He declared that the extremities were still warm and that death had been recent. He added that in all his experience he had witnessed no such appalling mutilations as accompanied this dastardly crime.

The body was removed to the Whitechapel mortuary and inquiries at once instituted in order to establish the identity of the woman. Meanwhile the frenzy prevailing in the district was indescribable. What awful specimen of monstrous humanity was moving in their midst?

The Portuguese sailor, whom we met in the Friend of Man public house, made application to view the remains. He explained in broken English, and with an air of great anxiety, that he feared the victim might be his sister, who had been living a loose life in London's East-end. The inspector in charge was dubious. However, it was of the utmost importance that the actual name of the victim should be discovered, and the foreigner was admitted. The white sheet covering the poor remains was reverently removed and the corpse of Mary Ann Nicholls, the face still smeared with blood, was revealed to view.

The Portuguese shuddered. 'A fearful spectacle,' he said. 'God grant that it may be my task to find this desecrater of the dead.' The officials regarded him with some suspicion, for he had dropped, or forgotten, the foreign accent with which he had begged admission, and now stood up erect, alert, dignified – a marked contrast to the timid alien who had first approached them.

'Do you know anything of this?' He was asked. 'Can you identify the woman?'

'Her name was Nicholls – Mary Ann Nicholls,' said he. 'So much I can tell you. She is known at the Friend of Man public in Thomas Street.'

'Perhaps,' said the inspector, ironically, 'you can also tell us the name of the brute who murdered her?'

'He calls himself "Jack the Ripper"', was the calm reply.

'We shall detain you,' said the official, 'until you can prove that you are not yourself connected with the crime. Where do you live?'

The foreign sailor, if such he were, turned away from the body.

'In Gower Street,' he said. 'You don't appear to recognise me, Parkins.'

'I do not,' remarked the puzzled Mr Parkins, 'and my duty is clearly to detain you. Why, you may have done this yourself.' He pointed towards the corpse.

'Tut,' was the answer. 'My name is Blake – Edmund Blake, and I am very much at your service.'

'Good Lord! Mr Blake it is,' said the astonished officer. 'I really beg your pardon, sir; but the excellence of your disguise must plead my excuse. I trust we shall have your aid in this inquiry?'

'I can give important evidence,' was the reply. 'I visited this neighbourhood in the full expectation that such a murder would take place. Let me see Detective Crow and Mr Ellis without delay.'

An hour later Blake was in a hansom on the way home. He gave a groan. 'I might have saved that poor woman,' he said. 'Oh, that I had kept her in sight at all hazards! I feel almost that her blood is upon my head. I will devote my life to the discovery of this monster. I will die in the cause if need be.'

8. On the Track

Edmund Blake was deeply concerned at the horrible murder of Mary Ann Nicholls. Convinced by the letter he had received after the first crime that other horrors would be attempted, he had gone to Whitechapel disguised, in the hope of learning something of his mysterious correspondent. He had overheard the conversation at the Friend of Man, in which the poor woman had been chaffed by her acquaintance for walking with a man obviously much her superior in station. He had already formed a theory that the criminal was an educated man. He determined to follow Mrs Nicholls and watch her encounter with her 'swell' admirer. As we know, he missed her in one of the labyrinths off the Whitechapel Road, and the poor victim went blindly to her fate.

Blake sat long over his untasted breakfast the next morning. The daily papers were piled about his chair. Their reports threw little additional light upon the tragedy. No immediate discovery was expected. The man 'Slogger', whose real name proved to be Turner, and whom Blake himself interviewed in his rooms, proved to be unable to give a very explicit description of the person with whom he had seen the dead woman in conversation. He was dark, and dressed in black. That was all Mr Turner was prepared to swear. No cries had been heard by persons residing near the scene of the murder, and no suspicious character had been seen hurrying away from Essex Wharf. There was, in fact, no clue to the mysterious assassin.

Blake had shown the letter he had received – the one signed 'Jack the Ripper' – to the police, but the authorities did not attach great importance to it, and seemed inclined to regard it as the work of the ubiquitous practical joker. A few days later they began to receive similar communications themselves in the same handwriting, and Blake was convinced that those were written by the actual murderer. Again and again had he compared the letter written by Mortemer Slade to Miss Penrose with the one he had himself received. The writings were in every way dissimilar, but the extraordinary use of the word Freedom could hardly be explained away as a mere coincidence, and each letter was inconsequent and disconnected in style. The Slade letter hinted at fresh horrors that were to follow every appearance of the writer before Miss Penrose. The Jack the Ripper letter suggested additional crimes in a similar strain. Blake told himself that there must be some connection between the two. Not wishing to drag the name of the Peer's daughter into the inquiry, he had not informed the police that Mortemer Slade had written to that young lady. But he had ventured to express the opinion to the Scotland Yard authorities that the murders were the work of a madman, and to remind them that Slade, a maniac and escaped from confinement, was still at large.

'Catch Dr Kent's patient,' said the detective, 'and it is quite possible – mind you, I do not say it is probable – that you will lay by the heels the murderer of these fallen women.'

The officials had pooh-poohed the idea, expressing themselves confident that Mr Slade, 'who,' they said, 'in any case was perfectly harmless,' was dead.

Later on, when other and even more awful crimes had been enacted, great efforts were made by the police to trace the whereabouts of men who had been released from asylums, private and otherwise, as cured.

A theory prevailed in the vicinity of Buck's Row that the woman had been murdered elsewhere, and the body placed afterwards in the mouth of the stable yard, where it was found. This notion found favour in the eyes of police at first, for very little blood could be seen where the corpse was discovered. Blake, however, learnt that a woman had washed the stains away from the pavement with two or three buckets of water after the body had been removed to the mortuary. The young detective was therefore confident that the murder had taken place precisely where the remains were found in all their ghostliness.

After many hours of anxious deliberation, Blake determined upon a course of action. It had always been clear to him that Mortemer Slade must have been assisted in his only too successful attempt to escape from Dr Kent's asylum. If that were so, Slade, he considered, must have paid pretty heavily for the aid rendered him. The man or woman whom he bribed to assist him might still be in the neighbourhood. He – or she – might even know where the madman was now in hiding. Indeed, such a thing was probable, for Slade would have to continue to bribe his assistant to keep his mouth closed. The man who helped a lunatic to make his escape was likely to make the latter pay him highly for his freedom.

'I'll go down to Dr Kent's place and see what I can glean there,' thought the detective. 'Failing that, there is one other desperate method by which I can place my hands upon this Slade – yes, just one other. If I am forced to make use of the Honourable Phyllis Penrose in order to discover his retreat, it will only be when all other means have been failed. I have sworn to leave no stone unturned to find this murderer, and I will keep my word. The first thing I have to establish is whether or not Mortemer Slade and Jack the Ripper are the same man.'

He swallowed a few mouthfuls of bacon, now gone greasy, and buttered toast, now grown hard, dressed – with his usual care – and drove to Liverpool Street, where he caught a train for Broxbourne. Arrived at that pretty place, he chartered a fly and drove out to Grange House, first, however, calling at a roadside inn about three-quarters of a mile from Dr Kent's mansion. It was from this inn that Dagenham had procured the horse and trap which had conveyed the escaping patient to London.

Blake entered the bar-parlour and called for a glass of sherry. A young girl served him with the fiery liquor, at which the detective, after putting his lips to it, could not avoid making a wry face.

'Public house sherry with a vengeance,' he thought. 'There is no need for me to poison myself in my anxiety to get information of Mr Slade.'

He turned to the girl, who was glancing admiringly at the handsome young stranger.

'Your father in, my dear?' he asked, lighting a cigarette.

'Mr Baxter is at home, sir,' she replied with a coquettish glance. 'I am his niece.'

'Is he engaged?' said Blake.

'I don't think he is very busy just now, sir,' she replied. 'If you wish to see him, I'll ask him to step in the bar.'

She was a little astonished that this distinguished-looking young man should seem to prefer the presence of her uncle to her own. She would have thought he would rather make his inquiries of her.

'The fact is, I'm quite a stranger here,' said Blake, 'and admiring the place very much and thinking the air would agree with me – I assure you I'm very delicate, though I don't look it – I thought of taking a little house and settling down here. I'm not a married man and I'm easy to please, but I should like to know a little about the place before deciding, and I thought your father – I beg pardon, your uncle – would be just the man to put me up to a few wrinkles.'

The young lady was all smiles. Mr Baxter, she explained, himself owned a small villa near at hand which might suit the gentleman. It would be most agreeable if they could come to terms. Broxbourne was a little dull, and so was its neighbour, Hoddesdon. There was society of a sort, of course, but–! She shrugged her pretty shoulders expressively and went off in search of her relative.

Mr Baxter was a hale, healthy, and hearty old gentleman who delighted in a little gossip, and who loved to hear himself discourse. Any information that Mr Baxter could give was Blake's for the asking. That gentleman settled himself comfortably in his chair and prepared to pump Mr Baxter as soon as a bottle of sherry – of a superior class – had been brought up from the cellar and decantered. This sherry was six and sixpence a bottle, and Mr Baxter himself liked it. The young stranger who sat confronting him was a customer whom Mr Baxter delighted to honour. He wished indeed he could meet more like him.

Together they discussed Broxbourne and Hoddesdon, the manners and customs of their inhabitants, the advantages to be derived from a lengthy stay at either place, and such small drawbacks as – in the landlord's opinion – mitigated their value as pleasure resorts. Mr Baxter did most of the talking and Blake listened with exemplary patience. He filled the old gentleman's dock glass with frequency and gave him a cigar, which rejoiced him exceedingly. Then he steered the conversation towards the object of his visit.

'What's the big house over yonder?' he said carelessly. 'The place standing in its own grounds. Quite a lordly affair, isn't it?'

'Finest mansion in these parts,' Mr Baxter replied. 'Pity is as none but luneys live in it. That's Grange House, Dr Kent's private lunatic asylum. Why, some o' them blessed madmen are worth their thousands a year.'

'Grange House?' said Blake reflectively. 'Oh, of course! Why, that's the place where the murder was last year.'

'In October,' said Mr Baxter. 'A young doctor was found in the road just outside the grounds, less than a mile from here, with his skull beat in.'

'Let's see! They never found the murderer, I think?'

'He hasn't been found yet at any rate,' was the cautious reply. 'The police never thought to come ask me questions, or I might have put them on the right track.' Mr Baxter looked important. Blake suitably expressed his contempt for the authorities at failing to avail themselves of the information which a man of the world like Mr Baxter unmistakably was might be expected to have at his disposal.

'Wait till you hear,' continued the latter, 'and you'll be more surprised than ever. There was a wealthy patient in residence at Grange House about the time of the murder. He escaped from the asylum that very night.'

'Well?' said Blake, as the old man paused significantly.

'Well,' replied Mr Baxter, 'that night a young chap named Dagenham, who was employed as a groom by Dr Kent, comes to me to hire my horse and trap for a week. He says he is commissioned to hire the conveyance for a friend of Dr Kent's, who is staying a week or two in the neighbourhood. Methinks that rather queer, for the doctor has plenty of horses and chaises and things up at the stables, and could lend his friend a trap without depriving himself or his patients of driving or riding exercise.'

'Exactly,' said Blake. 'It was queer.'

'It was very queer. However, Dagenham, he puts down a five-pound note and gets a receipt from my niece, and he says he'll call for the horse and trap in an hour's time. He comes for it, looking pale and flurried, I thought, about nine, and drives off in the direction of Grange House. I don't see him again for two days, when he returns with the trap, looking pale and more worried than ever.

"Here's the turn-out," he says, abrupt like, "the gentleman won't be wanting it longer."

"All right," I says. "But I let it out for the week, and I ain't prepared to refund any o' that fiver. Please understand that," I says, sharp-like. "Keep your — fiver," says Master Dagenham. "The gentleman ain't short o' fivers, and I ain't neither." With that he orders a glass of bitter and starts a-readin' the newspaper. "Shockin' murder near your place," says I, "I liked Mr Welman. Think that escaped lunatic had a hand in it?" He looks up at me quite angry-like. "Mind your own business, Mr Baxter," he says. "That's my advice to you. Don't go a-meddlin' in things as don't concern you," he says. I calls him a surly dog and pays no more attention to him.'

Blake considered a moment. 'He seemed to have plenty of money, I suppose?' he suggested, after a pause.

'He only remained in these parts two or three weeks after that,' Mr Baxter replied. 'He threw up his job with the luney-doctor, and he went to London. He came here to say goodbye one night in November, and stood treat to all in the house. I changed a ten pun' note for him.

"Well, Dagenham," says I, "you and me had a few words last time you came to me house, but I wish you no harm, and here's to our next merry meeting." "Thank 'ee, Mr Baxter," he says, with a gloomy shake of his nut, "I'm afraid there ain't goin' to be many more merry moments for me at all. Money ain't everything, Mr Baxter," he says, and that's the last ever I see of Jack Dagenham. He had been a bit sweet on my niece Alice, but I never cared much for the chap myself.'

'He went to London, Mr Baxter,' said Edmund Blake. 'I suppose you have no idea to what part he betook himself?'

The landlord thought a moment. 'I heard something about it,' he said, after reflection, 'but I didn't take much notice at the time. My niece Alice would know.'

'It's of no consequence,' said Blake, carelessly, 'no consequence at all. Take another glass of wine.'

Mr Baxter complied, finishing the bottle, and in a few moments the detective rose to take his leave.

'I've enjoyed our little confab very much, Mr Baxter,' he said. 'Men of ripe intelligence are always pleasant company, if I may say so. I'll try and find you a tenant for the cottage, if I don't take it myself. I have your card. Good day! Good day!'

In the passage leading to the porch of the pretty inn he encountered Miss Alice Baxter.

'I would like to speak to you a moment, sir,' she said in a low voice.

'I am at your service,' he replied, surprised.

The flightiness of manner which he had observed in the young girl had departed, and she looked pale and anxious. She opened the door of a small private parlour and motioned Blake to enter.

'I heard you speak of Jack Dagenham to my uncle,' she said hurriedly. 'I am sure that your inquiries were not as idle as you made them seem. Tell me, do you mean to make use of what you have heard to his injury?'

'Indeed, no!' Blake replied, looking with surprise at the girl's serious face. 'I merely wish to put to him a question or two which he can answer or not as he pleases. I have no wish to injure him, and I know nothing to his detriment. On the contrary, if I knew where at this time he is to be found, I could, I think, be of use to him.'

'You swear that?' she asked eagerly. 'You mean it?'

'Yes,' he replied, simply.

She looked him straight in the eyes, and said, 'I think I can trust you – that Jack can trust you. You have a good face. There is his address. Save him, if you can, sir, save him. I love him. He is all the world to me. Save Jack Dagenham.'

She gave him a half-sheet of paper, pressed his hand, and was gone.

'A strange girl,' said Blake, musingly, when he had re-entered the fly. 'What superficial judges we are. I thought her a mere coquette.'

9. Mr Blake Entertains Mr Dagenham

Mr John Dagenham, late groom to Dr Samuel Kent, MD, of Grange House, Herts, was the anything but proud possessor of a tobacco, stationery, sweet and newspaper shop in a side street near the present electric tram terminus at Tooting. Seventeen years ago that precocious suburb was not so extensively built over or plentifully populated as it is at the present time, and Mr Dagenham informed his acquaintances that the place was 'a hole' and the business 'a fraud'. Customers, either for half-ounces of shag, ha'porths or cough lozenges, or the morning paper, were like angels' visits, few and far between. 'A beautiful place to starve in.' That was Mr Dagenham's unhappy but appropriate description of the 'snug little business' which he had been induced to purchase on the strength of the all-too-glowing representations on the part of the agent who had the disposal thereof. As a matter of fact, the takings amounted, on the average, to about eighteen shillings a week. Mr Dagenham had somewhat expensive tastes for a young man of humble, not to say obscure, origin, and he frankly avowed himself both unable and unwilling to live upon that sum. Billiards, cards, horse-racing, and theatre visits are costly luxuries at all times, but Mr

Dagenham had persuaded himself that they were actual necessaries, and he did not intend to do without them if he could help it. He had paid £65 for the goodwill of the little shop in Fulton Street, Tooting, and he was now on the look-out for someone, as confiding as himself, to whom he could, at a price, hand over the business, which had proved a mere delusion and a snare.

Until the last few months, Dagenham had been an amiable young man, somewhat weak, somewhat vain, somewhat given to minor vices, but inoffensive withal, and by no means devoid of good qualities. These latter Miss Baxter, of the roadside inn near Grange House, had fully appreciated, and Miss Baxter was a good judge of a young man, and a critical. Young Dagenham had liked Miss Baxter. He had not been deeply in love with her, perhaps, but he had rather 'fancied' himself as a relative of the well-to-do landlord of a comfortable and fully licensed tavern. He would have proposed to Miss Baxter and been accepted, I think, by that impressionable young lady had the escape of Mortemer Slade not changed the whole tenor of his life.

The barbarous murder of Mr Welman, which he had witnessed and at which he had almost connived, had had a great effect upon young Dagenham's mind. A vague suspicion had attached to him, though nothing tangible could be brought forward to connect him with the crime. But there had been dark suggestions of the village wiseacres that 'John Dagenham knew summut of the murder', and to these his own manner greatly contributed. He became morose, gloomy, taciturn, and even quarrelsome. When he announced his forthcoming departure from the neighbourhood, a feeling of relief permeated the social atmosphere. All – except Alice Baxter, who really loved young Dagenham – were glad he was going, and Mr Baxter was even unfeignedly thankful.

His sweetheart bade him a tearful goodbye.

'I ain't good enough for you, Miss Alice,' he had said, as he held her hand and devoutly wished he had never accepted Slade's one hundred pounds, 'and I'm not blackguard enough to ask you to link your life with mine. I'm not my own man, in a manner o' speakin'. I've done a wrong thing and a foolish thing, but I need not tell you I never touched a hair of that dead man's head. I'm innocent of that, thank God. But I'm no fit mate for you, and the best thing you can do is to forget Jack Dagenham.'

'Jack!' she had replied, 'I can't, and I wouldn't if I could. At least, let me hear from you now and again, as – as – as a friend.'

He shook his head gloomily. 'I'll tell you where I'm going, Alice,' he said. 'And perhaps some day – but there! Least said, soonest mended. What's done can't be undone. Thank you a thousand times for your faith in me, and God bless you.'

It was in this spirit of gloom and despondency that Mr Dagenham embarked

on his little mercantile enterprise in Fulton Street, and the lack of trade and of congenial society only served to further depress his soul.

'I'll have to give the place away,' he said, in a moment of desperation, 'if I don't find a purchaser soon.'

One afternoon in August – a hot, perspiring, lazy sort of day it had been – Mr Dagenham emerged from his little parlour into the dark and stuffy shop and walked towards the open door to procure a little air. He was in his shirt-sleeves and presented a dejected and slovenly appearance. He had been the smartest of the smart as a groom; he was certainly an untidy and seedy-looking shopkeeper. He looked out into the hot street with an air of listless indifference. He felt too hot, too tired, and too idle to even take the trouble to light the stump end of an El Destino – he had won half a dozen of them the previous evening at shell-out – which was stuck in one corner of his mouth. His brown boots were unlaced, his tie was askew, his hair was rumpled. Mr Dagenham was a picture of neglected misery.

He looked out on the street. A slatternly girl, who had been in the act of cleaning a second-floor window on the opposite side, regarded him with idle curiosity from her perch aloft. A sturdy butcher's boy was flattening his shiny nose against Mr Dagenham's window. Some children – it was holiday time – were debating on what sweetstuff they should expend a halfpenny possessed by one of them. It was not an inspiriting scene, and Mr Dagenham groaned as he surveyed it. A small boy pushed past him into the shop whom Mr Dagenham reluctantly prepared to serve. He produced a penny and demanded that coin's worth of papers and envelopes, at the same time requesting the loan of the *Daily Telegraph* for his father, and the time of the clock for his mother, who was washing – whether herself or the family linen did not transpire. Having attended to the wants of this not-too-profitable patron, Mr Dagenham returned to the door and resumed his disgusted survey of the outer world.

'I wish I knew where that brute Slade got to,' he muttered. 'He'd find the money for a voyage to America, or I'd know the reason why. Go it, Jack Dagenham! Helpin' dangerous lunatics to escape, helpin' to hide murdered men, and now contemplatin' blackmail! You're an improvin' kind of beauty, ain't you? Oh! Dear no! I don't think.'

A gentleman, walking quickly, came round the corner of the street and paused as if in doubt some two or three doors from Dagenham's establishment. Jack glanced at him admiringly in spite of himself.

'Blest if you belong to Tooting,' he muttered, as he studied the exquisite cut of the stranger's lounge suit, 'unless Poole has opened a branch in this benighted part. You've got the West-end hallmark, you have, stamped on every link. What's your lay, I wonder?'

The gentleman stepped out into the road and inspected the names over each shop-front. Then he approached Mr Dagenham.

'Excuse me,' he said, 'but are you not advertising a business for sale?'

The ex-groom pulled himself together.

'Precisely, sir,' he replied, 'I am.'

'No other,' said Dagenham, eagerly, 'and a capital little concern it is – nice trade, good, steady returns, splendid neighbourhood. Suit young married couple.'

The gentleman smiled.

'Or a single young man?' he asked.

'It's my opinion,' said Dagenham, with conviction, 'that this business was especially intended for a single young man.'

'May I inspect the premises?'

'With all the pleasure in life. Come in, sir. I assure you I'm only selling it because I'm going to be married and my future wife already has a tidy business, which she wants me to manage, down in Staffordshire. I do about £8 per week.'

Inwardly Mr Dagenham prayed for forgiveness, and led the way into the shop.

The pair inspected the small house thoroughly, and the stranger described himself as well-satisfied with what he had seen. Indeed, he would probably buy the business if other inquiries proved satisfactory. He would announce his final decision two days from then. In the meanwhile he handed £2 to the delighted Dagenham for the trouble the latter had been put to in the event, unlikely enough, of no business resulting. 'Do you know, Mr Dagenham,' he said, 'I have taken quite a fancy to you. I have, indeed. We are both lonely young men, apparently, with few friends and no relatives in this city. It would give me great pleasure if you would dine with me tonight. Could you possibly close the shop and–'

'Could I? Can a duck swim? Why, we shan't take a rap after – I mean, nearly all the trade done is in the daytime, you know,' returned Dagenham, enchanted at the prospect of a good dinner and genial companionship. 'I'll join you and glad enough to do so. Where and when?'

The other smiled affably. 'Let us say the Café Lombard at seven o'clock,' he said. 'Will that suit you?'

'I'm your man,' was the reply. 'I say – no evening dress?'

'Oh, dear, no, I'm a busy man in my way and can't afford such fopperies. Seven o'clock, then. Café Lombard, Villiers Street. You'll see me waiting for you outside. Good afternoon.'

'So long,' said Dagenham. 'Count on me. Jack, my lad,' he added, 'this is a stroke of luck. Two quid if he doesn't buy. Sixty if he does. A big feed in any case. This is good biz. I'll close the blessed place, have a wash, and go and get a drink at the King's Head.'

Mr Edmund Blake alighted from a hansom at the Café Lombard as the clock struck seven. 'Now for Mr Dagenham,' he reflected, 'and all I want to know.'

His guest appeared five minutes later, a trifle flushed, the least bit unsteady on the legs, and a little thick in his speech. His drinks at the King's Head had been legion, for they were many. But Mr Blake was known at the Lombard, a quiet, decorous and inexpensive restaurant, near Charing Cross, and no notice was taken of his rather loudly-dressed companion, who swaggered in for all the world as though the place belonged to him. Mr Blake nodded to the obsequious waiter and ordered the repast: Hors d'oeuvre, fried soles, *poulet roti*, saddle of mutton, *omelette aux fines herbes*, *meringues glacés*, and dessert. To accompany these viands, the detective ordered a pint of a very special sherry and a bottle of Rhudesheimer to follow. All these arrangements Mr Dagenham regarded with grave approval. It was not until the hock had been finished and they were sipping their crème de menthe – Blake, with a thoughtful air, and vis-a-vis with the manner of one who has dined wisely and well – that the former judged it to be time to commence his campaign. He handed Dagenham his cigarette case with his pleasant smile.

'And when,' he said, affably, 'did you see Mr Mortemer Slade last, Mr Dagenham?'

That worthy dropped the heavy silver cigarette case as if it had been red-hot and gazed at his host with an air of rueful dismay that was almost comical. Mr Blake continued to smile with extreme geniality. At length he lit a cigarette and repeated the question between preliminary puffs, thus: 'And when' – puff – 'did' – puff – 'you see' – puff – 'Mr Mortemer Slade last' – puff, puff, puff – 'Mr Dagenham?'

The ex-groom was ghastly pale. He continued to regard his companion with frightened eyes. 'Did – did – did you say Slade?' he said at length.

'Yes,' was the smiling reply. 'Mr Mortemer Slade. Don't you think, Mr Dagenham, that you ought, in the interests of justice, you know, to give him up?'

Mr Dagenham looked sullenly at the nutshells upon his plate. The dinner was a failure after all. Everything with him was a failure. This easy-going, pleasant-spoken gentleman was a menace after all. It was sickening!

'What do you know?' asked the ex-groom desperately.

'Less than I would wish,' returned Blake, playing with his liqueur glass, 'but a good bit for all that. Take, for instance, the murder of Arthur Melnot Welman–'

'I never did it,' said Dagenham doggedly. 'I never hurt a hair on his head.'

'Of course not,' Blake replied, soothingly. But you know who did.' Dagenham said never a word. 'You were foolish enough, and – forgive me if I hurt your feelings – wicked enough to assist a maniac to escape, with the result that a useful life was needlessly thrown away. It was plainly your duty to inform the authorities that you knew the author of this crime, if only to protect others who might suffer at this man's hands. You did not do so, and I am sadly afraid that your indiscreet conduct – I put it mildly – has made you an accessory after the fact.'

Dagenham groaned. 'What are you going to do about it?'

'I am, for private reasons, extremely averse to doing you any injury, John Dagenham,' said Blake, gravely. 'You have rendered yourself liable to a criminal prosecution, but I have no intention of invoking the law against you. I want to know, however, and I must press you to tell me, where Mortemer Slade is at this time?'

'I don't know. I swear I don't know. I'll swear that I've never clapped eyes on him since that frightful business. I think he's dead. I hope he's dead. On my Bible oath, sir, I don't know where he is.'

Blake gave him a keen glance. 'I believe you,' he said. 'But I can assure you that Slade is very much alive.'

'You've seen him, perhaps?' asked Dagenham, with a fearful glance around the now deserted restaurant.

'No. But I know those who have. Now, Dagenham, I shall want to avail myself of your services for a little time. It may be for days only, it may be for weeks, it may be for months. I shall pay you well, and all I ask of you is to be discreet and faithful.'

'You can depend upon me, sir,' said the crestfallen youth. 'How can I serve you?'

'You would, of course, recognise Slade again whenever you should see him?'

'Recognise him? I'd know the fiend under any disguise,' said Dagenham, with a kind of tremor. 'Why, I've seen his face in my dreams again and again nearly every night, on and off, since then. Since he killed him, you know, sir. Recognise him? No chance of ever forgetting him, curse the devil!'

'I shall want you to accompany me to Whitechapel and the surrounding districts at nights occasionally,' said Blake. 'Meanwhile, keep your shop going, and be ready to carry out my instructions at any time. I suppose you can get someone to take your place when you are engaged with me?'

'Oh, rot the place!' exclaimed Dagenham. 'Why, I don't take enough to keep a canary-bird in Woodbines. Excuse me, sir, for speaking so straight, but that blessed business sticks in my gizzard.'

Blake laughed. 'You told me a more flattering tale, like Hope, this afternoon, Master Jack,' he said. 'We must try to find you something better before long. Meanwhile, I will pay you well for the little nightly jaunts I shall want you to take with me. And – a word in your ear, Master Jack! Write to a certain young lady down Hertfordshire way and relieve her mind in regard to your worthless self.'

'I will sir, I will! Worth her weight in gold is Miss Baxter. I'm very obliged and grateful to you, sir. I'll serve you well.' Blake produced his card. 'Keep that,' he said, 'and you'll know where to find me if at any time you hear or see anything of the party I am in quest of.' He paid the bill and rose to depart.

Outside the restaurant the two men paused. It was raining heavily, though the day had been fine and bright. 'I thought we should get it,' said Blake, 'a storm has been threatening all day. You'd better take a cab back to Tooting. I'm going to the club.' He pressed some loose change in Dagenham's hand, and the commissionaire secured two hansoms. 'Now, remember,' said Blake, as he entered his, and lowered the glass. 'Rely on me, sir,' returned Dagenham, and sprung into the other cab. 'Thirteen, Fulton Street, Tooting,' he called out to the Jehu. 'What? Six bob? Rats! Five, and a drink at the Horns!' The cabman whipped up his steed, and, with a last wave of the hand to the departing detective, Dagenham disappeared into the darkness.

The commissionaire, delighted with Blake's tip of a shilling, re-entered the brilliantly lit restaurant. A darkly dressed man, tall and spare, appeared from the shadows. He gazed up the street at the fast-receding cabs.

'Blake, the detective,' he muttered, with a strange smile, 'and my horsey friend Mr Dagenham. I swore I'd never kill another man, but really I shall have to keep an eye on young Dagenham. I heard the address. Lucky!'

He vanished, going towards Hungerford Bridge.

10. Miching Malecho: It Means Mischief!

Stephen Darrell could not but be but sensible to the marked changes in his sweetheart, which others, with eyes less fond and anxious, might have failed to notice. It was not that she had developed any slackening of affection for him. On the contrary, she appeared more devoted and attached to her handsome and talented fiancé than ever. But day by day at more about this period, Phyllis Penrose grew more and more dejected. She had been a lively girl, full of the joy of life, and extracting from the flower of existence all the honey it contained. Now she was silent, reserved, depressed, a victim to nervous headaches and hysterical fancies. Even her father, not the most observant of men, noticed the change that had come over his last-born, and wondered at her spiritless and listless demeanour. He could not account for it at all, and spoke of it rather grumblingly to her sisters, of whom the Countess of Shincliffe advised a change of scene and air.

'Stephen Darrell is a charming young man,' said that expert when questioned as to the possible cause of Phyllis's dejection, 'and no doubt very estimable; but he is exacting and almost too aggressively attentive. My advice is, Dad, that you take Phyllis abroad for a little time. The marriage need not be hurried. They are both very young. Take Phyllis to Rome or Naples for a little time – Aunt Malyon will be glad to go with you, and I might join you later – and she'll soon recover her spirits.'

The Earl stared.

'You speak as if you thought Stephen was boring the girl,' he complained. 'Why, she's madly in love with him.'

'So was I with Shincliffe,' was the reply – this, by the way, was not strictly true – 'but I was glad to have a respite even from his society now and then. Phyllis wants change, I tell you.'

'I suppose you know best, Edistre,' said Lord Caversham, resignedly. He had a great respect for this one among his daughters. 'But I didn't want to miss York Races this year, and the Continent gets more expensive every season. Still, it can be managed. I'm trusting to Seabreeze to win me £10,000 over the St Leger.'

His daughter frowned.

'I really think you might give your thoughts to more serious things,' she said severely. 'I'll tell Phyllis to order her maid to pack up, and you'd better be off next week.'

'She'll want frocks,' said the peer.

'She can give an order to Celeste today,' was the reply. 'I'll drive round for her at twelve. The child must have what she wants, of course.'

All this was arranged, and though Stephen was inconsolable, at the temporary loss of his sweetheart, he was obliged to agree that the change of air, scenery and surroundings might do her good. For himself, he was likely to be busy in town. He had to prepare for his diplomatic appointment, and, moreover, Mr Lestrange, to whom he was secretary, was in charge of a certain important Bill, which would require much of Stephen's time and services. The Radical member was not brilliant, and was ever glad to avail himself of Stephen's superior knowledge and attainments. It was decided that Lord Caversham, Miss Penrose and the Honourable Mrs Malyon – a widow, who acted as Phyllis's chaperon – her aunt, should proceed to Rome by easy stages on 8 September. The fashionable columns of the *Morning Post* announced the interesting fact, and thus their projected departure came to the knowledge of a gentleman calling himself Maidment, who had an obscure lodging in Stamford Street, Blackfriars.

Mortemer Slade no longer thought himself in love with the bright and proud young beauty, who had once declined the honour of his hand. Steeped in blood as he was, even he knew that Phyllis Penrose was as far beyond his reach as the steadfast stars which seemed to gaze upon him during his nightly prowls in filthy courts and unsightly alleys. He was now, and always must be, a pariah, the enemy of the human race. All men's hands, he knew, must forever be against him. If ever, he often told himself, he were detected at his appalling work, he would be stamped out of existence by the furious mob as a mad dog is kicked, and struck, and buffeted until life departs from it.

If, as he well knew, he were at last caught by the authorities, life-long imprisonment in Broadmoor as a homicidal maniac would be his inevitable lot. He had no room, therefore, in his warped mind for tender thoughts and ordinary passions. He could neither love nor hate. He was a monstrous inception, he told himself, who must harbour not one of the ordinary attributes of mankind.

But maniacs delight in mischief, and though Slade no longer loved Miss Penrose, he experienced an unholy delight in the thought of tormenting her. He could not make her love him, but surely – surely he could make her fear him. That, he thought, were joy indeed. Hence the midnight visit to Eaton Square on the occasion of the ball. Hence the unexpected appearance at the Hotel Oriental.

'She shall not escape me,' he said, as he pictured her look of dread and horror at the sight of him on each occasion. 'I'll make her a sort of unconscious partner in my East-end orgies by appearing to her every night before my bath of blood. Rome! Why, I'd follow her to the heart of the African forest if need be.'

Animated by those agreeable thoughts, Slade began to conjure up in his mind other means of persecuting the unfortunate Phyllis. His gloomy reflections reverted to Stephen Darrell, towards which innocent young man he felt a supreme hatred. He had contrived to procure a photograph of that unconscious youth, and at night, in his dingy bedroom, would inflict such indignities upon it, maniac-like, as sticking pins through the features and writing foul epithets upon the back.

'I'll separate the pair of love-birds,' he vowed again and again. 'I'll tear them apart. I'll place a barrier between them that nothing shall ever tear down. I'll break her heart. I'll drive him to drink, or suicide, or madness. Do they think, the hare-brained fools, that they have done with Mortemer Slade?'

In pursuance of this pleasing design, Mr Slade, a veritable wolf in sheep's clothing, prepared to cultivate the acquaintance of Mr Stephen Darrell. A scheme had suggested itself to him, and he did not propose to delay its execution.

'I'll have him attacked by two ruffians,' ruminated the maniac, as he walked slowly towards Liverpool Street one night early in September, 'and then come to his rescue at the psychological moment. First, though to procure my ruffians.'

He strolled towards the coffee-stall at which he had recently encountered the two Hooligans who had insulted the old gentleman, and the sight of it reminded him of those chivalrous youths.

'The very creatures for my purpose,' he muttered, 'if I should chance to see them. They'd murder a man for five shillings. As for me' – he smiled sardonically – 'I murder for nothing. But I am an artist, with the largest of capital As!'

He approached the coffee-stall and ordered a cup of tea, pouring into the cup some spirit from his flask. Two ladies were engaged in rather a heated argument over their coffee. The 'bloke' or one of them, it appeared, had transferred his migratory affections to the other, and this act of desertion she described with a wealth of language, which a hansom cabman, listening from his box and occasionally throwing in a word to each by way of encouragement, heard with envy and admiration. The lady who had been deserted concluded her spirited discourse by expressing a hearty wish in regard to the future state of her rival's eyes, and incidentally challenged her to come down to her court 'one of these nights and fight it out'. The lady whose household had been enriched by the addition of the other's 'bloke' was herself endowed with a fairly liberal vocabulary, and it is devoutly to be hoped that Slade, the coffee-stall keeper and the admiring cabman were sufficiently impressed and edified. The last-named, having expressed a desire to 'have his bit on the one with the ginger hair', and enquired very tenderly if the 'bull and cow was to be under the Markis o' Queensberry's rules', winked elaborately at Slade, whipped up his steed, and drove off, singing a mournful stave, of which 'Woman, Lovely Woman' appeared to be the subject. A constable shortly after requesting the good ladies to 'sling their hooks in double-quick time', they departed their several ways, keeping up the while a running fire of abusive epithets like minute guns at sea!

The street was deserted. Slade was about to move on when his attention was arrested by the gestures of the proprietor of the 'gutter hotel', who had whistled him back, and was pointing to a door from which two figures were emerging.

"Scuse me takin a liberty, gov'nor,' he said in hoarse tones, 'but there's Bleater and his pal Blinder a-comin' – them two young varmints as you put it acrost the other night.'

Slade appeared to regard this staggering information with indifference, not to say disdain. Nevertheless, he was pleased.

'Perhaps they want another good thrashing,' he remarked, with his grim smile.

'Perhaps they'll use their knives this time,' replied the man contemptuously.

'If they can use them as effectively as I wield mine, he said, 'they're dangerous indeed. Pests! Do you imagine I care for a couple of stunted, undergrown boys?'

Those unconscious youths reached the stall and gave their order. Their faces lengthened when they observed Slade, and they nudged each other.

'That's 'im,' remarked Bleater.

'Sure enough,' replied his friend, who generally acted as a sort of chorus, concluding Bleater's sentences, which were apt to be incomplete.

'He can 'it 'ard,' said Bleater, devouring bread and butter.

'Darned 'ard,' answered Blinder, expectorating before gulping down his steaming coffee.

When they had finished, Slade drew nearer.

'Have some more?' he asked.

The two roughs grinned sheepishly.

'Don't mind,' said Bleater.

'If we do,' added Blinder.

They had coffee, hard-boiled eggs, oily looking 'sardines', which may have been sprats or pilchards, bread and butter, and cake. They munched in appreciative silence. When they had satisfied themselves and Slade had paid, they requested 'fags'.

'I'm afraid,' said Slade, 'I don't quite–'

'Cigarettes,' said Bleater.

'Woodbines,' explained the chorus.

An additional sixpence from Slade procured them half a dozen packets, and their mean little souls rejoiced.

'Now, boss,' said Blinder, for once speaking without a lead from his friend, 'Wot's the bloomin' game?'

'We're ripe,' added Bleater, with an oath, 'for anythink – pitch and toss to manslaughter.'

Slade gently took their arms and led them away.

'A little matter of business, gentlemen,' he said, 'up west. Do you know the Ottoman Club?'

'Lor' love a duck,' exclaimed Bleater, 'you ain't a-goin' to introduce us there?'

'Hardly,' Slade replied. 'Abilities such as yours, my friends, would not be appreciated at their true value. Nor would your personal appearance meet with that approval which is your due. You are Nature's noblemen, and the Ottoman Club object to the species.'

'G'arn!' said Bleater.

'Stow it!' remarked his confederate.

'With all the pleasure in life, if I had the remotest idea what you mean,' said Slade, 'but the fact is, I have a little commission for you. I thought that neither of you would object to earning a couple of pounds each.'

The youths were expressive.

'For about five minutes' work,' said Slade. 'No more and no less.'

'We're on,' said Bleater.

'Dead on,' said Blinder. 'Is it tonight?'

'No,' was the reply. 'I want you to come to the Ottoman Club with me now, and to take particular note of a gentleman I will point out to you. He will leave about one o'clock, I expect, and his way home is through the park. Being a fine night, he will probably walk. He usually does walk home. Tomorrow night you will follow this gentleman, and, at a a suitable moment, attack him.

'Do you want us to "out" him, gov'nor?' asked Bleater in a whisper.

'He'll certainly show fight, and I expect you'll have to hit him rather hard. But, if possible, avoid a struggle with him. Get behind him if you can, and strike him down with a stick. Stun him if you like, but I don't want him seriously injured.'

'All right,' said Bleater, 'it's as good as done.'

'I shall be close at hand,' Slade continued, 'and will come to his assistance, whereupon, of course, you take to flight. I'll bring the money to the coffee-stall. There's ten shillings now as an earnest of my intentions. You both understand?'

'Oh, yus!' from the Bleater.

'We tumbles,' from his 'pal'.

They walked rapidly and in silence towards the Ottoman Club, which was situated in St James's Street, Slade keeping a little ahead. Arrived outside that well-known institution, they took their stand in a recess near the stone steps leading to the entrance hall. Slade remained in the background, so that he could not be seen by anyone emerging from the club. It would not do at all, he told himself, to be noticed by Darrell, to whose rescue, in the role of a good Samaritan, he was to come tomorrow. The clock struck one o'clock, and they waited, Slade in the shadows and the two ruffians near at hand. They had no desire to attract the attention of any passing police officer.

Stephen Darrell kept early hours. He was a hard-working young fellow, with his way to make in the world, and dissipated London was almost a *terra incognita* to him. He had Phyllis to think of. But he was a good clubman, and, as a rule, paid a nightly visit to the Ottoman. On this occasion he had accompanied Phyllis to a theatre – the Hon. Mrs Malyon in close attendance – and had come on to the Ottoman for a bit of supper and a smoke after seeing the ladies back to Park Lane. Phyllis had been a little brighter during the evening. Loth to leave Stephen, she yet looked forward to a brief sojourn among the Ancients. She had never been to Italy, though the French shores of the Mediterranean were familiar to her, and she knew her Rhineland tolerably well. In three days – it was now the 5th – they were leaving London. Stephen thought, with a sigh and some vague presentiment of evil, of the moment when he would see the boat train wafting away to sunny Italy the being he cared for most in all the wide world.

At twenty minutes past one he rose to leave the club. He announced his intention of walking home, his rooms being near the Marble Arch and the night being fine, though rather dark. Of his friends, Ralph Thorpe offered to accompany him.

'I want a walk,' he said, 'and you can give me a final Scotch and 'Polly' at your place. Your bachelor days will soon be over, Darrell.'

'They never will be missed, as the gentleman in the 'Mikado' says,' remarked Stephen gaily, as he wrapped a silk muffler – he was in evening dress – round his neck. 'I'm not funking the marriage yoke a little bit. Well, good-night, you fellows. Pleasant dreams and don't forget I shall want my revenge tomorrow.'

He and Thorpe walked down the broad staircase to the street, and turned Sharply to the left.

Slade darted towards Bleater and Blinder, who were gazing fixedly at the retreating figures.

'The tall one,' he whispered, 'in the blue saque overcoat. Did you see his face?'

'Yes,' said Bleater.

'We did!' acquiesced his friend.

'You will remember?'

'Trust us.'

Slade released their arms.

'Follow them into the park,' he said, 'and select a suitable little spot for tomorrow night's comedy. Meet me at the coffee-stall at midnight. Remember, stun him, but no worse, mind, no worse!'

11. A Cruel Life

Occasionally in the misfortunes of mankind, there comes to them a sense of impending calamity, a foreboding of evil, the cause of which is difficult to explain, the source of which is hard to trace. Few among us in this work-a-day world have not experienced this eerie feeling of pending catastrophe in greater or lesser degree. It is as if some warning premonition comes to us that danger lies ahead. The sentiment may be vague and transient, but we have it nevertheless, and, as often as not, it is followed by some disaster to justify its uncanny presence.

It was with this indefinite feeling of approaching trouble that Stephen Darrell walked to the Ottoman Club on the night of the attack planned by Mortemer Slade. He felt unaccountably gloomy and depressed. He had dined at Park Lane, quite *en famille*, with Phyllis and her aunt, Mrs Malyon, who were to leave for Rome two days later, whither the Earl would follow them early in the ensuing week. Something, perhaps, of his fiancée's dejection had communicated itself to her lover who, though he tried to be bright and entertaining as usual, failed signally to show himself in his customary spirits. Mrs Malyon, an excellent woman of jovial temperament, and a grand constitution, who attributed every disease on this planet to indigestion, rallied the young people on their mutual air of depression, believing, good soul, that their forthcoming separation was the origin of their trouble. 'You'll have Phyllis back in a few weeks,' she said gaily, 'the very personification of robust girlhood. The change will do her good, and, in any case, she could not possibly have remained in London throughout summer.'

Stephen agreed. 'I suppose not,' he said. 'I am not so selfish as to wish her to stay in town. I shall try to get away for a fortnight or so, myself.'

'For a fortnight only, Steenie?' Phyllis asked, concerned for her lover.

'Well, I'm hard at work on Lestrange's Bill,' the young man replied. 'He's very keen about it you know, and as long as I can be of use to him, I feel bound to stick to it. Never mind, Phyllis! We will have a long holiday when we're married – not the mere conventional three-week honeymoon, but a long spell of delightfully idle happiness before we settle down at the embassy.'

Phyllis smiled a little sadly. She, too, had premonitions of coming disaster with which was associated in her impressionable mind the sinister figure of Mortemer Slade. Much of woe, and misery, and pain might happen in six months. The course of true love, she told herself, in her new-born spirit of pessimism, never did run smooth.

The young lovers had a long and earnest conversation that evening after dinner, when Mrs Malyon had discreetly retired to her boudoir. They had not many opportunities for private discourse in their busy social life, and they were glad of an occasional chat about the golden future which lay stretched before them. It was nice to have Phyllis to himself now and then, Stephen thought; to tell her how much he loved her and how indissolubly his happiness was bound up in hers. The moments slipped away, and, when an hour had passed in sweet converse and Mrs Malyon returned and begged Phyllis to sing, he began to feel that his vague fears and indistinct forebodings were but the outcome of hard work and late hours. He stayed till nearly eleven, and left Park

Lane a little brighter than when he had entered that patrician thoroughfare, and less downcast.

He walked to his club, the night being fine and the distance not excessive. Approaching it, he became absurdly gloomy again, and even hesitated, as if averse to entering its friendly portals.

'Pshaw!' he said. 'What the deuce is the matter with me? I'm like a nervous girl, with no mind, or will, or spirit of her own. Buck up, Stephen! Have a whisky and soda, a hand at cards, or a game of billiards, and bid the blue devils take flight and be hanged to them! What have you got to worry about, you fortunate young ass?'

Thus apostrophising his own weaknesses, Stephen ran up the stone staircase two steps at a time and joined a noisy party of friends in the spacious card-room.

On the strength of defeating Lucian Greece, the club champion, by eighteen in a game and 250 up, and winning eleven sovereigns at poker, Stephen imbibed more whisky and soda than he allowed himself customarily of that exhilarating beverage, and, at one o'clock, he left the Ottoman with his spirits revived, and a feeling that the world was less 'out of joint' than he had suspected. He paused on the steps, uncertain whether to drive or no.

'A stroll home through the Park will do me good,' he thought. It's confoundedly hot, too, and I don't feel like wooing the drowsy god yet awhile. No, I don't want a hansom, Simmons' – to the military-looking commissionaire on the façade of the club – 'I'll walk home.'

Simmons got the usual generous tip, however, and Stephen crossed the road and proceeded towards the park.

It was a dark night, though fine. The moon was obscured by heavy banks of cloud, suggestive of a downpour before London woke up to her daily toil. Stephen stepped out with the easy tread of a man in prime condition, swinging his stick, and humming the refrain of the rather 'sugary' ballad which his lady love, blessed with a fine soprano voice – of good quality and accurately trained – had sung to him earlier that evening.

'Dear little girl!' he thought. 'The Lord knows I have no cause to be melancholy, secure of the love of the prettiest and nicest girl I've ever encountered. Soon, in so many weeks, in so many days, in so many hours, she will be mine.'

He entered the Park gates and turned towards the right, intending to make for the Marble Arch, near which landmark his rooms were situated. Beneath a tree – the spot was dark and solitary – he paused a moment to light his cigar. He looked at his watch. It was a quarter past one. As he moved away he observed the tall, spare figure of a well-dressed man emerge from the shade cast by a belt of path in the same direction as himself. He saw no more, for at that instant he was struck down by a blow on the head, the instrument used being a heavy chisel, administered by some person who had been in hiding behind the tree beneath which he had been standing He fell to the ground like a stricken ox, and lay, stretched out on the gravel path, stunned and motionless. Two forms appeared from behind the shelter of the tree.

'You've outed him,' said Bleater with an oath.

Blinder hurriedly placed his weapon in the pocket of his greatcoat.

'Hurry, you fool!' he growled. 'Take the blighter's timepiece before our man comes along. What's two quid apiece? Let's 'ave his bloomin' vallybles as well.' Bleater hesitated and was lost. 'We was told to 'it 'im on the 'ead softlike,' he expostulated. 'You've done it on 'im proper, but we weren't told to go down 'im, and I ain't inclined to exceed my instructions.'

Blinder cursed him for a fool, and told him to turn out the pockets of the prostrate man while he himself kept guard. Reluctantly, as though yielding to a show of superior force, the Bleater complied with the demand and, stooping, had just removed a breast-pin from the white silk muffler about the victim's throat when the tall spare figure of Slade appeared in front of them.

'Lor', gov'nor,' exclaimed Blinder, innocently, 'how you startled me!' Bleater rose sheepishly to his feet, and endeavoured to pocket the purloined article. 'Yes,' he said, 'you did jump out on us sudden-like.'

'Give me that pin,' said Slade, sternly, 'and get you gone, both of you, before the police come.'

Blinder frowned at his comrade, as if admonishing him to defy this mandate; but the latter quietly delivered up the pin, and meekly prepared to depart. To Blinder Slade handed another two sovereigns. 'You've done well,' he said, 'and I may employ you again. But if you stay here an instant longer, I'll summon the police, and you will be arrested. Now, go. I know where to find you if I want you. Go.'

'Horl right gov'nor! We're a-goin'. We've done our work and we've been paid for it,' replied Blinder, 'with a little bit of over-weight thrown in. Come on Bleater. Let's leave these two gents to settle their little differences alone. Good night, sir.'

'Good night,' said Slade gruffly. He was on his knees beside the body of poor Stephen, and was taking steps to restore him. The two young ruffians slunk off down the path, and soon breaking into a run, were speedily back in their East-end den, where the honoured the occasion by getting very drunk and violent with some spirits previously laid in.

Slade was left alone with Stephen. He had supported his head, which bore a deep and severe cut, against his knee, and was endeavouring to pour some brandy down the throat of the unconscious man. 'It was a nasty blow,' he muttered, 'but it has only stunned him, and he'll come to shortly. He'll have a headache tomorrow, I expect, and he'll feel shaken and weak, but he's got a fine, sound constitution – curse him! – and would soon recover from worse injuries than this. And now to procure assistance and get him home.'

Some minutes elapsed before anyone appeared in sight, but a belated reveller, on his way home, at length paying attention to Slade's repeated calls for help, with the aid of that wayfarer, the arch schemer was able to get his charge to the gates of the park. There a policeman came to their assistance; a four-wheeler was procured; and Darrell, who had not yet recovered consciousness, placed therein with as little fuss and discomfort as was possible in the circumstances. To this officer, whose mind could not grasp more subtle affairs than the customary 'drunks and disorderlies', Slade explained the facts and handed his card. 'I am a medical man,' he said, 'and I take a somewhat grave view of this gentleman's condition.' 'Is he a friend of yours, sir?' asked the constable, who was reluctant to miss a chance of distinction. 'If you like, we'll drive him to the station and–' 'By no means,' returned Slade, in a determined tone. 'He is an old acquaintance of mine. I've known him since he was quite a boy. It's my duty to take him home, where he will receive every attention, and

to superintend his case myself. Tell the man to drive to 12, Frobisher Crescent, near the Marble Arch. You'd better report the case one of assault, with intent to rob, I fancy. It is fortunate I appeared in time. You have my name and address? Goodnight, constable. Goodnight to you too, sir, and many thanks for your timely aid. Drive on, coachman.' He slipped some loose silver in the hand of the policeman, bowed politely to the gentleman who had helped to carry his victim and put up the window of the cab. 'Lucky,' he muttered as they drove away, leaving the constable and the good Samaritan to compare notes and formulate a theory if they pleased, 'that I had those visiting cards done. They won't find Dr John Emmett in the Medical Directory but that won't matter. Nor will they find him at the address on that card. It will serve, however, to establish my *bona fides* with Mr Stephen Darrell here when the right moment comes.'

On the way Stephen showed slight signs of recovering consciousness. He sighed heavily once or twice, moved uneasily, and murmured a few incoherent words, but Slade's keen ears caught the name of Phyllis. 'I should like to hear your next conversation with Miss Penrose,' he said aloud. 'It should be both interesting and affecting.' What a choice morsel I am about to give the society papers! How astonished the great world will be when it learns that the expected marriage between the Earl of Caversham's daughter and Mr Stephen Darrell will not take place!'

The cab entered Frobisher Crescent and came to a standstill outside number twelve, where Stephen had his bachelor establishment. Slade put his head out of the window and directed the driver to ring the bell.

'You'll see a brass plate with certain names and numbers on,' he said. 'Press the electric button opposite to the name "Mr Stephen Darrell" after the outer door is opened, and then give me a hand here.'

The cabman did as directed, and a night-porter appeared at the hall door, evincing much astonishment at the spectacle of Mr Darrell, whom he knew to be the model of propriety, unconscious in the arms of a stranger. He came down the steps and opened the door of the cabs.

'I beg pardon, sir,' he said, 'is the gentleman ill?'

'Mr Darrell has met with an accident, but it is of no serious consequence. I am Dr Emmett, an acquaintance of his. Assist me to get him upstairs,' said Slade authoritatively.

'I'll call Mr Darrell's servant, sir,' was the reply, 'if you will allow me. I know he is waiting up for his master.'

He pressed the electric bell and then assisted Slade and the cabman to get Stephen on his feet. The latter's valet appeared as the procession ascended the steps from the street, and seemed greatly relieved when assured by Slade that nothing serious was the matter. The cabman paid and discharged, he assisted Slade to undress his master and put him to bed. The self-styled Dr Emmett then prepared a bandage for the patient's head and administered a sedative with which he had happily provided himself, perhaps because he expected just such an emergency as had arisen!

Stephen's man – a faithful, attached servant – was named Cawte, and to him Slade explained what had occurred.

'It was most fortunate that I happened to be passing,' he said. 'I was just in time to prevent the ruffians from robbing Mr Darrell of all he possessed. Possibly they would have resorted to greater violence had I not so effectually disturbed them. Your master got a nasty blow, as it was; but he will be quite right again in a day or two with a little care, and, I've no doubt, will laugh at his unpleasant experience.'

The valet seemed troubled. He hesitated.

'Mr Darrell is engaged to be married, sir,' he said a little dubiously. 'Do you consider it necessary that the family of the young lady should be informed?'

'I think not. I hope not,' replied Slade. But in any case nothing can be done tonight, or, rather, till later this morning. I hope that it will not be necessary to alarm Miss Penrose. I shall be able to say definitely after my patient has had a good sleep. Meanwhile, if you can give me a shakedown–' He gazed round the handsomely furnished apartment. 'There is a spare bedroom, sir,' said Cawte respectfully. He was glad to have an expert opinion on the premises, so to speak, in case Stephen should suddenly be taken worse. 'If you will excuse me, I'll prepare it for your reception. Will you take some refreshment, sir?' He placed decanters and a syphon on a side table, and a gold box filled with Turkish cigarettes, a present from Phyllis Penrose, as the embossed lid informed the keen eyes of Mortemer Slade.

That gentleman, left alone, leisurely examined the treasures of his unconscious host. There was a large painting of Phyllis in a riding habit, the work of a renowned R. A., and photographs of the Earl of Caversham's beautiful daughter could be found in almost every portion of the room. One the various brackets and cabinets were framed portraits of men and women prominent in the world of sport, of politics, of art, and of letters, all signed by the distinguished individuals they represented. Stephen Darrell had been a great sprinter even after his university days were over, and here were a few of the silver trophies he had won. He had been the 100 yards amateur champion for at least three seasons. Handsome bronzes, costly silver, and choice paintings adorned the walls and tables, for Darrell, though far from rich, lived discreetly, had no debts and few vices, and was able to indulge, with moderation, his taste for artistic furniture and pretty bric-a-brac.

'You have here,' muttered Slade, stalking about the bright room like a spirit of of evil, 'ease, comfort, elegance, even luxury. I cannot deprive you of these, indeed; but tomorrow you shall lose something more dear to you than all, more cherished than all else the world possesses. When I have separated you forever from the being you love; when I have condemned you, with half a dozen words, to sudden death; when I have destroyed every hope you have; when I have deprived you of the joy of life, I'll leave you and return to my labours down east. Why, even now I hanker for the society of my female outcasts, my bedraggled Delilahs, who await my coming in those noisome, stifling alleys. I feel free as a soaring eagle there. Here I am as a caged bird. In forty-eight hours, no more, no less, I'll hie me to Spitalfields, and then, hey! For number three, ho! For my third victim.'

The valet returned. 'Your room is quite ready, sir. Will you allow me to show you to it?' Slade threw away his cigarette and prepared to accompany the man, after a final look at his patient. 'Bring me some hot water,' he said, 'at eight o'clock. I do not expect that Mr Darrell will wake before.'

It was twelve o'clock when Stephen awoke from a deep, but uneasy sleep, and the rays from the mid-August sun were pouring into his bedroom from the opened window. For some little time he had no notion where he was. The familiar objects on his dressing table seemed strange and new to him. The pattern of the wallpaper assumed novel and grotesque shapes. Sounds in the street of passing vehicles seemed extraordinarily dim and distant. He lay for some minutes blinking at the sunlight, only conscious of a splitting headache, and a severe pain across the eyes. Something enveloped his head, but what manner of thing it was he could not tell. There was a ringing in his ears, and his sight was blurred and indistinct. He endeavoured to raise his head from the pillow and to take in some impression of his surroundings, but the effort was beyond him, and he fell back with a groan. Someone, however, had approached the bed from behind him, and he at length realised that his man, Cawte, was gazing at him with some wonder mixed with compassion. Stephen stared back at him, and at last spoke in a weak voice. 'Is that really you, Cawte?'

'Yes, sir.'

'Could you enlighten me, do you think – if you tried – as to what has happened to me?'

'You met with an accident last night, sir, I understand. You are not seriously injured, I'm happy to say, but you received a blow on the head, and it has left you dazed and feeble. Do you find the light too strong for you, sir? Shall I lower the blind?' Stephen shaded his eyes with his hand. 'If you please,' he said. 'And I should very much like a brandy and soda. I feel as if I had fallen off a very high tower; indeed, I think I dreamed that I had done so. What is the time?'

The valet consulted a respectable silver watch. 'It is a little after twelve o'clock, sir, he said. 'I received instructions from the doctor to inform him when you awoke. With your permission, sir, I'll–'

Stephen made a spasmodic attempt to raise his head. 'Doctor?' he asked. 'Oh! It's been a case for a doctor, then?'

'A Dr Emmett appears to have discovered you in an insensible condition, sir, and to have brought you home. He evinced much concern at your mishap, and insisted on remaining the night in the event of medical aid becoming necessary. He is now in the dining-room.'

'Extremely considerate of Dr Emmett,' said Stephen. 'But he will find me a refractory patient if he attempts to forbid me to get up. Miss Penrose is leaving London tomorrow, and I have an appointment tonight at Caversham House. Get me a drink, Cawte, and I'll endeavour to dress.'

The valet mildly expostulated. 'I beg you, sir, that you will permit me to consult the doctor first. The wound on the head must be dressed, and—'

'Ask him if his treatment permits a B. and S.,' Stephen remarked, impatiently. 'And be so good as to understand that, under any circumstances, I must and will get up. What's this confounded thing round my head?'

'It was necessary to bandage it, sir,' Cawte explained, 'and the doctor was obliged to shave the hair away from the injured part.'

Stephen groaned. 'A pretty sort of guy I expect you've made me look between you,' said he. 'However, get me a drink, there's a good fellow. Give me the hand-glass and the Eau de Cologne from the dressing-table. Deuce take it! I feel as weak as a kitten.'

Cawte speedily returned with a message from 'Dr Emmett'. The brandy was out of the question for the present; but if Mr Darrell would drink the draught which the doctor had prepared for him, and which the valet bore with him on a tray, the patient would find his condition almost immediately improved. He might then dress if he wished, and Dr Emmett would hold himself at his disposal. In the meanwhile, Cawte was to apply a fresh bandage to his head, and this was speedily effected.

Whatever Slade's concoction may have been, it proved decidedly efficacious. The headache disappeared almost magically, and beyond a little not unnatural shakiness, Stephen felt little the worse, when, leaning on the arm of the servitor, he entered the room in which his guest was waiting. Cawte led his master to a seat near the window, poured out fresh coffee, and retired, leaving the two men face to face. Slade had been breakfasting. He seemed quite at his ease, and rose and bowed gracefully as his host entered the room.

'You look remarkably fit, considering,' he said in a gratified tone. 'I assure you, Mr Darrell, I was really concerned about you last night, but this morning you look almost well.'

'For which happy consummation I have you to thank, sir,' replied Stephen. 'I am extremely indebted to you for your timely aid. I cannot express how grateful I feel. Not many would have acted so considerately towards a stranger.'

'Not exactly a stranger,' Slade remarked. 'I knew your late father, Mr John Grant Darrell, very well, and esteemed him quite as much. My name is John Emmett. You may remember hearing your father speaking of me?'

'Of course I do,' said Stephen, enthusiastically. A John Emmett, in the medical profession, had been among his father's friends, although he had been dead some years, a fact unknown to Stephen. 'He always spoke of you in the highest terms. I am glad that I fell into such excellent hands. May I ask you to explain to me how I came in this condition?'

'I was walking through the park,' Slade replied, 'on my way home from a visit to a patient. In a lonely spot I saw you struck down by two ruffians who were about to rob you. I rushed to your assistance and the cowards made off. You had, I found, a nasty cut on the head, and were quite insensible. I procured help, and, discovering your name and address by an examination of your card case, I was able to bring you home in a cab. I am only thankful that the little adventure has ended so happily.'

'I am deeply obliged and grateful, doctor,' answered Stephen. 'I have an important appointment for this evening which I would not have missed on any account. I feel quite strong enough to go out. You have heard, perhaps, of my engagement to Lord Caversham's daughter?'

'I must confess I had not done so,' said Slade. 'I only practice my profession in a private capacity at the present time, but I am, nevertheless, a busy man, and hear little of what is going on in society. Allow me to congratulate you, Mr Darrell. As the son of my old friend, I sincerely trust that you will be happy.'

'I am seeing Miss Penrose tonight,' Stephen explained after a little pause. 'I should wish not to alarm her if it can be avoided. Will it be possible for me to remove these bandages, doctor, during the day?'

'I do not think it advisable,' Slade replied. 'But I will examine your head before I leave, and perhaps we shall be able to come to a sort of compromise in the matter. By the way, you will, I suppose, report the fact of your being attacked to the police?'

'*Cui bono?*' asked Stephen, lightly. 'I got off very easily, I consider, thanks to you. I ought to have been more on my guard, I suppose. I wore a diamond pin, rather foolishly, in my silk scarf, and the gewgaw probably attracted the attention of the blackguards. I don't think it was a planned affair.'

'You must avoid night walks in the parks for the future, then,' said Slade. 'As a matter of fact, I mentioned the affair to a constable I encountered, but I'm afraid he believed to the case to be one of the 'been on the spree' order, so I do not suppose you will hear anything of it.'

He paused.

'Mr Darrell,' he said suddenly, 'I am not one to alarm anyone without the excuse of dire necessity. But a medical man must perform his duty, however uncongenial the task may be. I must speak plainly to you. I know that you will forgive me, and comprehend my motives.'

Stephen seemed surprised at the grave tone which the doctor had infused into the words. He was regarding him, too, with a peculiar look of kindly pity and esteem.

'Do you feel that you are able,' the calm, even inexorable voice went on, 'to hear bad news?'

His serious tone seemed to strike a sudden chill to the heart of his hearer, and all the vague fears of the future, the indefinite forebodings, which he had experienced of late, returned with recruited strength to Stephen. He thought of his peerless Phyllis, and felt with a horrid certainty that the bad news this friend of his hinted at involved her, too. He pulled himself together with an effort.

'I am at a loss, doctor, to even guess what bad news you can possibly have for me,' he said. 'But I am sure I can hear it with fortitude whatever it may be. May I ask you kindly to speak plainly, and to speak at once?'

Slade elaborately sighed, as though reluctant to fulfil a painful task. Secretly, he rejoiced at the anxious expression which Stephen had assumed, and which all his resolution could not disguise or subdue.

'Your general health of late,' he began. 'How has it been?'

'Perfect,' was the reply. 'I have never had a day's serious illness in my life.

'Slade's face still wore an expression of pity and grief. 'You have never had occasion, or thought it advisable, to insure yourself?'

'Indeed, no. However, I thought of doing so rather extensively in view of my approaching marriage. Why do you ask?'

'From no idle motives do not doubt,' returned Slade, with increased gravity. 'In ascertaining the nature and extent of your injuries while you were lying unconscious this morning, I had occasion to make a brief and not very full examination of your heart. Mr Darrell, have any of your relatives suffered from heart complaint?'

Stephen smiled. 'Well, yes, now I think of it,' he replied. 'My grandfather on my mother's side – General Horncastle, of the Indian Army – died suddenly at the dinner table. My mother has often spoke of the shock it was to them. But surely, Dr Emmett, you do not believe that my heart is in any way affected? Why, I have never really known that I had such a commodity. I think,' he said softly, 'Miss Penrose – Phyllis – first convinced me that I possessed the organ.'

'I cannot be absolutely sure without a complete examination,' said Slade, 'but I noticed disquieting symptoms. Mr Darrell, many apparently strong and healthy men suffer from organic heart trouble without being the least cognisant of the fact. I have made the heart my special study. I am rarely deceived. I cannot say, on the strength of my cursory examination of this morning, whether your condition is serious or no – I hope to God that it is not – but I am bound to tell you that you will have to exercise great care – very great care indeed.'

Poor Stephen stared blankly at his tormentor, and there was silence. An ormolu clock on the mantelpiece ticked with merciless precision, and seemed to say, 'Heart affected – heart affected – heart affected,' over and over again with bewildering reiteration. A canary in a pretty gilded cage sang merrily a stave, which seemed to have a similar refrain. Stephen's collie pushed open the half-closed door, walked across to the mat in front of the fire-place – a tiger-skin – sat down, and surveyed his master with grave and wistful eyes. Across the table, as though he were a judge sentencing to death a miserable criminal, Stephen saw the inscrutable face of Slade, the sinister eyes fixed on his own in a horribly suggested compassion. He saw him draw from a case beside him, which he had not noticed before, a stethoscope. Stephen's gaze reverted to that instrument with a look of horror. Phyllis, from her portrait on the wall, seemed to be looking at him with mocking eyes. A piano-organ in the street commenced a lively air. Stephen could hear the voice of Cawte speaking to the woman who came in daily to sweep and dust his rooms; but the sound seemed far away. What was this dreadful doctor, sole arbiter of life or death, misery or happiness, about to reveal?

'I can speak more confidently,' the suave voice went on, after a pause of seconds which, to Stephen, seemed like hours, 'if you will allow me to continue the inspection begun early this morning. I may be able to reassure you. I do not know. But if you would wish to learn the truth–'

Stephen regained the control of his voice with an effort. 'Instantly,' he exclaimed, in tones unlike his own. 'I am no poltroon, Dr Emmett. Whatever the truth may be, I can bear to hear it. I demand that you tell me the worst. The happiness of others, more dear to me than my own, depends upon the truth being spoken. Do your professional duty, sir.' He rose, closed and locked the door, and drew the curtains of the window. He removed his coat and vest, took off his collar, and bared his broad chest. 'Now, sir,' he said, 'I am ready. Speak, and spare not.'

Slade made the examination. Again and again he applied the stethoscope, till he seemed satisfied with the results obtained. He motioned his victim to a chair, but Stephen elected to stand. He boldly faced the man who held his fate in his grasp.

'Well,' he said, bravely.

'It is as I feared,' came the measured reply. 'There is valvular disease, long-seated, but unsuspected. It is probable that you will never experience the least pain or physical discomfort arising from your condition. The merest chance – the attack upon you in the Park – has revealed the fact.'

'How long may I expect to live?' asked Stephen, in a stifled voice.

'My poor young man, I cannot tell you that,' said Slade. 'The period of your existence is on the knees of the gods. You may – I confess I do not think it likely – live for some years; you may – though Heaven forbid – die at any moment, as your grandfather died. Any sudden emotion, any protracted exertion might, and, indeed, probably would, be fatal. The heart is gravely affected, and–'

'My God! My God!' cried Stephen in a burst of agony. 'Do you know what this means? It is not for myself I care. But Phyllis, my Phyllis – it means – Oh! Heaven! It means the instant, irrevocable loss of her.' He sank into a chair, and, burying his face in his hands, burst into a fit of uncontrollable despair. They were not selfish tears. He had no craven fear of death. He had a true belief in a hereafter. But all his thought was of the loving, trustful girl, whose affection for him was not the less deep and sincere because it as undemonstrative. He knew the worth of the girlish heart, the extent of the girlish love. She was lost to him forever. The die was cast. In a few hours they would be parted forever.

Slade eyed him with a savage delight. This was power, he told himself as he watched his quivering victim. He had inflicted more pain with a few words than ever he had achieved with his sharp knife and relentless arm in the mean courts of the East-end. He had effected his object. Phyllis Penrose, who had refused his hand, would never marry Stephen Darrell.

He made an effort to comfort and console his victim. With care, he said, Darrell might live some years. Such cases he had known. He gave him advice as to how best to keep at bay the ever-encroaching danger. He recommended a certain treatment and a course of drugs. He suggested a voyage should distract his thoughts. Of all this, however, and much more, Stephen heard never a word. Phyllis was lost to him. His mind could grasp no fact less stupendous than that one. 'I beseech you to leave me, doctor,' he said wearily. 'I have much to do and require time to think. You have been the harbinger of woe, but you have done your duty. It is well that I should know the truth in time. My task lies before me. My duty has now to be done. I pray that the Almighty will give me strength that I may not shirk from it.' He drew his chequebook from his breast pocket. 'In the meanwhile I beg you to accept–'

Slade's pale face flushed. For the first time he looked uneasy. He raised his hand deprecatingly. 'Mr Darrell, I thank you, but I must ask you kindly not to do that,' he said with dignity. 'I knew your father. I sympathise with you from my heart. My services have been cruel but cruel only to be kind. I entreat you to not to let the sordid question of money–' He flushed again and was silent. Stephen understood. With a promise to visit him again, Slade rose to depart, and the two shook hands.

Slade strode away from Frobisher Crescent with a long, last gaze at the house his evil presence had afflicted.

'No,' he said, 'By —! I could not take his money. I've ruined his life, as I said I would. But take his money! No! And now to arrange another dramatic appearance before Miss Penrose. I wonder if my blood-red sunset will fail me this time.'

12. The Effects of the Lie

When Slade had departed, Stephen despatched his man with a note to Phyllis, and sat down at the open window to think. He felt sick and giddy, partly from his misadventure of the night before, and partly from amazed distress at the disclosures of the self-dubbed Emmett. Not for one instant did he question the correctness of the doctor's summary. How could he, indeed? Dr Emmett, whose name Slade had assumed, had been a close and intimate friend of his own father, and was not in the least likely to mislead him as to the condition of his health. The doctor, Stephen remembered, had always been regarded as *facile princeps* where diseases of the heart were concerned, and it was most improbable that his diagnosis could be wrong. Dr Emmett had, in reality, long since gathered to his forbears, but it must be understood that Stephen was ignorant of the fact. Slade had impressed him as a man well-versed in all the intricacies of the medical profession, and it was worse than useless to question any decision at which so eminent an authority might arrive. Stephen accepted without a scintilla of doubt the expert's plain statement that his heart was affected, and that, at any moment, his life, so precious to him since love had come into it, might end abruptly and without warning.

It was an appalling thought. Men, healthy apparently, young, strong and full of the exuberance of life, cannot be expected to realise that the grim spectre of death is with them at every instant of the day and night, and that at any moment they may be called upon to obey his summons. They think of death, if ever they think of it at all, as some abstract thing to be contemplated many years hence, but with which they at present have no concern. Egotistical in their health and strength, they cannot imagine that they, even they, stand perpetually on life's precipice, and that at any instant they may without warning be forced over the brink.

The knowledge that he stood face to face with sudden death came to Stephen with all the force of a supreme and irresistible blow. He was powerless, he felt, to strike in his own defence. He could, he knew, do nothing to avert the catastrophe. Prayers were unavailing; regrets were of no account. He must abide the issue and all that it involved. All he could do was to await the inevitable blow and to bow his head to the decree of inscrutable Providence. 'Two women shall be grinding at a mill: the one shall be taken and the other left.' He was to be taken when the old and feeble were left behind, and it was useless to rebel.

Arrived at a determination to confront his fate like a man, his one thought was of the girl he loved. He told himself, with no uncertain voice, that the projected marriage must immediately be cancelled, that the engagement, more dear to him than life itself, must be broken off without an instant's delay. To act otherwise were the deed of a coward. To marry Phyllis, knowing that his life was not worth a moment's purchase, would be to brand him in his own sight as a villain. Stephen was not a selfish man. To give up his sweetheart, to renounce the being he loved beyond everything in the world, meant misery for such remaining days, or weeks, or months, or years, as were vouchsafed to him. To continue the engagement and to marry his well-beloved, knowing what he knew, were villainy unspeakable, and meant greater mental anguish even than could come of an instant and everlasting separation.

He gazed out upon the quiet street. He felt that in the last hour his whole nature, his general outlook upon all things, had changed. He had been condemned to death. He felt that he had nothing in common with the happy, careless beings who pursued their daily avocations as though Death and Dissolution were not ever-present facts, but the phantasmagoria of a disordered brain. A butcher's boy, mounted on a stout pony, was leaving meat at the house next to his own, and seizing the opportunity to flirt with the pretty serving-maid who looked up at him from the area steps. What had he to do with death? A postman was delivering the mid-day mail and whistling blithely as he went his round, the embodiment of contentment and rude health. What had he in common with the grave? Two hours ago Stephen Darrell was as happy and careless and indifferent as these. Yet death, he told himself, must come to them when the grim reaper so willed. If his relentless scythe cut down Stephen ere the corn was ripe, why should he repine? Come soon, come late, all human beings must be garnered in.

He debated in his mind, gazing idly at the passers-by, what form his interview with Phyllis should take. It was, he told himself, quite impossible to announce the truth. In the first place she would be terribly distressed, and, in the second, she would – he knew her unselfish devotion – insist on the marriage taking place. He feared her soft pleadings, her tender sympathy, her perfect love. Together they would shake his resolution and make a cur of him. He must tell her nothing. He must let her go, in doubt, in anger it might be. It was his duty to release her; his honour demanded that she should go free.

Then he pictured his future without her. He saw himself hope-bereft, despairing, alone, uncared for, awaiting the unavertable end. He prayed humbly that when he had cut his love adrift from his life, the end might be soon. What could life supply in the place of love? What could fill the void the loss of her created? He had thought to bid her good-bye, this day, for a few weeks, and had felt wretched at the thought. This day he was about to say goodbye to her forever.

He sat down at his desk and wrote two letters. They did not take him long. One was to Mr Lestrange, informing that gentleman that it was impossible, owing to circumstances over which he had no control, for him to continue to act as his secretary, and adding that all papers and documents bearing on the Bill in which they were interested would be returned that evening. He told Lord Caversham that he had that day released Miss Penrose from her engagement. 'I cannot,' he wrote, 'give any of the explanation to which you have undeniably a right. I ask you to believe that in thus depriving myself of all that I have found most joyful, I am actuated by no motives other than those of duty. I love Miss Penrose. I shall ever love her. It is because I care for her too well to link her life with mine that I have destroyed my happiness with one blow. Forgive me, and forget me. I can say no more.'

With agonised mind and ashen face, he collected together the letters he had received from Phyllis, her portraits – reserving one – and three or four trinkets, a locket, a signet-ring, a pin, she had given him at different times. He made a packet of these, and arranged with Cawte, who had returned from Park Lane, for their delivery. The valet was struck by the changed aspect of his young master. That something more serious had occurred than the midnight affray in the park he felt convinced; but there was that in Stephen's face that debarred him from inquiry, however well-meant. This was not physical pain; it was clearly acute mental torture which his usually high-spirited young master was enduring.

'The message was, sir,' he said, 'that Miss Penrose would be there at six.' Stephen nodded. 'I am going to my room to lie down,' he said. 'Please don't let me be disturbed. I have left some letters on my desk. Kindly see that they are delivered. By the way, Cawte, we shall be going abroad next week. You will hold yourself in readiness.'

'The diplomatic appointment, sir?' asked Cawte respectfully. He was an old servant, and was privileged.

Stephen smiled sadly. 'I shall decline the appointment,' he said. 'Ask me no more questions, my good fellow. I am tired and worried. Let me rest.' He retired to his own room, leaving the valet to wonder what had transpired to so grievously upset his master.

A few hours later Stephen met Phyllis by appointment near the Marble Arch. He was waiting for her, and she dismissed the carriage when she alighted, and together they entered the park. They found two chairs in a quiet and secluded part and sat down, Phyllis rallying her lover on his lack of spirits and monosyllabic answers. 'Dear boy!' she thought. 'He is unhappy at the idea of our being parted for a few weeks. I am sorry too. He will be hard at work in hot, sultry London, while I am basking in the Italian sunlight. Poor old Steenie!' These reflections induced her to gently press her lover's hand, and recalled him to the painful task he had set himself. How pretty and sweet she was! She was dressed, he noticed, in some clinging material of a strawberry-pink tint, and was wearing a wonderful picture hat, a cunningly devised affair, to match. She held his hand between her small, white-gloved ones, and was thoughtfully turning round and round the plain gold ring upon his finger. He watched her expressive face, the tendrils of soft, golden-hued hair about her shell-like ears, the little sad mouth, and the long, dark eyelashes. She was good as she was beautiful, and she loved him. And his task was to make her tear him out of her heart forever. His duty, self-imposed, was to try to destroy forever the love she bore him.

'How is it you wished to see me here, Steenie?' she asked, after a silence of some minutes. 'You impatient boy! Could you not wait till tonight? I declare I believe that you had actually forgotten that we were going to Lady Tartuffe's tonight, and that I had promised you – oh! I forget how many dances!'

Stephen gently released his hand. How could he tell her? What was he to say? His heart died within him. It was at a dance he had proposed to her. They would never dance together again.

'I have something to say to you, Phyllis,' he began in such an altered voice that the girl turned to gaze with wonder at him; 'something, my dear love, of the most vital importance to – to both of us.'

She continued to look upon him with a sort of pained surprise. She noticed now how pale, how haggard he appeared. He was white to the lips, and he did not look at her. His gaze was fixed straight ahead as though he looked out upon a land, a future which was invisible to all other eyes. Was this the Stephen Darrell she knew and loved?

He moistened his lips with his dry and parched tongue, and went on in the same strange tones of measured calmness.

'Our marriage, Phyllis, cannot take place; our engagement must end now and here.'

She started and looked at him tremblingly.

'Stephen,' she whispered in faltering accents, 'what ails you? Why do you look like that? What mad words are you saying?'

'The words,' he said gravely, and with averted gaze, 'of sanity, of justice, and of reason. God gives me strength to go through this ordeal. I am no fit mate for you. I cannot reconcile it to my conscience to destroy forever the happiness of her I love best, oh! Most best, in all the world. Marrying me, you would be miserable. Do not ask me how or why. I dare not tell you; I cannot tell you. God in heaven! Give me the power to do my duty.'

She seized his hand. 'Stephen!' she cried. 'What has come between us? What phantom have you conjured up that can ever separate you from me? What wild imagination is this? Speak!'

'Phyllis,' he said, in the same tone of desperate and determined calmness. 'It is Providence, Fate, the will of God, that has come between us. No human effort can remove the bar that prevents our union. Between you and me there is a great gulf fixed, which no human endeavour can bridge over. I love you more – much more – than ever I did now that you are lost to me. It is because I love you more than happiness, more than life itself, that I restore to you your freedom. Forget me! Utterly forget me! If you cannot do that learn, oh! Learn, my dearest, to pity and forgive. I knew not of this bar to our marriage last night. I knew not of it twelve hours ago. But it exists, and it has divided us as completely as death itself.' He buried his face in his hands and his whole frame was torn with the force of his emotion. The girl laid a trembling hand upon his heaving shoulder.

'Stephen,' she said, 'Steenie! If there is anything wrong that you have done, my love is strong and can forgive. If some false pride prevents you from confiding the whole truth, however painful – nay, however shameful – to me, have faith and trust in the extent of my affection. Speak, Steenie! See! I entreat you, beseech you. Trust me, confide in me. Try the strength of my love. Tell me all.'

'I cannot,' he said hoarsely. 'You stab my wounds afresh!'

She looked at his bowed head, his convulsed frame. What had he done, she thought, that she could not forgive?

'I will not accept my freedom,' she said, with womanly dignity, 'unless you say you wish it. Is it your own freedom you are eager to secure?'

He dug his nails deeply into the flesh of his hands, and bit his under lip till the blood came.

'Answer me,' she said. 'You wish to annul our engagement?'

'I do not wish it,' he said. 'A higher power compels me. To marry you would be to steep my soul in selfish and sinful dishonour. You do not understand. You cannot understand Phyllis! Miss Penrose! My own manhood tells me that I am doing right.'

'Mr Darrell,' she said, rising. 'I will ask you one more question before I bring this painful interview to a close.'

'Speak,' he said. He looked up and revealed to her a face bearing all the traces of the extremities of human suffering.

'If this obstacle you speak of were known to me, do you believe that I would wish the engagement to continue, or should I, do you think, agree with you that it must end?'

'In your unselfish devotion,' he replied, 'I fear that you would elect that our engagement should go on. It is from that I wish to save you. I am going abroad, Miss Penrose, never, I think, to return. After my death, I swear to you that you shall know the truth. You will then understand and pity and forgive me.'

'After your death?' she exclaimed, breathlessly. 'Oh, Stephen! Stephen! What wild and whirling words are those?'

'The truth. Ask me no more. In pity leave me.'

'I am going,' she said. Her beautiful eyes were full of tears, though she bravely kept them back, and her loving, faithful heart had no room for aught but grief and compassion. She drew off her engagement ring and slipped it, softly and silently, into the pocket of his coat. Poor little token of their love! No other ring should ever take its place.

'I shall be faithful to your memory,' she said. 'I do not ask to know your motives. If they seem right to you, so be it. But if ever you want a friend, Mr Darrell, not a very wise or experienced one, I fear, but a loving, and a faithful, perhaps you will think of me.'

'You gentle angel,' he cried, 'you can forgive me?'

'I can,' she said. 'I do. I hope, indeed, I hope, that you will be happy.'

'Happy!' he groaned in bitter anguish.

'Goodbye,' she said. 'Goodbye, and may God bless you.'

She hurried away up the gravelled path towards the Park Lane entrance. The tears that she had restrained so bravely were flowing fast now, and when she looked back – once only – she could scarcely see his solitary figure, his arms upon the back of the seat, and his head sunk down upon them, for the mist that gathered before her eyes.

'He has broken my heart,' she said, simply. 'What will become of him – and me.'

She walked swiftly towards her father's house, hoping to enter unobserved. She would plead a headache, and thus escape the long and dreary dinner with father and her aunt, and the dance at Lady Tartuffe's which was to follow. Meanwhile, Lord Caversham would learn from Stephen what had occurred, and the match would be formally broken off. Broken off! Her engagement with Stephen Darrell! She could not, even now, realise that her brief dream of love was over, her vision of happiness gone forever.

As she left the park, the figure of a tall, spare man in black clothing attracted her attention. There was something familiar in the sinister, cadaverous face, the pallid complexion, the thin lips, and steely, penetrating eyes. She hurried past him and involuntarily raised her tear-dimmed eyes to his face. He smiled, a cruel and wicked smile, and pointed towards the heavens.

'Look at the sky tonight,' he whispered in her ear as he strode past her. 'The third tonight, Miss Penrose, the third tonight. Remember your own motto. "*Tout pour l'amour*," you know. Goodnight.'

She saw, with startled eyes, that it was Mortemer Slade. She tore up the steps of the great house and beat, in a frenzy of terror, mute and unreasoning, at the door. By the time it was opened he was gone.

That night the sun went down in a crimson glory that reminded one of blood.

13. The Third Tragedy

During the afternoon on which the events of the previous chapter occurred – on 7 September 1888 to be precise – Mr Jack Dagenham received a telegram from Edmund Blake requesting him to close his shop and come to his – the detective's – rooms in Gower Street.

'Something in the wind, I suppose,' muttered the ex-groom, as he changed his clothes preparatory to his expedition; 'perhaps Mr Blake has got on the track of that beast Slade, and wants me to be on the spot to identify him. Well, I ain't one to give anyone away, but hang me if I don't feel it my plain, unvarnished duty in this case. I'll do a good deal to oblige Mr Blake, too. He's treated me 'andsome, and I ain't going to do the crook on him. Besides, he's going to help me to a good job when I've chucked this hole, and I may yet prove myself worthy of Miss Alice Baxter, who ain't the sort to desert a cove when he's down. That little feed with Mr Blake may yet prove the makin' of you, Jack, my boy!'

Thus ruminating, Mr Dagenham polished his boots, brushed his bowler hat, adjusted his tie, and went out into the street, shutting and locking the shop door behind him. His departure was witnessed by a tall, gaunt, dark man, of shabby-genteel appearance, who had, for some time previously, been observing the small establishment from a doorway on the opposite side. This personage followed Mr Dagenham at a discreet distance, and did not lose sight of him, taking care the while himself to be unobserved, until he had entered a house in Gower Street. Then he walked forward and took stock of the premises in question. A brass plate outside the front entrance attracted his attention, and he smiled as he read the name displayed thereon.

'As I thought,' he murmured. 'Mr Blake has enlisted the services of my Grange House accomplice. Tonight they will hunt in couples. Blake is an acute hand, wary and strong on the scent, but the fox is not less cunning, and he will work havoc among the geese again tonight, and keep his brush safe from the hunters. I shall give you a fine run, Edmund Blake, a fine, sporting run; but you are clever and painstaking, and perhaps – who knows? – you may be in at the death.'

He went his way towards King's Cross, and was soon swallowed up in the crowd.

Meanwhile, Dagenham, all unconscious that he had been shadowed, sat in Blake's study, sipping spirituous refreshment and smoking one of his host's admirable cigars.

'I came, sir,' he said, 'as soon as ever I read your wire.'

'You did right,' was the reply. 'I want you to accompany me to the East-end this evening. Probably we shall be out till the small hours. I cannot tell for certain. I propose to make a sailor of you for the occasion.'

Dagenham stared.

'Just as you like, sir,' he remarked, resignedly. 'I'm willing. But I feels it only right to tell you that, except for an hour's trip in the *Skylark* at Brighton and a three-hour voyage in the *Clacton Belle*, I ain't had much experience of life on the ocean wave.'

So I supposed,' Blake said, with a smile. 'But a sea-faring man I mean to make you all the safe. It's merely a question of a suitable disguise.'

'Oh! I begin to tumble,' the ex-groom replied, with an air of relief. 'Well, sir, I daresay I can "shiver my timbers" as well as another for an hour or two. May I ask, sir, if you expects to land that shark, Mr Mortemer Slade, in your net tonight?'

'I am afraid that we shall have to go fishing long and oft before he bites, to pursue your metaphor,' Blake replies. 'He is wily enough to see the hook behind the bait. But I have some reason to think that he haunts Whitechapel and the surrounding districts, and I want you to point him out to me if we should run across him. There is £50 for you, remember, when you can say to me "There! That is the face of Mortemer Slade." If I can identify Slade with the mysterious double-murderer of the East-end, there will be other and larger rewards, and those we will share.'

'I think, sir, that I should know him.'

'He is certain to have resorted to some disguise, remember,' said Blake. 'He has cunning and intelligence of no mean order.'

Dagenham drew a deep breath.

'I saw his face when he killed that poor young man, sir,' he replied. 'I've seen it, sleeping and waking, ever since. I think – I really do think I should know him again anywhere and at any time.'

'I hope you may prove a true prophet,' was the reply. 'Now, come into my room, and we'll see what sort of a salt we can make of you.'

At eleven o'clock that night two foreign sailors – presumably Spanish or Portuguese – left the Gower Street rooms of Mr Edmund Blake, walking with a lurching gait suggestive of a life ''midship', and neither the mother of Mr Blake nor the maternal relative of Mr Dagenham would have recognised, in them, their respective offspring had those good ladies revisited these glimpses of the moon and encountered them on the stairs.

Unfortunately, however, for Mr Blake's theory, and still more unfortunately for the interests of justice, the two foreign sailors were seen to leave the house by a tall, gaunt man, of sinister aspect, who was looking out at them from the public bar of the big 'hotel' at the corner, and who kept them in view until they reached the commencement of the Whitechapel Road. There he abandoned them to their own devices. 'So,' he muttered, 'you expect to find your bird here, do you? Vain, indeed, is the snare of the fowler! Since you are working for my trail down here, I'll take wings to see the region of Spitalfields, and there astonish the natives. Goodnight, Mr Blake. You shall have pleasant reading tomorrow.' He walked swiftly away, going through Osborne Street, Wentworth Street, Thrawl Street, Flower and Dean Street, and so into Brick Lane, along which thoroughfare he proceeded until he reached the commencement of Hanbury Street. He waited there for a few moments as if expecting to meet someone; but, some women accosting him, he walked across to Dorset Street, which is a turning out of Commercial Street. There was a common lodging

house there – at No. 30 – and outside this establishment he remained for some time, pacing up and down and regarding the dismal and unsavoury premises with ill-disguised impatience.

'She's late,' said Mortemer Slade, to himself, as the clock of St Saviour's church struck the midnight hour. 'She seemed a timid, suspicious sort. Yet she'll come – she'll surely come if only for the money.'

At half-past twelve a woman emerged from the passage of the lodging house and went slouching up the street. Slade gave a quick glance at her face as she passed beneath a street lamp, and then followed with swift and noiseless tread. She was about forty-five years of age, five feet in height, of fair complexion, with wavy hair of a dark-brown tint. She had blue eyes and a large and somewhat prominent nose. Two teeth were missing from the lower jaw. She was poorly dressed, though clean and decent. Not yet had she lost all womanly pride in her appearance, for bits of ribbon were noticeable about her dress; a faded rose was in her bodice, some cheap feathers in her hat, and three common brass rings on the finger of one hand. Go back, 'Dark' Annie, go back to the kitchen of your sordid house while you are safe! Look behind you and beware of the awful presence of one who even now follows you with the blood-lust in his soul, and the knife clasped tightly to his breast! Avoid him, fly from him as you would shun the tempter of mankind! There is yet time to escape from his murderous maw! Go back, Annie Chapman, go back while you are free. When once he lays his hand upon your arm, and bids you stay, you are lost indeed. But no! You will not be warned. You go on – on – on to your fate, and the destroyer draws closer and closer till he reaches your side, and turns his bloodless face and cruel lips and gleaming eyes upon you. It is too late. Only a miracle can save you now.

'I know a likely place,' she says, speaking in superior tones, for Annie Chapman married a veterinary surgeon in a good position and had well-to-do relatives, whom her habits and course of life had long since alienated; 'down Hanbury Street. There is a backyard at the rear of the houses. No one will disturb us there.'

'That's capital,' he says. 'You're the sort for my money, "Dark" Annie.'

She leads the way, and they enter a sombre and dismal lane at the back of Hanbury Street. She pauses at one door, the back entrance to No. 29, and listens intently. Nothing is stirring. The people in the house are early risers, whose work commences almost as soon as it is light, and they seek their rest when the public houses close by them are doing a roaring trade. At one in the morning they are all in bed, sleeping the sleep of the weary, if not of the just. It is quite safe to enter the backyard of No. 29, Hanbury Street at that hour. As the woman has said, no one is likely to disturb them there. It is a good-sized yard and a few steps – stone-made – lead from it to the passage within the house. They stealthily approach the flight of steps and look through. The house-door beyond is wide open.

'People here return at all hours,' 'Dark' Annie explained in a horse whisper, 'so they're obliged to leave the door open all night. We could have got through that way if the back door had been locked.'

He nods in silent acquiescence of her words and notes the fact that he can escape that way if occasion arises. They sit down – oddly assorted couple – upon the stone steps, and the woman makes a bargain, the best she can. He shows her money, some loose silver, to give her confidence, and she is satisfied. She covers him with coarse caresses, and he responds with endearments of a sort. The moon rides high above them, pale and majestic, in the heavens and the woman, gazing up, wonders idly what lays beyond.

'I suppose,' she says, 'it's all an idle tale, eh?'

'What, my dear?' he asks.

'Oh! Heaven and a Saviour and the Angels,' she returns; 'All of it is a fairy-tale, I suppose, eh? Yet I sometimes think I'd like to believe that every word of it is true, and that we shall meet again those who loved us and those we used to love.' He remained silent. If a tender thought should spring up in this rough soil, if a gentle hope should animate this scarred breast in this, the woman's last hour on earth, let it be. He had come to maim and mutilate the body. He had no jurisdiction to hurt or harm the soul. But time waned. It would soon be dawn. His palm itched for the knife, his nostrils quivered for the smell of blood, his eyes longed for the sight of torn flesh and lacerated muscles. Haste then, thou man of blood. Hurry with thy monstrous handiwork. The night is far spent, the day is at hand.

She lay, as the others had lain, upon her back, the eyes wide open and staring with awful sightless gaze toward the heavens. The throat was cut with such appalling force that the murderer, thinking he had severed the head from the body, had tied a handkerchief about it to keep it on. The abdomen had been completely ripped open, the heart and the viscera had been neatly arranged by the victim's side, and the entrails were wantonly strewn around. What words can paint such hideous facts as these?

The house was one of three storeys, and was inhabited by fifteen different families. In the top floor front resided a Mr and Mrs Davis, an old couple, with three grown-up sons. One of them was a carman, and had to go to his work at an early hour. On descending the stairs at a quarter to six that morning, he turned to enter his backyard, and there saw the body of the woman, lying on its back, close to the short flight of steps. Blood was everywhere, in dark, forbidding pools, and had even splashed into the passage from back to front. The horrified man rushed into Hanbury Street and gave the alarm. The police poured into the street, and took charge of the slaughterhouse, which was besieged by frenzied crowds. The neighbourhood was up in arms. Women were wild with alarm. Men were mad with rage. Children cried for very sympathy. The dreaded Jack the Ripper was at his fell work again.

Slade, walking calmly away from the scene of this atrocity, was in Stamford Street before the discovery was made. Crossing Blackfriars Bridge he threw into the water three common brass rings. 'The fools,' he muttered, as he watched them strike the water, 'will assume the deed to be that of a wretched thief, who took them to be of gold. They are gone, like the woman is gone. My work proceeds apace.' He had dried and cleaned his blood-stained hands upon his handkerchief when he left the body. This he burned in the fire-grate of his room, after wiping with it the knife with which the deed had been done. He then made the usual examination of his clothing. There were no tell-tale stains. He had removed from the body a certain organ. The operation had been deftly done. His surgical knowledge told him where to look and how to cut. This had been done in a spirit of maniacal mischief. 'It will give the doctors something on which to air their views,' he thought, 'and provide my friend Blake with a fresh theory.' There, however, he was wrong, for the fact confirmed Blake in his notion that the murders were the acts of a man conversant with modern surgery.

It was twelve o'clock in the day before the detective returned to Gower Street, though he had dismissed Dagenham some hours before. Blake had learnt of the murder at Commercial Street police station shortly after its occurrence, and had at once hurried to the scene of the crime. He had been permitted to view the body, and had sickened at the awful spectacle it presented. He at once instituted certain inquiries, and was able to assist in the establishment of the identity of the poor victim. He interviewed the neighbours, and made some important discoveries. A woman, having occasion to go into the yard of the home next to No. 29, had heard voices in conversation speaking from the rear of those premises adjoining. They were those of a man and a woman. She reported that she heard the woman say 'No' twice, and had then caught a sound, suggestive of a human body falling against the fence which separated the two yards. Yet she had not, unfortunately, been curious enough to look over the fence and see what was occurring. Had she done so, she might have given an alarm, and the murderer would have needed all his courage, cunning, and resource to have effected his escape. The fingers of the poor corpse gave evidence of rings having been torn from them, but this Blake regarded as only a blind. Two highly polished farthings were in one of the pockets of the dead woman. Had these been given to the victim by the murderer, and had she taken them for half-sovereigns? It was possible. Another woman came forward to say that she had seen Annie Chapman talking with a dark man, apparently about forty years of age, near the London Hospital, and that she had heard the man say, 'Will you?' and the woman respond in the affirmative. But Mrs Chapman had paraded the streets night after night for a long time, and might easily have spoken to half a dozen different men in addition to her murderer. On the whole, Blake remained convinced that the ferocious deed was that of the same dangerous maniac who had murdered the other two woman, and that Mortemer Slade was the madman in question. 'I'll search every nook and corner of London,' he told himself, as he drove home, 'but I'll find him. I feel that my peace of mind, and the happiness of many others, depends on this man's capture or destruction. In a day or two I suppose they'll issue a reward. I want no reward. I want the honour and glory of ridding the world of a monster.'

On reaching home he did not attempt to rest. He had a bath, changed his clothes, swallowed some coffee, lit a pipe, and sat down to think. Whatever his deliberations were, they occupied him for more than two hours. Again and again he filled his pipe, and again and again he knocked the ashes from the bowl out on to the ashtray. He shifted his position many times, and for over half an hour paced about the room, deep in thought, and oblivious of time or place.

At last he spoke aloud, though there was no one there to hear. 'There is nothing for it,' he said, 'but a decoy. Do I know the woman cool enough, brave enough, wary enough? Yes, by the Lord, I do. One who can be trusted to act with calmness and decision. One with more presence of mind than anyone I know; resolute, strong, determined. Yes, I'll try a decoy, Jack the Ripper. And I know the very woman. I'll send for Sarah Watts. Let's see what my splendid Sarah can make of you.'

14. Sarah Watts

Mrs Watts, whose services Edmund Blake wished to enlist in his campaign against the Whitechapel fiend, resided at the village of Denham, not far from the town of Uxbridge, in Buckinghamshire. A more remote and old-world spot than this it would be hard to find in any English county. When you stand outside the White Swan Hotel in the centre of this ancient and attractive hamlet, you can imagine yourself seventeen hundred miles away from the metropolis, whereas, as a matter of fact, you are not above seventeen good miles from the Bank. At a lonely cottage in this place, situated close to the main Oxford Road, down a picturesque and leafy lane, occurred in 1870 a horrible series of murders, the work of one man. His crimes, however, which startled the country in that eventful year, were committed from motives of plunder and revenge, and in no wise resembled those of which Jack the Ripper was guilty. Nevertheless, the case of the brutal murder of the Marshall family revived itself in Blake's mind as he drove past the ancient parish church, in the graveyard of which the seven victims of John Owen's ferocity lie side by side. He left the fly which had brought him from Uxbridge outside the White Swan, and strode through the quaint village streets to the rustic cottage in which Mrs Sarah Watts resided. It was a pretty place, a very pretty place. A small stream flowed peacefully past the little house, the front garden of which was approached by a short bridge. It contained only four rooms did this cottage, and the whole front of it was covered with a clinging creeper and white and red roses. The garden was full of flowers of the homely kind, hollyhocks and gillie flowers and pansies predominating, and the air was heavy with the scent of them as Blake walked up the narrow and trimly kept path which led to the front door. At the back was the fruit and vegetable garden, and the rosy-cheeked apples, of which Blake caught a momentary glimpse, and the purple plums would have reflected no discredit upon their grower at a swell show. A large and sleek black cat came gracefully forward as the detective advanced, and, seeing nothing in his appearance to occasion feline alarm, rubbed itself against his legs and purred with a warm approval. Above the porch a large raven in a great wicker cage regarded him with a critical air of scrutiny, and from the garden at the back came the deep baying of a hound disturbed at the foot treads of a stranger. A little serving maid, neatly attired and obviously deft-handed, came to the door in response to his gentle tap, and ushered him into the front parlour with the intimation that Mrs Watts, to whom he had written and who exacted him, would be with him in a few moments, and that he might, if he liked look at the books on the table till she came. These were not very gay as to their outsides, nor very enlivening as to their interiors. Fox's *Book of Martyrs* is not the most cheerful reading in the world of literature, and *Don Quixote* is not altogether to the universal taste. The window of the room, however, was open, and there Blake remained listening to the music of the birds singing from many a leafy bower, and drinking in great health-giving draughts of the pure and rose-scented air.

The room was neat and well-ordered, testifying to the methodical habits and tidy care of its presiding genius. The furniture, though old-fashioned and somewhat severe-looking, was good and substantial. Portraits in oil of the first Mrs Watts and of the departed Ephraim Aston Watts adorned the brightly papered walls. There was a large, three-quarter portrait of Sarah Watts over the mantelpiece executed by a local celebrity, no doubt, whose principal object in the exercise of his art would appear to have been to make his 'subject' seem as supremely silly as was possible. In this task the painter had evidently succeeded only too well. The room possessed other treasures in the shape of crewelwork, antimacassars, waxen fruit and flowers in glass cases, and stuffed birds in gay plumage and impossible attitudes. A cottage piano stood in one corner of the apartment, and a small harp in another. On the shelves and brackets were framed letters from members of the aristocracy, the whom Mrs Watts, in the exercise of her peculiar talents, had rendered distinguished service at various crises. A duchess had actually presented the useful Sarah with a photograph of her portly self, signed, indeed, by her ducal hand, and a countess had sent her 'dear Sarah Watts', a daguerrotype of herself on the occasion of her marriage to the Earl of —!

While Edmund Blake is leisurely examining these and other mementoes of a peculiar career, we may seize the opportunity to give some account of Mrs Sarah Watts, who was really, in her own way, a remarkable and even distinguished person.

She was the only child of a sergeant-major in the Army, and had received a good education. Her capital abilities, natural talents, and anxiety to learn had endeared her to her masters when, through the instrumentality of influential friends, she was sent to complete her scholastic career at a first-class seminary for young ladies between Portsmouth and Havant. Her father died when she was twenty-five years of age, and she inherited a sum of £1500, which, invested, brought her a small but certain income of some 30 shillings a week. But Sarah was not without her ambitions in her way, and she did not wish to live a life of absolute idleness. She secured an appointment with a well-known and respected firm of private inquiry agents, in whose service she soon proved herself well-nigh invaluable. She was discovered by her employers to possess tact, discretion, resource, and courage in no common degree, and it was not long before she could count upon being sent in for cases of the most delicate and intricate nature. She had her limitations, of course. She had not, it is true, the analytical powers of Edmund Blake, nor his acute penetration; but in all other respects she was his equal, and in one or two, his actual superior. She did not reason. She had no need to. She relied upon her intuitive abilities, her quick insight into human nature and its motives, her keen instinct, and her feminine adroitness. For presence of mind and resourcefulness she was not excelled by any detective alive.

At thirty-five years of age she had placed her resignation before the firm by whom she had for ten years been incessantly employed and twelve months later she had married Ephraim Watts, a distant cousin of her own, who had been left a widower, and who was desirous of a help in his declining years. This bucolic and good-natured person died in 1885, when Sarah was forty years of age, and at his demise she inherited the little cottage in which, a widow and childless, with none but very distant kin, she was now installed. Even now, however, she could not be idle, and on several notable occasions she was called in to assist in delicate investigations which those concerned therein desired to hide from the prying eye of either the police or the press. It was in connection one of these 'hidden mysteries' that Edmund Blake had first encountered her, and he had immediately discovered her abilities. He told himself with absolute sincerity that she was a woman in a thousand and that, with her to assist him, he would not fear to face the most acute criminal intellect, or the results of any secret investigation on which they might be engaged. The moment had now come when his high opinion of her capacity might be tested to the full. 'Slade,' he thought, as he found himself gazing at the demure little lady of the house, who welcomed him so profusely, 'has all the devilish cunning of the maniac; but if it comes to a tussle – as I hope it will – Sarah and I – *place aux dames*! – ought to be a match for him.'

Mrs Watts was a little woman with wavy brown hair and sharp, beady eyes. She was slim and rather gracefully made, and had the long, sensitive hand of the musician. She always dressed in black, summer and winter, and was careful in respect to her shoes and gloves, these, indeed, being her pet extravagance. Her garments were plain, and somewhat old-fashioned in style, but the material of everything she wore was of the best and the fit perfection. She held herself rather aloof from her neighbours in the quiet and secluded village, and was by them regarded as a mysterious female, of romantic temperament and eccentric ways. She received her visitor with every show of graciousness. She had a great respect for Edmund Blake's brilliant talents, displayed in many a case in which she herself had been associated. She gave him her hand which the young detective, with graceful gallantry, respectfully carried to his lips. She was over forty years of age, but she looked pleased at the little attention, and actually blushed. She was of the type of woman who keep their youth even to sixty and seventy years of age.

'What breeze has blown you down here?' she asked, as she seated herself opposite to Blake at the window. 'I am a vain woman, Mr Blake, and I suppose I always shall be; but I can't think that I am altogether the attraction.'

Blake laughed.

'I always try to combine business with pleasure,' he replied, 'and in this instance have happily succeeded. I'm engaged on a case, a peculiar and intricate one, in which I should like your assistance above all things. You can, I think, help me to success.'

Her long, slender fingers, which were rarely still, toyed with the leaves of a sixpenny weekly paper on a table near her. 'I should be most happy to do what I could,' she said, a little diffidently, 'although I am supposed to have retired from the private inquiry business, and find plenty to occupy my time and my mind down here. What do you want, Mr Blake, my advice or my active participation?'

'Both,' he said, 'are like a virtuous woman – above rubies! I should be glad to receive either. I know your worth, Mrs Watts, and, allied with you, would fear no mystery, however involved.'

'This – the case you are engaged in – is a difficult one, then?'

'Undoubtedly,' he replied, with increased gravity. 'The case bristles with difficulties.'

'If you wish me,' said Sarah, 'to join forces with you, you will explain it all, not necessarily for publication, but – etc., etc.!'

Blake did so. He told her of the escape of Slade from Grange House, and of the contemporaneous murder of the asylum doctor. He explained how Phyllis Penrose had been alarmed by the appearances of her mad admirer, and how those appearances had been followed by the three appalling murders in the East-end. He showed her the letter he had received signed 'Jack the Ripper', and a copy of the extraordinary epistle sent to Miss Penrose. He told her of Dagenham's association with Slade's escape, and explained to her that the ex-groom was in his own pay. He gave her his reasons for believing the Whitechapel crimes to be the work of a homicidal lunatic possessed with a mad lust for blood. He told her that their future adversary was bold, cunning, and resourceful, and warned her that he would almost certainly stop at nothing to achieve his ends and effect his escape. 'If those murders, hideous and revolting as they are, are to cease,' he said impressively, while she watched him with keen and eager eye, 'this man must be laid by the heels. Mortemer Slade is a dangerous and a menace to all the world. I am convinced that he is Jack the Ripper, and nothing can shake my conviction. You have all the facts and can now form an opinion. What do you advise?'

She considered a little while before replying.

'Do you believe that he is still attached to, or that he still fancies himself attached to, Miss Penrose?' she asked at last.

'The facts point that way,' he remarked. 'He seeks her out on certain occasions, and those occasions have invariably been followed by a barbarous crime. He is seeking, I think, to punish her for her refusal of him when he proposed marriage some time ago. I think that she still exercises considerable influence over his mind.'

Mrs Watts acquiesced. 'I think so too,' she said, 'and if our surmise is correct, we may be able to get on the track of this mad gentleman by a judicious use of her name. Where is Miss Penrose now?'

'I understand,' Blake replied, 'that she, her aunt, Mrs Malyon, and the Earl of Caversham are travelling in Italy.'

'Is that fact known to Slade, do you suppose?'

'I cannot say,' he replied, 'but their departure has been announced in the public prints, and he may have read them. To all outward seeming, he is, remember, a perfectly rational being, and he may conceivably read his *Times* or *Telegraph* like any other.'

'It is probable,' said the little woman, in her brisk way. 'But the fact need not interfere with our scheme. Miss Penrose's maid might be remaining in England, and for the purposes we have in mind, I might be Miss Penrose's maid.'

'Exactly what I was about to propose,' Blake ejaculated with enthusiasm.

'Then,' Sarah Watts returned in her animated way, 'the question arises how am I, in the guise of lady's maid – a role I have adopted successfully before, by the way – to get into communication with our gentleman?'

'I suggest,' he replied, 'an advertisement.'

'It would mean delay,' she objected, 'and, quite possibly, disappointment. Nevertheless, it is certainly worth trying. I understand that you have never seen Mr Slade?'

'To my knowledge, I never have,' he replied. 'His appearance, of course, is well-known to the man Dagenham, who declares that he would recognise Mortemer Slade in any disguise, but he has no idea where is at the present time, and we failed to come across him through we were actually in Whitechapel on the night of the last murder. I am afraid we must put our trust in the press.'

'Yes,' she said. 'There is nothing for it but the agony column.' He took his notebook from his breast pocket, and a silver pencil-case came from another. He scribbled a few words, tore out the page, and handed it to his companion. 'How's that?' he said, laconically. She read it aloud.

M. S. – I am in Rome. If you would wish to hear of me, and to learn that I still love you, answer through the medium of this column. Secrecy inviolable. Be watchful. All for love is my motto – P. P.

'In what newspaper,' she asked, returning the paper, 'will you cause this to be inserted?'

'In all the London dailies,' he said. 'The day after tomorrow.'

'Mortemer Slade will, you think, imagine himself to be the "M. S."referred to?'

He nodded. 'I am sure of it. The motto, "All for love", will fetch him, it is the Caversham motto, you know.'

'Will the family like this?' she asked.

'I can explain my motives to Mr Stephen Darrell, who is engaged to Miss Penrose, and with whom I am friendly,' said Blake. 'The end justifies the means. The young lady has been greatly alarmed by the strange visitations of this man, and could not be otherwise than relieved to know that he is no longer at liberty to persecute her. If he is the awful murderer I take him to be, it is my duty to avail myself of any means, however painful, to effect his capture. I will answer for it that the Earl of Caversham himself will not blame me for the step I am about to take.'

'And the next move, if Slade replies?' asked the woman, with kindling eye. It was clear that already her heart and soul were in the chase.

'Would you be afraid to meet him?' he asked, scanning her closely.

She gave him a glance that was almost scornful. 'Afraid!' she said. 'I have never been afraid. I don't know what fear means. I would face your madman in this cottage tonight, alone, unarmed, and have no fear of him. You have tried me, Mr Blake, you should know.'

'Mrs Watts,' he answered, 'I am certain that your presence of mind and cool deliberate courage would pull you through. If it comes to an encounter between you, I should be inclined to lay odds on you. I must be going now. You will not find me slow to recognise your services, or to requite them.'

She shrugged her shoulders.

'As to that,' she said, 'you have assigned to me a task that is merely a labour of love. I will do my best, I promise you.' They parted, and Blake, confident in his new and able confederate, hurried back to town. At one of the Kensington stations between Uxbridge and London, he purchased a copy of the *Globe*, which contained the day's intelligence concerning the latest Whitechapel horror. There was nothing new. In a column of society gossip the following paragraph caught his eye, and set him wondering:

> We are asked to state that the marriage arranged between the Honble Phyllis Penrose and Mr Stephen Grant Darrell, recently appointed to the British Embassy in Paris, will not take place.

'Well, I'm dashed,' said Blake aloud, as he stuffed the pink paper into one of his pockets. 'What's in the wind now?' He got into a hansom and was driven home.

15. Stephen Comes to Say Goodbye

Three or four mornings later, Edmund Blake, carefully scrutinising the last page of that day's *Telegraph*, observed the following advertisement in the agony column:

> M. S. to P. P. – Should be delighted to see your representative. Let her be at Marble Arch at nine o'clock tomorrow night, wearing a spray of cornflowers. All for love.

That was all. The words were not many, but they were much. They satisfied Blake that the fish had taken the bait, and that there was a distinct chance of landing him at last.

'I hardly thought,' he said, as he carefully cut the paragraph from the paper and placed it in his notebook, 'that we should get a reply so soon. Mr Slade evidently reads his morning paper very thoroughly. I am glad of it. At last I am likely to stand face to face with this monstrous miscreant, and I do not think that he will escape again.' He reached for a sheaf of telegraph forms and scribbled out a wire to Sarah Watts. 'It will cost my plucky little friend a bit extra to have this brought from Uxbridge,' he reflected, 'but she won't mind that in the good cause.' He read the telegram aloud. 'Mrs Sarah Watts, Laburnam Cottage, Cheapside, Denham, near Uxbridge. Be at Marble Arch at half-past eight tomorrow night, wearing a bouquet of cornflowers. Slade has answered. – Blake.' He rang for his housekeeper and handed the telegram to that estimable lady to be dispatched at once, arranging for the prepayment of the reply. 'I'll be there before you turn up, Mrs Watts,' he said to himself, 'and give you your instructions, which you'll carry out faithfully and faultlessly as usual. I can rely on you for that. Between us, we shall bowl out our murdering maniac and rid London of the Red Horror which stalks among its poorest and least fortunate. I'll have Dagenham with me, so that there can be no possible error as regards identification.'

Half an hour later his housekeeper knocked at the door of the room where he sat writing, entered, and produced a card. 'A gentleman here to see you, Mr Blake,' she said. The detective glanced at the card. 'Show Mr Darrell in here at once,' he said, and added, when she had withdrawn, 'Now to hear the truth as to the estrangement between Mr Stephen and the Earl's pretty daughter. It's folly, I suppose, but I cannot, for the life of me, help associating the abandonment of the projected marriage with the baleful presence of Mortemer Slade. We'll see if I'm right or wrong.'

Stephen entered; such a changed Stephen, so pale, so worn, so hollow-cheeked and sunken-eyed, so grim of visage, so dull in demeanour, so mirthless and subdued, that Blake hardly knew him. Was this the clever, healthy, sprightly young man that he had heard spoken of as quite one of the popular pets of society? Was this the sprucely attired young dandy, full of life and spirits, the embodiment of hope and health, whom he had met and dined with only a few days before at the club? Edmund Blake was too well-bred to affect to observe the change in his visitor; but he told himself, as he placed a chair for the young man, that Stephen Darrell had been hard hit, and was not likely soon to get over the effects of the blow.

Stephen dropped wearily into the easy chair placed opposite to Blake, after he had shaken hands with his friend. He declined a cigar, and did not seem anxious to commence the conversation. Desirous of dissipating his melancholy, and setting him at ease, Blake began a long and somewhat incoherent discourse, during which he spoke of nearly every topic under the sun, referring to the latest cricket and racing news, criticising the newest play, mentioning the most-talked-of novel, the most recent political moves, and the latest and most spicy society gossip. He even exhausted the subject of the weather, that never-failing source of futile conversation, but, to all his remarks, poor Stephen replied with an indifference, and a brevity which brought even Blake's flow of eloquence to an end at last. Then, for some moments, they sat in silence.

'Look here, old fellow,' said Blake at length, 'we have not known each other very long, and it is possible that you may resent what I am about to say as an impertinence. But I can't help that. It requires no remarkable amount of perspicacity to see that you are in trouble; but, believe me, Stephen Darrell, believe me, your remedy is worse than the disease.

Stephen started uneasily. 'What do you mean?' he said, half-angrily. He kept his eyes upon the ground.

Blake reached over, across the table, and laid a friendly hand upon his shoulder.

'Mr Darrell,' he said, 'forgive me! Cocaine never cured the heartache yet, and never will.'

Stephen traced out the pattern on the carpet with the pointed toe of his patent-leather boot.

'Who told you I took that – or any other drug?' he said.

'You told me,' was the firm reply. 'Or rather, your very expressive face did. He who runs may read. I think your left arm could show traces of the injecting needle. Believe me, it is – not wise!' He spoke with a gentle, kindly firmness which disarmed resentment. Stephen sighed, and his anger was wrong.

'Hang it, Blake,' he said. 'I might have guessed that you would perceive what the trouble is. Well, I don't attempt to deny the impeachment. I've flown to cocaine and morphine, I admit. I've – I've – well! I've not been sleeping, you know. I've been restless at nights, and had to take something. I've not been eating, and any amount of Hennessey and soda won't bring forgetfulness. I've tried it, so I know.'

'It's a pity, said Blake, 'a great pity. I should not have thought that you, of all men, would succumb so easily.'

'You saw the announcement in the papers, I suppose?' Stephen asked.

'Yes, and I was shocked and surprised. I intended writing to ask you to come to see me.'

Stephen groaned. 'It's broken me up, Blake,' he said. 'I'm a doomed man, doomed in a way that even your keenness cannot fathom.'

'Nonsense,' said Blake, sturdily. 'A little misunderstanding, I am sure, between the young lady and yourself which a temporary separation and time will soon put right. That, I am sure, is the extent of your misfortune.'

'Would to Heaven that it were,' returned the other. 'Nothing that you can conceive in this world, no miracle, no act of man or woman, can bring Miss Penrose and me together again. We are severed forever.'

'Suppose,' said Blake, 'you were to tell me all about it? I promise that from no motives of idle curiosity, quite the reverse. I need hardly say that I shall respect your confidence. At least' – as Stephen shook his head – 'at least convince me that this man Slade is not the cause of the entanglement.'

'Good heavens! No,' cried Stephen. 'How could that lunatic come between us?'

Blake smiled. 'I only surmised it,' he said quietly. 'Well, you've satisfied me my suspicions were wrong.'

'I'll tell you all,' replied Stephen, 'knowing that my secret will be safe with you. I am positive of that.' Blake merely nodded.

'You will acknowledge that, as an honourable man, no other course was open to me than to insist upon Miss Penrose receiving back her liberty. To have married her, knowing what I know, would have been to commit a ghastly crime.'

Blake looked at him in open wonder. 'Proceed,' he said, quietly.

'Do I look,' inquired Stephen, 'like a man who might die at any moment, who is doomed to a sudden death, quick as a lightning stroke, which no power of man can avert?'

'Frankly, you do not,' was the reply. 'I know no one in my acquaintance less likely to meet such a fate. You are overwrought and unstrung. Your nerves are disordered. The drugs have begun to have their customary effect. Leave off the use of narcotics, take plenty of open-air exercise, live quietly, keep early hours, try to cease to worry, and I'd be glad to insure your life on very reasonable terms.'

Stephen smiled bitterly. 'I am suffering from acute valvular disease of the heart,' he said, 'and may die in this chair at any moment.'

'I cannot believe it,' was the reply. Blake looked shocked.

'Nevertheless, it is true. I have been carefully examined by an expert physician, who pronounces that my heart is vitally affected. The least exertion may kill me. I almost wish it would.'

'Mr Darrell,' said Blake, 'this is midsummer madness! I cannot think that your state is as bad as you say. You say that you have taken expert opinion?'

'The highest expert opinion. My case is hopeless.'

'When did you discover this, and how?'

'A week ago. By accident. Two roughs attacked me in the Park, returning one night from the club. I was rescued from their clutches by a gentleman, a doctor, who returned home with me, and who proved to be an old friend of my father's. He examined me the following morning, his suspicions as to my dangerous condition having already been aroused, and pronounced my condition to be most grave. I saw Miss Penrose, and, without explaining my reasons, broke off the match. I deliberately destroyed my one chance of happiness in this world. Phyllis is forever lost to me.

'I think,' said Blake, after a pause, 'that you would have done wiser to have made Miss Penrose acquainted with the facts.'

'That would have been unfair,' Stephen replied. 'She would, like the good angel she is, have insisted on sacrificing herself. She would have married me.'

'You have behaved nobly, Mr Darrell,' Blake replied, 'and I honour you. I might have been less quixotic, and more selfish. However, let that pass. Does the Earl of Caversham know the cause of the cancelling of the engagement?'

Stephen shook his head. 'No. I preferred to keep the matter altogether secret. Phyllis went to Rome the day following, and is there now. As for me, I have renounced everything: love, place, ambition, hope. I have refused to accept my diplomatic appointment, and am going abroad almost immediately. I'm going to Central Africa to shoot big game. There, in some primeval forest, thousands of miles from all the world holds that is dear to me, let the end come when it pleases. I've done with life, and I'm ready to die.'

'A nasty, fatalistic sentiment,' said the detective reprovingly. 'Mr Darrell, threatened men live long. You may have years of usefulness before you. But, tell me, did you have the opinion of your medical friend confirmed?'

'I did not. What was the use? Dr Emmett, who saw me, is a specialist in heart trouble.'

'Dr Emmett?' asked Blake, curiously.

'Yes,' was the reply. 'He was a friend of my father's, but I had never met him before.'

'What is his Christian name?'

'John. John Emmett. He is about sixty years old.'

Blake considered a moment. 'Did he write a series of articles for *The Medical Times* on gout on the heart in 1885?'

'That's the man.'

'And a treatise on aneurysm, published in 1883 by Lewkes and Paul?'

'Yes,' said Stephen. 'I remember my father speaking of the publication, and praising it highly.'

'Then,' said the detective, impressively, 'you have lighted upon a mare's nest, for your man is a rank impostor. That Dr Emmett died two years ago.'

Stephen leapt to his feet, a gleam of hope in his eyes, and a bright colour in his cheeks. Then he sat down again despondently.

'You must be wrong,' he said. 'Who would impersonate a respectable physician like my father's friend, and why?'

'I'll tell you that presently,' Blake answered. 'Meanwhile, let me satisfy you that I am correct as to Dr Emmett.'

He rose, went to his bookcase, and took down a copy of the Annual Register for the year he required. He turned to the pages devoted to the obituary record for that year, and brought the volume to Stephen. There, in cold, black print, the latter read the announcement of the sudden death of Dr John Emmett at Weston-super-Mare, and a list of the achievements of that gentleman in medical science. There could be no doubt about it. The man who had succoured him, had called himself his father's friend, and had sentenced him to death, was an impostor, as Blake had said. Stephen sank back in his chair; the effect of this surprising discovery was almost too much for him. It was too good to be true. His heart beat furiously, and the room seemed to be whirling round. He felt faint and ill. He swallowed a little cold water brought to him by Blake, and permitted that gentleman to bathe his temples, and to chafe his hands. Was it all a hideous mistake? Was his heart sound, and his life, ordinarily speaking, likely to be prolonged? Yet he could not hide from himself one possibility, that the man he had seen, though using a name and title to which he had no right, might yet be a doctor, and that his diagnosis might yet be true. Still, hope had come into his heart, and he could not drive it out. The love of life, the longing for years and honours, came over him again, and he hated himself for the coward he had been. He had taken refuge, like a poltroon, in the use of drugs, and had drunk to drown his misery. Now he no longer feared to hear the worst. If another medical man confirmed the opinion of the mysterious man who had blasted his life, he would face the future, whatever it might bring, like a man, and endeavour to live his few remaining days in honour and discretion.

He heard the voice of Edmund Blake as in a dream.

'Who else but Mortemer Slade, that arch-fiend, could have done this thing?' the detective was saying, as he paced the room with impatient stride. 'Who else could have devised such a devilish plan to rob you of love and life? Who else has an object in your removal? Who else has anything to gain by your loss of your betrothed? This man hated you because Miss Penrose loves you. His medical knowledge enabled him to impose upon you. He bribed the two roughs to attack you, and he took you home. Up with you, man, up with you! Dash your face in cold water in my room, get your hat, and come with me to Spencer, over the way. I've just seen him go in, so we are sure to catch him. He's as clever a chap as I know, and if he doesn't say your blessed heart is a damned sight sounder than mine, I'll devote my entire income to a society for the Doing Away of Doctors! Heart disease, forsooth! You're as strong as an ox and as sound as a bell.'

Thus adjured, and with the sense of hope strong upon him, Stephen accompanied his friend to Dr Spencer, and underwent an examination, over which the medico spent something less than a minute.

'You're a little shaky and run down,' he said, 'nerves are a little shattered; young

gentlemen's nerves often are at the end of a London season. Too much dancing, too much champagne, too much cards, too late hours, and so forth, *ad nauseam*! Take a little rest and plenty of exercise, and you'll be right as a trivet in a fortnight, I promise you.

'But my heart?' cried Stephen, rapturously.

'Heart? Your heart is as sound as a rock, sir; never sounded a better. Heart? Pooh, pooh! Wish mine were as good. Thank you, but I really couldn't think of accepting so large a sum–'

'Oblige me, doctor, by putting that in your pocket. Nay, I insist on it, and you are retained as my medical adviser forever and ever,' exclaimed the delighted Stephen, as he thrust two £10 notes upon the astonished practitioner. 'You have conferred upon me an eternal obligation.' He turned excitedly to Edmund Blake. 'Blake, dear old chap,' he said, 'I can't find words to thank you!'

'Tut!' said the detective, 'what have I done? Thank me when I lay hands on Mortemer Slade.'

'What shall I do? What do you advise? How can I put things straight? Oh! What a mountainous, monumental ass I have been.'

'My advice is this. Make it right about your appointment, and then go home, pack a portmanteau, and get off to Rome as fast as train and boat can carry you,' said Blake.

Stephen pressed his hand, patted him on the back, seized his hat, and was gone. Dr Spencer turned to Blake inquiringly. 'Strange young man your friend,' he said. 'Is he a little–'

'Sane as you are, doctor, ordinarily, but just now mad with happiness,' Blake replied.

A few minutes later he was again in his own sitting room. 'And now,' he thought, 'having put that little matter straight, let my thoughts revert to Jack the Ripper.'

A telegram lay on his desk. He opened it, and read it aloud.

'I will be there,' it read, 'Sarah Watts.' He chuckled. 'Good,' he said, 'Good.'

16. Mortemer Slade Foils the Detective

Punctually at half-past eight on the following evening there alighted at the Marble Arch from Paddington omnibus a slight, elderly-young lady, attired in a neat black dress. She also wore a black straw hat and a veil of neutral tint. The only spot of colour her personality revealed was provided by a great bunch of blue cornflowers, which she wore pinned carelessly to the front of her bodice. The lady, prim, neat, self-possessed, was Mrs Sarah Watts, from Denham, that old-world village near Uxbridge.

A few moments after her appearance there Edmund Blake arrived in a cab. It was a warm day, but he was wearing a long, loose overcoat, a white wrapper round his neck, and a cap. It would not have been easy to recognise the usually smart private detective. Perhaps he had no desire to be easily recognised.

He spotted Mrs Watts – and her cornflowers – in an instant, and saluted her.

'I knew I could count upon you,' he said eagerly. 'We have half an hour. At the end of that time Mortemer Slade should be here.'

'Don't be too sure, Mr Blake,' she replied. 'He may have fathomed the motives which prompted our advertisement, and taken alarm.

'In that case, would he have replied to it?' asked Blake. 'No! I think that at last, I shall see the greatest criminal of modern times.'

'Has he any suspicion that you are on his track? If he had he will take the advertisement to be mere bogus, and yet frustrate us.'

Blake shook his head.

'He cannot,' he replied, 'have the least notion that I am interested in the case. Possibly, he has never even heard of me.'

'You belittle your reputation,' was the smiling rejoinder. 'Still, we must remember that, after all, this Slade is mad and therefore not indisposed to take risks which would alarm an ordinarily minded man.'

'And,' added Blake, 'we must remember that he is in love, or rather, he was in love, with Miss Penrose. Depend upon it, this bait is the only one to catch him.'

Though this conversation was uttered in a low and hurried tone, much of it was heard by a tall youth of brutal aspect who had a bundle of special *Standard*s under his arm and was calling out the chief items in the day's news in a hoarse and monotonous undertone. Close at hand, leaning up against the park railings, idly watching the passengers hurrying off the multitudinous buses, was a similar young rough, who contrived to keep a pretty close watch upon the little lady in black, her tall companion, and the ruffianly newsmonger.

'Come into the Park,' said Blake, regarding the last-mentioned with stern disfavour – he had thrice refused a paper thrust into his hand; 'we can talk better there. I have certain instructions to give you.'

They entered the great gates, and Blake selected two chairs near the railings.

'It is not my intention to arrest Slade tonight if he should turn up,' he said to his attentive and keen-eyed companion. 'Indeed, at this juncture I have hardly the power to do so, since he was never actually wanted for the murder of poor Welman, and I have no direct evidence connecting him with the Whitechapel murders. It is my present intention to have him constantly followed and watched. I'd like, if possible, to capture him in the East-end itself – perhaps in the very act of another murder.'

'That means another victim,' said Mrs Watts.

'Not necessarily,' was the reply. 'We should arrive in time to prevent that, I hope. Now, as to your part.'

'I am all attention.'

'You will, of course, keep up the idea that you are an ex-servant of Miss Penrose's, and that she has paid you to act as her representative. You will represent the young lady as no longer in love with Mr Stephen Darrell. You will imbue the madman with the hope that he himself may in time be reinstated in her affections. You will make another appointment with Slade, or agree to keep any appointment he may himself arrange. You will keep him long enough in conversation to enable Dagenham and myself to procure a look at his face. He won't, can't possibly, indeed, recognise the former should he notice him, for I have disguised him, and me he has never seen. But I need not waste words instructing Sarah Watts how to proceed. She,' he added, admiringly, 'could hardly make a mistake in word or deed, if she tried.'

Mrs Watts smiled demurely. 'I will try to deserve your praise,' she said. 'Had I not better be getting back?'

He glanced at his watch. 'Yes,' he said. 'It is ten minutes to. I'll leave you here so that you can walk back to the Marble Arch alone. Dagenham and I will keep you in sight from the other side.'

They parted, and Sarah, adjusting the blue flowers at her breast, walked towards the gates. The ruffianly newspaper-lad was still there, and gave her a rapid glance as she passed. Blake, joining the disguised Dagenham, stood at the corner of the Edgware Road, and waited and watched.

Waited and watched. Ten minutes passed – a quarter of an hour – twenty minutes – half an hour – three quarters, and still the detective could see the little lady in black slowly walking backwards and forwards, forwards and backwards, outside the Marble Arch. No one joined her. No man spoke to her. No one noticed her even. It was plain that Mortemer Slade, in spite of his answer to the advertisement, had seen through the scheme and decided to keep away. There was nothing for it but to abandon the vigil and trust to better luck next time. Blake was bitterly disappointed.

'Curse the man!' he cried. 'He foils me at every turn.' Dagenham looked rueful, too. 'He never came near,' he said, 'I'll swear to that, gov'nor. I'd know him anywhere, the devil take him.'

At the expiration of an hour, Blake, despairing of a favourable issue to the adventure, dismissed Dagenham, crossed the road, and rejoined the patient Sarah.

'No go,' he said, blankly. 'He either smelt a rat or something prevented his coming. Let's hope it was the latter, and that he may make another appointment through the agony column.'

'We could put another in ourselves,' said Sarah.

'I think it would be wiser to let him make the next move. I'm very sorry you've had all this trouble for nothing, but one – two – three – six – a dozen rebuffs are not going to baulk me of my prey. Mortemer Slade, I'll have you yet.'

At the corner of the Edgware Road he procured a four-wheeler and directed the driver to take Mrs Watts to the Paddington terminus.

'How will you get from Uxbridge to Denham?' he asked. 'It's rather late. Can you get a fly something?'

'Oh, I'll walk,' she said. 'Two miles is nothing to me.'

'But it's such a lonely road,' he objected.

'I like it,' she said, calmly, and there was nothing for it but to say goodnight and direct the cabman to drive on. He raised his hat and strode away towards his club.

Instantly a young rough, running across from the opposite side of the road, hailed a hansom. ''Ere,' he explained breathlessly. 'Follow that there keb.' He made to clamber in.

'Who are you orderin' about?' the jehu demanded indignantly. 'Get you o' my cab, you murderin' looking young villin. I don't go in for luxuries in the way of fares.'

'I've got money,' said the other with an oath. 'Look. Five bob to follow that there growler. Blast it! Make up yer mind, can't yer? The — keb will be out o' sight while you're a-considerin' of it.'

'Get in,' said the man. 'You ain't a very 'ansome or creditable lookin' fare, I'm blessed if you are. But I'll chanst it. I ain't 'ad a grand day, and five bob's five bob from anyone's pocket.' He whipped up his horse, speedily overhauled the crawling four-wheeler, and kept immediately behind it until the two vehicles arrived at Paddington.

Bleater – for it was he – leapt from his cab and discreetly followed Mrs Watts, who had thought it prudent to discard her cornflowers, into the great railway station. He guessed that she would have a return ticket to whatever place she was going to on the line, so he simply shadowed her and listened when she made certain inquiries of a railway official. 'The one on the right for Uxbridge,' he heard the latter say, and when he had seen the

little lady safely installed in a second-class compartment, he raced back to the booking hall and procured a third-class ticket to the same place. 'Jack's orders,' he muttered, as he tore along the platform to the train, 'was to foller 'er and see where she went. I ain't a-goin' to lose sight of her on no account till I'm able to tell 'im where she 'angs out.' He sprung into an already crowded carriage, hot and perspiring, but satisfied that Mrs Watts could not leave the train without him seeing her.

At Uxbridge he was almost the first passenger to alight, springing from the carriage before the train had come to a standstill. It was three or four minutes before he perceived the slight figure of the woman he was watching, making her way towards the stairs which led to the station exit. He preceded her out to the road beyond and waited in a dark corner to continue the pursuit.

Mrs Watts gave up her ticket and walked briskly out of the station, making for the main Oxford Road. The shops in the town were shut, and the public houses – to Bleater's disgust – had been closed for at least a quarter of an hour. Few people were about at this hour in the quiet town, and the night was dark and rather threatening. But the indomitable little woman, with a lonely walk of two and a half miles before her, stepped out with a resolute tread and a determined mien which nothing could dismay.

The ruffian, keeping well within the shadows, slunk after the retreating figure.

'I 'opes yer ain't agoin' fur, me lady,' he growled. 'I'm a-gettin' a bit tired o' this job, well as Jack 'as promised to pay me. He does pay out orl right, I'll say that for 'im. Wonder what he wants with this 'ere shrimp of a female? Wot's 'is game, I wonder? Wot's 'is game?'

The road between Uxbridge and the village of Denham was not then illuminated by any kind of lamp, and Bleater found himself easily able to follow the woman without himself being seen. Only two persons passed them all the way, and with one of these, a woman living at Uxbridge who had relatives at Denham, Mrs Watts stayed and spoke for a time, during which the Hooligan remained concealed in the friendly obscurity of a hedge. At length Mrs Watts turned to the right, down a narrow road, and Bleater, following, observed a post painted white, on which could be read the legend, 'Half a mile to Denham Village.'

'Ho!' said the young ruffian, 'yer lives at Denham, does yer? Well, we ain't a-goin' to part company till I see yer safely 'oused. Jack's orders, you see, ma'am. Wot's 'is game, I wonder? Wot's 'is bloomin game?'

Bleater found it expedient to draw nearer to the woman, when she entered the village, for fear she should enter one of the houses in the quaint little street and disappear from his view before he could ascertain for certain where she actually lived. There was a risk of discovery in this, for she had looked round once or twice in the narrow part of the lane, and he had been obliged to step suddenly on one side and take refuge in the hedge or behind a tree. Right through the village they went, follower and followed, until Bleater, from the obscurity of a great oak, observed the little lady cross a tiny bridge over a little stream and enter a cottage, admitting herself with a latchkey. For an instant she stood at the front door and gazed out into the night. Then she entered, and softly closed the door, and, an instant after, a light appeared in the window of the front room. 'That's where she lives,' said Bleater, 'and my job's done. Lor' love a duck! What a nice walk I've got 'ome! Know what I'll do. I'll 'ave a doss in one o' them there fields and catch the first train up from Uxbridge in the mornin'. Won't Jack be eager to 'ear my noos, not 'alf, I don't fink!'

At twelve o'clock the following morning he met Mortemer Slade, as arranged, at a little ale house in the New Cut. Blinder, the role of newspaper lout now abandoned, was with his employer, and hailed his approach with an approving shout.

'Looks as if yer'd 'ad a bad night, me Bleater,' he said. 'Did the little old girl lead yer a pritty dance, eh?'

Blinder sniffed contemptuously. He would have preferred the task assigned to Bleater, and was frankly jealous.

'You followed her?' asked Slade.

'Yus. First to Paddington; then to Uxbridge; then to Denham, a village about two and a 'alf miles from the town. Stepped out like a fair old ped, she did. Can't she use her trotters, neither. Walked me bloomin' well off me 'am and eggs, she did.'

Slade smiled sardonically. 'You know where she lives?' he inquired.

'Yus,' was the reply. 'Last cottage on left-'and side of main village street. Bit o' a brook in front of the garding and a little bridge reachin' to 'all door. Roses and suchlike all over the front, and a big garding at the back. Laburnam Cottage painted on green gate in front. You can't mistake the plice, gov'nor.'

'You've done well,' said Slade. 'I told you I expected to be able to employ you again, and no doubt I shall have other and even more agreeable work for you. But, hark'ee both, of you! Don't try any tricks with me. Don't go seeking to find out my motives for this or my reasons for that; don't go prying into any business of mine, or try to do the crook on me. If you do, I'll kill the two of you with as much pleasure as a terrier would a couple of rats. I pay you well; I'll always pay you well. But I warn you to play fair with me, or to look out for squalls. Now, take this money and go. I know where to find you when I want you.'

Bleater and Blinder slunk off to their own haunts. 'What a nice man he is,' said the latter, clinking the money in his pocket. 'So agreeable and perlite, eh Bleater?'

The latter grunted and led the way into a tavern. 'I want some beer and bread and cheese,' he said. 'That's what I wants. I've been out all night. As to the bloke we know as Jack, wot's 'is game, I wonder? Wot's 'is bloomin' game?'

Slade strode hastily home. 'I dreamt,' he thought, 'the other night, that my defeat and discovery were ultimately due to a woman. I fear this little person in black, who advertised as though she had been commissioned by Phyllis to communicate with me, and who met Mr Edmund Blake before the time of the appointment with me. Is she instructed by Blake, I wonder? How fortunate I engaged those two blackguards to watch who turned up. I'll put you safely out of the way, my little lady in black, you've chosen to cross my path, and you'll have to pay the penalty. I'll add you, whoever you are, to my list of victims. I'll go home and prepare a scheme. Then I'll pay you a visit and we'll see what comes of it. You meet Blake by appointment, do you? Well! Well! We'll see! We'll see!'

He went towards Stamford Street, and, after a hasty meal at a fifth-rate coffee shop near that thoroughfare, betook himself home and lay down to think. His reflections were evidently pleasant ones, for he smiled once or twice, and once indulged in a fiendish chuckle which had, however, little of mirth or enjoyment in it.

'I foil you at every turn, Mr Edmund Blake,' he said exultantly. 'Tomorrow, I'll rob you of your fair confederate, and for the future you'll have to fight with me without her aid.'

17. Mrs Watts Disappears

A morning or two later, at about noon, Edmund Blake and Sarah Watts sat together in the *sanctum sanctorum* of the former. The detective had before him a newspaper, and sat staring at a paragraph in the agony column. The woman, calm and stolid as ever, sat facing him, with her gloved hands in her lap, and her face wore its usual expression of self-conscious strength and determination. Had Blake announced that Mortemer Slade had been seen to disappear heavenwards in a chariot of fire she would have evinced no surprise, and would probably have merely remarked that he was, in any case, an undesirable personage, who was best out of the way.

M. S. to P. P. Ask your representative to meet me at King's Cross Station at two o'clock on Tuesday next. Wear bunch of cornflowers. All for love.

These words Blake read slowly and thoughtfully aloud. He glanced up at the imperturbable Sarah, who was steadfastly regarding him.

'Will he turn up, I wonder?' he said. 'Or is this to be another wild goose chase like the last?'

'I think he'll come,' the woman replied. 'This advertisement is not merely one in response to ours. It is spontaneous on his part. He is anxious to hear of Miss Penrose, and he fully believes that he is in communication with her representative. Yes,' said the little woman in her most decisive style, 'I think he'll show up this time.'

'I'm inclined to agree with you,' Blake answered. 'I have taken the precaution to wire to Dagenham. He will be there soon, and he will accompany you to the rendezvous. He will then be in a position to tell me if it really is Slade who appears or merely a tool of the latter's.'

'A good plan,' said Sarah. 'You will, I presume, keep away yourself?'

'Yes,' he replied, 'I shall give instructions to Dagenham to follow Slade unperceived. I shall then learn the whereabouts of his hiding place, and be able to put hands on him at any time. I wish, if possible, to conclusively establish his identity with that of Jack the Ripper, and, with this view, it may be expedient to delay his capture till circumstances compel me to take action. If it can be done without imperilling the life of another unfortunate woman of a certain class, I'll arrest him in the very act of one of his atrocious crimes, and thus rid London, East and West, of this terror for all time.'

'I hope,' said Mrs Watts, 'that your plans may be successful. I seem to think they will.' As she spoke, Dagenham was ushered into the room. The ex-groom looked pale and excited. He was breathing hard, as though he had been running, and his usually well-oiled locks were dishevelled and awry. He leant heavily on the arm of a chair and stood surveying his employer with a comical expression of fear, not unmingled with a sort of glad relief. He bowed respectfully to Mrs Watts, who returned him an encouraging smile.

'You have come home in haste?' she said. 'It is hot weather for hurrying, Mr Dagenham.'

'It is, ma'am,' was the reply. 'I'm all out of breath.'

Blake put the newspaper on one side, lit a cigarette, after obtaining the gracious consent of his fair visitor to smoke, and leisurely surveyed Mr Dagenham.

'Sit down,' he said, pushing a chair towards him, 'and let me tell you your news. You've seen him?'

The young man started. 'Well, sir,' he said, 'I have, but how you know, that is a fair licker to me, begging the lady's pardon.'

'Tush,' said Blake. 'Little else would have so excited you. You have seen Mortemer Slade.'

'And spoken to him, I think,' said Sarah Watts, quietly.

'I have seen him and spoken to him,' said Dagenham, wiping his perspiring forehead with a large red handkerchief. 'You are quite right, sir, and so, too, are you, ma'am.'

'Where?' said Blake, eagerly.

'When?' asked Mrs Watts, her keen eyes fixed on the dismayed face of the groom.

'Half an hour ago,' was the reply. 'Near Waterloo Station.'

'Tell us all, please,' said Blake, setting himself in his armchair with an air of expectant enjoyment. 'Leave out nothing. The most minor facts may prove to be of importance.'

The ex-groom nodded. 'There's not over much to tell,' he began, 'but I'll tell you all there is. I got your wire, sir, at a quarter to eleven. I washed myself, dressed, and arranged to leave my lad in charge of the shop. I left my door at Tooting at eleven o'clock and walked to where the horse-trams start for the bridges at Westminster, Blackfriars, and Waterloo. At a quarter to twelve I alighted at the latter station, and I crossed over to the Lord Hill – excuse me for mentioning the fact, ma'am – to have a modest quencher before coming on here. I ordered my half-pint tankard of stout and burton – I'm partial to that there mixture, ma'am, when I takes anything at all, which ain't often, since I met the gov'nor here – and was just about to raise it to my lips when a young cove, a rough sort of bloke, comes up to me, and, touching me on the shoulders, says, "You're a-wanted outside by a gent." "What gent?" says I, a-thinking of you, Mr Blake. "Oh," says my flash youth, "don't you ask no questions – you'll see who it is when you gets outside." I drinks up my beer, and I walks outside the hotel, and looks up and down the street, my young covey a-standin' by and a-grinnin' like mad. "Now look 'ere," says I in a rage-like, "If you think I'm a bloomin' countryman up here to be fleeced or made a fool of, all I can say is you've struck the wrong chap, young gallows face, and you're simply wastin' your precious time. Take yourself off, while you're safe," says I. At that, up strides a tall, dark man and takes my arm. "Don't waste words on him, Mr Dagenham," he says, "but just attend to me." I shakes my arm clear away from his grip and

looks straight at him, intendin' to ask what he meant by interfering with me. "Look again," he says, with a grin. "Perhaps you'll know me then." I did look again and I sees, underneath the false wig and moustache, the devilish face of Mortemer Slade. I knew him in an instant. I gave a desperate look round, meaning to denounce him to the nearest policeman. "You daren't do it, Jack Dagenham," he says, "you daren't do it. Breathe my name aloud, and I'll stab you here, instantly, in the heart, as you stand. I'll do it," he says, "and chance what happens to me.'"

'What did you do?' asked Blake, intensely interested, and wishing above all things that he had been at hand.

'Stood still staring like an idiot, sir,' was the uncompromising reply. 'You can't tell the power that this man possesses over you; you can't tell how he seems to hold you and to force you to do his bidding. I stood still, and I daresay trembled like a babby. "I know you, Mr Dagenham," he goes on, "you're a dirty spy, that's what you are. But you daren't split on me, even to oblige your smart friend, Mr Edmund Blake" – them's his words, sir, not mine – "because you know I'll cut the liver out of you if you did. Tell your master," he says, "to look out for me down Whitechapel way in a few days, and to be careful I don't steal another march on him in a few hours. Your Mr Blake is no match for Mortemer Slade," he says, "and no match for Jack the Ripper, either." Then he strides off towards St George's Circus, calling out, "Come on, Blinder," to the nice, gentlemanly young party who had followed me into the Lord Hill. I watched him disappear into the crowd and came on here, sir, in a cab.'

'You hardly behaved like a hero,' said Blake, after a moment or two's reflection, 'but I'm not inclined to strongly blame you, the time is hardly ripe yet to arrest Mr Slade, and I have another plan in store. You will accompany this lady to King's Cross Station, and, without being seen yourself, will observe all who approach her. If Slade speaks to her, keep him in sight and follow him wherever he goes. For this purpose, you will have to disguise yourself again. Go and get ready. I'll give you full instructions on your return.

Half an hour later, Mrs Watts and the discomforted Dagenham – disguised for the occasion of a bearded sea-faring man – left the Gower Street rooms in a four-wheel cab and proceeded to the Great Northern terminus. There Mrs Watts alighted and entered the bus station yard, the ex-groom following not too conspicuously in the rear. Blake had not forgotten to procure a spray of the pretty blue cornflowers, and these adorned the trim waist-belt of the little lady as she took her stand close to the bookstall and waited for Slade's appearance. Dagenham waited near at hand, and Blake remained at his rooms.

In a few minutes Blinder – the aggressive youth who had accosted Dagenham that morning – entered the station and at once engrossed all the ex-groom's attention. It was clear, the latter told himself, that this young ruffian was more or less in league with Slade, and it might therefore be his duty to follow him and see what became of him rather than wait for the master-villain himself. He was debating this point in his mind when Blinder approached, and, at once recognising him – to Dagenham's surprise and dismay, for he was, of course, disguised – as the sailor he had seen with Blake on a previous occasion, said mysteriously, 'I've just seen your gov'nor, Mr Blake, and he says you're to come to him at once.'

'Stow that,' said Dagenham, threateningly, 'you're the cove that followed me into the Lord Hill this morning. You're in league with Mr Mortemer Slade, who is wanted by the police for murder, and I've a good mind to give you in charge of suspicion. Mr Blake wouldn't entrust the likes of you with any messages.'

He glanced anxiously round. He saw the slim figure of Mrs Sarah Watts standing by the bookstall. No one was with her. It was clear that Slade had not turned up yet, if, indeed, he meant to keep the appointment at all.

'Give me in charge, would yer?' cried Blinder, menacingly. 'You're a nice sort o' beauty to talk about givin' in charge, you are, I don't fink! I brings yer a message from yer boss, nice and civil-like, and this is 'ow yer receives of it. I'll go back to Mr Blake and tell 'im as 'ow 'is 'igh and mighty assistant is too proud to do 'is biddin' and refuses to carry out 'is 'orders. Why I've 'alf a mind to–'

'What?' cried the exasperated Dagenham. He was a stout-built young fellow of uncertain temper, and he felt an uncontrollable longing to call this young street rough to account. The latter approached yet closer and appeared to entertain some designs of pulling Mr Dagenham's rather prominent nose.

'I've 'alf a mind to deal yer out one,' he said. He then administered a slight push to the ex-groom and snapped his fingers aggressively in his face.

Dagenham was not of long-suffering temperament, and this was more than he could stand. He pushed back, straight with his shoulder against the advancing figure of his burly young adversary, and nearly knocked him off his feet. A row on the station was exactly what the Hooligan had been retained to contrive. He hit out wildly, and Dagenham, ducking his head, closed in and got in one or two heavy blows on the head and face. The rough replied with vigour when he had recovered himself, and a pretty little set-to between two evenly matched rivals was in progress when, a small crowd having assembled, a couple of station constables and two or three of the railway officials stepped in and broke up the ring. Dagenham found himself being hustled off the station. Three stalwart policemen had hold of him, and were dragging him towards the street.

'Fighting and brawling won't do here,' said one, 'you had better go quietly, or you'll be taken where you won't like to find yourself when you've slept yourself sober.'

'Sober!' said poor Dagenham, vainly struggling with his captors. 'Why, I've only had two drinks all day. Here, let me go, I say! I'm engaged to watch a lady on the station by Mr Edmund Blake, the great private detective. I'll get in no end of a row if I leave here.'

'You'll get in no end of a row if you stay here,' was the reply. 'You're a well-known character, and so is the chap you were fighting with. Think we don't know your game, getting up a sham fight, so that your pals can run the rule over the crowd while you're at it. Get along with you.'

Sham fight, indeed! This was hard lines on poor Dagenham, who was conscious of a cut lip and a nasty swelling about the left eye. His only hope was that he had adequately tampered with the countenance of his opponent, who himself was being conducted to the street in another and opposite direction. But the latter was chuckling at having achieved his object, which was merely to find a pretext to get Dagenham away from the station. He had succeeded. A final shove deposited the first-named into the crowded road outside the terminus.

'Don't you come back here again,' said one of the constables, taking a last look at his disconsolate figure, 'or you'll get what for. No lip, now,' – as Dagenham attempted an expostulation – 'try your game on here again, that's all.' He went back to his duties, leaving the expelled one a picture of mortification and disgust.

'What on earth will Mr Blake say?' he groaned. 'He gave me strict orders to keep the lady in sight, and this is how I carry 'em out. If I catch that young blackguard again I'll mark him so as his mother won't know him for her own highly promising offspring. Meanwhile, I must go and explain to the gov'nor. Lord, help us! Slade may have come and gone by the time I can give Mr Blake the office.'

The latter was anxiously awaiting the return of either Dagenham or Mrs Watts, or both, at his own rooms. He looked his surprise when the first-named returned alone. Dagenham was so embarrassed he could hardly speak.

'Tell me, man,' the detective exclaimed impatiently, 'Did Slade turn up?'

'I don't know, sir; leastways' – began the unfortunate groom.

'You don't know?' Blake repeated, angrily. 'Don't be a fool, Dagenham, and understand I'm not in a humour to be trifled with. I ask you did Slade keep the appointment?'

'I don't know, sir,' was the reply. 'I was turned off the station. The young villain who was with Slade this morning attempted to assault me. There was a bit of a row – I struck him – and we both got turned off the station by the railway police.'

Blake leapt to his feet. 'Good God, Jack,' he said, not unkindly, 'what does it seem to you that I employ you for? I impressed upon you again and again that nothing was to induce you to leave the station till Mrs Watts herself came away. Then you were to follow the man who had been speaking to her and to return here. Those orders were simple enough and explicit enough, goodness knows. Can't you see, you foolish fellow, that this row in the station was a got-up job arranged by Slade for our defeat and discomfiture? But we may still be in time. Let us get back to the station now. Slade may be with Mrs Watts. I'll follow him myself. By heaven! If he escapes me again!'

They tore off to King's Cross Station in a hansom, and reached the terminus in seven minutes' time. Blake left Dagenham in the cab, and entered the precincts of the railway depot alone. He went to the entrance gates of every platform; searched every refreshment room; peered into every corner and crevice of the great building; interviewed porters and ticket-collectors; made every possible inquiry; but nothing could be learnt of the whereabouts of the demure little lady in black whom Dagenham had seen pacing up and down before the bookstall. Sarah Watts had utterly and completely vanished. She was – and was not! She had been – and was no more! He hung about the station for over an hour, after sending Dagenham back to Gower Street in case the missing lady had returned there. He sent a pre-paid telegram to Denham, in the supposition, unlikely though it seemed, that she might have returned to her home, without first seeing him. But it was not till late that evening, when he learnt that Mrs Watts had not returned to the Buckinghamshire village since she left it early in the morning, that he became seriously alarmed. Where was she? What had happened to her in the short interval of time between Dagenham's departure from the station and his own arrival there?

Here was mystery indeed!

18. Trapped

Mrs Watts watched the encounter between Blinder and Dagenham with no little concern. At one moment she felt inclined to interfere on behalf of the latter; but wiser counsels prevailed, for she had no wish to miss Mortemer Slade if, as she fully expected, he appeared at last. She saw the groom forcibly removed from the station, struggling and expostulating; but she remained true to her trust, feeling certain in her own mind that her plain duty was to carry out the orders of Mr Blake regardless of any side issues whatsoever.

It was now the right moment for Bleater, who had remained on watch throughout the fracas between Blinder and Dagenham and had seen the latter expelled from the precincts of the railway station, to play the part allotted to him in the plot so artfully arranged by Mortemer Slade. Dressed in the shabby and faded livery of a hired coachman, and respectfully touching his greasy high hat, he approached Sarah Watts and said, with a mysterious air, "'Scuse me, ma'am; be you the lady who represents P. P.?'

Sarah was on the *qui vive* at once. At last, thought she to herself, the real drama is about to begin; at last the curtain has risen on the play. 'If you want to know,' she said quietly, 'if I am the person who has been advertising in the agony column respecting a certain young lady and a Mr Mortemer Slade, I answer yes. Why do you ask?'

'Because,' said Bleater, assuming an air of humility and respect little in accordance with his villainous aspect, 'I am 'ere to take you to Mr Slade if so be as you are willin' to come.'

'Cannot Mr Slade come to me?' asked Sarah suspiciously.

'No,' said the assumed coachman. 'He can't. Mr Slade is a much-injured gent as has got many enemies. For aught he knows, you may be in league with them.'

Mrs Watts was not above romancing in a good cause. As a matter of fact, she could, when expedient, lie like truth itself.

'I might,' she replied, 'indeed; but I happen not to be. How much you know of Mr Slade's affairs is, of course, a matter between you and him alone. I presume he trusts you.'

'With a bit,' said Bleater, with a sinister grin; 'but not with much.' In reality, Slade had told him and his companion as little as possible. He had ferreted out facts about their by no means blameless pasts which enabled him to use them, rascals as they were, with perfect security.

'If the gentleman you speak of wishes to hear of the young lady I represent, he will see me without delay,' said Sarah, whose one idea was to come face to face with the escaped madman, and who entertained not the least fear of him or the consequences of the encounter. 'I am willing to accompany you.'

'Right you are, Missis,' was the reply. 'Come along o' me.' He led the way into York Road, that interminable thoroughfare which extends to Highgate and beyond. A few yards down this road, Sarah Watts, looking anxiously around for any signs of Dagenham – who was, by this time, on his way back to Gower Street – observed a closed carriage with the windows down and the blinds pulled halfway across them. The vehicle, which had two horses in the shafts, looked like one of those used by commercial travellers in their daily rounds. The horses' heads were being held by a street loafer picked up outside the public house opposite, and two or three itinerant news vendors and a bootblack were gazing at the 'turn-out' in anything but silent admiration. These spectators Bleater elbowed on one side with little ceremony. They scattered right and left, and the young rough held the door of the carriage open for the lady to enter. 'A little drive into the country, ma'am,' he said in her ear. 'Mr Slade ain't a frequent visitor to town. It ain't good for 'is 'ealth, nor 'is safety neither.' Sarah Watts hesitated. Courageous as she was, the idea of rushing into the lion's den in this way staggered her a little. If Blake's version was correct, the man she was going to interview was a dangerous lunatic, guilty of the most frightful crimes, and capable of others still more dreadful. Yet her duty, she told herself, was to take the risk. It was not, she thought, possible that Slade could have divined the truth. Almost certain was it that he believed that he was about to hear of and from Phyllis Penrose, and it was for the sake of that he was thus daring to make his whereabouts known. 'I'll face him,' thought the brave little woman, 'but I'd give twenty pounds to be able to send a message to Mr Blake without this coachman of his seeing me.'

Bleater still held the door of the carriage and surveyed her curiously. 'If you're a-comin', ma'am,' he began, 'we'd better–'

'Yes! Yes! I'm coming, of course. Have we far to go?'

'A matter of ten miles into the country,' he replied. An idea struck her.

'I've already had a long and tiring journey,' she said, 'I came away from home without breakfasting. If we are to go so far, perhaps you would not mind obtaining me some refreshment from the tavern opposite.' She produced her purse. Bleater looked doubtfully, but with a longing glance, at the tavern on the corner of the Pentonville Road. 'It's agin my orders,' he muttered, 'to delay. Still, five minutes ain't no great 'urt neither way.'

'Of course,' said Sarah, exhibiting a two-shilling piece, 'you'll take something for yourself, coachman, before you drive?'

Bleater, a thirsty soul at most times, was unable to resist this invitation. Slade, he considered, was not likely to hear of this little dereliction from the strict path of duty. He could drink a pint at a draught and be out again from the public in two minutes. He held out his hand for the money.

'What'll you take?' he asked, an idea flashing across him.

'Get me a flask of sherry,' Sarah replied, 'and some sandwiches. There is three shillings, is that sufficient?'

He seized the coins without staying to reply, and darted towards the tavern. In an instant she produced from her reticule a small pocketbook and a pencil. She scribbled a few words on one of the pages and hastily tore the note from the book. A knowing-looking urchin about ten years old stood by; him she accosted.

'Here, my lad,' she said, 'take that note to the address written on it.'

'Yus, mum,' said the boy with alacrity.

She gave him a shilling.

'Gower Street,' she said, hastily, 'is not far up the road. Anyone will show you the house. Give the note into Mr Blake's own hands, remember. I have asked him to reward you. You are sure you understand?'

'I'm fly, mum,' was the boy's eager reply. 'Gower Street? Why, I'd find me way there blindfolded, strike me I would. I'm off now.'

He darted away, mixing with the crowd at the corner, just as Bleater emerged, wiping his lips, from the tavern.

'I've put Blake up to the move,' thought the inflexible Sarah. 'Now, I'm ready for you, Mr Slade. We'll see who scores in this little encounter.'

She got into the carriage, and Bleater, having handed her a small packet of sandwiches and a pocket-flask containing sherry diluted with water, sprang upon the box and drove off at a rapid pace. Sarah Watts was tolerably conversant with her London and with the main arteries out of town. She lowered one of the carriage windows, and gazed out into the crowded streets. The vehicle was speeding up the Gray's Inn Road, and presently entered Farringdon Road, and so into Blackfriars Road over the bridge. At the Obelisk it turned into the New Kent Road, and soon was speeding towards Deptford. On and on it went, driven by Bleater at the same furious speed, and before long the suburban streets were left behind, and Sarah noticed that they were entering a district that was almost rural in comparison to that which they had passed through. 'We've come a good ten miles,' she thought, gazing out at the long, white, dusty road which stretched in front as far as the eye could see, 'and must be somewhere in Kent on the way to Sevenoaks, I should think. I'll ask the coachman how much further we have to go.'

Bleater turned on his box without slackening his rate of progression.

'Not far now,' he bawled. 'We finish a little bit this side o' Chislehurst, lady. Three-quarters of an hour ought to do us.'

He applied his whip to the tiring horses, and drove on without waiting for her reply.

Sarah Watts felt exhausted and hungry. It was a hot, sultry afternoon, and the dust, coming in at the open window in great clouds, had given her throat a dry, parched feeling which was the reverse of pleasant. She had had no lunch, and had left home early that morning without partaking of her customary hearty breakfast. She felt faint and famished.

'My kingdom for a cup of tea,' thought the little woman, 'but as I have no tea, I must make do with this,' and she swallowed half the contents of the flash of sherry. 'Humph!' she thought. 'I'm not a judge of wine, I admit; but there's a very queer flavour about that public house sherry with a vengeance! I'll try a sandwich.' She ate a couple of these and moistened her throat again with the peculiarly flavoured liquid from the flask. Then she looked out on the high road, now lined by thick hedges, beyond which were the fair market gardens of beautiful Kent. Orchards, the trees in which

groaned with the weight of fruit, abounded on all sides, and the smell of flowers and the hot autumn air combined were almost overpowering. She leant back in the carriage and closed her eyes in an almost irresistible desire to sleep. The feeling of intense drowsiness was almost overwhelming. There seemed a strange humming in her ears, a throb at her temples, a peculiar blight before her eyes. The sounds of rustling leaves, of running water, of carolling birds, came to her as from a vast distance. The noise of the carriage wheels, the crack of the driver's whip, seemed hushed and subdued. Was she awake or dreaming? Was this consciousness or insensibility? Where was she? What time was it? Where was she going, and who was taking her? Her heart began to beat furiously and strange, fantastic lights began to dance before her eyes. Her head ached furiously. She was conscious of that if of nothing else. She made an effort to rise and lean out of the carriage window. She felt as though she were being stifled. She tried to call for help, but no sound save an indistinct muttering came from her parched throat. Again she essayed to rise, but fell back helpless. Then, as it appeared to her, the carriage approached a high, dark precipice – drew nearer and nearer – tottered on the edge as the horses took the plunge – and then down – down – down into the blackness and nothingness. She slipped off the seat and fell insensible to the floor of the carriage.

A mile and a half before Chislehurst, on the edge of an open and desolate heath, Bleater pulled up his horses, dead-beat and reeking with perspiration, and descended from the box. He glanced into the carriage without opening the door.

'He told me to give 'er a dose,' he muttered, 'if I could, and I done it. Her askin' for that there sherry-wine give me the opportunity. Now, she won't give me trouble like. I can't abear a screamin' woman. Always makes me feel inclined to give 'em a 'it on the 'ead with a sledge 'ammer or somethin' light and 'andy.'

He looked across the heath in the direction of a lonely and dilapidated dwelling some half-mile distant on the top of a small ridge. Not a soul was near. He drew the horses to the side of the path and left them to nibble the fresh grass in peace and comfort while he sat on the edge of the common cutting up twist with a murderous-looking pocket-knife. 'Blessed if I can tumble to this 'ere Slade,' he thought. 'If that's really the blighter's name, what does he want this 'ere woman brought 'ere for? What's 'e goin' to do wid 'er when 'e gets 'ere? Well, I never were good at riddles, and I give 'im up.' Looking up presently, he saw the subject of his ruminations crossing the heath with long and telling strides. He put his pipe away and stood at the horse's heads, ready to obey orders.

'You've got her?' asked Slade abruptly.

'Yus, gov'nor,' was the reply. 'She's in the kerridge. I give 'er a few drops o' what you give me, and it sent 'er to bye bye.'

'That's well,' said Slade, opening the door of the conveyance. 'You've done your part well. What became of Blinder?'

'Oh, 'e went and tackled that there sailor-cove we saw with Blake, the detective, the other night. They gets up a little bull and cow, and they both gets warned off the station.'

'Did this lady come willingly?'

'Like a lamb to the slaughter 'ouse,' said Bleater. '"Are you the lady as represents P. P.?" says I. "Yus," says she. "Do you wish to see M. S.?" says I. "I does," she says. "Come wid me,"

I says, an' she jumps in like a bird. I got 'er a drink at the pub, and I slips the stuff you give me into the bottle.'

'She'll remain in the state she is for at least two hours,' said Slade, feeling the pulse of the little woman, who was lying huddled up on the floor of the carriage, breathing stertorously. He raised her in his arms with no more effort than he would have required to pick up a kitten, and placed her on the seat against the side of the carriage. Then he entered the vehicle himself and took the opposite corner.

'Drive across the common,' he said, 'to the house yonder.'

He shut the door, and, without a word, but with much speculation in his mind, Bleater drove, along a narrow path, towards the desolate building standing, bold against the sky, upon the hill. It formed part of a deserted farmhouse, and consisted of eight or ten rooms bare of furniture, carpets, and the ordinary conveniences of habitation. Report had it that the place was haunted by the ghost of an old miser who had been murdered there many years before – shortly after, indeed, the well-remembered butchery of Mr and Mrs Bonar, by their manservant, Philip Nicholson, at Chislehurst – and none of the inhabitants of that quiet country town and its adjacent villages would go near it under any circumstances whatever. Mortemer Slade had recently taken the house at an absurdly low rental, and had paid six months' money for it in advance, his object being to have a place at which he might secrete himself in the event of his having to retire from London.

'This lady will be staying here under my care for two or three days,' he said, when Bleater pulled up just by the house, which was surrounded on all sides by a thick and impenetrable hedge. 'Open the gates and lead the horses to the front door.'

With some difficulty the rough swung open the heavy iron gates and led the horses up a short drive to the main entrance of the house. The paths and garden bore a neglected aspect, and were covered with a tangled brushwood and obnoxious weeds. Mortemer Slade lifted the inanimate body of poor Sarah Watts from the carriage and, turning to Bleater, said, 'Drive back now to where I met you and wait for me. I shall not be long.' He stood on the moss-grown stone steps with the unconscious woman in his arms until Bleater and the carriage were out of sight. Then he opened the door with a large rusty key and entered the house. He threw open the door of a room on the ground floor at the back of the premises. This apartment looked into a wild and uncared-for garden, at the end of which a high hedge divided it from the lonely fields beyond. The nearest house was a mile or more away, and no scream or cry for help could be heard in these dreary wilds. The room in which Slade now stood was fairly clean, as though some recent effort had been made to render it habitable. In one corner, furthest from the windows, a mattress lay on the floor, and attached to a ring in the wall above this was a steel chain. The maniac viewed these preparations with a sardonic grin of satisfaction. Placing the unconscious woman on the mattress, he arranged the chain about her waist in such a manner that, though it would be possible for her to stand up or lie down at will, she could not advance more than 3 feet from the wall, and could not free herself from the grip of the stout steel links. The ends he padlocked together, and pocketed the key. Sarah Watts was thus a prisoner securely chained to the wall. He surveyed his handiwork with grim approval and prepared to depart.

'That,' he said, 'effectually accounts for one of my enemies. Cry or scream as you will, you will not be heard, my dear lady. Beat your wings how you will against your cage, none will open your prison to let you escape. Here you will die of starvation or thirst – and, as like as not, you'll be a madwoman when the end comes. I'll then dispose of your body and turn my attention to Mr Edmund Blake. But first to Rome, for another crisis in my life approaches. I have to offer up to London my fourth sacrifice. My next victim shall be Mistress Elizabeth Stride, and the scene shall be Barners Street. Prevent it if you can, you bunglers of the police. I defy you all.'

He went to the windows and drew the heavy curtains across them. 'It will be dark,' he said, 'when she recovers.' Then he made for the door, and, with one last look at his victim, who was stirring uneasily, locked it behind him, and went out into the front garden. Joining Bleater, they drove to Sevenoaks, and from there Slade caught a train to town, leaving the former to return the horses and carriage to the mews proprietor from whom they had been hired.

And some little time later, darkness having supervened, unmerciful consciousness returned to Sarah Watts, and the full knowledge of her awful situation burst upon her.

19. Slade and Phyllis

Rome! The city of a thousand wonders, of very many memories. Rome! The capital of the ancients, the historic foundation of all most dear and enduring in our modern civilisation. Rome! The abode of the Immortals, the eternal resting place of the old-world giants of literature and art. Rome! The depository of a million secrets, of a million faiths. The theatre in which was played many a humans drama, many a tragedy of life. Rome! The seat of ancient learning, the home of luxury and vice; the burial ground of glories undimmed in the passage of ages. Rome! The most wonderful city the world has ever known. Still, in all her splendour, she rears herself above the capitals of the world. Still she attracts to her shrine worshippers of a bygone age and an historic past. Age cannot wither her, nor custom stale her infinite vanity!

It was to this crown gem in the diadem of sunny Italy that Phyllis Penrose came after the painful scene with Stephen Darrell. Her love for the latter was deep and abiding. Intensely hurt as she was at his refusal to explain his motives for cancelling the engagement, much as her pride revolted at the knowledge that she was unable to forget him, she still knew that her love for him was supreme and unconquerable. Her father and her sisters urged her to plunge into a vortex of gaiety and to forget a young fellow who, as Lord Caversham remarked, never was 'really worthy of her serious regard'.

The projected match, said the great world, was never so brilliant a one that the Honourable Phyllis Penrose, who might have married a duke, should for long bewail its abandonment. After all, said her friends, Stephen Darrell was all very well in his way; a clever, painstaking man no doubt; but a daughter of the Earl of Caversham, whose sisters had done so well in the matrimonial market, might look much higher for a male. Poor Phyllis could not disguise from herself the fact that Stephen had behaved very badly. He had refused her the explanation which was her right, and had broken off the match, apparently, in pure caprice. It was, no doubt, her duty to detest the offender; but instead she found herself loving the sinner more tenderly than ever, and finding a thousand excuses for him in her overwrought mind. She racked her brain with idle speculation as to the real cause of Stephen's defalcation. She felt convinced, against her better judgement, that he loved her still. At their last interview, it was apparent that he was suffering the most acute pain at the mere idea of parting with her. There was no indifference, no apathy on his side. Phyllis could read in his eyes, in his voice, in his attitude, the grief he was experiencing at the loss of her. Why, then, was he voluntarily severing himself from all that he held most dear? Why was he sacrificing his happiness, and to what? Phyllis asked herself those questions again and again, but could frame in her mind no plausible reply.

Rome was fairly full. London had sent the Immortal City her complement of visitors, and America had dispatched her usual army of wealthy pilgrims. There was no lack of gay society, of dance, dinners, picnics and routs. Phyllis had been presented to King Humbert and his gracious consort, and had been voted one of the most beautiful girls even born in the Island Empire with which Italy had for so long been on terms of sincere friendship and generous sympathy. She had no lack of admirers, nor, for that matter, of suitors. She was a *persona grata* everywhere, and if a few noticed her depressed air and spiritless demeanour, those were attributed to the icy reserve of the average British maiden, and applauded accordingly.

Phyllis had one especial delight – to escape from the society of her gay friends and to penetrate, alone and unattended, to the ruins of St Marco Pistola, an ancient monastery situated in a lonely part of the suburbs of Rome. This place, unsuitable to picnic parties, being remote, inaccessible and mountainous, was a haven of rest to the distressed mind of Phyllis Penrose. There, seated on a rock, surveying with admiring eye the valley below, stretching far down to the Tiber, she would remain for hours, book in hand. Sometimes she would attempt a sketch of ruined tower or ivied wall, but the pencil or brush would fall idly from her hand, and her distraught mind would revert to her absent lover and to the cause of their separation. One fine afternoon in September, in this sombre and reflective mood, she set out alone for her favourite ruin. She usually left word at the chalet which the Earl had rented where she could be found if occasion arose; but it was understood that she wished to be alone, and no one followed her to her lonely destination. Phyllis was a typical English girl, brave and self-confident. She entertained no craven fear of brigands or of beggars, and went about the town unattended and unmolested. She had never yet met with any misadventure and felt no fear.

The sun was sinking in crimson glory as she climbed the heights on which stood, in bold relief against the blood-red sky, the ruins of St Marco. Two grey stone towers crowned the edifice, but the interior had sunk, with the ravages of time, into a mere heap of rock and boulder. A few old, ivy-clad walls alone remained of the old-time glories of the picturesque monastery. The place was silent, solitary, remote. It was above an hour's walk from Rome, and few of the visitors cared to face the hill in the heat of the day. Phyllis, however, was strong and hardy, and to her the climb was a mere nothing. In England, at home, she had always been a lover of outdoor exercise. She seated herself at the base of one of the great towers, on a grassy mound, and gazed down at the green valley of the old river, the proud old father of Rome, the Tiber, glistening and gleaning in the setting sun. Where, she thought sadly to herself, is Stephen now? Where was the man she had loved and hoped to marry? Had he gone abroad, to the Cape, as it was reported? Was he eating his heart out in the interior of Africa, divided from the one who so faithfully loved him by a gulf which nothing could bridge over?

'Stephen! Stephen!' she cried aloud, stretching out her arms in supplicatory gesture to the cool river in the broad, green valley below. 'Would you were with me; would this dark cloud had not come into the bright day of our love. Shall I ever see you, Stephen, my Stephen, again?'

There was a stir behind her as of someone moving in the grass, and she looked hastily round as a hand was lightly laid upon her graceful shoulder.

'My dear Miss Penrose,' said a suave, smooth voice, which seemed to her strangely familiar, 'I am afraid I startled you.'

The girl rose to her feet. She was as white as death. The eyes of the sinister-looking being who confronted her were the eyes of Mortemer Slade. He was the one being, perhaps, in all the world who could bring fear – real, absolute fear – to the heart of Phyllis Penrose.

She turned as if to fly down the hill. Slade laid a detaining hand upon her arm.

'Nay,' he said, gently. 'I have come far to see you. Surely you will not leave me so soon?'

She flung off his hand with a gesture of disgust.

'Sir,' she said, 'it is impossible that you can have come here to see me. In any case your visit is unsolicited, and your presence now is disagreeable to me. You are, by birth and station, a gentleman. It, therefore, should not be necessary for me to say more.'

'My dear young lady,' he replied, his burning eyes fixed upon her own – against her will she had to lower hers – 'when I became what I am I ceased to be that conventional being – a gentleman. I acknowledge no laws, no rules. I have made my own, and to those alone I subscribe. I told you that my fate lay in your hands. If I am a monster, an unutterable being unfit to breathe the same air as your saintly self, it is you who have made me such. I am of your creating.'

'I cannot talk to you, sir,' she replied with proud disdain. 'I leave it to your own perception to discover why it is impossible for me to hold communication with such as you.'

'I am, I suppose, beyond the pale?' he said with a sneer.

'What you are is best known to you,' she replied with spirit. 'I have no wish to be a judge of your actions. But I trust, Mr Slade, that you will not compel me to seek protection of my father.'

'Your father?' he said; 'why, your father, the poverty-stricken peer, up to his eyes in debt – struggling to keep afloat – would have sold you to me, my proud beauty, mad as they say I am.'

'You lie,' she said. 'Or rather, you know not what you say. You are mad.'

His face turned livid. 'Beware, Phyllis Penrose,' he cried, 'how you trifle with such a thing as I. There is blood upon my hands, blood upon my heart, blood upon my soul. So far I have only shed the life fluid of the outcast and the social leper. Beware lest I experiment on women of a gentler breed, a nobler race. Your blood is blue, for you are patrician. Beware lest I spill it to learn that it is only the same as that of any poor wanton in a London slum.'

'The Earl of Caversham,' she cried, 'shall protect me from your insolent persecution. Let me pass.'

'Why not appeal to Mr Stephen Darrell?' he said. 'Is he not your natural protector? Or has he thrown you over; has he jilted the Honourable Miss Penrose? Methinks I have read of some such scandal.'

Her cheeks flamed scarlet. How could she escape? Not a soul was in sight. She walked rapidly down the hill, Slade following and speaking into her ear as he strode along.

'Look at the sky,' he said, 'and recall what I wrote you. On the eve of every crisis in my life I would appear to you. Today is Monday; on Sunday next there will be another fearful murder in the East-end. You can, if you will, spare me the commission of that frightful fate, a wretched woman whose only faults are that she is poor and ignorant and idle and drunken. A word from you can save that drab.'

She hurried on. Would she never reach the white, dusty road below?

'A word from you and I will spare her,' he continued. 'Give me your love – I will spare them all. Speak but one tender word of affection to me, Phyllis Penrose, from the heart, and you can save me and them. Their fate, the lives of these poor, lost wretches, lies in your hands. And mine, too. You can, with but a word, save me from myself.'

She turned and faced him, her little white teeth clenched, her cheeks burning, her eyes aflame.

'Leave me,' she said, 'madman and murderer. I know you for what you are. You are the midnight fiend that stalks abroad in London and spreads death and desolation as you go. Attempt to follow me farther and I'll denounce you to the first person I meet. You are a dangerous lunatic, escaped from justice, and even now the police are searching for you. So far you have preserved yourself, but the hour of doom is not far distant. You will have to answer for your hideous crimes and the penalty will be exacted to the full.'

'Then perish, Elizabeth Stride,' he said, brutally, 'and half a dozen after her. I will continue to run my course until the end is reached. Look for the blood-red sky this weekend and know that you might have saved her and those that come after her. I'm going back to England to murder, rapine, lust and sudden death. Back to the noisome alleys, the darksome dens, the filthy courts. But first – I'm going to have one kiss from those proud young lips. I've come some miles from it, and that one kiss I'll have.'

He seized her by the wrist, and, despite her struggles and cries for help, drew her to him in a close embrace. His hot breath fanned the curls upon her broad white forehead; the glare from his eyes seemed to burn into her own. He pressed his lips to hers in one mad moment, and in the next received a staggering blow from a strong manly arm. He threw her from him and turned to face his assailant. It was Stephen Darrell. The two men glared into each other's eyes. Phyllis lay prone upon the ground as she had been flung by Slade.

'I know you,' cried Stephen in exultant tones. 'You are the man who came to me as my father's friend, and told me that my death, through heart disease, was certain and imminent.

You are the escaped madman from Grange House. You are the murderer of Mr Welman and the suspected slaughterer of poor women in the East of London. You are Mortemer Slade. By heavens! You shall not escape me now!'

Slade drew himself up to his full height. 'Attend to your sweetheart, sir,' he said coldly, 'and spare me these heroics. I heed not your throats. Permit me to pass.'

'Never,' said Darrell, and flung himself upon him with such force that Slade, whose muscles were of steel, was borne to the ground. Phyllis gave a slight scream. 'Stephen! Stephen!' she cried, in an agony of fear. 'He will kill you!'

Deaf to those cries and heedless of all but their mutual hate and rage, the two men rolled over and over in a desperate struggle. Darrell was the younger and the more agile, and he heeded not the furious blows which Slade, unable to rise or to loosen the grip upon his throat, inflicted upon his head and face.

'Release me,' hissed Slade, writhing beneath his adversary's grip, 'or I'll kill you.'

'Never!' was the reply, 'Till I hand you over to the police.'

Unobserved by Stephen, the madman contrived to extract from his pocket a clasp-knife. This he skilfully opened with one hand. The next instant he had plunged the weapon into his opponent's side. With a groan Stephen fell back powerless and sank into merciful oblivion, the blood pouring from the thrust. Slade leapt to his feet and tore down the hill. Phyllis threw herself upon her prostrate lover, and, crying for help, staunched the wound with her handkerchief and the lace she had been wearing about her throat. Two peasants, attracted by her screams, at last appeared, and the insensible body of Stephen, alive, but dangerously wounded, was borne back to the city.

Mortemer Slade, however, got clear away.

20. The Rescue of Sarah Watts

Slowly, laboriously, and painfully did consciousness return to Sarah Watts. She lay for some time in a state of semi-torpor, the effects of the narcotic administered to her. Occasionally a low moan escaped her lips as she tossed about on the hard mattress to which she was confined by the steel chain attached to the bare and paperless wall. Her throat was parched and dry, her eyes red and inflamed, her temples throbbed incessantly, and her whole frame seemed weak and shaken.

When at last she was restored to sensibility – though she still felt sick and feeble – all the incidents of the previous day recalled themselves to her mind – the drive to meet Mortemer Slade, the drugged wine, the sudden death-like unconsciousness and the black nothingness that ensued. Where was she now? A prisoner in the hands of a homicidal maniac; that fact was clear. But the curtains of heavy, dark material had been drawn across the windows, and the bare room was in almost total darkness. How long she had lain there she could not even guess; nor could she tell whether it was now night or day. She feebly felt for her watch. It was still fastened securely in her waistband, but was of no service to her, as she could not see the time by it in the dark and gloomy room. Feeling for her watch, her hand came in contact with the chain which her enemy had clasped and padlocked round her waist. She was a captive, indeed. She made an effort to rise, but fell backward with a deep groan. Her head ached and throbbed, and her limbs refused their office. She must wait. Strength would return in time, and then she would attempt to secure some notion of her surroundings. At present she was as powerless as a newborn babe.

She fell to pondering over the wonderful fortune enjoyed by this Slade, whom now she fully believed to be the monster of the East-end whose unspeakable crimes had already filled the world with horror and amazement. Three murders, in addition to that of young Welman, had he already committed; and yet he had contrived each time to get clear away and to defy the best efforts of the police to lay him by the heels. Even Edmund Blake's campaign against this spirit of evil had so far abjectly failed. Even she, used to the ways of criminals and an adept in the detective art, had fallen into the simple trap this mad murderer had prepared for her. She had evidently been watched on the occasion of the first appointment with Slade at the Marble Arch. He, or some confidant of his, had seen her talking to Blake, had probably followed her, and had thus enabled Slade to discover that the advertisements in the agony columns of the papers were only a ruse. This, she told herself, she could not have foreseen, but she need not quite so readily and thoughtlessly have fallen into the trap so artfully laid for her.

She recalled the fact that she had been prudent enough to dispatch a boy with a message to Blake before embarking on her hazardous undertaking. On his promptitude, sagacity and courage her hopes of escape and rescue would perhaps depend. On those qualities she knew she could rely; but Blake would have no idea to what part of the country she had been taken, and would thus be unable to discover her prison-house. Nor had she even the satisfaction of seeing Slade face to face. She had been unconscious when he met the carriage, had been brought to the place where she was, and made a prisoner without being able to denounce her gaoler. He had evidently gone, and had left her there, a prisoner, alone.

She managed to raise herself sufficiently to lean upon her elbow and to listen intently. Was there anyone in the house besides herself? The place was absolutely silent, but then it might be dead of night for all she knew of the time or the place of her captivity. She had not yet the strength to cry for help, nor had she any hopes of release by such a means. Slade had left her because he knew that, cry as she would, there was no one that could hear. On her own ingenuity, courage and resource she must rely if Blake could not contrive her release.

These were now her only weapons, and her spirits rose as she remembered how often they had served her in good stead. In the pocket of her dress were four or five sandwiches, and on these she could exist, if necessary, for some forty-eight hours. She had no feeling of hunger now, but she would have given her slender income for a whole year for cool, clear water to bathe her aching temples and moisten her cracked and swollen lips. Passing her hand to the chain about her waist, she felt the length of it, and discovered that it was attached to a rivet in the wall. She could stand up and move about to the extent of some three feet. She ascertained that the floor was bare of covering and the wall paperless. This fact lent strength to her theory that she was in an empty house. Probably, too, it was situated in some remote country district, with no other human habitation near at hand.

The steel links were so tight about her waist that she found it impossible, with the utmost exertion of which she was capable, to shift it more than an inch in either direction. Slade had seen to that, she thought. The chain would neither go down over her hips nor up over her chest. Escape in that way was utterly out of the question. She became conscious that a little light was penetrating through the curtains where they joined. The room was certainly a little less dark. It might be dawn breaking. She knelt upon the mattress and delivered up a silent prayer to heaven. As if in answer to her supplication, her ears, intensely keen to the least sound in the silent house, plainly heard a slight noise outside the curtained windows of the room. She started up, listening intently. There was silence again, and she greatly feared that she had been deceived. But no! The sounds came again, and it was now quite clear that someone was approaching the room by the window. She could hear the light footsteps on the tangled grass outside. Presently there was a sound as of a glazier's diamond cutting out a pane of glass and in a few moments the glass fell into the room with a light crash. The curtains were thrust aside and a dirty hand undid the latch of the window. The room was suddenly flooded with light, and Sarah Watts, springing to her feet, prepared to face her enemy. But though she had not yet set eyes on the face of Mortemer Slade, she knew that the man, unkempt, ragged, and dirty, was not the gentlemanly ex-physician whom she dreaded, yet wished, to see. No; the man entering the room by the now open window was of a different calibre. His appearance was not in the least prepossessing, but somehow she felt reassured. Escape might come this way.

The man paused in the act of climbing in at the window and gazed at the woman chained to the wall with an expression of great astonishment. Then he spoke.

He said, 'Well, I'm damned!' Having delivered himself of those words, he sat on the edge of the window and stared at Sarah Watts in mute amazement. The latter, her courage all recovered, said with spirit, 'Are you concerned with the murderer Slade in keeping me a prisoner here?'

The stranger came slowly into the room and closed the window gently enough.

'I ain't concerned with no murderer, mum,' he said. 'I'm a bad 'un, but I draws the line at murder.'

'Then,' replied Sarah, with kindling hope, 'if you are not in league with the wretches who brought me here, perhaps you will be so good as to tell me with what purpose you came here, and why you came by the window.'

'I came,' said the man, stubbornly, 'to see if there was anything I could nick.'

'Oh!' said Sarah.

The man advanced and examined the chain and rivet in the wall to which it was attached. 'It's like this 'ere, mum,' he said. 'I'm a tramp, I am – a bit of a beggar, a bit of a thief, and a bit of a poacher. I came down to this place to try to get a bit o' 'opping, but I ain't got a altogether spotless character, and the blokes round 'ere won't take me on. I was living 'idden behind a furze-bush last afternoon on this 'ere common, and I sees two men a-carryin' a woman wot appeared to be dead into this 'ere 'ouse. Leastways, the tall one – a dark, foreign-looking cove – takes the woman in 'is arms and carries 'er 'ere, leavin' the other chap to look after the kerridge. When that there tall man come out alone, I begins to think it rummy, 'specially as this 'ouse don't appear to 'ave any inhabitant. Thinks I I'll wait till night or early mornin' and I'll pay that there 'ouse a visit and see if I can't do meself a bit o' good, and find out what become of that there dead woman. I allers keeps me diamond wid me to do a bit o' window-cuttin', if necessary, so, as them winders are nearly level wid the ground, I 'as no great trouble to effect a entrance. When I sees you a-standin' up alive on that there mattress, a-chained to the wall in this 'ere empty room, it give me a bit of a start, I tell yer. I don't know as 'ow I've quite got over it yet.'

Throughout this speech, which he uttered in a half-familiar, half-respectful tone, the tramp was examining the chain and making desperate endeavours to force the rivet from the wall. 'It's a screw,' he said, at last. 'That's wot it is. If I'd got a thin poker or somethin', I could use it as a lever and force that there screw out of the wall.' He scratched his head in comical despair. 'Even then, though, he remarked, you'd 'ave the rest of the chain on, and I don't suppose you'd care to return to your sorrowin' friends with an ornament like that on.'

'I have money in my pocket,' said Sarah, 'and more at home. I will give you £5 to release me from this wall, and another £5 to rid me of this chain.'

'Lor' bless yer, mum,' was the reply, 'I'd put yer at liberty for nothin' at all, come to that. I don't know what you've been a-doin' of, but I know that there foreign-looking cove as brought you 'ere ain't got no right to keep a woman chained to a wall like a dog. So I'm a-goin' to set you at liberty if it can be done.' He turned to the windows. 'I'll go and 'ave a look over the garden 'ere,' he said. 'I might find some sort of thing to take that there screw out. Blowed if I can bear to see you a-tied up like that.' He lowered himself down, and Sarah could hear him trampling down the long grass and overgrown weeds as he moved along. Escape was at hand. She was saved. Unless Slade, or one of his confederates, returned at once, which did not seem likely, she and her rescuer could get clear away unmolested. Her active mind suggested a means by which the steel chain about her waist might escape observation till she could have it forcibly removed. She had brought a long, loose dust-cloak with her and this had been placed beneath her bed to serve as a pillow when she had been laid unconscious on the mattress. She could twine the yard or so of steel chain about her waist and hide it from observation beneath the cloak if her unknown friend should be unable to release her from the coils. Providence had indeed watched over here. If the beggarman-tramp had not been hidden in the furze close to the building in which she was confined, death, from thirst or starvation, would have been her fate. Brave as she was, she shuddered at the thought. Mortemer Slade expected to return to this lair in a few days and find her dead upon the floor. Her body would doubtless have been disposed of in some cunning way, and her fate would have remained an impenetrable mystery to the end of time. She fell on her knees and offered up a grateful prayer to heaven.

Presently her rescuer returned, clambering through the window. His face wore a benignant expression, and he had in his hand a strong, though rusty and discoloured file.

'You're in luck, mum,' he exclaimed. 'I found this 'ere weapin in a old tool-shed down at the end of the garding. A file is the werry thing I wanted for the little job of settin' you free. Now, if you'll be so good, lidy, to come a little closer to this 'ere wall and to 'old the chain tight in yer 'ands – so – I'll be 'elpin' yer to get out of that winder in a brace o' shakes, for I expec's the door has been locked outside by the blackguards as brought you 'ere.'

'You shall be well rewarded,' said Sarah. 'I owe my life to you. You must tell me your name. If there is anything I can do for you or your family, I'll willingly–'

'Thank yer kindly, mum,' said the tramp, hard at work with his file. 'I ain't fond o' givin' my name and address as a gineral rule, 'cos I may or may not be wanted by the perlice; in fact, I 'ardly knows for 'ow long I shall be at liberty as it is. I will take a few bobs from you since you're so kind.'

'Bobs!' said Sarah. 'Pounds, you must mean,'

'No, mum, thankin' you all the same. Bobs it is. But I've got a little nipper in London, 13 Mossle Court, Chenies Street, Bermondsey – a good woman, though poor, looks arter 'er – and if you'd go up and see 'er and cheer 'er up a bit, takin' a pictur-book or a packet o' sweeties with yer, I'd take it kindlty, I would indeed. I'm a vagrant myself, by eddication and nater, and pounds would be no use to the likes o' me.' As he spoke, the file went clean through one of the links of the chain, and the steel waistband which, for some hours, had encircled the trim little form of Mrs Watts, fell to the floor with a crash.

She seized the tramp's hand and shook it heartily. 'Thank you, my man,' she said. 'I'm free now, and I shan't forget my preserver, nor his little one in London. I'll just write down that address you gave me, and if you'll tell me for whom to ask when I call, I'll go to see her tomorrow and take her with me to my little place in the country. A stay in Buckinghamshire will do her good.'

'Say, mum, as how you come from Smiler, that's me,' he replied. 'They'll understand, and my little Mary will take to you, I know.'

'Take this card,' said Sarah, 'and don't lose it. If ever you want any help or advice, don't be afraid to come to me. Keep out of trouble if you can, and I'll see if I can't find you some nice suitable work in the country which will enable you to have your little daughter always with you.'

He shook his head doubtfully. 'I'll remember your kind words, mum, and bless you for 'em.' He could not be prevailed upon to accept more than a few shillings, and even these he took reluctantly. He assisted the little woman to descend into the disordered garden at the rear of the house, after she had taken one long last look at the room in which she might, but for Providence, have met with a fearful death. On the edge of the common they shook hands and parted, though 'Smiler' kept her in sight for some time after, as though afraid that some attempt might be made by her foes to retake her. At the turn of the road across the heath towards the London Road, Sarah waved a last farewell to her rescuer, and hurried on. Slade, or some of his confederates, might even now be in the district, and she was anxious to get back to town and relieve the mind of Edmund Blake as to her fate. Even more anxious was she to get upon the track of Mortemer Slade, the dreaded 'Ripper', from whom other and still more terrible crimes might yet be expected.

At a decent cottage, not far from the station, she ascertained that the first train to London left in something under an hour. She asked permission to wash and rest herself here, and the homely villager, gladly consenting, made her some breakfast, and the warm tea was especially comforting. Soon after Sarah Watts was speeding towards London, where Blake, who had only just received the note she had given to the street urchin the previous afternoon – the boy had been run over on his way to Gower Street and taken to hospital – was making every possible inquiry as to her disappearance.

'You won't catch me napping again, Mr Slade, said Sarah, exultantly, as the train steamed into the terminus. 'Once bit, twice shy. I'm prepared for you now, and the next time we meet I may do the scoring.' But – and it was a disappointment to her until the hour of her death – Sarah Watts was not destined to have part or lot in the final undoing of Mortemer Slade.

21. Slade's Narrow Escape

Mortemer Slade returned to London from Rome early on the morning of 29 September. It was raining hard as he strode over Hungerford Bridge towards the Surrey side, and he had the collar of his ulster turned up almost to his eyes. The leaden skies and pouring rain seemed in harmony with his sombre thoughts. He felt nervous and depressed for once, this iron-willed man who had waded through oceans of blood to gratify his unnatural hatred of all humanity. He felt less confident of himself than ever he had done, and less secure against detection. The London papers which he had seen in Rome had kept him enlightened as to the desperate measures now being taken by all the forces of the law to bring the career of 'Jack the Ripper' to a close. Every court and alley in the densely populated East-end was now being keenly watched and patrolled; every second man one met as one took one's way through the sordid streets was a detective, amateur or professional, in disguise. House-to-house visitations were being secretly conducted; suspicious characters were being followed and watched; and ordinary wayfarers were being stopped and asked to give explanations of their presence in the district affected by the 'Whitechapel Find', as the press described the unknown miscreant. Scotland Yard, the object of much unmerited abuse, was on its mettle. The Chief Commissioner of Police, Sir Charles Warren, was not spared from adverse criticism by thoughtless persons, who could not understand the exceptional difficulties under which the police laboured. Serious thoughts were not entertained of utilising the services of trained bloodhounds, who might conceivably trace the murderer to his lair. The unfortunates, too, who plied their pitiable calling in the East-end were now afraid to speak to any strange man, however harmless-looking, and roamed the streets in parties of two or three for mutual protection. Slade told himself that victims might, for the future, be hard to find. Then again his attack upon Stephen Darrell might lead to his discovery. Steps would now be taken to secure the escaped lunatic who had actually intruded himself upon and dared to threaten the daughter of the Earl of Caversham. Stephen, smarting under the injury he had done him, would spare no pains to bring about Slade's capture. Had not he – Slade – nearly succeeded in separating him – Stephen – from the girl of his choice? That offence so ardent a lover was not likely to forgive. Yet even if he were arrested none, he told himself, could prove that Mortemer Slade and the dreadful assassin of fallen women were one and the same man. Blake might suspect it, since he was making such tremendous efforts to get upon his track, but it would be hard for the detective to prove that he was the mysterious murderer of the east. They might accuse him of the murder of Welman on the night of his escape, and of the attempted murder of Stephen Darrell; but the worst that could happen to him then would be his incarceration in Broadmoor as a dangerous homicidal lunatic. The worst! Why, that was just the worst!

'I'd never go back to a madhouse,' he thought bitterly. 'It's a living hell to a man with brains, and desires, and promptings like mine. No, I'll kill myself first. But I have not run my course. The hour of doom is not yet. My freedom is not yet seriously endangered. I must find a fresh disguise – if need be, a fresh lodging. If Stephen Darrell recovers, as I think he will, he will move heaven and earth to encompass my death or capture. But the play is not yet over. There are other acts to come.'

Later in the morning, having snatched a hasty meal at a cheap eating house, he went to his lodging and removed his few belongings in a carpet bag, informing his landlady that business called him abroad. He paid the woman a week's rent in lieu of notice. This she accepted somewhat grumblingly, for 'Mr Maidment' had been in all things a desirable lodger, and she was loth to lose him.

'I 'opes, sir,' she remarked, with an air of injury, 'that you'll be as comfortable in them furrin parts as I've tried to make you. Many's the time that I've said to Mrs Cadsby, next door to number seventeen, as 'ow–'

Her loquacity perished under the sinister glance which Slade bestowed upon her. She delivered herself of a sniff which was full of significant meaning and prepared to depart to her own regions.

'Oh!' she said at the foot of the stairs, 'A gentleman called yesterday to see you. Perticlar anxious, sir, he seemed, too.'

Slade, with an effort, suppressed his surprise. 'A gentleman to see me?' he said. 'Curious that, I have no friends or acquaintances in London.'

'So I thought, sir. You ain't 'ad many callers, nor letters. As I said to Mrs Crunch, who lives at number twenty-one – the widder of a pea captain with a cork leg–'

Slade gave a gesture of impatience.

'Spare me these revelations, madam,' he said. 'Did the gentleman leave his name?'

'No, sir,' said the woman. 'I can't say he did. He asked me if I knew when you'd return. I says no, you'd been called out of town.'

'Did he ask for me by name?'

'No; he asks for the dark gentleman lodger, the one who goes out so frequently at night. Well, I sees as he means you at once, and I says, "Mr Maidment, you mean." He asks me for how long you'd been with me, and I tells him. He was very pressin', I must say, but quite the gent, I do assure you, sir.'

The woman had had excellent assurances of the latter fact. The gentleman at parting had begged her acceptance of half a sovereign in return for such information as she had been able to give, though it did not occur to her to mention that fact to her departing lodger.

In the dark recesses of his inmost mind Mortemer Slade cursed the interfering folly of this harpy. Who was the man who had called? Clearly someone who had penetrated through his disguise. Had Bleater or his companion betrayed him? It was unlikely. He paid them well, and knew enough of their pasts to clap them into gaol. True, they knew his real name. He had been obliged to mention that when one of them had interviewed Sarah Watts at King's Cross station. Even now the house might be watched. He might be followed and seized. If Blake or the criminal authorities had got wind

of his retreat, a guard would certainly have been set upon the house. In this emergency what was his best course? A way out suggested itself to his mind. There was a man staying in the same house – he inhabited a back attic – named Robbins, who lived upon a pension derived from some mysterious source. Nearly all this stipend he spent upon drink, and, when out of funds, would do a very great deal in order to procure some fiery liquor. Slade had occasionally exchanged a word or two with this drunken fool upon the stairs, and had on one or two opportunities treated him to what Mr Robbins called 'a morning quencher'.

He turned to the woman and asked if this person were then in his room.

'I'd like to bid him goodbye,' he said, 'if you have no objection.'

'Quite natural and proper that you should, sir,' was the reply. 'Yes, he's in. He don't often go out when he's short of cash. Will you knock at his door, Mr Maidment? I'm rather busy downstairs, and–'

'Don't let me detain you,' Slade said, hurriedly.

He did not wish the woman to see him leave the house. She descending to the kitchen, and Slade made his way to the room of the inebriate Robbins. That gentleman, who had a red nose and a decidedly wolfish air, welcomed him gladly in a somewhat thick and bibulous voice. Yes, he could do a drink, he candidly admitted; indeed, he could comfortably do with two or three if Mr Maidment would be good enough to pay for them. He expected a remittance soon, but until it came – ! Slade pressed upon him the loan of a sovereign, and would take no denial.

'Pay me when you can, sir,' he said; 'you are welcome to the loan, I assure you. Besides, I was about to ask you to do me a little favour.'

'Name it, my dear sir, name it,' said the trembling man as he hastily donned his jacket and boots.

'We'll walk so far as the Lord Hill,' aid Slade. 'I have a theory that a man can so disguise himself that his most intimate friends will not know him, and I'm anxious to put it to the test. Now, if you'll put on this ulster and hat and this wig and beard' – he deftly removed them from his face – 'neither of us will be recognised by our landlord, who is in the public in question, and I shall win my wager.'

Mr Robbins gazed in some wonderment at the change in the appearance of his friend. Slade was now his clean-shaven self. Robbins had only seen him, of course, fully bewigged and with a close, dark beard. The drunkard thought the circumstance rather curious and suspicious, but he was half-muddled with liquor, and he wanted the sovereign and two or three glasses of spirits. He allowed Slade to fix the beard and wig upon his head and face, and enveloped his shaky self in the long ulster. The two men were nearly of a height and of similar build, so Mr Robbins now looked remarkably like 'Mr Maidment'. They descended the steps and reached the street without encountering the landlady, whose strident tones reached them from the lower regions. At the corner of Stamford Street, just outside the Lying-In Hospital, Slade observed a man standing at a point commanding a view of the house from which they had just emerged. He affected to take no notice of this person, who, believing himself to be unperceived, unobtrusively followed them, and saw them enter the well-known hostelry named the Lord Hill, opposite Waterloo Station. The man being close behind them, and within hearing as they entered the hotel, Slade took the opportunity of addressing his companion in a careless way two or three times as 'Mr Maidment'. The bait took. The emissary of Edmund Blake who was shadowing them at once assumed poor Robbins to be the man he wanted. Slade called for drinks and remained with his dupe for a few minutes. Presently he emerged on the pretext of requiring a certain newspaper, leaving Robbins standing at the bar. The man who was watching glanced at him as he passed, but made no attempt to follow him, being convinced that the real Slade was the man in the long ulster and slouched hat, now drinking in the Lord Hill.

Slade slipped down one of the side-streets opposite the terminus and hailed a passing cab, bidding the driver to take him to Victoria.

'Whew!' he said, wiping the perspiration from his forehead, 'a narrow escape. It is as you thought. Your movements are being watched, Mr Slade. I did well to leave Stamford Street, and was only just in time. That drunken reprobate will be taken in my place, and, when they find out their error, the hue and cry will begin more ardently than ever. I must for the future bestir myself over my murders. How about two in a night? That will stir them on a bit. I'll try it; I'll try it tomorrow.'

Arrived at the station, he booked to Chislehurst, and was soon speeding towards the lonely house in which reposed, as he believed, the corpse of Sarah Watts. Alone in a first-class carriage, he opened the bag he carried, and with a few deft touches effected an almost total change in his outward appearance. A fair wig and a light moustache completely transformed him, and the gentleman who left the train at Chislehurst was as different to the one who had entered it in London as he well could be. Now he felt safe. Once more he had contrived to put the hounds off the scent.

He walked across the silent and deserted heath towards the lonely house in which reposed the remains of his latest victim. His idea was to dig a grave and bury the body in the tangled overgrowth in the garden. He would spend the night over the task and return to town in the morning.

'I am quite safe here,' he assured himself. 'No one knows of this retreat.'

Arrived at the 'haunted house', as the locals termed it, he let himself in, entirely unobserved, with his latchkey. The place was silent as the grave. Death had evidently long since claimed its victim in the room at the back on the ground floor. Outside the door of that room he paused for a moment, listening intently, with his hand upon the knob. There was not a sound. He inserted the key in the lock and slowly turned it and opened the door, flinging it wide open, as though he entertained some apprehension as to what might be lurking on the other side. Great beads of perspiration stood out upon his forehead, and he trembled, this awful man, like an aspen leaf. He had never shaken at the sight of blood. Murder had never made his pulse stir or quicken. But in this case he wondered what he should see: the body of the woman who had starved to death, or who had died a raving maniac, with distorted features and dishevelled hair? With an effort he summoned up his courage and strode into the room. He gave one glance around, and staggered back against the wall with an exclamation of dismay. There was no woman in the room – alive or dead. There was no horror there to chill the blood or dim the eye. Upon the floor rested the metal chain he had locked upon her waist, and one of the links had been filed through. That he took in, at one lightning, amazed glance. Then he saw that the window had been broken or cut, and that her escape had been effected by that way. Beneath the green and rank weeds were trodden down as with heavy hob-nail boots or shoes. A rusty file rested on the window ledge. He turned to the door by which he had entered. There was a paper pinned upon it, neatly written upon in a feminine hand. He darted towards it and read it in a strained voice aloud.

'I know you for what you are, murderer and madman. Your plot to encompass my death has failed. I have escaped you. Your course is drawing to its close. Your race is nearly run. You have a furious woman now to deal with. Beware!'

A curious oath escaped him, and he looked round like a hunted thing. This place, then, was closed to him too. Even here he was not safe. This house might be watched. Sarah Watts would betray his retreat to the authorities or to Edmund Blake, and at any moment the lonely house might be raided by the police. He felt that it was not safe to return to town by rail. The trains at Chislehurst or Victoria might be watched. The local police at the quiet Kentish town might be warned. 'I'll tramp to London,' he said. 'It will be early morning when I get back. I'll prove to Blake and this woman that Mortemer Slade is not foiled yet.' The sun went down that evening in floods of crimson glory.

22. Blake and Sarah Watts

By the success of Slade's cunningly devised ruse, Edmund Blake's scheme for his discomfiture was again reduced to failure. It becomes necessary tat this juncture to hark back to explain to the reader the method by which the great private detective hoped to bring the murderer-maniac to book. Let us, accordingly, return to the morning of Sarah Watt's escape from the empty house near Chislehurst.

Blake had awaited news of her with the utmost anxiety. It will be remembered that Sarah had dispatched a youthful messenger to his Gower Street rooms with a note intimating that she had gone to meet Mortemer Slade. Unfortunately, the message was not delivered for some hours after. The lad entrusted with the note had not delayed in starting for Gower Street, but, by unhappy chance, he had met with an accident in the street on the way. He had fallen beneath a Paddington–King's Cross omnibus and the offside wheels had passed over one of his legs. He was conveyed to the Royal Free Hospital, in Gray's Inn Road, and there it was found that the limb had been severely fractured. The note addressed to Edmund Blake was found upon him, and that gentleman sent for early the next morning. He saw the little sufferer, who related how he had been commissioned to take a message by a lady who had driven off in a closed carriage. Blake left some money for the parents of the injured boy – poor people, to whom a few shillings were something equivalent to a godsend. Then he returned to his rooms and wondered what steps he should now take. He knew the resourcefulness and courage of his feminine coadjutor, and relied largely upon her well-known presence of mind. But he also realised the cunning and malignity of the enemy with whom they had to deal, and sighed as he thought of the possible fate of his confrère, and his impotency to arrest it.

Returning to his chambers, he commenced to take steps to ascertain whither the vehicle containing Sarah Watts had been driven. This presented less difficulties than might be supposed. Exhaustive inquiry revealed the fact that the carriage had been seen in the Old Kent Road, and he ultimately succeeded in tracing it to a certain point on the Sevenoaks–Chislehurst road. Returning from his peregrinations at about noon, he entered his rooms to find Sarah Watts sitting moodily by the open window; a little pale maybe, a little weary-looking, a trifle less alert than usual, but otherwise herself, indeed. She turned as he approached her, and rose to greet him.

Blake heaved a great sigh of relief. A load was removed from his mind. Here was his Sarah alive, and, apparently, little the worse for her interview with one of the greatest criminals of all time. He could not disguise from himself that he was, more or less, responsible for any adverse fate that might have been hers. He had sent her to her doom, had asked her to beard the lion in his den. It would have been forever upon his conscience if Mrs Watts, faithful and courageous, had met her death in his service. He seized both her hands.

'Thank God,' he said. 'I began to dread what your fate might be and to torture myself that I had sent you to it. But you look pale and worn. Let me give you something – some wine.' He seized a decanter from the sideboard and poured out a tumblerful of capital old sherry.

'Drink,' he said, 'before you speak a word.'

Sarah obeyed him. Even she, iron-willed and of splendid constitution, was beginning to feel the reaction of all that she had passed through. Her limbs were stiff and painful, her head aching, her spirits depressed, and her voice hoarse and indistinct. Like a sensible woman, she swallowed the contents of the glass almost at a draught, and pronounced herself better. She put down the tumbler with a sigh.

'Now,' she said, 'I feel that I can talk to you.'

Blake seated himself opposite to her in his favourite attitude – his head recumbent upon his rent hand, the arm resting on the table.

'I need hardly say that I am prepared to actually devour all that you can say,' he remarked. 'I am literally all ears.'

'I am afraid you will be disappointed,' began Sarah quietly. 'I have not seen Mortemer Slade.'

Blake started, and opened wide his eyes. 'Not seen him?' he repeated.

She shook her head. 'Yet I have been in his presence, too.'

'You speak in riddles,' said Blake, almost impatiently. 'My good Sarah, explain.'

'When Dagenham and I reached King's Cross station,' she said, 'he left me as arranged by you, and I waited for Slade to keep the appointment. Meanwhile, Dagenham appears to have involved himself in a disturbance with the railway officials, and he was forcibly removed from the terminus. I did not go after him, but waited for our man to turn up.'

Blake murmured his approval.

'Presently – Dagenham now being out of sight – I was accosted by a rough-looking youth attired as a coachman. He asked me if I were waiting for a person of the name of Slade, and I replied that I was. He said that he was instructed to take me to that gentleman. After a little consideration, I decided to accompany him. We left the station by the entrance, or, rather, exit, leading to York Road. There, just outside, I noticed a closed carriage, a man at the horses' heads. My driver informed me that we were about to drive some way into the country, and requested me to get in. It then occurred to me to send you a message informing you of my intention, but I was unwilling to do so in the presence of the coachman, who was obviously a creature in the employ of Slade. I found a pretext to get rid of the man for a moment. I requested him to obtain me some refreshment for the journey, and he left me and hurried over to the hotel at the corner for that purpose. Availing myself of his absence, I scribbled a note to you–'

'I received it the next day – in fact, a few hours ago,' Blake interrupted. 'Pray go on.'

'And handed it to a little lad standing near the carriage. I gave him instructions to take it at once to your address.'

Blake leaned forward. 'He started for Gower Street,' he explained, 'and was run over and injured by an omnibus. Proceed.'

'The driver of the carriage returned immediately after,' Sarah went on, 'and we started on our journey. We proceeded towards Chislehurst and Sevenoaks, on the main Maidstone road. The drive was hot and dusty, and beyond Eltham I felt tired and sleepy. To enliven myself I had recourse to the flask of sherry which the man on the box had procured for me.'

Blake gave a groan.

'Drugged, of course,' he murmured. 'What fools this man has again made of us.'

'Drugged, as you say,' she replied, 'though I can hardly blame either your sagacity or mine. How were we to know that Slade had discovered the motives for the advertisements, and had penetrated through our carefully planned design?'

'I might have guessed,' Blake murmured. 'A madman's cunning is a thing apart.'

'Well, to continue,' said Sarah, in the same quiet tones, 'I drank the wine, and almost immediately began to feel an intensity of drowsiness, which it is impossible for me to describe. The air seemed stifling, and the hedges which I looked upon from the windows, and the green fields and trees, seemed to be going round and round. I had sense enough to know that the wine had been tampered with, and made an effort to call for help; but my tongue clove to the roof of my mouth, and I was unable to ejaculate an articulate sound. My heart seemed to be bursting and my brain to be beating like a hammer upon an anvil. I endeavoured to rise, staggered, fell back, and remembered no more.'

'Would to God!' groaned the hearer, 'I had come upon you then.'

'It was not to be,' said Mrs Watts, seriously; 'fate decreed that even now I was not to see this man face to face. The drug I had been given was efficacious, and the effects of it lasted long. I woke up at last – woke from as troubled, restless, uncanny a sleep as ever I remember – to find myself in an empty room, alone. I had been placed upon a mattress, and a steel chain tightly clasped round my waist. This chain was attached to an iron rivet in the wall. I could move about for a matter of two or three feet and no more. The room was in almost total darkness, and I seemed to realise that I was the only breathing thing in the whole empty, silent, deserted building. It was useless to scream; my cries for help could not be heard. I had been fastened up there like a wild beast, and left to starve and die.'

Blake clenched his hands.

'What fiendish ingenuity,' cried he. 'Madman or murderer, you yet shall pay the penalty of such misdeeds.'

'You wonder how I am here?' said Sarah. 'My escape seems almost miraculous: a tramp, who had seen me carried insensible into the house by a tall, dark man, enveloped in a great cloak, forced his way towards morning through the window of the room in which I was imprisoned – the apartment was, luckily, at the back of the house, almost level with the garden – and rescued me. In a deserted tool-house this man found a rusty file, and the steel chain which kept me captive was soon lying at my feet. I was free. I rewarded my deliverer, and returned to town. Here I am, at liberty, uninjured, but as ignorant of the whereabouts of Slade as I was before.'

Blake considered a little while, biting his nails, a habit of his only when he was thinking deeply.

'You would remember the house?' he asked.

'Oh, yes,' was the reply. 'It is situated about a mile from Chislehurst, and is apparently the only dwelling on a bleak and desolate heath. But will the man return to it?'

'Almost to a certainty,' said Blake. 'He will think that your bones, my good Sarah, lie bleaching on the mattress in that solitary chamber, and he will return to dispose of your remains. I will have the local police instructed and the stations watched. Did the man who freed you describe the appearance of the man who carried you into the house?'

'As well as he could,' she replied, 'but he was lying behind a furze-bush on the common some little distance away.'

'The description, together with that supplied by Jack Dagenham,' said the detective, 'will suffice.'

He produced a sheaf of telegraph forms and scribbled out some wires.

'I'll send these at once,' he said; 'Victoria, Charing Cross, and Ludgate Hill will be watched, and the intermediate stations before Chislehurst.'

Alas! Edmund Blake little knew that when Slade returned to the latter place his appearance would be totally changed. In place of the dark, sombre, sinister man, with black beard and moustache, there was destined to alight at Chislehurst station a tall, fair man in light and well-cut clothing. This all-important fact, however, was, of course, unknown to the detective. His wires dispatched, he and Sarah sat down to a substantial luncheon, to which the lady, at least, rendered the fullest justice. They had barely concluded the admirably served meal when Dagenham was announced. That young gentleman, still rejoicing in the black eye he had received on the King's Cross platform, looked excited and dishevelled.

He rushed across the room to where Blake was sitting.

'I've seen him,' he cried; 'I've seen him again, and I know where he lives.' He sank into a chair.

'The plot thickens,' said Blake, uneasily. 'You allude to Slade?'

'Yes, sir,' said Dagenham, 'and to no other.'

'When and where have you seen him?'

'I saw him leaving Victoria Station last evening, about half-past eight,' said the groom.

Blake and Mrs Watts exchanged glances. Dagenham, it was quite clear, had seen Slade returning from Chislehurst.

'And then?' said the detective, abruptly.

'I followed him,' was the reply. 'I determined to make sure of him this time. I followed him without his observing me, and I kept him under notice all the time. I kept in the shadows and slunk into corners, and–'

Blake leapt to his feet.

'Man,' he cried, 'if you know where he is now, out with it. Lives depend upon his capture now, today, at once. Where did he go?'

'I followed him down Victoria Street to Westminster Bridge. He turned down Commercial Road, into the Belvedere Road, and so into Stamford Street. I stood by a public house called the Glass House and watched him disappear into one of the dwellings on the opposite side of Stamford Street. He opened the hall door with his latchkey. I hung about for an hour, but he did not emerge. It was clear to me that he lived there. Here is the number.'

Blake fairly grabbed at the paper which the groom handed him.

'At last,' he said; 'at last.'

But – well, the 'best laid plans of mice and men oft gang agely.'

We know how Slade, returning to the Stamford Street address, discovered that the house was being watched, and how cleverly he had contrived to slip out of the morass in which he was so nearly enmeshed. Blake was beside himself when he learnt of the mistake made by his representative at the Lord Hill. Slade had got clear away again, and the detective could only, in the words of Alexandre Dumas, 'Wait and hope.'

23. Two Murders in a Night

We left Mortemer Slade, afraid to venture by train, tramping to London after his startling discovery in the deserted house at Chislehurst. He left the Kentish town about eight o'clock on a Saturday night, preparing to set out when it was quite dark and little chance existed of his being followed. A market-cart, laden with fruit and vegetables, overtook him when he had walked some nine miles on the silent and abandoned road, and he bargained for a lift to town. The vehicle brought him some miles nearer to his destination, and before the public houses closed he found himself in the crowded streets of the East-end.

Let us see what hideous things this arch-fiend accomplished there. Early on the Sunday morning – the date, forever memorable in the annals of crime, was 30 September – the body of a woman was found with her throat cut in a court in Berners Street, Commercial Road, Whitechapel. A man named Eagle had passed through the court at about twenty minutes before one o'clock, and had not observed anything unusual about the premises. There was a club run by Jews for Jews in this court, and this Mr Eagle was a member of it. Had the body been in the place in which it was found when he entered the court on his way to this club, he must either have seen it or or tripped over it, and as the dark deed was discovered some twenty minutes later, it is a fair inference that it was committed in that particular space of time.

At any rate, the body was found by a Russian Jew named Diemschitz, a travelling jeweller, and steward of the International Club, at precisely one o'clock. This man had driven down to Sydenham in the pursuit of his business, and he drove back into the yard at the time mentioned. His pony shied at something which lay huddled up almost in its path, and a brief scrutiny revealed the corpse of a poorly clad woman in a heap at a corner of the yard. There was a terrible wound in the throat, the vertebrae being severed, but there were no other injuries. The body was still quite warm, and blood was flowing freely from the great cut which had meant a sudden death to its recipient. It was quite clear, said the friend from the club whom Mr Diemschitz had summoned to the spot, that the murder had only just been perpetrated. Had Mr Diemschitz driven his pony into the yard but a few moments earlier than he actually did, he must have discovered the barbarous murderer at work. Indeed, it was quite feasible that the pony's steps had disturbed the midnight fiend at work, and that the mutilation which had accompanied all the previous crimes was thus, in this individual instance, frustrated. This was proved by the fact that the assassin had immediately proceeded elsewhere to find another victim on whom to vent his savage lust for blood.

On the arrival of the police, summoned by the panic-stricken members of the club, the yard was cleared, and the body was carried off on an improvised ambulance to the mortuary. It was soon recognised to be that of an unfortunate, a Swede, named Elizabeth Stride, alias 'Long Liz'. In the left hand of the victim, tightly clenched in the death agony, were found some cachous, which fell to the ground when the doctor made his examination. There were marks suggestive of a short, if severe, struggle upon the shoulders, but it was doubtful if the unfortunate woman had been able to give forth more than one agonised cry for help, or piteous prayer for mercy. The medical men who examined the corpse opined that she had been seized by the shoulder, pressed to the ground, and killed. She was on her left side when the gash in the throat had been administered, and the cut, as in the previous cases, was from left to right. The police, the detectives, the secret agents, the press, the public – all who had studied the previous crimes with bated breath and silent tremors – were face to face with yet another 'Ripper' murder. The excitement and alarm caused thereby baffle all attempts at adequate description. It had been assumed that the victims of the unknown miscreant were drugged into insensibility, but, in this and in other instances, no trace of anaesthetics or narcotics could be found in stomach or viscera. The clothes of this poor murdered woman had not been disturbed. The victim, accompanied by her destroyer, had voluntarily placed herself down, at full length, upon the spot on which she was found. The man had stooped over her, and, with a smile of treachery, or Judas-like caress, had seized her by the shoulder, had held her down as in a vice, and drawn his long, thin, razorlike weapon across the exposed throat. She had given one gurgle and had died instantly. About to commence the usual horrors, the sounds of the pony trap approaching the yard had reached the savage's ears, and he had fled into the darkness of the night to seek another victim. To glut his lust for gore upon yet another poor unfortunate. To murder, and maim, and mutilate, and to desecrate God's image as only he knew how.

He sought the City, and there found his fifth successive victim.

As Police Constable Watkins, 881, of the City Force, was patrolling his beat in Mitre Square at 1.45 on Sunday morning, 30 September 1888, he noticed the body of a woman lying on her back in the south-western corner, her feet being towards the square. Never in that officer's life, and never perhaps would he see the like again, had he been called upon to examine so terrible and awe-inspiring an object. The head was hanging to the neck by the merest thread, the stomach had been ripped open, and the bowels protruded to the gaze. The face was extraordinarily mutilated. There was a cut a quarter of an inch long below the left eyelid, dividing the structure completely through. Both eyelids were nicked. There was a frightful cut over the bridge of the nose, extending from the left border of the nasal down to near the angle of the jaw on the right side, across the chin. This cut entered the nasal bone and separated all the arteries of the cheek, with the exception of the mucous membrane of the mouth. The tip of the nose had been cut off and lay on the cheek. The mouth, at either end, had been cut into, and the skin had been deliberately peeled off the cheeks. The liver and spleen had been stabbed, the walls of the abdomen laid open, and a certain portion of the body removed. And other wounds – rips, cuts, stabs, slashes – there were innumerable, which it would be unpleasant to describe. A more appalling murder, one more meaningless in its ghastly savagery, has never been recorded in the whole lurid, bloodstained history of crime. The identity of the victim of this barbarity was soon established, and she proved to be one Kate Eddowes, who had for some years been living with a man named Conway, who, however, was easily able to clear himself of any complicity in the frightful crime. To Mr George Lusk, the chairman of the Mile End Vigilance Committee, was sent, shortly after the inquest, a small cardboard box. It contained a gruesome object, which the writer described as half the kidney he had removed from the

both of the murdered woman. The other half he declared he had eaten after he had cooked; but the object sent was so far advanced in decomposition that it was quite impossible for the surgeon to discover whether it was part of a human kidney or that of an animal.

Rushing away from the scene of this unutterable crime, the murderer passed through Gouldstone Street, Whitechapel. In this thoroughfare he wiped his bloodstained knife upon a piece of coarse apron and threw it away into a passage leading to the staircase of Nos 108–119. Mortemer Slade was becoming careless, it would seem. Continual immunity from pursuit and capture had made him indifferent to risk, perhaps. In his pocket he had a piece of chalk. No one was about, and he took it out and gazed carelessly at the wall just above the spot where he had thrown away the scrap of rag still wet with blood.

'A little message,' he said, with a grim smile, 'to entertain my friends the enemy. Now, what shall I write? What piece of balderdash shall I scribble on this wall to puzzle and mislead the authorities? I am safe from pursuit. I have time to leave here what mysterious message I choose.' He tried the piece of chalk upon the wall. It wrote clearly enough.

'There's been some idle talk,' he muttered, 'about my work being the work of a Jew. Why, I don't know, any more than I know the origin of half a hundred reports, and rumours and theories radiating around my name. Here goes.'

He commenced to write. Slowly he traced upon the wall, standing upon the second step of the stone stairway for the purpose, the words:

The Jews are the Men that will not be Blamed for Nothing.

This done, Jack the Ripper glided swiftly away.

The bloodstained piece of apron and the writing upon the wall were ultimately discovered by a constable named Alfred Ling at five minutes to three in the morning. Neither were there when he had passed about three-quarters of an hour before that time.

At the inquest the coroner, in summing up, suggested that a verdict of wilful murder against some person or persons unknown should be given at once, there being nothing to be gained by postponing it until the evidence had been gone through again. The vocal cords, he said, must have been cut with such rapidity as to prevent the least sound issuing from the throat of the victim. All the evidence showed that no noise had been heard. Not only had the woman been murdered, but the mutilation had been such as to render identification very difficult. Shortly after 1.30 a man and woman were seen talking at the corner of Church Passage by some gentlemen leaving the Imperial Club in Duke Street, one of whom stated his opinion that the clothing he had seen at the station was like that warn by the woman he saw. At half-past one a constable went round Mitre Square, turning on his lamp, and seeing nothing amiss. At sixteen minutes to two the body of Mrs Eddowes was discovered. The murder and mutilation must have been accomplished in so short a space of time as fourteen minutes, but according to the medical evidence, the injuries might all have been inflicted in five minutes. The history of the case, quoth the coroner, was very painful. The deceased, it appeared, was first living with a man named Conway for some fourteen years. Her drunken habits compelled him to part company from her. There were several children, and even they did not appear to know what had become of her. There was nothing to suggest that either Conway or Kelly had anything to do with the murder. Conway appeared to be an inoffensive man, and Kelly at the time in question was in bed at a cheap lodging house. Kelly had heard that deceased was locked up, but knowing the City custom of discharging persons charged with being drunk as soon as they had recovered, made certain that she would return soon. They had, this man Kelly and she, been 'hopping' for the last six weeks, getting back on the Thursday before the murders, when they procured a night's shelter in Shoe Lane. On the Saturday Kelly saw her for the last time at eight o'clock in the morning. She was then going to find out where her daughter was. It was believed the latter lived in Bermondsey. There was no evidence to show what became of her in the interim. Evidently she had been drinking. There was no question but that the unfortunate woman had been murdered by some person or persons unknown. Indeed, he might say by one person, as only one, seemingly, could have been implicated. A munificent reward had been offered by the Corporation, and might – he hoped would – lead to the apprehension of the miscreant.

The usual verdict was returned.

Blake had a long consultation with the authorities. He fully explained his theory in regard to the crimes, and related the circumstances of the attempted murder of Sarah Watts at Chislehurst. The fact, as stated by Blake, that Mortemer Slade, the homicidal lunatic, was alive and at large, received startling confirmation two or three days later, when news came to hand describing the attack upon Stephen Darrell at Rome. It then became clear that, even if Edmund Blake's suppositions were wrong, and that Slade was not the mysterious murderer of the East-end, he was at least a most dangerous lunatic whose capture it was necessary to bring about with as little delay as possible. The house at Chislehurst was accordingly raided by the police, but nothing likely to lead to Slade's apprehension was found there.

24. Stephen and Phyllis

Stephen Darrell lay hovering between life and death. Dangerously wounded in the struggle with Mortemer Slade, and with his life's blood apparently pouring from the gash inflicted by the maniac's cruel knife, he had been removed to the National Hospital at Rome, and there he had lain unconscious for many hours, and only kept alive by the assiduous care and devoted skill of the Italian doctors and nurses. The knife had penetrated the side to a considerable depth, and had missed a vital part by the narrowest of margins. As it was, the injuries were of a highly dangerous character, and the surgeons of the hospital expressed themselves as extremely doubtful of his recovery. It was almost a miracle, they declared, that the stab had not proved instantly fatal. By great good fortune, and thanks to the invalid's temperate living and fine constitution, a fatal issue might possibly be averted; but they could not promise a recovery, and their faces were grave and concerned when inquiry came from the English colony at that time quartered in Rome.

Phyllis's own health had been seriously endangered by reason of the attack upon her lover and the shock of meeting with Mortemer Slade. Though strong and robust, she was of somewhat emotional temperament, and her association with the unspeakable criminal she believed Slade to be, accidental thought it was, had made a terrible impression upon her mind. Her sister, the Countess of Shincliffe, was telegraphed for, and arrived at the Italian capital with a retinue of servants and a veritable mountain of trunks and boxes. She was a strong-minded young woman, and immediately took charge of the situation, as it were, and settled down to bring Phyllis to what she called 'a reasonable frame of mind'.

'The whole affair seems very extraordinary,' she remarked to her father. 'I understood that Mr Darrell had himself annulled the engagement. Yet, apparently, he follows her to Rome, and makes a dramatic and wholly unexpected appearance by a ruined castle just in time to save Phyllis from a madman, and to receive fatal injuries himself.'

'I am almost as much in the dark as you are,' said Lord Caversham. 'Poor little Phyllis is almost beside herself with grief and anxiety about Darrell, and seems scarcely able to give a reasonable account of the sad affair.'

'How was it this Slade was not caught?' asked his eldest daughter. 'The Italian police seem to have been very remiss.'

'They did all they could,' was the reply. 'But he got clear away. It is thought that he escaped in a cargo boat, and there is some talk of his having been traced to Marseilles. Of course, the Scotland Yard authorities have been informed, and we shall hear of his capture, I fancy, if he sets foot in England.'

'Has Phyllis received any explanation of Darrell's temporary infidelity?'

'I cannot say,' answered the earl. 'She has not confided to me, and I have not liked, in her present weak and hysterical condition, to press the point. You, Editha, are the one to ascertain from her the exact position of affairs.'

'I suppose,' said Lady Shincliffe, with a little grimace and a deprecatory sniff, 'she is as fond of him as ever?'

'I am sadly afraid so,' he replied. 'I dread the consequences this young man's death may have upon her. She seems to think, absurdly enough, that she has been the cause, in some indirect fashion, of the fate he has met with. She reproaches herself continually, and refuses to be consoled.'

'Is there any likelihood of Mr Darrell's recovery?'

'I am afraid but little,' was the grave reply. 'He is young and strong, and may just possibly pull through. We must all do what we can. Phyllis's happiness and peace of mind are at stake – perhaps even her life and reason.'

'Are these Italian doctors efficient, father?' Lady Shincliffe asked.

'I have every reason to think so,' the earl replied. 'But for our own satisfaction and that of Darrell's family, I have telegraphed to Sir Edward Leger, the great surgeon, and he will arrive from London tonight. Young Darrell must be saved if human effort can achieve it.'

'What of Phyllis?'

'She declines to see anyone, and remains alone in her room.'

'She will see me,' said her sister in her decided way. 'She will have to. I'll go to her at once.'

The Earl of Caversham saw his eldest daughter depart on her mission of comforting his youngest with some misgiving.

'All my daughters are a little obstinate,' he reflected, as he lit a cigar. 'Dear girls, but a little pigheaded. Phyllis has her share of the family trait. Still, if Editha insists' – he shrugged his shoulders and prepared to depart to the English club – 'I'll lay a shade of odds that Editha gets her way and sees her.'

He proved to be right. Lady Shincliffe had a long interview with Phyllis, and left that maiden in a rather happier and resigned frame of mind.

'It's no use giving way, my dear, like this,' she said, stroking the young girl's pretty hair. 'Stephen Darrell is not dead yet, and these young men take a lot of killing. Sir Edward Leger arrives today and will have a consultation with Dr Coecini and Professor Marcantonio. By tomorrow we may have good news for you. Dry your eyes, get your maid to make you look presentable, like a good child, and come for a drive with me.'

There was nothing for it but to comply, and the Earl of Caversham, returning two hours later from the club, had the pleasure of beholding his two daughters driving through the streets of the capital in an open victoria. He stared after the carriage with an amused smile.

'Clever woman, Editha,' he chucked. 'Generally gets her own way. Just like her poor dear mother in many respects. Heigho! What the deuce will I do till the London papers come?'

It was decreed that Stephen Darrell should recover. The eminent surgeon from London declared that his condition was indeed grave, but very far from being hopeless, and he advocated a certain operation of the most intricate and delicate kind which would almost certainly save the life of the patient. The local specialists agreed, and the operation was performed successfully. Lord Caversham speedily had the satisfaction of being able to inform his child that her 'recalcitrant lover' as he termed him, would certainly recover.

'When can I see him?' demanded Phyllis, overjoyed.

'Oh, not for some days,' was the reply. 'Besides, unless Mr Darrell has tendered you, and is prepared to tender me, some explanation of his extraordinary conduct in London, it would be hardly seemly for you to see him at all.'

To this view Lady Shincliffe, a devotee of propriety, instantly subscribed.

'The young man must see dad and explain his motives for breaking off the match,' she said, 'before we can acknowledge his right to see you.'

Phyllis's face, bright with newly awakened hope, fell as she regarded him.

'Dear father,' she said, softly and shyly, 'Dear Editha, I know what you say is right. But Stephen had some very strong reason, the strongest possible reason, for acting as he did. I am satisfied that he will act now as an honourable gentleman. He has my whole trust and my whole love.'

Three weeks later Stephen, pronounced to be out of all danger and fairly on the way to recovery, though weak and enfeebled, wrote from the hospital the following letter to the Earl of Caversham:

My Lord – I have been kept informed of the sympathetic inquiries which you have kindly caused to be made as to my progress almost daily, and, being for the first time able to write, I hasten to express to you my grateful thanks. I am most desirous, dear Lord Caversham, of tendering to you a full explanation of the motives, not altogether discreditable to me I hope, which compelled me to mar my own happiness some weeks ago, and to which I need not now more particularly allude. I love Miss Penrose, if that be possible, more devotedly than ever, and I only await her father's sanction to obtain her pardon, and to renew my suit.

I am,

Your grateful and obedient servant,

S. Grant Darrell

Next day the interview, solicited in this letter, took place. Returning to his chateau the same evening, the Earl sent for Phyllis, and, kissing his daughter with more demonstrative affection than he usually betrayed, said kindly:

'I have seen Darrell, little girl, and I am perfectly satisfied with the explanation he has offered to me. He is a noble fellow, and I'm deuced sorry that I ever misjudged him. Indeed, I asked his pardon, and we shook hands the best of friends.'

'Father,' Phyllis exclaimed, nestling to his breast with more tenderness than she had evinced since she was a child. 'I love to hear you speak like that. I knew Steenie was in the right.'

'You love him still and wish to marry him?' asked the Earl, stroking her peach-like cheek, and softly pulling her pearl-like ear.

She hid her face against his shoulder.

'Need you ask?' she said simply.

A week later, the interval of time being all too long for Phyllis, the meeting between the lovers took place. Stephen, rapidly gaining strength, was now able to get up and, attired in a silk dressing gown, to sit on the piazza fanning himself in the warm Italian sun. It had been arranged that the Earl of Caversham and his family, now reinforced by another of his daughters, should return to England in a few days, and that Stephen should accompany them if he maintained his present rapid improvement. He was eagerly looking forward to a return to active life. Hope had entered into his heart again, and he was happy, if a little impatient, under the restraint which was still necessary for his complete recovery.

'My love,' he murmured, feeling the beating of her heart against his own. 'My little faithful, long-suffering, devoted love. What have you thought of me, what could you have thought of me, all this weary while?'

She stood silent in his arms.

'Life,' he said solemnly, 'is a joyous thing, not lightly to be flung away when love comes into it. I have thanked God that He has spared me for this hour. I pray to Him that, for the future, I may be a better man, and worthy of the great gifts of love and life that He hath bestowed upon me.'

He reverently kissed her lips. There ensued a little silence. Their hearts are full, and words seemed idle things.

'When I deliberately freed you from he bond that united us,' he said, clasping her yielding form still closer in his arms, 'I believed that I was a man liable to die at any moment of an incurable disease. I had been assured so most positively by a man masquerading, for some cruel purpose which now I can divine, as a doctor, and my father's friend. I was in honour bound to release you. It broke my heart almost, but I did it. A little later, thanks to Edmund Blake, a valued friend whom I must make known to you, I learnt the truth. Shall I tell you, love, the name of the villain who lied to me?'

'No need,' she murmured, with a little shudder. 'It was Mortemer Slade.'

'It was,' he said gravely. 'When I discovered how cruelly I had been imposed upon, I tore off to Rome intending to beseech you for forgiveness, and to tell your father all. That was Blake's advice again. My wife' – he held her proudly to him – 'will come to like and value Blake as I do.'

She silently pressed his hand.

'I called at the chateau, rented by your father, and was informed by the servants that you had taken your favourite walk. The situation was described to me, and I determined to brave your resentment, and beg you to hear me and the truth. I saw that villain threatening you. I tore up the hill, and came upon him from behind. The rest, dear love, you know.'

A tremor ran through her whole frame.

'Oh, Steenie,' she cried. 'He – this man – forms the one black cloud in the bright vista of our future life together. My blood runs cold at the mention of his name. I dread to hear it breathed. Oh, how devoutly I pray that we may never encounter him again.'

He endeavoured to calm her fears.

'He will be taken,' he said. 'I am certain that his capture is imminent; I have had a letter from Edmund Blake, in which he assures me that Slade's arrest cannot be long delayed. He has a scheme for his undoing, which even his maniacal cunning will not circumvent. Cheer up, beloved, and have courage. I feel – I know – I understand that his "day is far spent, his night as at hand"!'

25. The Red Light in the Sky

The Earl of Shincliffe's private yacht, the *Violet Melrose*, brought the Caversham party back from Italy to England. They left Rome one morning in the first week of November, embarked at Naples, and made for Dover, the weather being fine and propitious. The party consisted of Lord Caversham, the Countess of Shincliffe, the Hon. Mrs Malyon, the Hon. Miss Penrose, Lady Marion Minting, Mr Stephen Darrell, and their respective servants. On the afternoon of 8 November the white cliffs of old Albion hove in sight. The brief voyage and the keen sea-air had achieved wonders for Stephen Darrell, who, now completely recovered, was the life and soul of the little coterie which assembled nightly in the handsomely furnished and commodious saloon after a magnificent repast each evening. He was his own man again. Secure in the love and steadfast devotion of Phyllis, happy in the improvement in his worldly prospects which the unexpected death of a distant and rich relative had assured him, he was now the gayest of the gay, and full of bright plans for the immediate future. The Earl of Caversham's consent to an early marriage had been secured and Stephen felt that his future happiness, and that of the girl of his heart, was certain and assured. He brought Phyllis up to the deck to watch the white cliffs of Kent grow closer and closer, and the two stood together, apart from the others, gazing out upon the enchanting view before them. It had been a mild and beautiful day for the time of year, and, if the weather could be accepted as an augury, their return to 'England, Home, and Beauty' was indeed happily and opportunely timed.

'Look,' he said – they were hidden behind the companion way, and it was quite safe to encircle her slender waist with his muscular arm; at any rate he did so – 'see, we are leaving the dark clouds behind us and gradually entering into the bright and genial light. Where are the usual November fogs and early winter mists? Have they fled away at your approach, sweetheart, like the wicked goblins before the good fairy of our storybooks?'

She turned a laughing face to his.

'The skies,' she said, 'are in unison with us. We are happy, and so are they. Steenie, I am so happy that sometimes I am almost afraid.'

'Of what, dearest?' he asked. The light laughter of the others, standing amidships, floated towards them on the gentle breeze. 'Of what, and whom?'

'My idle fancies, I suppose,' she said, quietly. 'But while that man is free–'

'Think no more of him,' he said. 'His course is nearly run. I feel that he will never trouble us again. Forget, my own, that so dark a shadow ever crossed your path.'

'I try,' she replied, with a sigh, 'and sometimes I succeed. But I see him in my dreams, a terrible figure, endowed with supernatural powers, and waging an eternal war upon the poor and weakest of frail humanity. I see him overcome at last, dethroned, defeated, destroyed; but not till he has accomplished ages of untold evil and waded through unfathomed seas of innocent blood.' She shuddered. 'Such poor, such despised, such outcast creatures he has sent, all unprepared, to their account. Steenie, if we become rich–'

She paused, and gazed up at her stalwart lover with the pure look of love.

'Well, my love?'

'If we become really, truly rich, I'd like–'

'Go on, my pet.'

'To do what little we could for the poorest outcasts of the slums. For the women especially. They have sinned, perhaps, but who can tell how vastly they have been wronged. Stephen was almost a rich man now. He vowed that if wealth and power would be given him in the fullness of time, he would do his utmost to ameliorate the lot in life of those of a class from which the monstrous Slade had chosen his victims. He nobly kept his vow.

'Listen, Phyllis,' he said, producing a letter. It had been written to him by Edmund Blake, and had reached him an hour or two before the yacht had sailed from Naples. 'It is against my wish to remind you that this miscreant Slade still lives to torment the human family. You will, however, like to know what my friend writes on the unsavoury subject.'

'I should, indeed,' said Phyllis.

Darrell flattened out the closely written sheet upon the rail of the bulwark and read as follows, though he had some difficulty in preventing the wind from blowing the paper away:

Gower Street,

2 November 1888

My dear Darrell,

Yes, you can certainly count upon me meeting you at Dover. The blow will do me good, for these East-end outrages have done me out of my annual holiday this year. I shall put up at the Lord Warden, and there await the arrival of the good yacht *Violet Melrose*. I am looking forward to meeting the Hon. Mrs Darrell that is to be. The Earl will remember my name, I think. I was fortunate enough to be of some slight service to him on a certain occasion.

Of Mortemer Slade I have nothing to report; so you know, my plan for his capture unhappily miscarried, and the failure of the scheme was immediately followed by the double murder. I had ascertained in what street he had been hiding; had penetrated through his disguise, and planted a trusted man outside the place to watch for his return after his attack upon you in Italy. But '*l'homme propose, et Dieu dispose!*' Master Slade cleverly disguised a fellow lodger as himself and my representative first shadowed, and then arrested the wrong man. I was very disappointed at the frustration of my hopes. Indeed, my loss of temper, under the circumstances, may, I think, be forgiven me. That we shall hear of him again, I feel confident, though Whitechapel and the surrounding districts are so closely watched as to render it difficult for him to continue the horrors without great risk of discovery. Yet something 'in my innards' tells me that the long, stern chase is drawing to its close. The police theory is that his body will be fished out of the river one of these days. But I think differently. I continue to receive letters purporting to come from the murderer, and I am confident that they emanate from Mr Slade.

Well, *au revoir* till we meet,

With every good wish,

Believe me,

Yours sincerely,

Edmund Blake.

'There,' said Stephen, as he carefully folded up the letter and placed it in an inner pocket. 'Thus writes one of the smartest and cleverest men I know.'

'Yet he has so far failed signally to capture the man,' Phyllis observed, a little wistfully.

'The task has been one of extreme difficulty,' Stephen replied. 'The elucidation of these mysterious crimes in the London streets has proved beyond the powers of the detective faculty the world over. From Paris, New York, Berlin, Vienna, St Petersburg have come criminal experts anxious to assist their English confrères in the capture of the unparalleled murderer. All have failed, all efforts have been

unavailing. A great reward is on offer to tempt a mercenary to betray his master; but Jack the Ripper has done his fell work alone and unaided and no one appears to have seen him either going to meet or returning from a victim. The detective instinct, keen as it may be, is only human, and everything human has its limitations. I do believe, however, that if this fiend is destined to be caught, he will fall before the sagacity and courage of Edmund Blake.'

While Stephen spoke, the sun had been gradually setting in the west. Looking up at the conclusion of his remarks, Stephen observed upon the face of his sweetheart a curious expression of fear and awe. Her eyes were fixed upon the slowly setting sun, which was darkening the sky with purple splendour. Soon the heavens, the whole canopy of the firmament, were bathed in a crimson glow. The skies were a blood-red, the whole aspect of the clouds grand, impressive, formidable.

'A crimson sunset,' she said almost inaudibly, with a little shiver.

'It will be a fine day tomorrow,' said Stephen, watching her uneasily.

'Will he keep his word, I wonder?' she murmured half to herself. 'Will he appear to me tonight? Has a new crisis come into his terrible life?'

Stephen wrapped a light shawl gently about her shoulders and led her below, but for the rest of the evening she was silent and constrained.

It was nine o'clock at night when the yacht found anchorage off the Admiralty Pier. Lord Caversham's secretary had procured a suite of rooms for the peer and his party at the Lord Warden, as they did not intend to proceed to London till the morrow. Edmund Blake came on board while the luggage and other impediments were being removed to the shore, and was warmly welcomed by the Earl, who had never forgotten how skilfully Blake had solved the mystery of the burglary at Caversham House some three years previously. He was introduced to Phyllis and to the other members of the noble family, and it was some little time before he was able to snatch a few moments' private conversation with Stephen.

'You look as fit as the proverbial fiddle, my boy,' he remarked, critically regarding Stephen's admirably proportioned figure. 'A stab in the left side looks like a blessing in disguise, to judge by the healthy aspect you present.'

'I'm all right,' replied Stephen, lightly. 'What do you think of her?'

'Charming,' was the reply. 'A very lovely girl indeed. I heartily congratulate you and wish you all possible happiness. But I fancy she looks a little pale and distrait. Perhaps she's tired.'

'Not altogether that,' answered Stephen. 'You know that she imagines that a red sunset portends another visitation from Slade? Did you notice the sky tonight?'

'A crimson sunset has preceded every one of those murders,' said Blake. 'But Slade will have all his work cut out to bring one off in the streets. Every alley, every court, every recess is still being watched, though just on six weeks has elapsed since the last crime. If he attempts a murder in districts he has hitherto haunted, his arrest – perhaps in the very act – must follow as the night the day.' The two men were talking in Stephen's cabin. Lord Caversham entered.

'Your man has come on board, Stephen,' he said, 'and wants to see to your baggage. Can he come down? We are just going on shore.'

'I'll join you now,' cried Stephen. He put on an overcoat and a white silk muffler and prepared to ascend.

The Earl followed.

'Of course, you'll join us at dinner, Mr Blake?' he asked, graciously. 'Or perhaps we'd better call it supper at this time. The ladies will take a light meal in their own rooms, for even my hardy Editha complains of being tired, and Phyllis is as pale as a sheet. You'll join us, Blake?'

'I am honoured, my Lord,' said the great detective, bowing. Blake came of an ancient stock, and the Earl did not count it a dishonour to meet him as an equal.

They reached the upper deck. The ladies had already left the vessel, and were waiting for the menfolk upon the pier. Stephen, leaving Blake to assist Lord Caversham, hurried after Phyllis, whom he could discern with Lady Shincliffe, Mrs Malyon, and Lady Marion, just passing through the turnstiles on their way to a carriage, which was waiting outside to convey them to the hotel. He distinctly saw, as he pressed forward through a crowd of people on the pier, the form of his betrothed fall, sinking into the arms of her aunt. It was clear to him that something was amiss, and that she had fainted. Indeed, he had heard her utter one pitiful little cry of alarm and distress. He rushed forward, reached the spot in an instant, and supported the fainting girl in his arms.

'What is it?' he cried in wild alarm. 'What has happened?'

Lady Shincliffe replied. She was ready with a bottle of smelling-salts, and with advice and aid.

'A man brushed past us rather rudely,' she said. 'He seemed to turn and to stare at Phyllis. The next instant he vanished, and Phyllis gave a little cry and fell.'

A crowd of curious onlookers was collecting, and these Stephen brushed to one side as he carried his inanimate fiancée to the carriage. Lady Shincliffe entered with him and Mrs Malyon and Lady Marion occupied the other. Arrived at the hotel, Phyllis was tenderly carried to her room, and restoratives applied. She soon recovered consciousness, but was seen no more that evening.

'What was the cause of her fright?' asked Blake, when Stephen returned from paying her a visit. 'No ordinary alarm would have brought about so acute an attack of nerves.'

'Deuced funny, I call it,' remarked the Earl. 'Phyllis was all right in the early part of the evening.'

'She is nearly prostrate with alarm and shock,' said Stephen gravely. 'These repeated frights are undermining her general health and will end in a serious illness if they cannot be made to cease. The man who brushed against her as she left the pier was Mortemer Slade.'

'Impossible,' cried the earl, 'Slade now in Dover?'

'Phyllis is positive it was he. I know that she is right. I am going out to find him, and to bring him back with me, alive or dead.'

Blake leapt to his feet.

'No,' he said, 'your duty is here to watch and mind the girl you love. It is my task to run this wolf to earth, and I will yield it up to no man. I go to do my duty. My lord, I wish you good night, and a pleasant journey to town tomorrow. Darrell, guard Miss Penrose as you would your life. Nay, I know I need not tell you that. You shall hear from me. You are wanted here. My task is elsewhere.'

He bowed to the Earl, shook hands with Darrell, and was gone.

26. The Great Chase Begins

Edmund Blake always carried a disguise in case of an emergency. There were several changes of raiment in the two portmanteaux he had brought with him to Dover, and these included a complete rig-out suitable to a village farmer of the old-fashioned type. The trunks were in his bedroom. It would take him, he calculated, about fifteen minutes to array himself in the garments of a veritable 'Farmer Giles'. A few deft touches to his clean-shaven face – he had, for some time, discarded a moustache – and he would easily pass muster as a rural agriculturist farming his own bit of land in some hamlet adjacent to the famous seaport opposite to Calais. It was necessary, however, to acquaint the manager of the hotel with his design, and this he did in a few well-chosen words. Instructions were given to the clerks and servants of the hostelry that they were not to take any notice of any rustic attired as a farmer should such an individual be seen to enter or go away. Blake did not wish his goings and comings to be noted and discussed. Secrecy was the keynote of the system of detection which had hitherto served him so well.

In twenty minutes from the time of his leaving Lord Caversham's private apartments, he left the hotel disguised beyond any possibility of recognition and discovery. Even the keen eyes of the man he was about to seek, who might or might not be familiar with his features, would hardly penetrate through so artistic and thorough a disguise. On that score, Blake, embarking upon the greatest struggle of his career, felt perfectly safe. He wore a loose, shaggy greatcoat of a dun colour, which reached below his knees and extended halfway down his leather leggings. In its capacious pockets he placed a pair of handcuffs – his own design – a loaded revolver, a small life-preserver, and a flash of brandy slightly diluted with water. The wind was blowing cold and drear from the sea, and it was quite possible that he might be out all night. He meant, if it were humanly possibly, to take the man this time. Never had he felt more resolute, collected, and cool. Slade should not escape this time if human endeavour could prevent it.

He had already half-formed a plan of campaign. The time had been about 9.15 when Phyllis Penrose, catching sight of the face she dreaded to see, had swooned away, and it was 9.45 when Stephen had announced to them the reason for so sudden a fainting attack. It was now 10.10. In the interval, one train had left Dover for London, and it was not improbable that Slade, having satisfied his purpose in seeing Phyllis, had caught that one. On the other hand, he might be waiting for the 10.55 train, which was the last leaving Dover that night, and happened to be an express. It will be understood that the only descriptions which the detective had in regard to the outward aspect of Mortemer Slade was that given him by Jack Dagenham, and, as we know, the former had completely altered his appearance on the occasion of his escaping from his abode in Stamford Street. Blake told himself that he had to look for a tall, dark, cadaverous-looking man, with beard and moustache, deep-set eyes, an aquiline nose, and thin lips, who invariably dressed in black. As a matter of fact, Slade was now attired in fashionable clothing and wore a fair wig and a flaxen moustache.

Providence, however, which had resisted all Blake's attempts to capture the murderer, now exerted itself on his behalf.

As the detective turned into a quiet and deserted street on his way to the railway station, he observed in front of him the shadows of two men sheltering in the doorway of a closed shop. Something – Providence, chance, luck, intuition, call it what you will – prompted him to pause and to take stock of them and his surroundings. The men were sheltered by two pillars supporting a stone portico, and he himself, standing flat against the wall a few yards from them, was screened from observation. They were talking earnestly in low tones. Blake, pressing himself closely to the wall, approached as near to them as he prudently could, and remained still, listening with absolute intentness, for, as he neared them, he had distinctly heard one of them pronounce his name. Now, from where he stood, he could hear all that passed between them.

'You say,' exclaimed the taller man – Blake could not see the face of either – 'that he entered the hotel with the others?'

'Yus, gov'nor,' said the other in the unmistakable tones of a Cockney rough. 'I see 'im right enough. It was the cove as we saw meet that there woman at the Marble Arch. Blake 'is name is, and he 'angs out in Gower Street. I knows 'im well enough. 'E's a terror to all the crooks. In course, I don't know what you've been a-doin' of, Mr Slade, but I'd much rather 'ave that there nosey Blake after you than me.'

'You talk like a child – or a fool,' was the angry retort. 'And, man alive, keep that name Slade to yourself if you value a whole skin. This man, this Blake, was still at the Lord Warden when you came away?'

'Yus,' the other replied. 'I waited there a few moments, and he did not come out. He's in there a-drinkin' with the nobs as sure as my name's Bleater. I found out from a ostler as I come across that he's a stayin' there. Now, then, sir, tip us your orders. It's a getting' late and cold, and the pubs will soon be closin'! What do you wish me to do?'

The tall man moved a little into the light. Blake devoured him with his eyes. This, then, was the London Terror. What eyes, bright as steel, cruel as a tiger's, cold as a slab of granite, the man had! 'They are the eyes of a dangerous maniac,' thought the detective, as he surveyed him. Their baleful light burned a ray into his soul. He would never forget the eyes of Mortemer Slade, now that he had once looked into their awe-inspiring depths.

Slade moved back with a restless, uneasy gait into the shadows.

'You'll keep that hotel under observation,' he said, in his suave, even tones. 'Not necessarily tonight, but from tomorrow morning. You will ascertain for me the time at which this Blake leaves here and his destination. You will report to me at the usual spot. Be vigilant and faithful, and I'll well reward you. Attempt to betray me, and I'll make you lament that your mother did not strangle you at birth. Here's money for your expenses, no rioting, remember! No drunken debauchery liable to land you in the hands of the police. Take the money and go.'

Blake, alive to the least sound, caught the chink of money, and saw Bleater receive it, and speed away like the wind. Mortemer Slade came out from the shadows of the portico, and gazed after the retreating figure of the rough.

'So far, so good,' he muttered, looking up and down the empty street. 'Mr Blake is so far out of the running. I can now hie me to London, and pay my long-projected visit to that charming female, Mary Jane Kelly.' With one swift, backward glance, he strode down the deserted street and took his way towards the station.

Blake permitted his enemy to get some little distance ahead, and then followed in his wake, debating in his mind what course to pursue. A picket of military police were slowly patrolling the road, keeping well in the centre, and glancing now and then at the soldiers as they made their way homewards to the barracks. Should he denounce Slade there and then, and enlist the services of these stalwarts in pursuit? Should he whisper a word to the policeman on his beat advancing towards him with measured tread? No. He preferred to have all the credit and glory of laying the monstrous madman by the heels. Slade had foiled and escaped him so often. He must take him himself, alone, or forfeit his own life in the desperate venture.

He saw his man enter the station. It was 10.45. He took a first-class ticket to London, intending, however, to enter the same carriage, whatever class, as Slade elected to travel in. He did not intend to lose sight of the man he was shadowing. His purpose was to follow him to the appointment with the woman he had heard him mention and arrest him then. That was his present plan; but circumstances, he told himself, might cause him to change his designs at the last. He would act as the situation seemed to suggest and trust to Providence and his own resourcefulness to pull him through. The London train – an express – was in, and Blake walked slowly up the platform as though seeking am empty compartment, or one in which he might smoke with impunity. He was conscious that Slade, who had not taken any particular notice of the elderly farmer in the long, shaggy greatcoat, was engaged in a similar search, almost immediately behind him. The detective had brought his cigar-case with him, and he opened his overcoat to procure the case from his breast-pocket. That simple act proved his undoing. The production of that cigar-case resulted in the complete and absolute failure of his plans. In pulling out the case Blake happened to drop, unnoticed by anyone but the man behind him, a small leather pocket-book. Slade stooped and picked it up, intending to return this owner. Indeed, he strode forward with that object, when the initials in the back – in silver – attracted his attention – 'E. B.' There was no mistaking them, flourishing, ornate, big capitals they were in filigree silver. His suspicions instantly aroused, Slade opened the case. Inside were a dozen or fifteen visiting cards and 'Edmund Blake' was the name upon them. He slipped the book into the pocket of his overcoat, and cast a sly and sinister glance at the figure of the farmer. So! That worthy old party in the rough coat, stout boots, broad-brimmed hat, and leather gaiters was none other than Mr Edmund Blake. The humour of the situation tickled him. The shadower shadowed! The pursuer pursued! Well, he would travel up to London with Mr Blake and see who had the laugh at the end of the journey.

'Now then, any more for London?' shouted a porter in his ear. 'Train's going on, sir. Take your seats.' A bell rang, doors were being hastily slammed, tickets were being examined. Slade leisurely opened the door of a first-class 'smoker' and took a seat in the far corner. A minute after the door of the compartment opened again, and he saw the tall and portly figure of the farmer who had dropped the card case jump in and take a seat. Passengers to town were few that cold November night, and no one else got in. The pursuer and the pursued had the carriage to themselves. In another minute they were speeding on their way.

Slade looked up from the paper he had been reading, as they passed through a wayside station at great speed, and regarded his companion with a smile.

'No stop, I believe, sir,' he said politely, 'till we reach Charing Cross?'

'Aye, that be so, sir,' returned the 'farmer' in a very rural accent. 'Fine weather we be havin' for time o' year.'

'Today was pleasant,' said Slade, still eyeing his companion with an amused smile. 'Been staying at Dover, I presume?'

'I lives hard by,' was the careless answer. 'I've a bit o' business in Lunnon tomorrow, and I prefers to travel when its dark loike, and I can sleep in the train. Won'erful place, Lunnon, sir, ain't it?'

'It's rather large,' said Slade, languidly, 'and very dirty. I can't say I am a great admirer of it myself.'

'Ah! Them as live there can't be expected to enjoy the soights and such loike as we rustics. I comes up twice a year, I does, regular. The missis she be lookin' after farm at present, so I–'

'Come up alone for a little innocent recreation, I suppose? Well, London is a wicked enough place, I daresay, if you know where to look for it. For wickedness, I mean.'

Blake sighed as an old man might who remembered that his days for skylarking of any kind were in the past. Slade could not but admire the skill with which he represented the role of the old farmer. But he was immensely tickled with the humour of the strange situation all the same.

He settled himself comfortably in his corner of the carriage, crossing his long legs, and opening his overcoat as though he found the air – both windows were up – a little oppressive.

'One meets, sir,' he said, 'with strange personalities and stranger adventures in the course of a roving life like mine. It is hard to say, sometimes, where comedy ends and tragedy begins. Things are not always what they seem, and people are not always what they make themselves out to be. The wisest amongst us is easily deceived. The world is filled with treachery, deceit, and bedevilment. Now, take yourself for instance. You have your little secret, I suspect; some skeleton is hidden in a neglected and forgotten cupboard at your farm. You shake your head? You have no family secret? You are plain John Smith of Apple Orchard Farm, in the village of Sleepy Hollow, and all that sort of thing? Well! Well! I'll take your word for it. You, at least, are all, and only, that which you appear to be. And that reminds me' – he paused, and slipped off his overcoat, placing it in the rack above his head – 'that time flies, and that we are some halfway to London. Allow me' – he smiled benignantly, and, turning a little to one side, cut the communication cord on his side of the carriage with a pair of scissors – 'Allow me to congratulate Mr Edmund Blake upon his admirable disguise. You really are, my dear Blake, old Farmer Hayseed to the very life!'

27. In the Train

The two men were face to face at last. Edmund Blake, essentially sane and normal, courageous, cool, daring, resourceful, faced Mortemer Slade, degenerate but cunning, calculating, brave, and physically powerful. It was a battle of giants – a case of Greek meeting Greek. Each was worthy the steel of the other. Would a madman's cunning prevail over the detective's skill? Would the mental equilibrium of the one overthrow the great bodily strength of the other? To which would go the victory in an encounter, the end of which neither could possibly foresee?

The train was tearing through the darkness with a rush and a roar at some fifty miles an hour. Blake, realising his position in a mental flash as drowning men see sketched out before them, in a moment of time, the whole of their past careers from childhood up, remembered that London would be reached in something less than half an hour. Could he master the desperate man who stood, at the further end of the carriage, steadfastly regarding him with that strange, set smile, or would the maniac triumph? He braced himself together by a grand mental effort and returned Slade's gaze with interest. Under that keen and undaunted look, the eyes of the mad surgeon dropped and sought the ground. But he was the first to speak.

'Allow me,' he said in courteous tones, 'to return to you the innocent instrument by which your identity was revealed to me.'

He threw the pocket-book which Blake had dropped on the platform on the carriage-seat beside his adversary, who, without removing his eyes from the other's face, picked it up and deposited it in an inner pocket.

'But for that little mishap, Mr Blake,' said Slade with a faint smile, 'I should never have known you.'

Blake sat down in his corner, but Slade remained standing by the opposite window.

'Since you do know me,' the detective said, with perfect sang-froid, 'there is no need for me to continue to pose as a country farmer. You are Mortemer Slade, for some time an inmate of Grange House asylum?'

'I am,' was the calm reply.

'You murdered Mr Edgar Welman, a young doctor, on the occasion of your escape from that retreat?'

'I did.'

'Since then you have perpetrated other crimes; such, for instance, as the attack upon Mr Stephen Darrell in Italy and the abduction and attempted murder of Mrs Sarah Watts?'

Slade shrugged his shoulders.

'I perceive,' he remarked, 'that you are well informed.'

'For these crimes,' Blake continued, 'some motive, however trifling and obscure, seems to exist. They are, if I may say so, at least understandable. Since, however, you are in so obliging a mood, and I have been fortunate enough to catch you when imbued with the spirit of confession, I should much like to know why you killed these poor women who had never wronged you in thought, word, or deed?'

'You are somewhat inquisitive, sir,' Slade replied, 'but that, I suppose, is natural in a detective, and I am not indisposed to gratify your curiosity. We are alone, Mr Blake, and there is no human witness to our conversation. I maintain, and have always maintained, that I was a sane man at the time I took up my residence with Dr Kent. I was, however, declared to be mad and I determined to do what little I could to justify that verdict. The newspapers of the last few weeks testify to the fact that I succeeded.'

He was still standing, leaning against the woodwork of the carriage in an easy position, the ends of the severed communication cord hanging down and across the window. Blake sat in his corner calmly regarding him.

'Mr Slade, he said, 'you have more than justified the specialists' description of your mental state. You have committed, in a spirit of pure, wanton savagery, a series of crimes unparalleled in this, or any other, country. The horrible nickname which you have assumed will live forever. Your deeds will be remembered when the actions of the just have long been forgotten; when the words of the sages have long ceased to influence the thoughts and deeds of mankind. Does it not occur to you that you have done enough? Are you not at last surfeited with the flow of blood? Shall we not call a truce? Shall not the butchery end? If you submit to me – as I mean, indeed, that you shall – man will not judge you, and God, who sent your affliction, will be merciful. Believe me, there are worse places than Broadmoor, and you will be king there, an emperor of crime whose sway none can dispute, to whose eminence none can ever hope to reach.'

He paused. Vanity, an all-consuming selfish vanity, he knew to be the keystone of insanity. Your madman is egotistical to the fingertips. He had touched a tender cord. Slade's eyes brightened and gleamed in the fitful light of the railway carriage.

'Yes,' he said softly. 'You speak truly. I should be enthroned and crowned as the greatest murderer of them all. Perhaps I am destined to such a pre-eminence in the end. But as yet I have not done enough to earn so proud a position in the criminal annals of our time.'

'Indeed you have,' said Blake. His fingers were playing with the handcuffs in his pocket. He bent his eyes upon the madman's, with a grim intensity of purpose. Would his will prevail? Would his mind beat down the mental resistance of the man he faced so bravely? If he could but get these wristlets on–!

Under this baffling gaze, Slade turned restless. His eyes were directed towards the floor, and he shuffled uneasily. Beware, Edmund Blake! Beware of the madman's cunning! Now, at this juncture, when he seems conquered and subdued, he is the more subtle, the more cunning, the more desperate, the more dangerous. Beware!

'You think I have done enough for fame?' Slade asked complacently.

'You stand out,' said Blake, 'head and shoulders above them all – a triton among the minnows; a giant among pygmies. Jean Baptiste Troppmann, who exterminated the Kink family; John Williams, who removed the families of Marshall and Williamson; John Gleeson Wilson, who slaughtered Mrs Henricheon and her children; William Godfrey

Youngman, who slew his mother, brothers and sweetheart; John Owen, who decimated the village of Denham, all pale their ineffectual fire before you.'

'There is,' said Slade, with his curious smile, 'much reason in what you say.'

'They, poor bunglers, suffered at the hands of the law, or committed suicide,' Blake continued; 'but you will be allowed to live, to recount your tales of lust and blood, and to fight your battles, in peace, comfort and security, over again. Come, Mr Slade! The whole world pants for an account of how you killed these wretches. It is for you to speak. All humanity will wonder and shudder at your words. Is that not fame?'

He rose and approached the other. Slade, whose face wore a dreamy expression of ineffable pride and self-glory, allowed him to come quite close. They stood up together, each man tall and athletic; Slade the more powerful, Blake the more agile and active. But – beware!

Only for an instant of time the detective, about to produce his handcuffs, removed his eyes from those of Slade. With an inarticulate cry that was like no human sound, the murderer threw himself upon him, clutching at his throat with fingers of steel, and endeavouring with desperate strength to hurl him to the floor. Taken by surprise, Blake nearly went under, but he recovered his balance with a superhuman effort, and, in the attempt to force those choking, strangling fingers from his throat, rained blow after blow with his naked fists upon the face of his assailant. But the iron grip never relaxed. The clutch tightened about his neck, and Blake felt that he was gradually being forced backward towards the window of the carriage by which he had been sitting. His hands were free, but he was much hampered in the furious struggle by the thick and clinging overcoat he wore. His right hand sought the pocket of his coat. If he could get his revolver or his life-preserver. Half-choked, he felt that he could not breathe much longer under that grip of iron. His hand clasped the barrel of the pistol, and, raising it aloft behind his furious assailant, he brought down the butt-end of it with all the force he could command upon Slade's skull. The blow told. The madman released his grasp of the detective's throat, and staggered back with a horrible cry. But Blake, half-strangled, was weak and exhausted, and unable to follow up the advantage he had gained. With a backward blow he shivered the glass or the window behind him, hoping that the attention of the other passengers might be attracted by the crash. Slade seemed about to spring. Levelling his weapon, Blake aimed at his adversary's legs; but the revolver missed fire, and the furious murderer was again upon him. A terrific struggle ensued. Slade seemed endowed with supernatural strength. Slowly but surely, Blake resisting every inch of the way, he forced the latter back towards the other window. His muscular arms encircled him so that Blake could not reach the pocket in which his life-preserver lay, and he seemed not to heed the wild blows the detective rained upon his head and face. The wigs of each, assumed for the purpose of disguise, came off in the tremendous struggle, and they gazed each upon the other's real and genuine countenance. Blake's powers of self-defence were giving way. His breath came in great gasps, and the veins in his sweating forehead and temples stood out like whip-cord. He strained every nerve to keep away from the door of the carriage, but he was opposing a madman's strength, and he felt that the battle could have only one result. Slade's design was clear. He meant to fling him from the carriage on the rails.

The train was slowly slackening its speed. It was clear that the sounds of the struggle, and the noise of the falling glass, had attracted the attention of those in the next compartment. Blake could hear them knocking upon the woodwork. The communication-cord had been cut, but, in some way, the attention of the guard had been attracted, and in a few moments the train might be expected to come to a standstill. Could he resist till then?

As if realising his own risk, Slade redoubled his efforts to force the other towards the door. His gigantic strength enabled him to achieve that object. With one hand he opened the door, and thrust Blake, still struggling, out upon the line. As he fell backwards from the carriage the detective, however, with one convulsive grip, got his arms round Slade's neck and they fell out together, locked in a murderous embrace. Blake felt that he was falling from a great height. He seemed to see the train rush by. He heard the shouts and cries of people, and saw their pale and panic-stricken faces as they flashed by. A million stars appeared to dance before his bewildered eyes. A deafening roar, as of many waters, sounded in his ears. Then he seemed to hear a great clap as of thunder, and all was dark. He lay stunned and helpless upon the line.

Slade, brushing away the blood which poured down his own face and obscured his vision, rose from Blake's inanimate body, and glared wildly round. He was bruised and shaken, but had suffered no material injury in the fall. Fields, dark and desolate, lay on either side of the line, separated by a ditch and hedge. In the distance he could hear shouts and see the occasional fitful gleam of a lantern. The train had stopped some distance along the line beyond where they had fallen, and in a few moments the people travelling in it and the guard would be upon them. He had no time to lose. Cowering down he forced his way through the hedge and leapt the shallow ditch. It was a dark night, and he was not likely to be seen crossing the fields. Shaking his fist with malignant gesture towards the spot on the railroad whence the shouts proceeded, he made off across country as fast as his exhausted state would permit.

Blake was found a few minutes after. Bruised, battered, beaten, he was nevertheless alive, and, marvellous to relate, no limbs were broken. When he regained his consciousness he actually staggered to his feet and besought those who would detain him to allow him to proceed at once and to capture his assailant at all costs. His spirit was indomitable; his determination alone to take the murderer unquenched. He spent the night, however, at the earnest solicitation of a doctor, who attended to his injuries, at an inn outside the nearest village, and, though weak and much shaken, insisted next morning on catching the first train to town. There, almost upon arrival, he heard of yet another 'Horrible Murder in the East End!'

28. Mary Jane Kelly

Marie Jeanette Kelly her real name was, but her friends and acquaintances, most of whom resided in the neighbourhood of Dorset Street, Spitalfields, had a firm objection to these aristocratic-sounding appellations, and to them she was mostly known as 'Mary Jane'.

She had been married when she was sixteen years of age, and was at that time accounted a pretty girl. Drink and debauchery, however, are the sworn foes of daintiness and beauty, and little remained to 'Mary Jane' in the way of good looks at the time we are writing of. She had, indeed, sunk lower and lower in the social scale, and was now in no way dissimilar to the rest of her class, though she had at one time indulged in baseless dreams of better things.

The woman had been living with a man in Miller's Court for some months, but they had had a trifling quarrel, as such partners usually do, and Mr Bennett – for that was the gentleman's name – separated from her on 30 October, and sought fresh fields and pastures new. There was nothing, it transpired, known detrimental to his character, and with this story he has nothing to do.

Miss Kelly was born in Limerick but was sent to South Wales when very young, and came to London only four years before the date of this history. Her father's name was John McBride Kelly, and he had been employed at an ironworks in Wales. She had a sister who was in quite a respectable position, six brothers living at home, and one in the Army. At sixteen she had, according to her own accounts, married a young collier named Davies, and had lived with him till he was killed in a mine explosion. After that, in Cardiff, she took to dissolute ways, and, on first coming to London, lived in a fast house in the West-end. An admirer took her with him on a trip to Paris, and on her return she walked the streets in Radcliffe Highway, and lived with one or another for varying periods. When Bennett picked her up, they took lodgings together in Commercial Street, Spitalfields, afterwards migrating to Miller's Court – No. 13 – in which she encountered the fate we are about to describe.

About twelve o'clock on the night of 8 November 1888 – it was a Thursday night – 'Mary Jane' was walking in Dorset Street, and there she was joined by one of her cronies, who, like herself, had had more to drink than was altogether good for her. The name of her friend was Cox, and Mrs Cox was a widow.

'Well, Mary Jane,' quoth that good lady, as she steadied herself against the brick wall, and leered up into the face of her acquaintance. 'How's your luck, old dear?'

'Rotten,' was the reply, spoken in the soft accents of Hibernia.

'Sorry it is I am to 'ear you say so,' said Mrs Cox, 'for I wanted a drink o' beer and the loan of a tenner.'

Mary Jane took her arm.

'We can go in the "Spotted Dog" and have two four-'alfs,' she remarked, 'but it's never a tenner, nor a farthin', I've got to lend. But I'll have some tonight. Oh, yes. Sarah Ann Cox, I'll have some tonight as sure as we're both living women.

They entered the swing-doors of the four-ale bar in the hostelry alluded to, and Mrs Cox, though her friend paid, called for the beer.

'Got someone to meet, lovey?' she asked,
leaning a bare and brawny arm upon the bar
counter.

'Yes, I 'ave someone to meet, Sarah Ann
Cox. I don't deceive you. I'm going to meet a
real live toff wot's good for 'alf a James and a
bottle o' spirits.'

Ms Cox sighed. She was envious of so much
good fortune.

'Well, some of us is born lucky,' she observed,
sipping her thick and muddy-looking beer.
'Blessed if I've taken two bob in the 'ole week.
What time's your appointment, Mary Jane?'

Miss – or Mrs – Kelly winked elaborately at the unwholesome-looking pot-boy.

'Of course you'd like to know, old gell,' she said, 'and of course you ain't goin' to. I know
where and when to meet 'im, and that's good enough for me.' She drained her glass. 'Or
you, if it comes to that.'

The pot-boy paused in the act of cleaning glasses, and glanced up, not sorry for the
chance of entering into the conversation.

'I wonder some of you ladies,' he remarked, 'ain't afraid of encounterin' Jack the Ripper
some o' these dark, foggy evenings. We ain't 'eard the last of 'im yet, I think.'

Both ladies shivered and glanced uneasily round the bar. Mrs Cox even commenced
to make preparations for departure, wrapping her shawl tightly round her shoulders, and
fixing her dilapidated bonnet more securely upon her head. She expressed the opinion that
it was cold, and the belief that she would 'get 'er eye in a sling' if she didn't 'get back 'ome'
immediately. In passing out of the bar, she took occasion to whisper to her friend a word
of warning. 'Take care of yourself, Mary Jane,' she said. 'Don't go a-trustin' too much to
strangers. He may still be at his game. You never know.'

The other gave a scornful laugh. 'I ain't afraid of Jack the Ripper,' she said, 'and the bloke
I'm waiting for is a real swell, such as I used to mix with. Goodbye, Mrs Cox, ma'rm. Good
luck to yez. Come round to my place in the mornin', and you can 'ave 'alf a dollar if you're
'ard up.' By which speech it will be seen that poor, lost Mary Jane Kelly was not a mean or
close-fisted person, whatever failings of another kind might be alleged against her.

She procured another glass of ale, 'on strap', she termed it, and remained at the bar
till closing time. Then she returned to 13 Miller's Court, where she rented a room at
– at 4s 6d a week – which was level with the street, and which possessed a window with
a broken pane of glass in it. She had put a piece of curtain up before this hole in the
window to keep the icy blasts of winter from penetrating into the cold and cheerless
room. It was a wretched apartment, containing little more than a miserable-looking bed,
a rough deal table, and a dirty washing-basin resting on a rickety chair. This was the
'home' of Mary Jane Kelly. She was twenty-nine shillings in debt to the landlord of the
squalid den, but she had been promised the money by a 'gentleman friend' and she was
certain that he was 'as good as his word'. The landlord grunted and thought otherwise;

but some latitude for rent is allowed in those parts, and he was not disposed to request his tenant to get out.

The 'gentleman friend' to whom Mary Jane had alluded was not punctual, however, to his appointment. He was to have met the lady in Dorset Street at 12.30 to 12.45, and she, after lighting a vile-smelling candle and putting the bed 'to rights', had hurried back to see if he had arrived. There was no sign of him. Curving her impatience, Mary Jane returned to Miller's Court, and, occasionally between then and 2.30 in the morning, she went out as far as the street corner and looked out for him. He came not, however, and like the lady in the 'Moated Grange', she was 'aweary, aweary'. When making these brief excursions from her abode she was seen by several persons who knew and recognised her, and their testimony the next day went far to prove that she had anticipated her murderer's coming, and had arranged for it.

At 2.30, however, the court – you entered it from Dorset Street – was quite deserted. Mary Jane, standing at the door of No. 13, waiting and expectant, saw a man steal swiftly along in the shadow of the wall, and her heart gave a great jump. It was her 'toff', her 'swell', her 'gentleman friend'. But he presented a strange and unwonted appearance. One of his eyes was blackened and nearly closed. His upper lip was cut. There was a great bruise upon his forehead. His shirt was torn at the neck and his collar was gone. Strangest of all, he was now clean-shaven and his hair was much darker than when she had seen him last. All down the front of his jacket – he wore no overcoat – were spots of blood. His hair was dishevelled and his bowler hat was bent into an unnatural shape. Mary Jane could only stand and gaze at him with wonder. What had her 'toff' been up to? His pale face was unnaturally gaunt and haggard, and his eyes had a hunted, wolfish look, not pleasant to behold. He pushed past her with scant ceremony and entered the wretched room, sinking, as if exhausted, on the side of the bed. The woman, with astonished eyes and mouth wide open, still stared as if she had seen a ghost.

He cursed her for a fool.

'Have you never seen a man after he's had a fight before?' he demanded roughly.

'Have you been fightin'?

'Yes. What do you think I've been doing? Playing marbles? Or nursing babies?'

'You've got a bad eye, dearie, and a nasty bruise or two,' she said, a little doubtfully, 'but a basin o' cold water will do yet a world o' good. I 'ope yer gave back as good as you got?'

He gave a hoarse laugh.

'The man I fought with is good for a six weeks' stay at the nearest hospital,' he said, 'if he isn't dead.'

'Where did it happen?'

'Not far away,' he replied, 'it was that detained me. But here I am and here you are, and when I've washed off this blood and brushed my hair, and rubbed a little grease paint over these marks, why, we'll have a jolly time together.'

He rose and looked round the room. 'You've got that portmanteau I brought here?' he asked. 'You've not sold it or pawned it?'

'No, lovey, I ain't that sort.' She pointed under the bed.

'To give,' he said, as he pulled a leather trunk into the centre of the room, 'the Devil his due, I don't think you are. And what of my other instructions. You've told no one of my occasional visits here?'

'Not a soul,' she said.

He produced a key and opened the portmanteau, taking out a decent suit of blue serge, a clean shirt and collar, and a thick dark overcoat of Irish frieze. A cloth cap followed.

'I'll put these things on before I go,' he said, 'and these tell-tale, bloodstained garments I can leave, in the trunk, at one of the railway stations. I wonder if Blake is dead. I hope so.'

Having delivered himself of this kindly sentiment, he proceeded to bathe his face and hands while poor Mary Jane set forth, on the dirty table, the remains of a very small joint of cold beef, some bread, pickles, and cheese, and a bottle containing brandy. 'It's not what you're used to, lovey,' she said, 'I knows that. But if you're tired and hungry a bit of bite and sup will do you good.'

He drew the clumsy chair to the table, and, after a long draught of raw spirits, swallowed a few mouthfuls of food, Mary Jane watching him the while well pleased.

Poor, weak, depraved Mary Jane. He might have spared you, you who had not betrayed the secret of his visits, had harboured him, and had given him food and drink. You, whose wretched room came to him as a haven of refuge, a sanctuary for the time being. Could he not spare you an awful death and your body the frightful indignities he had inflicted upon your sisters in poverty, vice, and misfortune? Of all Jack the Ripper's murders, this, committed in the victim's own room, was the most cruel and the most cowardly. The horrors the fiend wreaked upon the corpse of the woman who had sheltered him are of nameless atrocity and cannot be described.

Four hours later – at 6.30 in the morning, to be precise – he stole from the room after one last, swift look at the desolate figure upon the bed, at the pools of blood upon the floor, and the collops of human flesh – sliced off her still-warm body – he had placed upon the table. He had attired himself in his fresh clothing and had covered his bruises, so far as his face was concerned, with grease-paint after the unutterable deed. He closed the door softly behind him, and glided out into the darkness of the dull November morning.

Go, thou Man of Blood! For the moment, thou art free. But thy hour is at hand!

29. The Pursuit Continued

Mortemer Slade, fresh from unexampled brutalities, stole away from Miller's Court in the chill of the November morning uncertain where to go or what to do. Some inspiration seemed to tell him that his career of unbridled territory was nearing its end. The events of the past few weeks, the free play he had given to his bestial passions, the blood he had waded through had had the not unnatural effect of adding fuel and flame to the fire of his insanity. He found himself less able to restrain his gusts of tempestuous rage, less able and less willing to disguise and hide from his fellow men the fact that he was mad. Despair and desperation had entered into his ghoul-like soul. The satisfaction he derived from his acts of brute-like fury only lasted during their commission. Away from his victim, away from the sight and smell of their blood, he found that he loathed himself for being the thing he was. He cared little when the end came, or what form it took.

Where should he go? Whither should he wander? He had only a few pounds left, and he dare not make application to his solicitors or lawyers for more. He had become a social leper against whom every man's hand was directed, and to make himself known to a living soul would be to court instant disaster and detection. Stephen Darrell, he knew – and Phyllis's influential friends – would move heaven and earth and the waters under the earth to secure his capture. Edmund Blake could not be less eager to run him to earth in the vent of that gentleman being still in the land of the living. Stamford Street, as a retreat, was impossible; the empty house at Chislehurst had been taken possession of by the police and was closely watched; the woman who might have hidden him and sheltered him lay wallowing in her blood, a shapeless, horrible, mutilated figure, in the silent room in Miller's Court. Refuge he had none. There was nothing for him but the high road and the fields.

Walking swiftly through the labyrinths of mean streets, with suspicious glance from side to side, with hunted eyes, and uneasy gait, he endeavoured to control his distorted mind, and to form some plan for the future; but his brain was running riot and would not answer to his demand. He could not, try as he would, direct his thoughts to any fixed resolve. He could only see before him a grim procession of the women he had slain, keeping him ghostly company, and mocking him as they pointed, with lean, outstretched fingers, to the wounds he had inflicted. At the head of this unsightly troop was his last victim, who had given him food and shelter, and who now lay, on her bed, a spectacle of horror such as might appeal to the stoutest heart. He found himself idly speculating at what time the body might be expected to be found. Who would first enter that close room, reeking with the smell of blood? Who first would look upon the sightless eyes, and the porticoes of human flesh which lay rotting on the table? He had scooped out the woman's stomach, and had wantonly placed the boots she had worn in the gaping, ghastly cavity. He had cut off her breasts and hung her entrails upon the nails on the door. Who first would shudder at these spectral sights?

Even he, the monstrous maniac, with hands and heart dyed red with innocent blood, sickened at these and similar thoughts. What curse had been set upon him that he would have found nerve, and will, and strength to perpetrate such deeds? For once, he – the arch-fiend, the record murderer – shuddered at the mental reflection of himself.

He was standing just outside St Paul's. The great dome reared itself majestically in the grey

of the coming dawn. The clock struck the hour. What should he do? Whither should he go?

An overwhelming desire to keep moving, to tramp on – and on – and on, he knew and cared not whither – took possession of his soul. A strong, north-east wind was blowing, cuttingly cold and keen; but he heeded not its icy blast, for the spirit of the gale seemed in harmony with his own. He determined to seek the open country, the river. Perhaps there, standing on some desolate bank of the wintry Thames, he might be able to control his thoughts, and form some plan by which he might escape from the fate which seemed in store for him. It might be that, alone with nature, he would arrive at some decision as to his future course. He would walk on and on, through the busy, teeming streets into the quiet, country lanes, and there seek rest and peace and some decision as to the time to come.

At twelve o'clock that day – he had come at a great pace, and had never paused or rested on the way – he found himself at Weybridge, and, through the leafless trees, could see the dark, forbidding river swollen by recent heavy rains. The long tramp had wearied him, stiff and sore as he still was with the great battle in the train. The skies were sullen and overcast and seemed to whisper warning of a coming storm. One or two wayfarers, hurrying homewards before the threatened rain, glanced curiously at him as they passed, but he heeded them not, and fixed his tired and haggard eyes upon the river.

Entering the outskirts of the little riparian village, he passed a pleasant-looking inn, outside which stood a wagon and two fat and jolly-looking horses. He paused irresolutely. The sound of men's voices came to him from the open window of the bar. The waggoner was regaling himself with a pot of beer and indulging himself in friendly discourse with the landlord and one or two locals. Slade, pausing beneath the window, heard most of what was said.

'You'll find I'm right,' said the landlord. 'Mr East told me just afore you come in. "Any news from town?" I asks. "Yes," says he. "There's been another poor woman foully murdered in the East-end." "You don't say so?" says I, startled like. "Hacked to pieces," says he. "Worst case of the lot. It seems," he says, "that the landlord sent his son to a house in Miller's Court to collect the rent off a woman as had got a room there. The chap could make no one 'ear, so he moves a bit o' stuff as covered a 'ole in the window-pane, and looks in. He gives a screech and runs off for 'elp. They finds 'er, pore soul, 'acked to pieces." That's what Mr East says, and I'll stand on 'im.'

The waggoner drank his beer and rose to depart.

''Anging's too good and easy for that cove,' he said, sententiously. 'I'd like to 'ave 'im fixed down the road and then permission give me to drive my cart, fully loaded, and my two 'osses over 'im. Even that death, though, would be too gentle-like, strikes me!'

Slade stayed to hear no more. That hideous thing upon the bed had been found then. He thought that they could have found little else. He had dropped the trunk containing the clothing he had warn at Dover over London Bridge in the darkness.

He wandered on. Proceeding down a secluded lane, he came upon a wood, the trees in which were bare and leafless, and the ground beneath damp and clinging. But he felt that he must try to snatch some rest and some repose. His brain seemed on fire and every fibre of him ached. If he did not secure some sleep, how could he face and overcome the dangers that might be? He flung himself at full length beneath a hedge where the earth was fairly dry, and closed his tired and restless eyes. Sleep! Would the balmy restorer of all ills come to such as he? Could he forget, in the oblivion of slumber, for some few moments, the horrors of the past, the fears of the future? Sleep! It might mean all to him.

He slept – an uneasy, restless, dreadful slumber, peopled with ghosts and spectres of his lurid past. Dreams came to him, dreams of all that he had been, all that he was, and all that he might become. He saw himself the centre of an admiring and cheering crowd of students outside his college at Oxford University. He had just taken high honours, and all were predicting for him a distinguished and honourable career. There he was amongst them, in cap and gown, a slim and graceful figure, tall and dark, proud of his reception, and glorying in the homage his friends. He saw himself again, the centre of a throng of furious men and women, clamouring for his life. The police had him in their charge and were bringing him up for trial. The people swarmed about them endeavouring to drag him from the protection of the law, cursing him, spitting at him, reviling him, and threatening to tear him limb from limb. The officers of justice battled to keep him in their midst, and to save him from the vengeance of the mob. They got him to the court, and there before him sat the judge in crimson and ermine who, with the twelve grave men in the jury-box, held his fate in the hollow of his hand. 'To be detained during Her Majesty's pleasure.' He heard the words pronounced and saw the wardens, stalwart, stern-faced men, motion him to leave the dock and follow them to the gloomy cells below. He heard his own last shriek of madness and despair, and saw himself, an inmate for life of the criminal lunatic asylum, re-enacting again and yet again the slaughter of those fallen women. He saw his own body at last huddled, lime-covered into a shameless, nameless grave. And he saw the devils below welcoming his spirit with hideous smiles and mocking gestures of welcome. So he slept and dreamed.

A man who had come upon him as he slept – who had approached the recumbent figure with soft and stealthy tread – stood over him and watched him as he groaned and moaned in this uneasy slumber. The wretched sleeper had talked aloud and raved, unconsciously, about his victims. The things, awful, unspeakable, which he had said made even this hardy listener's blood run cold. He gazed upon the dreaming man with fascinated horror.

'Yus,' he whispered, bending over to get a clearer view of his features. 'It's the very man – the man who carried that good lidy to the empty 'ouse and chained 'er to the wall. Left 'er to die, he did. Wanted to kill, he did, the lidy as has been good to my little one, and was werry good to me. If ever I see that man again, I was to communicate with Mr E. Blake. Well, I've seed him again, and I'm goin' to let Mr Blake now. 'ow? Why, the teligraft, in course. I'll just steal back to the village and I'll send that there message over the wires. Then I'll come back and I won't lose sight of you again, my sleeping beauty.' With gentle tread, the watcher stole away, and still the wretch slept on.

He awoke with a start and a cry. Soft rain was falling on his unprotected face, and dusk was creeping on. Even that nightmare of sleep, disturbed as it had been, had somewhat refreshed him, and his limbs no longer ached with pain and want of rest. He rose and stretched himself, shaking off from his garments a few decayed leaves and twigs. He was conscious of being hungry and thirsty, and of feeling cold. There was money in his pockets. He would buy food, and then, perhaps, he would collect his thoughts and decide for once and all upon some line of action. How irresolute, uncertain, undecided he had become. How he ceased to care when and how the end might come.

He left the wood and sought and found again the main road. Entering the village he sought about for a quiet, obscure inn where he might eat and drink and gain strength for a tramp through the night. Whither? It did not matter. Let blind chance lead him where it will. He would keep on.

He entered a small ale-house and took a seat by a rough table near the bar. His good clothing attracted some little attention from the woman who served him with beer and cheese, but not more so than his haunted, haggard looks. Two villagers were also in the room, drinking together from the same pot. Slade ate and drank with feverish haste. He could not remain still. He must be up and going. Whither? On. That was all he knew. He would keep on. A tramp, bronzed and jovial, entered the little bar and called for ale. He seated himself near Slade and on him the murderer turned his haggard gaze.

'You know the neighbourhood?' he asked, pushing away his empty plate and handing up his glass to be replenished.

'Man and boy,' said the tramp. 'I've known these parts for nigh on forty year. A stranger 'ere, gov'nor?'

'Yes. Is Pangbourne far away?'

'Pangbourne?' repeated the tramp, wiping his lips. 'Not far. You could heel and toe it in two 'ours and a bit. Pretty place, too, in the summer.'

Why had he asked? Slade did not know. But Pangbourne would do as well as another. He would get a bed there, and perhaps in the morning some plan might suggest itself to him. Perhaps he would decide to go abroad. In the morning. On. In the meanwhile, he would keep on.

'I daresay,' he said, 'they'd put me up at Pangbourne?'

'There's inns there, sir,' said the landlady.

'Try the Dog and Partridge,' remarked the tramp. 'I've 'eard as 'ow gents stay there in the summer.'

Slade rose and paid his score. He offered the men a drink. The two rustics accepted with alacrity a fresh supply of beer, but the tramp gravely shook his head. No, he would have no more just then. He was sure he would have no more just then.

Out upon the road again. Towards Pangbourne. The rain came down heavily and streamed off his hat and boots as he strode along. A night's rest and a warm supper would put him to rights, he told himself often as he walked. And brandy; plenty of brandy. Then he would make up his mind what it was best to do. Meanwhile, on! He would keep on!

30. The Pursuit Grows Warm

Filled with rage and disappointment – and disgust at his own carelessness in dropping the card-case which had given Slade the clue to his identity – Blake, stiff and sore, bandaged and plastered, returned to town. No bones had been broken in his fall from the train, which, fortunately, was then proceeding at a very slow rate; but his escape from death, or serious injury, was hardly less than miraculous. His *amour propre* was now intensely aroused. He had himself crossed swords with Mortemer Slade and had been worsted at all points. Blake was not devoid of a certain amount of self-esteem, and he burned to compensate himself for his colossal failure. He returned to London more than ever determined to capture Slade 'off his own bat' as he expressed it. His prey should not, he vowed, escape him again. But there might not, he told himself, come to him an opportunity again of bringing the East-end reign of terror to an end. Slade had got clear away, and it might be a matter of extreme difficulty to get upon his track again.

The detective heard of the awful discovery in Miller's Court with feelings of rage and astonishment. It was clear to him that, after this prolonged struggle in the train, his enemy had made his way across the fields and in some way obtained a lift towards London. A bicycle had been stolen from an outhouse close to the village near which the train had been stopped, and Blake, rightly enough, concluded that the murderer had used the machine to reach London, arriving in time to commit the awful crime which had again plunged the whole of England in a state of the utmost frenzy.

Early in the afternoon of the day on which this barbarity was discovered, Blake, sitting in his office at the Gower Street rooms, received a telegram. It had been handed in at Weybridge post office half an hour before, and ran as follows:

Blake, 74 Gower Street, London, W.C.
  Slade is here. I'm watching him. Come next train.
  Will meet it. – Smiler

The detective was overjoyed to receive the message. He looked up the next train and departed in the fastest hansom he knew of, one he customarily employed when engaged on work in which speed was of first importance. He had met Smiler. Sarah Watts had made her preserver known to him, and he was aware that the tramp, in his gratitude to the 'lidy' who had befriended his little motherless girl, was entirely to be trusted. It had been arranged between them that if, in his wanderings, Smiler should come across the man he had seen carrying Sarah Watts into the empty house at Chislehurst, he should instantly let Blake know, and should, pending the latter's arrival upon the scene of action, keep a close watch upon the movements of the wanted man.

'You scored last time, Mr Slade,' muttered Blake, grimly, as the train ran through a riverside station. 'But it may now be my turn.'

He alighted at Weybridge and was met by the faithful Smiler.

'Where is he?' was his first question.

'On the road, walking, between here and Pangbourne,' returned Smiler, touching his greasy, torn cap.

'You are sure?'

'Sartin. He asked me the way. He is going to stop the night there, and asked where he could obtain a bed. The Dog and Partridge was mentioned, and I suspects, sir, he has gone there. With a fast 'orse we could overtake him on the road. He's a desperit-lookin' villin, sir. I'm a angel of light by the side of him.'

Blake strode towards the exit of the station. No time was to be lost. At all hazards the madman must be taken, alive or dead.

'Can you drive?' he asked.

'Can a duck swim?' Smiler replied eagerly. 'Drive, sir? Yus, anything that stands on four legs – or three and a swinger for that matter.'

'Where can I hire a trap?'

'At the Castle, sir. If you'll go in the bar parlour and wait, I'll have the 'orse in the shafts, and the trap ready in a brace o' shakes.' So saying the willing Smiler – eager to oblige, in any way he could, a friend of the 'good lidy' – ran on, leaving Blake to follow at a more leisurely pace.

'I must be neither over-bold nor over-cautious,' thought the detective. 'Another personal encounter with this fiend might do for me altogether, though I reckon myself strong and in first-rate training. Well, I'll get to this inn, the Dog and Partridge, first, and let things shape themselves.'

In ten minutes, thanks to the energetic Smiler, they were bowling along the road to Pangbourne. The rain was falling heavily and the ground was muddy and sodden; but the horse was a good one – Smiler had seen to that – and they were doing their ten or eleven miles per hour even in the sticky 'going'. It was a dark night and a lonely road; indeed, they scarcely passed a single pedestrian upon the way. Smiler kept up a running conversation as they sped along; but Blake, muffled to the ears and sheltered beneath an umbrella, rarely spoke, and devoted his whole brain to the problem before him. He wished to take Slade himself, alone. It was dangerous work. How could it best be done?

He directed Smiler to pull up as they entered the deserted village street. From the cottages on either side of the road glowed many a lamp and candle, throwing a ruddy glare upon the pools of water which the heavy rains had formed. Blake sprung out of the trap.

'I leave you here,' he said, and felt for some loose change.

'Lor' love yer, sir!' Smiler replied, 'ain't yer goin' to let me assist you in the capture of the murderin' villin?'

Blake gave a gesture of dissent. 'My work must be done alone,' he said. 'You will take the horse and trap back to the inn from which we hired them. Then you will go to the local police station and hand this note, which I wrote while the conveyance was being prepared, to the inspector in charge. He will understand, and do as he is instructed. I don't question your fidelity or usefulness, Smiler, and I don't doubt your courage. But my game, successful or not, must be played alone. I have a long account of old scores to settle with this man. The place and the hour for a final adjustment have arrived. We shall meet again.'

He dismissed him with a nod and stood in the middle of the road watching the retreating trap, and the receding lights it bore, till it was swallowed up in the blackness. He was alone. The orchestra had finished, and the curtain was about to rise on the last day of the drama.

In the meanwhile, Mortimer Slade had reached the little inn, situated in the main street, to which he had been recommended. It was a pretty enough home, standing back in a garden, which in the summer months was a mass of roses, jasmine, and the stately hollyhock. Its brick walls were covered with ivy, the growth of years; and at the back flowed the Thames, now swollen to unusual and almost alarming proportions. They knew something of floods at Pangbourne, and the older villagers, gathered together in the homely taproom of the inn, looked wise, and shook their heads when the weather – or, for that matter, the river – was alluded to. Slade, tired, damp, and dispirited, entered the small bar parlour, which was dignified by the name of the Select Room, and was reserved, in the summer, for those tourists or fishermen who might be making the inn their temporary home. In the winter months a stranger in their midst was of rare occurrence, and his advent, had it been known, would have excited much speculation amongst the simple villagers drinking mild ale and smoking clay pipes in the public room.

A pert young barmaid – an importation from London – regarded him curiously. The stranger was well dressed, though he appeared to be nearly wet through, and seemed to her to be well spoken. His eyes, however, had a look which, as she afterwards explained, 'made her shudder, they went through her so!' To this young lady, beribboned and bejewelled, Slade addressed himself, she watching him the while.

'I am detained here,' he said, with an effort – 'sorely against my will, a riverside place like this being neither the most agreeable nor convenient of spots at this season of the year – on business which it is impossible for me to conclude till the morning. I should like to avail myself of the hospitality of this inn. Have you a bedroom vacant?'

'Oh, yes,' said the pert damsel. 'We don't get many visitors at this time of year. It will be half a crown.'

Producing that coin, Slade ordered six-pennyworth of brandy hot, and declined to order any supper. Then mental and physical exhaustion held him in their remorseless grip – despair and desperation preyed on his vitals – and food was out of the question. Rest was all he wanted, a night's rest. That granted, he would wake up a new man in the morning and ready to continue his daring game with fate.

A little later, warmed by the generous spirit, he ordered more brandy, and they brought him an evening paper which had just arrived. Its columns were full of the sickening details of the latest 'Ripper' atrocity, and Slade smiled a little grimly as he saw his own gruesome deed described. Much space was devoted to the appalling crime; and, by way of postscript, he read the following paragraph, which told him that his inveterate foe was alive and ready to track him down. The correspondent wrote:

> In connection with the awful murder in Miller's Court, we have to record that Mr Edmund Blake, the eminent private detective, who has devoted himself with tireless energy to the elucidation of this mystery, and who is known to hold very decided opinions as to the identity of the unknown miscreant, was the object of a murderous attack in a railway carriage while travelling from Dover to London. He was hurled from the train, but miraculously escaped all serious injury, and is now back at his rooms in Gower Street. His assailant escaped in the darkness, but we understand that he is known, and that his arrest is imminent.

He threw the paper aside with a muttered curse. Blake alive and uninjured! What respite would he give him ere continuing the pursuit? Would he escape if they should meet again? Was Blake, after all, destined to accomplish his overthrow?

He sat drinking morosely, and brooding over his own terrible thoughts, till ten o'clock, when he asked for a candle and the number of his room. The aggressive barmaid – amazed that a gentleman could consume so much brandy with so little effect – handed him over to a smart chambermaid, who ventured to indulge in some trifling verbal pleasantry as she conducted him above stairs. Most male visitors chucked attractive chambermaids under the chin when being lighted upstairs – or such, at least, was this one's experience. Slade, however, received her advances with an icy stare, which sent her below much quicker than she had ascended. He shut the door and locked it upon the inside, surveying the apartment by the light of the candle held aloft in his hand. It was a room of good size, looking towards the rear of the house, and substantially furnished. Below was the stable-yard and beyond that a meadow and then the river on the swollen crest of which, pale and watery, cast an intermittent gleam. The bed was a great four-poster of antiquated style, but the sheets and pillows were white as driven snow and looked cool and inviting. He went to the window, threw it open, and gazed out upon the night. The rain was still falling, and great banks of cloud sailed past in the dark and lowering skies. Voices reached him from the stable-yard. Two men were talking; ostlers or the like. He could hear them tending to the horse and conversing as they went about their work.

'Inspector Mannering,' said one, 'and a big detective covey from London. They come into the tap and orders drinks as cool as may be. "We were told to ask for Mr B.," says the London chap. "Has he left any message?" The barman does a stare and says he'll go and inquire. Comes back and says, mysterious like, "If you'll step into the dining room, gents, the missus will see you." What's in the wind, I wonder?'

'Dunno. Someone's been a-doin' somethin' he didn't oughter, I s'pose.'

'A few minutes after another gent – tall, with a long strip of sticking plaster on his forehead – comes in and says to Jack, the barman, "Tell your mistress Mr B. will see those gentlemen now," and he goes in and joins the others. Presently he comes out again, but the other two coves – that there Mannering from Weybridge and the other – are still in the 'ouse. Wonder if it's anything to do with them 'orrible murders.'

'T'ain't likely! I 'spects it's over that burglary business at Datchet. Dang that bay mare! She won't keep still.'

Slade crept away from the window. The police were here, in the house! And Mr B.! Who could that mean but his pursuer? What should he do? How could he escape? He was hemmed in on all sides. Blake had doubtless telegraphed for assistance, and the inn was surrounded. At any moment they might be knocking at the door, demanding admission in the queen's name.

31. The End of the Chase

Mortimer Slade stood in the centre of the room, a prey to a hundred conflicting emotions. The end had come at last, ten. Blake was determined to take no more chances. This time it was to be a fight to the finish. Well, all that remained to him was to sell dearly his life or his liberty.

He crept to the door and listened. A silence seemed to have fallen upon the inn, though it was barely closing time, and the voices of the few roysterers in the taproom were stilled. In what part of the house the detectives were he could not conjecture, but it was evident that Blake had left them there to prevent his departure while he himself was away. His one hope seemed to lie in Blake's absence. The detective obviously did not intend to immediately arrest him, or he, too, would have remained on the premises. Gathering his wits together, and concentrating his hitherto wandering thoughts with one mighty mental effort, he began to speculate on his chances of escape. But first he began to wonder how Blake had succeeded in running him to earth. He had not been seen to leave the house in Miller's Court, and no one had followed him on his tramp to Weybridge. But it was idle to ask himself such questions. The fact remained that Blake was here, and that, doubtful of the issue of another personal encounter, he had enlisted the services of the local police. Slade was unarmed. The keen, razor-like weapon with which he had hideously mutilated his victims he still retained, but a revolver would have been worth, in his present position, a dozen such. He cursed himself that he was unprovided with any weapon of offence. Had he had one, he might have shot Blake and then turned the weapon on himself, and thus involved the two of them in one common death.

He returned to the window, which was open at the bottom, and listened again. The two stable-helps had retired from the yard, and the place was silent and deserted. A clock near at hand struck eleven. It was closing time, and he could hear doors opening and shutting and retreating footsteps as the few customers remaining at that late hour betook themselves homeward. It was clear that, whatever Blake's plans might be, he did not intend to disturb him tonight. Doubtless a watch was kept upon the door and any attempts to escape that way would be frustrated. There remained to him the window.

He threw himself, dressed as he was, upon the bed and waited. In two or three hours the inmates of the house would doubtless be asleep, tired after a hard day's work. The detectives would be on the watch, but he did not despair of escaping from the back, and in any case, he was determined to make the attempt. 'It's life or death,' he said. 'I begin to feel that! I care little which it is.'

He heard it strike one, and two and three o'clock. At the latter hour he rose softly and again listened at the door of the room. Not a sound reached his straining ears. Silence reigned. He turned the key in the lock and, opening the door, glanced fearfully around. His room was the first, facing the staircase, of four or five in a long, low passage. The doors of the other rooms were closed, and it was impossible to tell whether or not they were occupied. Shutting and locking the door again, he stole gently to the window and opened it with as little noise as possible to its fullest extent. The drop to the ground was about eighteen feet. The ground was flagged beneath, and he did not relish the idea of a fall from that height upon the stones. He could not drop the distance without making a noise that would disturb the house. Absolute silence was the only chance.

Along the side of the window, just within reach of his hand, ran a drainpipe which emptied itself into the gutter below. There was room between this pipe and the wall for him to get a firm grip of it, and he would trust to luck to find a foothold. If he could lower himself softly and silently in this way he might get off under cover of darkness. There was a wall to be scaled at the further end of the yard, but this, he thought, would present little difficulties. He was stiff and more from lying on the damp ground, and from the struggle with Blake; but dread of capture had made him forget his bodily ills and had given him renewed strength and agility. He got out of the open window, and, clasping the pipe in his powerful hands, sought for a niche in which to plant his feet. The house was an old one, and, fortunately for him, the bricks in the wall were rough and uneven. Thus he obtained a foothold and was able, with infinite care to lower himself noiselessly to the ground.

He glanced fearfully about. Great clouds obscured the pale moon and a heavy rain was falling. The yard was very dark, and by keeping close to the wall which ran along its side he might hope to reach the end of it unperceived by anyone who might be at the window of the inn. He took two or three steps forward and paused. There rang out on the night air the deep baying of a hound. The animal was evidently chained up somewhere near at hand. Curse the dog! How it barked! He moved on a few steps, and he could now see a huge mastiff tearing at its chain in a vain effort to reach him. The hound's eyes glowed like coals alive with fire. Its deep bay, threatening, furious, would arouse the house, if not the neighbourhood. To scale the wall at the end of the yard it was necessary for him to pass the dog. Already he heard the sound of someone stirring and the opening of a window in the inn behind him. He drew forth the sharp stiletto he carried and moved on. With a roar like that of a lion the great dog sprang upon him and bore him to the earth. Its fangs fastened themselves in his throat. With a sharp, indrawn cry of acute pain, Slade plunged his weapon into the dog's side near the heart. Again and again he stabbed. The grip about his throat relaxed, and, with a sigh and a sob, the hound rolled over. It was dead.

He staggered to his feet. Was it his imagination, or did he really hear a shout behind him? Was there someone, a man, gazing at him from a window of the inn?

He seized a three-legged stool which stood near, and, springing upon it, reached the top of the wall. He flung himself over it without a look behind, and dropped on soft and sodden earth beneath. Up again, he darted across a meadow, at the end of which stood a belt of bare and spectral trees, beyond which the sullen, swollen river, now in flood, glistened and gleamed. He could hear the murmur of waters in the distance. The river was a roaring torrent about the weir.

He was on the river bank, the towing path. Heedless of where he ran, he tore along this path, fear lending him wings. Lower down he might cross the bridge and find his way into the main road. He would retrace his steps to London. With the start he had he might reasonably hope to give his pursuers the slip and hide himself again in the labyrinths of the great city. If he was to fail, if he was to be caught, then he would bare his own breast to the knife and die, cursing them all and laughing at their disappointment. He tore on. The floods had swollen the river to the very edge of the banks, and he could hear the water splashing about his feet as he ran. The wind and rain lashed the usually calm waters of the Thames into a roaring, seething sea. A great noise of tossing, foaming water, which came from a place some half a mile along the bank, told him that he was close to the weir. There he might cross the river and hide himself in the tangled brushwood of the opposite bank for a brief breathing space. He could not tell whether or not he was pursued. The rush of waters drowned almost any other sound. He held the dripping knife in his hand and ran on.

In a few minutes he had reached the lock. He could see, as the clouds about the moon momentarily lifted, great waves of water beating like mad furies against the woodwork. The gates were closed. The path by which he might cross was a narrow one, but he could guide himself over by the great beam and reach the opposite shore in safety. Near at hand was a cottage, the habitation of the lock-keeper. The place was in darkness. Doubtless the man was in bed and snoring. Nothing need be feared from him. He set foot upon the wooden steps leading to the narrow bridge and prepared to cross. As he took the first step the figure of a man standing on the drawbridge, halfway across the lock, presented itself before him, barring his path.

A great storm had been gathering which he had not observed. At the moment that Slade saw the figure in his path, a stupendous flash of lightning, following a peal of thunder, which echoed throughout the valley of the Thames, revealed the face of the man before him. He gave a startled cry. Before him stood Edmund Blake.

'Fool and madman!' cried the detective. 'To think that you could avert your doom. I watched your escape and came to this spot, for which I saw you were making, by a shorter way. Mortemer Slade, your career of crime is over. Your chances of escape are absolutely gone. Behind you the way is barred. Were the wind less high and the waters less disturbed you would hear the foot treads of the men I placed to watch your room in the inn. They are close upon you now. In front of you, to prevent your passage, here I am. Yield, then, and to me, for resistance is useless, and no human effort can prevent your capture.'

Again a roar of thunder and a blinding flash. Slade winced as the tongue of flame tore round him, seeming to envelop him in its fiery folds. But he rose majestically to the occasion. He braced himself for a great effort and drew himself to his full height.

'I have foiled you once or twice before,' he cried in a voice which even the gale and the roar of waters could not deaden. 'Upon your own head be your fate. Here you shall die. These greedy waves shall have your body, and may the devil take your soul.'

Throwing the bloodstained knife into the river, as though he disdained to meet his foe with other than nature's weapons, Slade advanced along the bridge of the lock. Blake did not budge. His trained hearing caught the sound of men advancing rapidly along the path by which Slade had come. He could even hear the voice of Inspector Mannering shouting his own name as he neared the lock. In a few moments they would be here to help him secure the madman. Meanwhile, he would trust to his own strength to detain his foe. He could have shot him dead, but he was determined to take him, his prisoner, alive.

Slade advanced. When only a few feet separated the two men he made a bound like a panther and seized Blake in his long and sinewy arms. There was a roar of thunder, like the crack of doom. A flash of light, turning the heavens into an inferno, illumined the scene. The two men, locked in each other's arms, tearing at each other's throats, gazed into each other's eyes. The madman, striving to beat away the hold which Blake kept upon the beam of the lock, endeavoured to force his opponent over the slender bridge into the wild gulf of waters below. Blake, intent on keeping his hold and balance with one hand, had a tight grip of Slade's throat by the other. This time they seemed equally matched. The dauntless courage of the detective equalled the maniacal strength of the other.

With shouts and cries, a party of men, five or six in number, headed by the inspector from Weybridge, reached the edge of the lock on the bank nearer to Slade. The family of the lock-keeper, too, had thrown open their windows, and were gazing in amazed wonder at the desperate struggle on the bridge.

'I can hold him,' shouted Blake, exultantly. 'Do not fire. He must be taken alive.'

Mannering lowered his revolver and prepared to cross the bridge and seize the murderer from behind. As he made the first step, however, the heavens above him seemed to crack and open. A roar, as of the accumulated artilleries of all the military powers of the world, rent and shook the earth. Following this peal of thunder came a flash of lightning which blinded and staggered the beholders. Mannering, falling back upon the bank, looked up and saw the awful light seize and wither the two men upon the bridge as a wisp of straw is consumed by the fire. It had struck them, inflicting an instantaneous death as by an act of God. The horrified beholders saw the two bodies, still entwined in a desperate embrace, totter and fall from the bridge into the seething, tumbling waters below. Without warning, without a last prayer for divine mercy and forgiveness, two souls had gone to their account. The murderer's career was indeed at an end, but his fate had involved the death of the man who had sworn to bring him to book. Faithfully Blake kept his word. A martyr to the cause of duty, he was dead.

Conclusion

Thus perished, by the visitation of the Most High, a monster such as the world may never see again. The body of the mad surgeon was recovered from the river many days after the great storm. His identity was established, and he was buried as a pauper in a nameless grave, his relatives refusing to associate themselves in any manner with his career or death. That he was Mortemer Slade, the escaped lunatic, the police were well aware, and many of them did not hesitate to privately declare that, with his fate, the career of Jack the Ripper was brought to an end. But the knowledge of the facts which might have proved beyond dispute his connection with the awful Whitechapel crimes died with Edmund Blake. Only the great detective, now lying in a watery grave – for his body was never discovered – could have established the exact truth.

Phyllis Penrose and Stephen Darrell were married the following year. Stephen decided to embark, now that he was well endowed with this world's goods, upon a political career. In this his unquestionable talents soon availed to bring him to the front, and in his real identity – for I have written of him under an assumed name – he is greatly admired and respected in the House. He and his beautiful wife devote much of their time and income to the amelioration of the conditions under which the poor live in the squalid courts and alleys of the East-end. A Home for the Poor, Destitute and Fallen Women owes its origin to him, and he is still the largest subscriber to its funds. His son is called Edmund, after the friend whose terrible death he never ceases to lament.

The Earl of Caversham died of gout upon the heart two years after the marriage of his youngest daughter. There was no heir to succeed the title and the rather impoverished estates, and the earldom is now extinct. He left behind him the materials for a work entitled *The Deterioration of our Race Horses and How We Can Arrest It*, which has since become a classic. Not by much else is his name remembered.

Mrs Sarah Watts, retired from any participation, active or passive, in the 'gentle art' of detection since the death of Edmund Blake, still resides in the little cottage at Denham, and is devoted to her flowers. She has enough affection left, however, to bestow a goodly portion upon Mary, daughter of the man Smiler who had rescued her from the clutches of Mortemer Slade, and it is whispered that this Mary, grown into a bewitching young woman, will be 'passing rich' when the 'good lidy' – as Smiler calls her – is taken away.

That last-named worthy still tramps the countryside, and contrives to keep himself, for the 'lidy's' sake, out of serious trouble. He was much concerned at the death of Edmund Blake, and is still secretly convinced that had he remained with the detective that stormy night at Pangbourne, his doom might have been avoided. He is a constant visitor to the cottage at Denham, and is not more proud of his pretty daughter than he is of the 'good lidy' who cherishes her so dearly.

Edmund Blake willed £500 to Jack Dagenham. Enriched by this sum, and rendered wiser and better in character by experience, that young man returned one day to Broxbourne and incontinently asked Alice Baxter to marry him. The maiden was nothing loth; and, though her father viewed the match with a disfavour which even time and circumstance could not overcome, the marriage proved a success. Mr and Mrs Dagenham are a very happy couple, and the former is a popular host of a pleasant little country hotel.

Those gentle youths, Bleater and Blinder, never learnt the nature of the fate that had overtaken their sinister and mysterious patron. They heard no more, and saw no more, of Mortemer Slade. He vanished from the environment of their sordid lives like a spent bubble. They often talked of him and wondered what had been his end. They regretted the loss of him on account of the sovereigns that came from his apparently inexhaustible purse.

'"E were a wrong 'un, that's certain sure,' said Bleater with a sigh on these occasions, 'but his quids were as good as gold.'

'Wish we could see the colour of 'em agin,' his friend would answer.

They ultimately got into serious trouble with the police, and were lost to sight, to memory dear, for a long time on account of a little burglarious miscalculation. Since then Bleater and Blinder have been in and out of prison with remarkable regularity. Gaol-birds they are, and such will they remain.

Other murders – of unfortunate women – followed hard upon the death of Mortemer Slade, and those crimes, mostly occurring in the 'Far East' of London, have been generally attributed to the fiend who will always be designated 'Jack the Ripper'. But they were merely fraudulent imitations of the real and genuine article. The Whitechapel demon died when Mortemer Slade went to his long account.

May the world be free for the future of all such wretches as semi-sane and dangerous as he!

3
Guy Logan's Later Career

The True History of Jack the Ripper attracted positive notice from the readership of *The Illustrated Police News*, and Guy's literary career was looking brighter than ever before. He became a permanent contributor to this newspaper, with a not inconsiderable output of poetry and prose, as well as several articles on the history of crime. It must have been a disappointment to him that none of his early novels were ever published in book form. Whereas *Violet Kildare* was admittedly a forgettable production, the title of *The True History of Jack the Ripper* alone would have sold thousands of books. It is a mystery indeed why no enterprising publisher took it on, when they could have bought the rights from *The Illustrated Police News* for a pittance.

It is of course unfair to severely criticise a novel that is more than a hundred years old, but it must be remarked that in spite of its exciting subject-matter and racy plot, Guy Logan's *The True History of Jack the Ripper* is a worthy exponent of the working man's fiction of the time.[1] Although definitely superior to many of the other cheap novels of the time, it is superficial, formulaic and shows signs of having been written in a hurry. Guy may well have assumed that the Ripper, aka Dr Mortemer Slade, had gone insane due to neurosyphilis contracted from a prostitute, but this is never stated implicitly in the novel, meaning that the reader is left to wonder what really drives this madman. If Slade's previous history is left unstated, it does not make sense for him to murder unknown prostitutes, whereas his former lady friend Phyllis Penrose, who jilted him and then left him to rot in the lunatic asylum, is only treated to a few frights. Too little is made of the novel (at the time) theory that Jack the Ripper knew Mary Kelly, and used her room in Miller's Court as his hideout.

As we know, Guy Logan believed that one plot was not enough for a novel. He probably had a pre-existing idea of a play or short story about a neurotic young man who is tricked by an evil doctor into believing that he suffers from some kind of lethal heart defect. After the young man broke up his engagement, believing that he would soon be a corpse, he left the field open for the said doctor to steal his girlfriend. This sub-plot was added to the Ripper novel, to unhappy effect. As for the great detective Edmund Burke, he is a carbon copy of Sherlock Holmes, complete with his Watson-like sidekick Ralph Thorpe. It is unfortunate that the stalwart Thorpe disappears in mid-novel, leaving the detective alone and unprotected when the time has come for some fisticuffs. Guy was probably a great admirer of Conan Doyle's Holmes stories, as judged by the profusion of great consulting detectives in his fictional output, and the two Reichenbach-like climaxes of *The True History of Jack the Ripper*.

Nor was the 'Lady Detective' Sarah Watts, who makes such a short-lived and anticlimactic appearance in the novel, exactly a new invention. Female detectives abounded in the cheap detective novels of the era: *The Illustrated Police News* had once serialised *The Romantic Revelations of a Lady Detective*, and one of George R. Sims' novels featured a successful female consulting detective named Dorcas Dene.[2] The bludgeon-wielding roughs employed by the Ripper hark back to Professor Moriarty's similarly armed accomplice in *The Final Problem*, and one is tempted to quote P. G. Wodehouse: 'A rough with a bludgeon! Gad, sir, if I were a fiend in human shape with a brain of the first order I would think up something a little better than roughs with bludgeons.'

*

Not long after *The True History of Jack the Ripper* had been published, Guy Logan met the young part-time actress Ellen Mary Norman. Although Guy was by now in his mid-thirties, and Nell, as he called her, barely out of her teens, they fell in love and wanted to marry. The problem was of course that Guy's estranged wife Melville was still very much alive, and cohabiting with Harry Verner at a farm in Whitehall near Dereham. To be able to marry Nell, Guy went to consult Morris & Rickard Solicitors, of No. 4 Mitre Court, and in March 1907, he made a petition for divorce in the High Court of Justice.[3]

In his petition, Guy Bertie Harris Logan, of No. 83 Palmerston Road, Wimbledon, pointed out that although he had married Melville Stroud in June 1891, and cohabited with her at Fife Road, Kingston-upon-Thames, and at No. 294 Kennington Road in London, she had deserted him in 1893, never to return. She had for many years been living with Harry Verner at Whitehall near Dereham, and had frequently committed adultery with this individual. One would have thought that after living apart from Guy for not less than fourteen years, Melville would consent to divorce him, but for some reason or other, quite possibly sheer spitefulness, she would not agree to a divorce. She and Harry Verner employed solicitors of their own to contest the petition, which was finally dismissed on 31 December 1907.

This rebuff from the High Court of Justice did not prevent Guy from cohabiting with his beloved Nell. The 1911 Census lists Guy Logan, now aged forty-two, as a sporting journalist, living with his 'wife' Ellen Mary Norman Logan, and their two children, two-year-old Leslie Guy and six-month-old Phyllis Muriel. Guy and Nell could afford to employ a nursemaid to look after the children, an indication that Guy had finally been able to save some money, or more probably that he had received a legacy from one of his wealthy relatives; nor can it be ruled out that Nell had some kind of private income of her own.

*

Since publishing Guy Logan's *The True History of Jack the Ripper*, *The Illustrated Police News* occasionally kept serialising various sensational novels, some of them with 'fierce' titles like Douglas Stewart's contributions *The Wild Tribes of London* and *The Fiend of the Bomb, or the Anarchist's Doom.* In 1910, Guy himself made a comeback with *The Dread Secret*, a sanguinary fantasy that owed part of its plot to 'Monk' Lewis and its title to Wilkie Collins' relatively little-known novel *The Dead Secret*.[4] It was followed by *The Green Room Mystery*, a feeble Sherlock Holmes pastiche.[5] His next offering, *Circumstantial Evidence, or the Making of Paul Menteth*, does not have the exciting action of *The True History of Jack the Ripper*, but it offers a more realistic plot.[6] The eponymous hero is a feeble drunkard and gambler, who has tired of life after his wife wantonly deserted him for a certain Frank Chalmers. One evening, when walking home from a country pub, Paul chances upon a stray dog. The animal leads him to the corpse of a murdered man, and Paul runs away in a state of hysteria. The racecourse blackguard Jerry Hawker makes sure that Paul is arrested by the police when attending the Gatwick Races. The murder victim turns out to be Frank Chalmers. But Paul's loyal sister Mary and her boyfriend John Pettifer are determined to prove his innocence. They hire the consulting detective Leo Sternhold to find the real culprit, and in spite of some fisticuffs with racecourse blackguards with names like 'Hackney Jem' and 'Smiler Jenkins', the great detective prevails in the end. It was of course Paul's former wife, a thoroughly modern woman who flirts with noblemen and consorts with crooks, who got tired of Frank Chalmers and paid a blackguard named Ginger Blake to kill him, before plotting to 'frame' her estranged husband Paul for the crime.

Guy's next offering, *The Mystery of a Second-Class Carriage*, is more interesting since it is clearly based on a real crime.[7] In 1897, the barmaid Miss Elizabeth Camp was found dead in a second-class carriage on the South Western Railway, beaten to death with a large pestle. In spite of a multitude of clues, the murder was never solved. In Guy's version, woman of mystery Elizabeth Strood is found battered to death in a second-class carriage, and Detective Inspector Bates investigates. He is helped by a young man named Archie Cairns, the private secretary of the wealthy Sir Dennis Dalrymple. It turns out that the real Sir Dennis has been murdered by a South African crook named Jack Donellan, who then usurped his name and title without any difficulty. Elizabeth Strood, another native of South Africa, came to England to expose him, only to be murdered by the pseudo-baronet as a precautionary measure. The prolific Guy went on to write *The Convict's Daughter*, thrillingly subtitled 'A Romance of the White Slave Traffic', and the theatrical melodrama *The Lure of the Limelight*. In *Dark Deeds, The Ordeal of Kenneth Kenworthy* the hero is the famous consulting detective Mortimer Stroud, and the plot is based on the murder of a man named John Miskin and his housekeeper Sarah Dyson, by a burglar named John Seaman. Again, this plot is loosely based on a real crime: the murder of Mr Levy and his housekeeper Sarah Gale by the burglar William Seaman in 1896.

At the outbreak of the First World War, *The Illustrated Police News* was ready for another orgy of ultra-patriotism. Admittedly, unlike the harmless Boers who had only amused themselves with the occasional strip-searching of English ladies, and the use of various dubious military ruses, the dastardly Huns excelled in brutal and sanguinary outrages. This time, the artists of *The Illustrated Police News* did not need to exaggerate when describing the German war crimes in Belgium and France: the wholesale murder of civilians, the burning of churches and cathedrals, and the shooting of Nurse Cavell. *The Illustrated Police*

News lost no time before employing their star author to produce another stirring novel to inflame the patriotism among its readers. As we know, Guy was something of a 'card', and he thought nothing of reusing the characters he had invented for *Violet Kildare* with their names slightly changed.

The early chapters of Guy Logan's *The Beautiful Spy* are quite hilarious, to a modern reader at least. Captain Eric Verner DSO, the son of Colonel Viscount Malcolm, is an upstanding, honourable young gentleman.[8] But unlike his father and fellow officers, Eric is a friend of Germany, and speaks the language. Nor does he share their opinion that the Huns are subhuman brutes, intent on war with the rest of Europe; in fact, he has married a beautiful German blonde named Hilda von Aussenberg. But at the outbreak of war, Eric catches Hilda stealing some important military documents entrusted to Lord Malcolm. She calmly tells him that she has been a German spy all along, and that the country of her birth comes first in her affections. As the dazed and stupefied Eric watches her leave with the military secrets, he realises that his fellow officers had been right all along: the Germans were really the scum of the earth! In a pathetic confrontation with Lord Malcolm, he takes the blame for the theft himself, since his sense of honour forbids him to accuse his wife of the crime. He promises to change his name and join the Army as a private soldier, so that his distinguished family is spared further dishonour.

In the meantime, Hilda hands the stolen documents over to the German spymaster, Count Paul Levigne. A thoroughly modern woman, she has enjoyed an affair with this sturdy, moustachioed cad for several years, and he is the father of her bastard child. But at a later meeting between these two, Count Paul addresses his paramour in terms of disrespect, and the Beautiful Spy, who possesses more spirit than Guy's other lachrymose heroines, pulls a small revolver and shoots him at close range.

Together with his loyal, lower-class friend Tom Peters, Eric Verner goes on to perform various heroics on the battlefields of Europe. He befriends an English nurse named Viola, and is always ready to deliver some punishing right hooks to various German cads who have lustful designs on her. The Beautiful Spy herself survives various hair-raising scrapes, before being shot by the dastardly Paul Levigne, who had only been winged by her earlier attempt on his life. Eric saves the wounded Lord Malcolm, who has led a cavalry charge in person. In the end, Nurse Viola persuades Hilda to confess all her misdeeds, on her deathbed. Lord Malcolm also dies from his wounds, and Paul Levigne is executed as a spy. All ends well for Eric Verner: he is restored to his proper place in society, obtains the Victoria Cross, and marries Nurse Viola.

In Guy's final *Illustrated Police News* offering, *Jack Leverton's VC*, the hero is yet another upstanding young gentleman with a high sense of family honour.[9] Jack Leverton, the eldest son of Sir William Leverton, is hated by his stepmother Lady Lutetia, since he stands in the way of her son Denzil inheriting the title. Denzil is a bad hat, who forges his father's signature to obtain money, and then asks his loyal brother for help. Jack agrees to see the moneylender who has been blackmailing Denzil, but he finds him dead and is arrested for his murder. The loyal Jack is willing to take the blame for his brother, who he presumed to be the murderer. But during the murder trial, the Old Bailey suffers a direct hit from a German bomb, and Jack escapes. He joins the Army as a private soldier, and performs various heroics, although the evil Lady Lutetia keeps plotting against him, aided by a certain Major Granger who turns out to be a German spy. But again all ends well: Jack wins the VC and marries his sweetheart, and Lady Lutetia confesses to the murder, before drowning herself.

In 1915, Guy must have been concerned that, as an able-bodied man of military age, it was his duty to fight for his country. But after his desertion caper back in 1891, joining the Army was out of the question. Instead, Guy managed to join the Navy, and he was posted to *Pembroke III*, a shore establishment belonging to the Royal Naval Air Service. Guy served there for two years, presumably in a clerical position, and advanced to become a Chief Petty Officer.[10]

*

There is nothing to suggest that Guy Logan had any involvement with *The Illustrated Police News* after the end of 1916. In the 1920s and 1930s, this once-vigorous newspaper went rapidly downhill, and it contained no fiction, nor any memorable contributions about the history of crime. It ceased publication in 1938.

In 1916, Guy and Nell had their third child, the daughter Evelyn, born in Hammersmith early that year. In January 1922, Guy Bertie Harris Logan, of No. 17 Dunravin Road, Shepherd's Bush, describing himself as a civil servant, filed a petition for bankruptcy. Two years later, he was released, with Mr Frank T. Garton, Official Receiver, Bankruptcy Buildings, Carey Street, London, as the trustee.[11] It may well be that Guy kept contributing the occasional racing news article or trial report to various London newspapers, but it appears that he was able to retire from his journalistic 'day job' some time in the 1920s. None of his plays had achieved lasting success, or brought him much money, and his novels lay forgotten in the pre-war bound volumes of *The Illustrated Police News*, which were sold as scrap paper in the 1920s, for sixpence. But by some stratagem or other, Guy and Nell managed to keep poverty from the door, and they could make sure that their children received decent educations. It was not until 1935 that Guy and Nell could finally get married, presumably after Melville had expired.

Guy also kept in touch with his eldest son Eustace, who had married Mary Payne, the daughter of the famous comedian Teddy Paine. Guy surely must have known Teddy Payne, who was active in the late Victorian and Edwardian theatre, with very considerable success. Eustace and Mary Logan soon had three sons named Brian Melville, Donald and Barry, and a daughter named Valerie. A Brian Melville Logan is listed to have been living at Cowes, Isle of Wight, as late as 2005. From comments made on the Teddy Payne page on an internet bulletin board, it seems likely that at least one of Guy Logan's three grandsons had issue.[12] As for Guy's younger son Leslie, he married Daisy Harris at Romford in 1933, and there is reason to believe that he died in 1971.

In the mid-1920s, Guy Logan finally decided to make some positive use of his encyclopedic knowledge of criminal history, and to establish himself as a writer on true crime. It was not easy for a little-known former penny-a-liner like him to get his first book published, however. In the 1920s as well as today, patronage and influential friends were important factors conducive to success in London's nepotistic literary world. George R. Sims had died in 1922, and he and Guy do not appear to have been close friends anyway. Although Sims had been an enthusiastic member of Arthur Lambton's Crimes Club, there was no hope for Guy to be invited to hobnob with the snobbish members of this select dining club. In fact, his only ally among Britain's true crime authors appears to have been Wynifried Margaret Jesse, a successful writer on criminal and other topics under her gender-neutral pen-name F. Tennyson Jesse. She befriended Guy in the 1920s and encouraged him to keep writing.[13]

It took until 1928 before Stanley Paul Publishers, a reputable London house, published Guy's first proper book, *Masters of Crime*, a study of multiple murders. A nicely bound and well-illustrated hardback, it sold for 12 shillings and sixpence. On the title page, he is introduced as the author of *Mystery of a Second Class Carriage*, *Chronicles of Crime* and *The Tragic Tale of Thurtell*, but these are some of his old *Illustrated Police News* serials, which their canny author had disguised as proper books to give the impression that he was an experienced and much-published writer. *Masters of Crime* is likely to be the first full-length book dealing with multiple murders. It begins with a long chapter about Jack the Ripper, reproduced later in this book. The Ratcliffe Highway murders of 1811 are also dealt with in full: unlike some later commentators, Guy does not doubt the guilt of John Williams, the man arrested for the crimes, who committed suicide while in custody.[14] Some of the shorter chapters deal with old 'friends' like Owen of Denham, Youngman the Walworth murderer, and Gleeson Wilson of Liverpool. The French multiple murderers Philippe, Troppmann and Lacenaire also receive mention, and the book ends with a long chapter on 'Scenes of Celebrated Crimes', in which Guy shows off his considerable murder house detection skills. He was wrong, however, in claiming that Palmer the Poisoner's house in Rugeley had been pulled down; according to competent local historians, it still stands today.

Although receiving few and lukewarm reviews, *Masters of Crime* sold well enough for Stanley Paul to commission its successor, *Guilty or Not Guilty*, arguably Guy's best true crime book. Published in April 1929, it consists entirely of British murder mysteries. Guy provides a brilliant retelling of the mysterious murder of Jane Clousen at Kidbrooke Lane, Eltham, in 1871, for which a young man named Edmund Pook stood trial and was acquitted. Guy clearly thought him a very lucky man. Guy resurrects the well-nigh forgotten mystery of Mrs Ann Reville, murdered in a Slough butcher's shop in 1881. A boy named Augustus Payne stood trial for the crime, but was acquitted; Guy instead hints, quite possibly with some accuracy, that Mrs Reville's husband Hezekiah might have been the guilty man. Guy also provides a superior account of another Victorian mystery: the disappearance of the baker Urban Napoleon Stanger from his shop at No. 136 Lever Street. Quite possibly, his remains were roasted in his own oven by Frenz Felix Stumm, another German baker, who had designs both on Stanger's wealth and his wife.[15] The book's other unsolved murder mysteries include those of Rose Harsent of Peasenhall, George Harry Storrs of Gorse Hall, and the North London railway murder of little Willie Starchfield.

Again, the sales of *Guilty or Not Guilty* proved sufficient for Stanley Paul to commission Guy's third outing in the true crime field: *Rope, Knife and Chair*, published in May 1930. A collection of celebrated British, French and American murders, its contents include the Louise Masset and Mrs Pearcey cases, and Guy also makes an early mention of that monstrous American boy murderer, Jesse Pomeroy. Just like *Guilty or Not Guilty*, this book was also published in the United States, by Duffield & Co. of New York. Guy's fourth true crime book, *Dramas of the Dock*, published in November 1930, is of higher quality, providing intriguing full-length accounts of the Euston Square mystery of 1879, and of the mysterious Manchester murder of Jane Roberts in 1880. Guy resurrected the almost unknown Northampton case of Andrew McRae, who murdered Annie Pritchard in 1893; he also managed to find and photograph the murder house in Dychurch Lane.[16] He dedicated *Dramas of the Dock* to F. Tennyson Jesse, 'to whom the author is beholden for much help and encouragement'. Reviews of these three books were mixed, with one critic lambasting Guy for 'resurrecting old and long forgotten crimes with a view to pandering to a morbid taste for deeds of horror and bloodshed'. Less squeamish reviewers praised his keen analytical sense and readable style, however.[17]

In June 1931, Guy released his fifth book, *Classic Races of the Turf*, a thoroughly researched and amusingly written account of horse-racing history, with a preface by the celebrated amateur jockey Sir George Thursby. It achieved better reviews than any of his previous books. *The Illustrated London News* gave it a full-page spread, admiring Guy's felicitous racing anecdotes; the *Saturday Review* praised its profound and encyclopedic knowledge of the annals of racing; Captain Coe of *The Star* cordially recommended it to all lovers of the Turf.[18] But in spite of all this publicity, the book sold only modestly, and it is today sought after by horse-racing enthusiasts, fetching as much as £30 for a good copy.

Just a few months later, in September 1931, the prolific Guy released his fifth true crime book, *Great Murder Mysteries*, a hodgepodge of British and foreign cases 'left over' from his earlier books. But although published in London by Stanley Paul, and in New York by Duffield & Co, this book was hardly reviewed at all, and sold very poorly. After *Great Murder Mysteries* had flopped in 1932, Guy must have hoped that his next Stanley Paul book, the novel *The Eternal Moment*, would be a success. Its preposterous plot highlights Guy's old-fashioned notions, outdated already by the 1930s. The hero, the dilettante painter John Angus Fleming, falls in love with a young lady named Margaret Neame, but she is seduced by his war-hero friend Roderick Mortimer, a drunkard and a cad. After Mortimer has fathered Margaret's child and refused to marry her, Fleming seeks him out at the Mortimer family seat near Ludlow. He greets his former friend with the words 'You are a rotten blackguard, Roderick Mortimer!' and tries to force him to marry Margaret. Baring his teeth like an angry cur, Roderick replies, 'You talk like the hero of a tenth-rate melodrama!' After a furious fight, Fleming kills Mortimer with a bludgeon. Escaping from the murder scene, Fleming is himself knocked senseless and robbed by an escaped convict, who is of course later arrested and charged with the murder of Roderick Mortimer. But the convict's brilliant barrister, Maxwell Power, clearly based on Marshall Hall, turns the tables on John Angus Fleming: due to a dropped cufflink, he is himself found guilty of murder and sentenced to death, only to be reprieved at the last possible moment. Rather understandably, no newspaper reviewed *The Eternal Moment*, and very few people bought it; it is today a very scarce book indeed. Its minuscule sales meant that Stanley Paul dropped Guy from their list of authors, for good. This must have been very disappointing for Guy, who had dedicated his only published novel 'to Nell, who is, to me, everything'.

*

As we have seen, Guy's first seven books were published by the London-based publishers Stanley Paul. Of his five true crime titles, *Guilty or Not Guilty*, *Rope, Knife and Chair*, and *Great Murder Mysteries* were co-published by Duffield & Co. of New York, but they did not sell in great amounts. In the mid-1930s, the London publishers Rich & Cowan published cheap reissues of *Guilty or Not Guilty* and *Rope, Knife and Chair* in a two-volume series called True Crimes. These books sold in respectable quantities and are today more common than the Stanley Paul editions.

It would take Guy Logan several years to find another publisher: Eldon Books, who normally specialised in cheap novels. His 1935 book *Verdict and Sentence* had a preface by Sir Basil Thomson, the former Assistant Commissioner at Scotland Yard, who had written several useful true crime books himself. Sir Basil admired the depth of Guy's research, and the fact that since the early 1890s, he had attended every important murder trial at the Old Bailey. The sprightly chapter on the Mannings includes a mention of Guy's grandfather, Major-General George Logan, who had met Mrs Manning in Edinburgh in 1849. Albeit a woman of a certain age, she had been very friendly to young Lieutenant Logan, whose advice she sought concerning how to dispose of the valuables of her former friend Patrick O'Connor, whose mangled remains she and her husband had left behind under the flagstones of their kitchen at No. 3 Miniver Place, Bermondsey. Guy's *Verdict and Sentence* also contains a curious chapter about the murder of Mr Paas by the bookbinder James Cook in Leicester in 1832. The murder house, said to be the smallest house in Leicester and situated down a narrow yard approached from Wellington Street, had been pulled down just a few years earlier. Another chapter deals with Christiana Edmunds, the celebrated Brighton chocolate-cream poisoner. The chapter entitled 'On the Scaffold' has tell-tale similarities with the long essay 'Last Words on the Scaffold', originally published in *Famous Crimes*. Guy's final full-length book, *Wilful Murder*, contains chapters on Courvoisier, Kate Webster and William Seaman, the Whitechapel murderer of 1896, among others. A brilliant chapter deals with the mysterious axe murders on board the American barkantine *Herbert Fuller* in 1896. The second mate, a man named Thomas Bram, was convicted for murdering the captain, his wife and the first mate, but he was later released on parole and pardoned by President Woodrow Wilson in 1919.

Guy Logan was always alert to chances to extend the profits from his books. In 1936, Dublin-based Mellifont Press, specialising in cheap popular novels and 'self-help' books, decided to make a corner into true crime. They recruited a number of authors to contribute to their 'Mellifont Celebrated Crimes' series. Shabbily produced on cheap paper, these small paperback books had a garish illustration on the front page, and sold for just threepence. Ludicrously, the protagonists were depicted as present-day gangsters and molls, even William Corder and Maria Marten, of Red Barn infamy. The retired detective Edwin T. Woodhall, a prolific author of low-quality crime books, was responsible for seven out of twenty-nine books in the 'Celebrated Crimes' series, including a confused account of Jack the Ripper's crimes, containing many inventions and inaccuracies. Guy agreed to contribute four volumes to the 'Celebrated Crimes' series, but our canny hero had his own ideas how to do so. The Mellifont titles *Guilty or Not Guilty* and *Rope, Knife and Chair* consist of chapters excerpted from the original Stanley Paul editions of these two books, and a third offering, *Studies in Crime*, also published in 1937, contained a selection from the remaining chapters from these two books. In contrast, Guy's fourth Mellifont book, *Monsters of Crime*, published in 1938, does contain some new material. Guy edited and improved some of the chapters from *Masters of Crime*, and also added a revised version of his account of Kate Webster, and a new chapter about the American serial killer Harry F. Powers.

Thus Guy Logan published seven full-length books on criminal history, apart from the four Mellifont concoctions. None of his books became anything like a bestseller, although all but *Great Murder Mysteries* sold enough to make the publication of its successor commercially viable. Guy's books can today be had for as little as £15 or £20 each, if eBay is made use of, and specialist booksellers avoided. The relative scarcity of his books has meant that Guy Logan has not received the recognition he is due. Well written and amusing, his true crime books are based on a lifetime of study of criminal history. Guy had personally attended the trials of many of his protagonists, and had kept accumulating material ever since. It has to be remembered that Guy was fifty-nine years old when *Masters of Crime* was first published; some of his coy and old-fashioned literary mannerisms hark back to Victorian times. Syphilis is referred to as 'a disease that should be nameless' and paedophilia is 'a crime which I cannot detail'. The major drawback of his books, for the reader with an academic bent, is that they all entirely lack footnotes and sources, even with regard to the origin of their illustrations. Still, the factual reliability of the books is very good, and they provide interesting sidelights on some curious British murder mysteries.

Already in 1935, Guy has announced that he was working on his masterpiece, *Murder Houses of London*, and in 1938 he may well have been putting the finishing touches to his life experiences as a murder house detective.[19] But a very sinister woman had other plans for our hero's future career.

*

In *Great Murder Mysteries*, Guy had included a chapter entitled 'More Deadlier than the Male' about some notorious murderesses. It has an epigraph from one of his own old plays:

Man is generally wicked from necessity;
Woman from choice.

Guy provided rather sketchy accounts of Catherine Hayes, Marie Manning and Gabrielle Bompard, ending up with a longer section about the American murderess Ruth Snyder.

In rather dubious taste, the book was illustrated with a photo of Ruth Snyder in the electric chair, after the current had been turned on. More crucially, the chapter briefly mentioned the notorious Frenchwoman Marguerite Steinheil, who had stood accused of murdering her husband and her mother. Guy hinted that he thought her very lucky to have been acquitted. But it would have been more prudent of him to keep quiet about his opinions about this case, since unbeknownst to Guy, Marguerite Steinheil was still very much alive.

In 1889, the pretty young French girl Marguerite Japy had married the Paris artist Adolphe Steinheil. He was twice her age and a far from attractive figure – a weakling with homosexual leanings – but he was a painter of considerable repute and could offer his wife some degree of social standing. They lived in Steinheil's comfortable Paris villa, and had a daughter named Marthe, presumed to have been fathered by the artist. Pathologically vain and with a great fondness for male company, Marguerite Steinheil become one of the leading courtesans of Paris. Her salon was frequented by men of eminence in French political and social circles, including Ferdinand de Lesseps, Jules Massenet, François Coppée, Émile Zola, and Pierre Loti. Her greatest conquest of all was President Félix Faure himself. She used to be admitted to the Elysée through a side door, providing access to the rotund president's private suite of rooms. The widely believed story that Félix Faure died of apoplexy during one of these illicit meetings must be considered 'not proven', however. The lurid rumours about Félix Faure's death in her arms exposed Marguerite Steinheil to the Paris gossip journalists, but she continued her old life like if nothing had happened. In 1908, she wanted to leave Steinheil and marry one of her lovers, the industrialist Borderel, but he was unwilling to marry a divorced woman.

On 31 May 1908, Marguerite's husband and mother were found dead in the villa at No. 6 bis Impasse Ronsin, just off the Rue de Vaugirard. Steinheil had been strangled, and Madame Japy had choked on her false teeth. Marguerite was gagged and loosely bound to a bed. She said that she had been tied up by four black-robed strangers, three men and a woman. Some newspapers speculated that they had come to her house in search of certain secret documents which Faure had entrusted to her keeping, possibly relating to the Dreyfus affair. The police immediately regarded Marguerite as the prime suspect, however, since the ropes she had been bound with were very loosely tied, and since her gag had no traces of saliva. It was presumed that one of her lovers had been her accomplice; Borderel had an alibi, but there were plenty of others to choose from. The wicked Marguerite attempted to frame her manservant, Rémy Couillard, by concealing a small pearl, which she claimed had been stolen at the time of the murder, in his pocketbook. She then tried to incriminate Alexandre Wolff, the son of her old housekeeper, but he had a solid alibi. She was arrested in November 1908 and taken to St Lazare prison. The crime created a sensation in Paris, and the trial was a great media event. It was revealed that Marguerite had had a great number of admirers, including a Russian grand duke, a bevy of French noblemen, and even King Sisowath of Cambodia. The rumours connecting the man-eating Marguerite with the Prince of Wales, later King Edward VII, again must be regarded 'not proven'.

The sensational trial finally ended in her acquittal on 14 November 1909: the wicked Marguerite had been saved by a plucky performance in court, and the exhortations of a first-rate legal team.[20]

After being acquitted of murdering her husband and mother, Marguerite Steinheil received many offers of marriage, but she turned them all down. She settled down in London and published her memoirs in both English and French. She avidly read about herself in the Paris boulevard press, and instructed libel lawyers if she thought the journalists had been too cheeky. In 1912, she took on the author Hargrave Adam, who had published some unfavourable observations about her in his book *Woman and Crime*, but Adam's publishers employed a French solicitor to dig up various unsavoury details from her past life, and she had to settle for a small amount. In 1917, Marguerite married her old admirer Robert Scarlett, Lord Abinger. A high point in her remarkable career came when she was presented to the king and queen at Buckingham Palace. But after her husband had died in 1927, his relatives inherited most of his estate, and Lady Abinger moved to a flat in Hove. She remained alert to any chance of a profitable libel action, and took £500 off the author Lovat Dickson, who had referred to her as a prostitute, in 1937.[21]

Lady Abinger had not read Guy Logan's obscure *Great Murder Mysteries*, but her moment came when the *Daily Express* and Syndicate Publishing Co. issued *The World's Greatest Detective Stories*, containing three chapters excerpted from Guy's book. After reading about herself in this book, the vindictive baroness took Guy and his publishers to court, the case being heard at the King's Bench Division on 15 November 1938. Lady Abinger's eloquent barrister, Mr John Fennell, bent the truth a great deal when he claimed that his client

> was a leader of Parisian social and political life, and so made many powerful enemies. In 1909 a tragedy occurred in her home. She was arrested and was in a Paris prison for 13 months awaiting trial. After a trial lasting 11 days she was acquitted and her innocence was conclusively proven. The first reaction of a young man who sat watching throughout the trial was to marry her. He afterwards became Lord Abinger.

The libels of Guy Logan had added a fresh stock of sorrows to one who had already suffered too much. Guy might well have wished to follow the example of Hargrave Adam, and investigate his opponent's colourful past a little closer, but his craven publishers 'chickened out', agreeing to pay damages of £2,000, and costs. The pathetic account of the baroness who had 'survived an experience containing all the ingredients of an Athenian tragedy', only to be libelled and mocked by an impudent cad of an author, was widely reported in the newspapers.[22] Lady Abinger celebrated her victory with a grand dinner for all her friends at the Metropole Hotel in Brighton: one of the guests was her current lover, a so-called Polish count, another the abortionist Dr Appiah, once the prime suspect of the first Brighton Trunk Murder of 1934.[23] Poor Guy was not invited, although he helped to pay for the fare.

After the dismal outcome of Lady Abinger's lawsuit, Guy Logan never published a word again. What happened to his *Murder Houses of London* is not known. In 1939,

Guy's twenty-three-year-old daughter Evelyn married Mr Henry Cowlin, a native of Weston-super-Mare who was not less than fifty-seven years old. Guy and Nell moved to Weston-super-Mare with them, and lived in a comfortable end-of-terrace house at No. 80 Milton Road (it still stands), not far from their daughter's house at No. 20 All Saints Road. Guy died at Milton Road on 10 February 1947, aged seventy-eight, from acute pneumonia according to his death certificate. It is sad but true that he has remained well-nigh forgotten ever since. Only two Ripper authors have commented on his theories about the case, and he is not mentioned in that hall of fame (or in some cases infamy) of Ripper authors and theorists, the valuable *Jack the Ripper A–Z*.[24] Even on the Internet, only the occasional Jack the Ripper and true crime buff has kept Guy's name alive.

But now the time has come to highlight Guy Logan's later theories about Jack the Ripper, through reproducing the relevant chapter from *Masters of Crime*.

Above left: 24. A signed photograph of Guy Logan, with his racecourse binoculars, from his *Dramas of the Dock*.

Above right: 25. The Northampton murder house in Dychurch Lane, which is no longer standing, in a photograph from Guy Logan's *Dramas of the Dock*.

Right: 26. The murder cottage near Bude, from Guy Logan's *Dramas of the Dock*.

Above: 27. Some of Guy Logan's books.

Above left: 28. The lurid cover of one of Guy Logan's Mellifont paperbacks.
Above right: 29. An advertisement for *Great Detective Stories*.

Above left: 30. Marguerite Steinheil in court, from an old postcard.
Above right: 31. Marguerite Steinheil, from her memoirs.

4

The 'Ripper' Murders: New Light on an Old Mystery, by Guy Logan

The dark and impenetrable mystery which surrounds the identity of the strangest and most terrible figure in criminal history is now never likely to be dispelled. Whoever 'Jack the Ripper' was, whether homicidal maniac with a special grievance against one class, lunatic doctor, or, as some think, an insane religious fanatic, he has taken his dread secret to the grave, and nothing is left to us but conjecture as to the man, his methods, and his motive. No real light has ever been thrown on a series of crimes which held the horrified attention of the world very nearly forty years ago, though many theories were then and have been since propounded.

Those of us who are old enough to remember the state of indescribable panic which prevailed in London's East End, that network of dark courts and fulsome alleys between Aldgate and a point in Whitechapel Road, even now cannot think of those days in the late autumn of the year 1888 without a shudder.

I recall the night I accompanied a newspaper colleague to that area of squalor, vice, and crime, when, with the Terror at its height, every second man one met was a detective or policeman in plain clothes, and the women of those dreadful streets crept about in companies of three or four, afraid to venture out alone, with blanched faces and faltering steps, seeing in every male they encountered a potential murderer. One remembers the public outcry against the police on account of their failure to lay hands on the midnight monster, the resignation of the late Sir Charles Warren, the tremendous efforts made by officials and private persons alike to bring the butcheries of outcast women to an end. Innumerable schemes for the prowler's capture were suggested and tried, vigilance societies were formed, bloodhounds were kept ready for immediate service, every dark corner and dimly lit court was closely watched, men were disguised as women decoys, every stranger passing along the Whitechapel Road late at night was stopped and questioned. Arrests of suspicious characters, harmless vagrants and travelling foreigners, were made in all parts of the country, every possible clue investigated and followed up, house-to-house searches made in such streets as might be expected to shelter the monstrous maniac. Again and again it seems as though his discovery was inevitable – on one supreme occasion he was almost certainly seen, spoken to, and closely observed – yet ever luck favoured him, always he got clear away; never, from the mass of information collected, was a clue obtained that could lead to his detection and arrest. No wonder that some imaginative people began to ascribe to him supernatural attributes, to declare that he was a ghoul or vampire, a hideous apparition from another world, able to come and go unseen by mortal eyes. These wild suggestions were put forward in all seriousness by those with a fancy for the occult, and, though we can laugh at them now, they were, in some quarters, quite gravely entertained at the time.

It did seem almost incredible that this friend in human guise was able, time after time, to evade capture, though as in the Berner Street instance, his victim's still palpitating body was found within a few seconds of her being foully done to death.

Apart from that was the fact that in every case the murderer must have been well-nigh smothered in blood. Where did he go after leaving his victim's mangled remains? How did he rid himself of his blood-stained garments? Who sheltered and sustained him? What kind of a lodging was it where such a man could be sure of a safe retreat? These, of course, were the real problems of the time, and they remain to this day as insoluble as then. I do not propose to tell the story of each of the 'Ripper' crimes. The object of this survey is to discuss the general bearings of the whole, and to relate some facts, never hitherto recorded, which happened to come within my own personal knowledge and review. The actual murders were so hideous in their atrocity, the bestial mutilations, especially in the later cases, so truly appalling, that, since there must be a limit to the horrible, I shall refrain from description except where such is absolutely necessary. The details of each murder rarely varied, except that they terminated in a very crescendo of horror; they were unquestionably the work of one man, and he left-handed; they were confined to one class, and that the lowest, poorest and most unfortunate of all, and they mostly bore one distinguishing trade-mark, the removal of a certain organ, as to which more presently. The means were invariably the same.

The man selected his victim without much, if any discrimination; the woman accompanied him readily and of her own free will, lured by the promise of a small sum of money; she placed herself in such a position as to render her an easy prey to the sharp knife; she died instantly after the one sweep across her throat; and the mutilations followed.

Most were murdered out-of-doors, in dark corners of dark alley ways, one, in Buck's Row, on the landing of a house, another – and this was the worst of them all – in her own miserable hovel in Miller Court, Dorset Street, Spitalfields.

That one took place on Friday, 9 November 1888, and followed hard on the double crime of 30 September, when Elizabeth Stride was butchered in Berner Street, and Catharine Eddowes cut to pieces in Mitre Square, Aldgate. In the Berner Street case a man, driving a trap into the courtyard where the body lay weltering in its blood, came upon it immediately after the deed, and the murderer must, unseen and unheard, have darted past him in the darkness. The woman had been slain under the very window of a Socialist club in which twenty or thirty men were at the time, and they never heard a sound. She had not been dead thirty seconds when the man's horse shied at the corpse. The husband and the children of this woman, by the way, had been drowned in the famous Thames disaster to the *Princess Alice*. After killing Catharine Eddowes in Mitre Square, within three-quarters of an hour of his earlier exploit, the man tore off a piece of her apron, and on it wiped his bloody hands and knife. He then walked to Goulston Street, where this scrap of apron was afterwards found, and, on the wall, chalked his famous and cryptic message, 'The Jews are not the men to be blamed for nothing.' An officious and stupid police constable sponged out the words lest a crowd collected and a riot ensued, but it was said that the writing much resembled that on a letter and postcard which had been received by the Central News some little time previously.

The postcard had been written in blood and bore the marks of blood-stained fingers. Both began 'Dear Boss', and threatened fresh crimes, though the letter contained a reference to 'respectable girls and women being perfectly safe.' They were signed 'Jack the Ripper' and were probably genuine, which is more than can be said for many of the communications bearing that dreaded signature. These were palpable hoaxes, the efforts of mischievous persons with a depraved sense of humour. The police and others were inundated with 'practical jokes' of the kind. The writing on the wall, however, was of the first importance, and it was the greatest pity that it was rubbed out. It is not generally known that Scotland Yard received a communication from the Russian police to which they were disposed to attach some importance. This took the form of a letter in which it was stated that similar murders had taken place in Moscow in, I think, 1885, that a man, whose name was given, had been caught red-handed, and, since he was obviously insane, he had been confined in a criminal lunatic asylum. He had made his escape from there in the early spring of '88 and had never been captured; at one time he had been a doctor. A description of him followed, and the London police were warned to look out for such a man, the more so since he had spent three years in London and knew the English language well. The letter added that this man was a religious maniac, that he believed that only by killing them could the souls of 'unfortunate' women enter into Paradise, and that there had been the same mutilations in the case of his victims. Without a doubt the London murderer had anatomical knowledge. He knew where the uterus could be found and how best to secure it undamaged.

In one case the left kidney had been removed, and this organ, in medical opinion, is particularly awkward to get at. It is a fearful act that, a few days after this particular outrage, the left kidney from a human body was sent, packed in a neat box, to the Yard with the usual 'Ripper' letter, full of rejoicings at what he had already accomplished and promising fresh horrors very soon.

If the letters to the Central News, however, were the genuine products of the murderer, the story of the escaped Russian is at once discounted. They were written in 'slangy' English and might have been penned by an American, but certainly no foreigner could have produced them. The writing was clear and precise, and the vulgar phrasing may, of course, have been purposely adopted to lead the police astray.

No doctor, even a mad one, would have written illiterate letters like these. Quite possibly, like all the others, they were 'fakes', but the postcard intimated the date of his next venture, and if that was only an anticipation on some trifler's part, it was a very intelligent one, for the next discovery was made on the very day predicted. Assuredly the sentence chalked on the wall in Goulston Street was the actual work of the mysterious miscreant, and, but for the stupidity of the constable, it might conceivably have led to his discovery.

At first it was thought that the motive of these crimes was to secure a human organ, which, to put it bluntly, had a commercial value to those in the know, but I do not hold with this opinion. The man, whoever and whatever he was, was bent on killing and maiming women of one class and calling, on wreaking his vengeance even on their inanimate bodies. The woman, Kelly or Watts, murdered in her own room, bore such mutilations as profaned the human form. They were of a kind unnameable, and could not have been perpetrated by the most ferocious wild beast.

It was the man's object to disgust and horrify, and, in that wretched room, he had time to wallow in his victim's blood. The doctor who was the first of his profession on the scene was struck dumb with horror at the sight the corpse presented, and the policemen were sickened to actual nausea by the spectacle. It seemed to be the work of a demon let loose. Nothing like it had ever been known in the records of crime. No sane man, however cruel, callous and bloodthirsty, could possibly have inflicted such shameful atrocities as were enacted in that garret; of that I am sure. It follows, then, that 'Jack the Ripper', though apparently sane and rational, was certainly mad, but there are, of course, degrees of madness, different forms of insanity, and we cannot express any definite opinion as to the nature of this creature's mental malady, which, in any case, he was clever enough to conceal. A type of erotic insanity, or epileptic furore, as in the case of Philippe, his French prototype, is suggested, but the latter never stooped to mutilations of the kind the London fiend delighted in. The London newspaper I was then representing sent me to interview that famous criminal pathologist, the late Forbes Winslow, who expressed the opinion that the murderer may have been normal except in moments of erotic frenzy.

'He may go home each time,' said the authority, 'and, by the morning, when the fit has passed off, not know or remember what he has done.' It is difficult, however, to reconcile this theory with the known facts, even though it was that of a recognised authority. A monomaniac, with whom a certain idea had become an obsession, might well have committed the Ripper crimes, but would a man such as Dr Forbes Winslow had in view have set out on each occasion with a definite purpose, armed himself with a deadly weapon, gone straight to the district where such victims as he sought could be most easily found, known how and when to approach them, and made so good, because so stealthy, an escape? The French 'Ripper', Joseph Philippe, who operated in Paris in the sixties of the nineteenth century, was animated by two motives, plunder and the lust for blood, and he chose his victims from that same class because they alone were not likely to reject his overtures.

The London monster's object is more obscure, but it is safe to assume that, for some reason, he had sworn vengeance on the frail sisterhood in Whitechapel, and that he was ready to proceed to any lengths to gratify his hatred and desire for revenge. One can only hint at that reason in these pages. A certain terrible disease, contracted in that neighbourhood, probably spurred him on to vengeance, remorseless and implacable. One of these outcasts had, morally and physically, ruined him. In his diseased mind, all were to suffer for the fault of one.

Was 'Jack the Ripper' ever actually seen and spoken to? I think that question can be answered in the affirmative, and I will now give my reasons. At 44 Berner Street there was then – it may be there now – a small fruit shop. It was kept by a man named Matthew Packer, who used to serve his customers through a window to save them the trouble of entering the small shop. At 11.30 on the night of Saturday 30 September 1888, there came to this window a man and a woman, whom Packer knew by sight. The woman, indeed, he was well acquainted with, for Elizabeth Stride – 'Long Liz' as they called her – was a familiar figure in that vicinity. Of the man he knew nothing, other than he had seen him two or three times, and had remembered his face.

This man stopped before Packer's window and, indicating some cheap black grapes, rather gruffly asked for half a pound, paying three pennies for the fruit. He seemed anxious to keep in the shadow and turned his face away when Packer happened to glance at him, but the latter was well able to describe him. He was a man aged about thirty, in height 5 feet 7 inches, or just on that, square-built, dark-complexioned, clean-shaven, and alert-looking. He wore a long black overcoat and a soft felt hat, and spoke in a quick, sharp manner.

Packer did not take him for a working-man, but rather for a clerk. The woman took the bag of grapes and the pair moved off, the man holding her arm. They went in the direction of the Socialist club, in the yard in front of which Elizabeth Stride's body was discovered less than twenty minutes later. Near her was the paper bag in which Packer had placed the man's purchase, and *a quantity of grape skins and stalks*. The woman had been eating the grapes as she talked with the murderer in that yard, only a stone's throw from Packer's shop. Three or four days later the latter saw the man again. To use the fruiterer's own words, 'I knew him instantly, and he remembered me. He gave me a dark menacing look, but I should have had him "nabbed" if it had not been that I was taken by surprise, and that I had no one at the moment to leave in charge of my stall. I told a shoe-black to follow him, but when the man saw me whispering these instructions, he suddenly darted off and jumped on the first passing tram. I can positively swear to its being the same man.' There can, I think, be no doubt that this was the murderer.

Meanwhile, fresh information was reaching Scotland Yard from abroad. In the winter and early spring of 1887–88 a series of fearful murders, accompanied by frightful and peculiar mutilations, occurred in Texas. The victims were Negro girls, of the same class as the London outcasts.

The murderer was never caught, though tremendous efforts were made to effect his capture.

He was presumed to be a foreign Jew, but very little light was ever thrown on his identity. The *Atlanta Constitution*, a leading Southern newspaper, gave a full account of these crimes while the London scare was at its height, and suggested that the unknown miscreant was the Texas murderer at work again. Then, in the early summer of 1889, an exactly similar series of crimes startled the people of Nicaragua.

These occurred at Managua, the chief town of that turbulent Central American republic. The 'Yard' got in touch with the chief of police there and received from him a report which, on the face of it, strongly suggested that the London assassin had made his way to Central America, after the last outrage in England. The circumstances were identical, the mutilations similar, the mystery just as dense and baffling. No one was ever arrested for the Nicaraguan crimes, or, rather, ever convicted, but a wild and unauthenticated story was afterwards circulated about a mad Englishman, once a doctor, confessing on his deathbed to being the author of these and the London outrages.

Similar tales, none of them capable of substantiation, have been spread about from time to time, and even now 'Ripper' revelations are not uncommon. I think it more than probable that the Whitechapel fiend, finding London at last too hot to hold him, deprived of the opportunities for his blood debauches, did betake himself abroad, and that he went to America. Further, I think it likely that he had come from the States in the first place, and that he was an American Jew. The two letters and the postcard sent to the Central News began with the words 'Dear Boss', and contained other significant suggestions of American origin.

The man Packer, who served him with the grapes, declared that the stranger spoke with a slightly guttural accent, and recognised no Yankee twang in his intonation, but he only spoke a few muttered words on that occasion, and may have purposely 'disguised' his voice. One woman named Lyons spoke to being accosted by such a person as Packer described in Hanbury Street, close to Dorset Street, on the night of the murder in Miller's Court, and she expressed the opinion that he was either an American or a man who had travelled in the States. 'He asked me to take him to any quiet spot I knew,' this woman said, 'and promised me some money. I was frightened, however, by the way he kept on looking up and down the street, as if to see that we were not being observed, and there was the outline of what I took to be a large knife in the pocket of his long, dark coat. I was scared by the thought of those other poor women. Whenever any person passed us he averted his face. Two or three women came along that I knew, and I made an excuse and left him.'

One of the earlier murders, that of Annie Chapman, on 8 September, had been committed in the back yard of a house in Hanbury Street, No. 29, the door of which was open day and night. Anyone could pass right through from the street to the yard of this tenement. A man happened to look out of the window on the stone stairway into this yard at a little after midnight and saw two figures in the shadow of the wall. He heard one of them, a woman, utter the words, 'No, no', in a rather excited way. A few hours later, by a man named Davis on entering this yard to get coals, the woman was found huddled beneath that same wall brutally slain. All the watcher from the window had noted of the man was his long dark coat. One pauses here to wonder if he used to take off this coat just before each murder, so as to keep it free from incriminating stains, while he made his way through the streets to whatever lair he had close at hand. Otherwise, surely the condition of his clothing must have attracted attention and remark, especially at a time when every peculiar and suspicious-looking stranger was liable to instant challenge. It is, indeed, one of the most singular features of the whole mystery that the blood-stained man, fresh from a new slaughter, should always have succeeded in getting through the cordon of police. Hundreds of innocent, harmless men were stopped and sternly interrogated, but the one guilty individual, never. A theory much in favour at the time was that of the escaped lunatic or asylum patient released as cured. Many terrible crimes have been committed by men prematurely released from proper control, but I feel a strong conviction that had the 'Ripper' been of that type, the murders would have been less purposeful and methodical. A semi-lunatic would have inevitably given himself away, sooner or later. The late George R. Sims was fond of declaring that, in the end, the murderer's identity was known to the police, that he was a doctor who had become insane, and that his dead body was found in the Thames soon after his last exploit, but nothing to establish this story was ever put forward, and I regard it as pure myth.

If the authorities had been in possession of such information they would certainly have published it if only to relieve the public mind.

To sum up, I believe that 'Jack the Ripper' was (1) a man, with some surgical experience, who knew both England and America well; (2) that he had suffered from a disease that must be nameless here, contracted in the neighbourhood of the murders; (3) that this had affected his brain and caused him to 'declare war' on the special class from which he chose his victims; (4) that the mutilations were the result of a blood-lust and a desire to wreak his hatred even on the lifeless bodies of these unfortunates; (5) that he had a secret lair or hiding-place in the district at which he was able to remove all signs of his fearful deeds; and (6) that there were those in London who more than suspected his proclivities, but were too timid to denounce him. In Mrs Belloc-Lowndes's remarkable story *The Lodger* this last theory is advanced in a very powerful way. To my own knowledge a quantity of blood-soaked garments were found months afterwards in a locked trunk in a bedroom vacated by a man whose movements had excited some vague suspicions.

This man left his lodging in the East End very hurriedly, saying he would send for the trunk, but he never did so. Among the clothes was a blue serge suit, the buttons of which bore the name of a Chicago tailor. The police made enquiries here, but nothing ever came of them, or, if there did, was ever allowed to transpire. Never, in this world, will this stupendous mystery be solved.

Among the weak-minded and depraved, crime of this kind is, alas! contagious. The 'Ripper' murders in London found many imitators during the three or four years following them, though, except in one case, the 'copies' lacked the devilment of the original. None could hope to expect to vie with the Whitechapel monster in enormities, but the murder of the little boy, Johnny Gill, aged eight, at Bradford on 28 December 1888, was quite as ghastly, and even more apparently motiveless.

This child left home between the hours of 7.00 and 8.00 on that morning to accompany a young milkman, whose name I shall suppress, on his round. At Walmer Villas, within 200 yards of his own home at 41 Thorncliffe Road, the little lad jumped down from the cart and said he would run home and get his breakfast. He did not, however, reach his dwelling, and, forty-eight hours later, his body was found in an entry to some stables in Meller Street, close to Thorncliffe Road, by a youth named Burke. The child's body was nude, but was wrapped in his own garments, the whole, in the form of a bundle, being held together by his braces. He had been killed by repeated stabs to the heart, but the infamies to which the corpse had been afterwards subjected defy description and exceed belief. The murder and mutilations had not been committed in the place where the remains were found; the body had been carried there between the hours of 4.30 and 7.30

a.m. on 30 December by someone who knew the district well. At 4.30 the constable on duty in Meller Street had tried the door of the wash-house in the entry, and had stood on the very spot where the mangled body was later found.

Further, there was no blood about the place. A case of grave suspicion was made out against the milkman, with whom the boy had been when last seen alive, but at the magisterial examination he was discharged. The Coroner's jury, however, having returned a verdict of 'wilful murder' against him, he was rearrested and committed for trial but, when the case came up at Leeds, the Grand Jury threw out the bill, and the man was released from custody.

This case was by far the most shocking and terrible of all the 'Ripper' imitations, and, since we must assume the innocence of the milkman, it remains an unsolved mystery to this day. In 1891 a little girl, Barbara Waterhouse, was lured to his home at a suburb of Leeds by a wretch named Walter Lewis Turner, and there most barbarously murdered and mutilated. His mother, with whom he lived, was out at the time, and, on her return home, noticed a suspicious-looking bundle under the stairway. She communicated her misgivings to a neighbour, who sent an anonymous letter to the Leeds police. Meanwhile, Turner, assisted by his mother, had carried the child's body to Leeds in a tin box and deposited it behind the Town Hall there. He confessed to the crime, was convicted, and executed. At the time of the murder of the boy, Gill, at Bradford, Turner was living in the same part of that town. The two crimes were extraordinarily similar, and it is not at all unlikely that Walter Turner was guilty of both.

My own belief is that the last genuine 'Jack the Ripper' crime in London was that of the woman Kelly, in Miller Court, though it is, of course, possible that the unknown was also responsible for the murder of the unfortunate, Alice McKenzie, on 17 July 1889, in the same district. In this case, however, certain of the former features were lacking, and the police were doubtful if it was the work of the same hand.

On September 10th in the same year the dismembered trunk of a woman, probably of the same class as the other victims, was found under an archway in Pinchin Street, Whitechapel.

Medical opinion was that she had been dead at least four days. The remains had been probably brought to the spot in a sack and there deposited, but as any person carrying a sack or bundle late at night in that district at that time would assuredly have been challenged by the first policeman he encountered, it was assumed that a coster's cart or barrow had conveyed it there, and that the sack may have been hidden underneath a quantity of cabbages or the like. The identity of this victim of a fearful murder was never established, but the crime was not at all after the 'Ripper' pattern, and was probably another 'imitation'. The murders ceased, I think, with the Miller Court one, and I am the more disposed to this view because, though the fact was kept a close secret at the time, I know that one of Scotland Yard's best men, Inspector Andrews, was sent specially to America in December 1888, in search of the Whitechapel fiend on the strength of important information, the nature of which was never disclosed.

Nothing, however, came of it, and the Inspector's mission was a failure. The story that Neill Cream, the poisoner of unfortunates in London a few years later, was really the 'Ripper', and that he confessed to the crimes on the scaffold, has no foundation whatever. This wretch, whose hobby was murder and a crude form of blackmail, was in prison in America at the time when most of the Whitechapel crimes were perpetrated, and the man Saddler, suspected of the murder of Francis Cole, in 1891, was at sea when most of the murders occurred. Some where, some when, this monster died, whether by suicide, in a lunatic asylum, or quietly in his own bed, and took with him his fearful secret. The truth can never be known now.

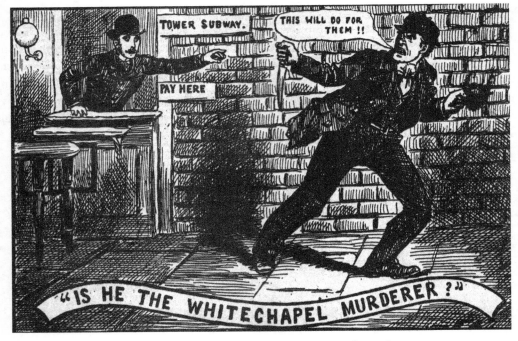

32. 'Is He the Whitechapel Murderer?', from *The Illustrated Police News*, 22 September 1888.

33. Women are arming themselves to take on the Ripper, from *The Illustrated Police News*, 22 September 1888.

FINDING THE MUTILATED BODY IN MITRE SQARE.

34. 'Finding the Mutilated Body in Mitre Square', from *The Illustrated Police News*, 6 October 1888.

THE FIFTH VICTIM OF THE WHITECHAPEL FIEND.

35. 'The Fifth Victim of the Whitechapel Fiend', from *The Illustrated Police News*, 6 October 1888.

36. Constable Watkins summons assistance, from *The Illustrated Police News*, 6 October 1888.

37. Bloodhounds are tried in the hunt for the Ripper, from *The Illustrated Police News*, 20 October 1888.

5
What Did Guy Logan Know About Jack the Ripper?

In his 1905 novel *The True History of Jack the Ripper*, Guy Logan had adhered to what can be termed the Macnaghten version of events, as originally outlined in Major Arthur Griffiths' *Mysteries of Police and Crime*, first published in 1898.[1] The Whitechapel Murderer had five victims and five victims only, and the major suspect was a doctor in the prime of life, presumed to be insane or in the borderland of insanity. He had disappeared after the murder of Mary Kelly, and was found drowned in the Thames a month after the Miller's Court atrocity. The journalist and author George R. Sims, who knew both Sir Melville Macnaghten and Major Arthur Griffiths, was another early proponent of the 'Doctor in the Thames' version of events. A successful playwright and poet in his time, and an early proponent of social reform, Sims has become almost totally forgotten.[2] It is not generally known that the author of 'Christmas Eve in the Workhouse' and other overblown poems was actually a journalist of some standing. Sims was fond of London's criminal history, an area where he was tolerably well informed. A blatant self-publicist, he was often fond of hinting that he possessed secret information about the unsolved mysteries of the great metropolis. He more than once speculated about the identity of Jack the Ripper in his 'Mustard and Cress' column in the *Referee* newspaper.[3] The bold Sims claimed that he knew that Jack the Ripper had twice been incarcerated in lunatic asylums, but each time, the benign alienists had let this monster loose to continue his sanguinary career. Another dubious addition from Sims was that the police had been in search of the doctor alive when they found him dead.

In a serial about 'My Criminal Museum' in *Lloyd's Weekly News*, George R. Sims provided some further useful hints about the 'Doctor in the Thames'.[4] The doctor had lived in a suburb about 6 miles from Whitechapel. He had suffered from a horrible form of homicidal mania, directed against women of a certain class, as Sims put it. He had once been an inmate in a lunatic asylum, but had been liberated and regained his complete freedom. After the murder of Mary Kelly, the doctor had disappeared, and his friends had made inquiries about him, detailing their own suspicions to the proper authorities. A month later, the doctor's body was found in the Thames, looking as if it had been in the river for nearly a month. It is not known what proportion of Sims' speculations were based on fact, and how much was invention. Nor is Sims' original police source known, but it is likely to have been either Sir Melville Macnaghten or Major Arthur Griffiths.

Guy Logan and George R. Sims moved in the same circles: both were playwrights and journalists, and they shared an interest in criminal history. Guy's 'Leaves from our Notebook' column in *Famous Crimes* indicates that he knew Sims, and that he quoted this senior journalist's opinion with respect. It is unfortunate that we do not know if these two were friends or just nodding acquaintances, but it is safe to presume that the plot of Guy's *The True History of Jack the Ripper* owes much to George R. Sims and his lucubrations about the Ripper's identity. Mortemer Slade is a doctor who makes sure he gets out of the asylum. He suffers from homicidal mania and murders five prostitutes, before he plunges into the Thames. Although Guy adds some sensational improvements to the story, including the Lady Detective and the two pseudo-Reichenbach episodes, he still adheres to what he believed to be the accepted basic facts about the mystery of the Whitechapel Murders, as presented by George R. Sims.

The story of the Doctor in the Thames is still debated today. The major problem has been that no medical man, of any description, was fished out of the river in the relevant period of time. When Sir Melville Macnaghten's original memorandum was rediscovered in 1959, the 'doctor' was named as Mr M. J. Druitt, however. There was immediate enthusiasm among the ripperologist community when it turned out that Montague John Druitt, a young barrister turned schoolmaster, had really committed suicide in December 1888. He had been sacked from the school where he had been teaching, and his mother had been certified insane and committed to a lunatic asylum. Montague Druitt's suicide note said that since he was fearful of going the same way as his mother, the best thing was for him to die. The note did not at all refer to the Whitechapel Murders.

For more than fifty years, the ripperologists have been searching for corroborative evidence against Montague Druitt, whose rather sad life has been described in some detail.[5] He had been quite talented as a young man, and a useful cricketer, but he failed to achieve anything worthwhile as an adult. The reason he had been fired from Mr Valentine's School, Blackheath, where he had been teaching for eight years, may well have been homosexual tendencies. But nothing has emerged to incriminate this rather inadequate young man, or to suggest that he was capable of committing a series of gruesome murders. It is left unexplained why Macnaghten, Major Griffiths and George R. Sims all described Druitt as a doctor, when he lacked any medical education, nor is there an obvious reason why Macnaghten stated that the suspect was forty-one years old, when Druitt was in fact only thirty-one. It has been discovered that as early as early as February 1891, Mr Henry Richard Farquharson, a West Country MP, told a journalist that Jack the Ripper was the son of a surgeon, and that he had committed suicide on the night of the final murder. Now the Druitt family came from Wimbourne in Dorset, not far from Farquharson's country seat at Tarrant Gunville, and Montague Druitt's father was a prominent local surgeon.[6]

The Macnaghten memorandum lists three Ripper suspects: Montague Druitt, a Russian thief named Ostrog who was said to carry knives and hate women, and an insane Polish Jew named Kosminski. Ostrog has since been exonerated, since he was in prison in France at the time of the Ripper murders. In contrast, Kosminski has remained a credible suspect. Assistant Commissioner Sir Robert Anderson did not subscribe to the 'Doctor in the Thames' theory, preferring the insane Polish Jew, who was later named by Chief

Inspector Donald Swanson as 'Kosminski'.[7] It is likely, albeit not conclusively proven, that this 'Kosminski' was identical to the lunatic Aaron Kosminski, who lived on in an asylum until 1919. As for Chief Inspector Frederick Abberline, he had his own suspect, Severin Klosowski, alias George Chapman, and he spoke up against Sims' lucubrations in 1903. Thus the 'Doctor in the Thames', aka Montague Druitt, was not *the* Scotland Yard suspect, rather one of several individuals suspected by different police officials at the time.

*

When he wrote about Jack the Ripper in his 1928 book *Masters of Crime*, Guy Logan had clearly moved on from his 1905 theory about the murders. Indeed, he sneers that 'the late George R. Sims was fond of declaring that, in the end, the murderer's identity was known to the police, that he was a doctor who had become insane, and that his body was found in the Thames soon after his last exploit, but nothing to establish this story was ever put forward, and I regard it as pure myth.' Instead, Guy was the first theorist on the Ripper case to suggest that the murderer might have been an American, and that after committing the Whitechapel Murders, he had returned to his native land. He speculated that the American might have contracted syphilis from an East End prostitute, and that he had developed neurosyphilis, resulting in a murderous mania against the class from which he chose his victims. Not unreasonably, Guy found it likely that the American had access to a secret lair in Whitechapel. Interestingly, he further speculated that there had been those in London who knew about the murderer's proclivities, but were too timid to denounce him.

It has been suggested that Guy Logan's musings about the American Jack the Ripper may well have been inspired by a letter sent to George R. Sims by the Detective Chief Inspector John George Littlechild, formerly of Scotland Yard, in 1913.[8] When Sims had been sniffing around for further information about the 'Doctor in the Thames', whom he interestingly referred to as 'Dr D.', Littlechild's reply was a startling one:

> I never heard of a Dr D. in connection with the Whitechapel murders but amongst the suspects, and to my mind a very likely one, was a Dr. T. (which sounds much like D.). He was an American quack named Tumblety and was at one time a frequent visitor to London and on these occasions constantly brought under the notice of police, there being a large dossier concerning him at Scotland Yard. Although a '*Sycopathia Sexualis*' subject he was not known as a 'Sadist' (which the murderer unquestionably was) but his feelings toward women were remarkable and bitter in the extreme, a fact on record. Tumblety was arrested at the time of the murders in connection with unnatural offences and charged at Marlborough Street, remanded on bail, jumped his bail, and got away to Boulogne. He shortly left Boulogne and was never heard of afterwards. It was believed he committed suicide but certain it is that from this time the 'Ripper' murders came to an end.

After the leading 'Ripper' collector Stewart P. Evans had purchased the Littlechild Letter in 1993, and realised its considerable significance, he made sure that the antecedents of this mysterious Dr Tumblety were properly investigated.[9] It turned out that 'Dr' Francis Tumblety, an American quack, had been in London at the time of the Whitechapel Murders. A native of Ireland, his family had emigrated to the United States in the 1830s. He established himself as a prominent member of America's booming 'herbal medicine' industry, and earned a good living on Tumblety's Pimple Destroyer and other well-publicised nostrums. When one of his patients died unexpectedly, quite possibly as a result of his ministrations, he could afford a good lawyer, and got off scot free. A flamboyant character with a liking for pseudo-military attire, the tall 'doctor' sported an over-large moustache and was accompanied by a favourite dog. A practising homosexual, he was said to be known for his misogyny and his hatred for prostitutes. He travelled incessantly, and more than once visited Europe.

It is a fact that Francis Tumblety was in London at the relevant time, since we know that he was arrested on 7 November 1888 on several charges of 'gross indecency', involving homosexual practices with various young men. Awaiting trial, he jumped bail and escaped to France using a false name, before leaving for the United States. The problem was that the good 'doctor', who was already notorious for his self-promotion and habitual untruthfulness, had accumulated a good many enemies within the American newspaper press. These individuals published articles about Tumblety's escape from London, hinting that his arrest had been connected to the Jack the Ripper murders, and even untruthfully alleging that Scotland Yard was trying to get him extradited. But the New York City Police, who kept Tumblety under surveillance, said that there was no proof of his complicity in the Whitechapel murders, and the crime for which he was under bond in London was not extraditable. Far from committing suicide like Littlechild had suspected, Francis Tumblety lived on until 1903, in comfortable circumstances.

The discovery of Tumblety as a bona fide Jack the Ripper suspect has meant that the good doctor's past life has been put under the microscope, but just like for Montague Druitt, there has been a distinct scarcity of additional incriminating evidence.[10] Tumblety lied and bragged, and cheated people with his dubious herbal medicines, but he did not seem to possess any violent tendencies. A very tall and broad-shouldered man with an enormous handlebar moustache, he would have stuck out like a sore thumb in the Whitechapel slums with his weak, effeminate voice and obvious American accent. And as a homosexual, he would be almost unique in the annals of male serial killers of women.

Are there any other Ripper suspects that fit Guy Logan's profile of the 'travelling serial killer'? One was the abortionist and serial poisoner Dr Thomas Neill Cream, who was said to have tried to confess to being the Ripper just before his execution, but he is recorded to have been in an American prison at the time of the Whitechapel Murders. Slightly more promising is the Hungarian Alois Szmeredy, once charged with murdering a woman in Buenos Aires, but evidence is lacking that he was in London at the time of the murders.[11] After the German seaman Carl Feigenbaum had been executed for murdering his landlady in New York City in 1894, his lawyer gave press interviews pointing out his client as Jack the Ripper. It has later been argued that a sailor visiting London occasionally on a German ship would have excellent opportunities to commit murder during these visits, before taking refuge on board ship, but again evidence is lacking that Feigenbaum was in London at the relevant time.[12]

Another, more promising 'travelling serial killer' was Severin Klosowski, aka George Chapman, convicted for murder in 1903. A violent man with a misogynistic streak, he left London in April 1891 and went to the United States. He returned to London in 1893, took the lease of several pubs, and poisoned three of his mistresses. Chief Inspector Frederick Abberline, Hargrave Adam and Superintendent Arthur Neal all considered Chapman a credible suspect, as has leading modern Ripper author Philip Sugden.[13] Chapman was the right age, had the right temperament, and knew Whitechapel well. There has also been speculation that Chapman was a wholesale serial killer, who committed not only the Ripper crimes, but also the so-called Thames torso murders, and that he also murdered four women during his stay in the United States before returning to London.[14] But on the other hand, it is strange for a serial killer to change his modus operandi so radically (i.e. knives to poison); whereas Jack the Ripper murdered (presumably) unknown street prostitutes, Chapman murdered women who were well acquainted to him. As Guy Logan put it in *Masters of Crime*, 'Some where, some when, this monster died, whether by suicide, in a lunatic asylum, or quietly in his own bed, and took with him his fearful secret. The truth can never be known now.'

Notes

1 The Early Life & Opinions of Guy Logan

1. Eugenie May Logan married Alfred Kemp in 1891, and died in 1952 aged eighty-four.

2. Guy Logan, *Wilful Murder* (London 1935), pp. 80–1.

3. Guy Logan, *Guilty or Not Guilty* (London 1929), p. 248.

4. Guy Logan, *Masters of Crime* (London 1928), pp. 200–1. Deeming was later arrested in Melbourne and executed there in 1892.

5. *Illustrated Police Budget* 13 Jan. 1906, pp. 7–8.

6. *Era* 26 Aug. 1895.

7. *Era* 5 Oct. 1895.

8. *Shields Daily Gazette* 1 Sept. 1896; *Era* 8 Sept. 1896; *Bath Chronicle* 24 Sept. 1896.

9. *Era* 26 Nov. 1898 and 19 June and 21 Oct. 1899.

10. Guy Logan's *Violet Kildare* was serialised in *The Illustrated Police News* from 28 April 1900 until 16 March 1901.

11. These poems are in *The Illustrated Police News* 22 Dec. 1906, 28 Dec. 1901, 25 Dec. 1909 and 27 Dec. 1902.

12. J. Adcock on the Yesterday's Papers internet home page has a biography of Harold Furniss.

13. Quoted in *Dundee Courier & Argus* 21 March 1893.

14. In *The World* newspaper, quoted in the *Derby Mercury* of 1 Aug. 1883.

15. *Western Mail* 16 Aug. 1894.

16. The British Library catalogue has added a mystification by claiming that there was one run of *Famous Crimes* published from 1903 until 1905 (shelfmark PP7616yf) and another published in 1908 and 1909 (shelfmark PP7616yg), but a close inspection has revealed the latter to be a misdated and incomplete run of the original publication.

17. Clifford Elmer Books, Catalogue 2, 2008. A bound volume containing twenty-six issues of *Famous Crimes*, *ex libris* Jonathan Goodman, was advertised for sale by Peter Harrington Books (Catalogue 65, #97) for £1,250.

18. These extracts are from *Famous Crimes Past and Present* 7 (82), 56 [Murder Houses], 7 (86), 128 [Murderers' Letters], 6 (73), 170 [Prison Poets], 5 (64), 279 [Taverns associated with Famous Crimes], 6(78), 248 [Criminal Lunatics at Large], 9(110), 304 [A 'Ripper' Anecdote],

10 (122), 104 [Great Criminals at Large] 10 (123), 148 [A Visit to Elstree], 10 (123), 142–3 [Towns and Their Famous Crimes] and 10 (125), 174 [Great 'Crime' Houses].

19. It was No. 4 Burton Crescent and the murder remains unsolved. The murder house no longer stands, having been demolished for the expansion of London University.

20. Guy is right that No. 3 Miniver Place became No. 103 Weston Street. It stood until 1960; see M. Alpert, *London 1849: A Victorian Murder Story* (London, 2003), p. 93.

21. The house was in fact No. 11 Montague Place. It no longer stands, having been demolished in 1904 when the British Museum was extended to the north.

22. Josiah Misters attempted to murder Mr Mackreth at the Angel Inn, Ludlow, and was hanged at Shrewsbury in April 1841. Some say that he meant to murder a solicitor but went to the wrong room by mistake. The Angel Inn still stands, and a historic old pub it is; although it is only an 'attempted murder house' I have enjoyed a small ginger ale – ahem! – there more than once when visiting Ludlow.

23. This crime took place as early as 1826. There is a Jolly Carter pub in Winton today, but Guy is probably right about the original murder pub being taken down.

24. According to an Internet source, Bill o'Jacks was demolished to make way for a plantation above Yeoman Hay reservoir.

25. Thomas Earlham and his housekeeper Mary Mohan were murdered at their tavern in Smallwood in February 1883, and the tramp Patrick Carey was hanged for the crime.

26. A man giving his name as Charles Y. Hermann confessed to the Ripper murders in New York, but he was not believed.

27. The murder victim's name was George Fell and the case remains unsolved.

28. The real name of the murder victim was James Wells, a butcher turned bookmaker. The murder was never solved.

29. The victim was never identified and opinions differed, at the time, as to whether it was really a murder, or a practical joke by some medical students.

30. The Eltham Murder, for which Edmund Pook stood trial, was actually committed in 1871. The Purton Tragedy involved the unsolved murder of an old man named John Grymes at his cottage in Purton, Wiltshire, in January 1874. There was no unsolved double murder in Kentish Town in 1878.

31. The child found murdered in Upton Park, Plaistow, was actually named Willie Barrett.

32. E. O'Donnell, *Strange Disappearances* (London, 1927), pp. 281–97; J. Oates, *Unsolved Victorian and Edwardian Murders* (Barnsley, 2007), pp. 88–95.

33. The Grimwood murder house was an unlamented victim of the reconstruction of Waterloo Bridge in the 1930s. The rumour that the man Hubbard fled to America was unfounded.

34. The Youngman murder house at No. 16 Manor Place has been demolished to make room for a new local police station, see P. de Loriol, *South London Murders* (Stroud, 2007), pp. 33–5.

35. Both houses still stand, although the Pearcey house is today known as No. 2 Ivor Street, Kentish Town.

36. Part of Henry Wainwright's murder house, namely the workshop where he concealed the body, still stands; the Seaman house has been reconstructed, but houses opposite show what it must have looked like.

3 Guy Logan's Later Career

1. L. James, *Fiction for the Working Man* (Oxford, 1963); R. F. Stewart, *Always a Detective* (London, 1980); also the articles by P. A. Dunae (*Victorian Studies* 22 [1979], pp. 133–50), J. Springhall (*Victorian Studies* 33 [1990], pp. 223–46 and *Economic History Review* NS 47 [1994], pp. 567–84) and S. D. Bernstein (*Criticism* 36 [1994], 213–41).

2. E. C. Miller (*Victorian Literature and Culture* 33 [2005], pp. 47–65).

3. National Archives J 77/906/7523.

4. Serialised in *The Illustrated Police News* from 19 Nov. 1910 until 20 May 1911.

5. Serialised in *The Illustrated Police News* from 25 Sept. until 11 Nov. 1911.

6. Serialised in *The Illustrated Police News* from 3 Feb. until 29 June 1912.

7. Serialised in *The Illustrated Police News* from 10 Oct. 1912 until 6 Feb. 1913.

8. Serialised in *The Illustrated Police News* from 7 Jan. until 24 June 1915.

9. Serialised in *The Illustrated Police News* from 21 Oct. 1915 until 6 April 1916.

10. National Archives ADM 188/565/48.

11. *London Gazette* 14 March 1922, 2192, and 29 Jan. 1924, 943.

12. www.ancestryaid.co.uk.

13. Her biography by J. Colenbrander, *A Portrait of Fryn* (London, 1984), does not mention Guy, however.

14. P. D. James & T. A. Critchley, *The Maul and the Pear Tree* (London, 1987).

15. See J. Smith-Hughes, *Unfair Comment* (London, 1951), 1–107 and *Eight Studies in Justice* (London, 1953), pp. 1–28.

16. It no longer stands.

17. *Western Morning News* 12 June 1929, 10 April 1930 and 12 Oct. 1931; *New York Times* 11 Aug. 1929; *Saturday Review* 15 March 1930; *Times of India* 13 May 1930; *Observer* 15 Nov. 1930.

18. *Observer* 31 May 1931, *Irish Times* 26 June 1931; *Illustrated London News* 6 June 1931, 970.

19. Guy Logan, *Verdict and Sentence* (London, 1935), p. 180.

20. A. Lanoux, *Madame Steinheil* (Paris, 1983); P. Darmon, *Marguerite Steinheil, Ingénue Criminelle?* (Paris, 1996); F. Delacourt, *L'Affaire Steinheil* (Paris, 1999).

21. E. Dudley, *The Scarlett Widow* (London, 1960), p. 190.

22. *Times* 15 Nov. 1938.

23. E. Dudley, *The Scarlett Widow* (London, 1960), pp. 5, 190–1.

24. Namely by S. Evans & P. Gainey, *The Lodger* (London, 1995), p. 230 and R. Odell, *Ripperology* (Kent OH, 2006), pp. 58–9. Guy's books are listed by B. Harrison, *True Crime Narratives* (Lanham MD, 1997), but surprisingly not by A. Borowitz, *Blood and Ink* (Kent OH, 2002).

5 What Did Guy Logan Know About Jack the Ripper?

1. A. Griffiths, *Mysteries of Police and Crime* (London, 1898), vol. 1, pp. 28–9.

2. On Sims, see A. Calder-Marshall (ed.), *Prepare to Shed Them Now: The Ballads of George R. Sims* (London, 1968), pp. 1–48, and W. J. Fishman, *Into the Abyss* (London, 2008).

3. *Referee* 22 Jan. 1899, 16 Feb. and 13 July 1902, 29 March and 5 April 1903, and 13 Oct. 1907. See

also G. R. Sims, *Mysteries of Modern London* (London, 1906).

4. *Lloyds Weekly News* 22 Sept. 1907.

5. D. J. Leighton, *Ripper Suspect* (Stroud, 2006). There are anti-Druitt articles by A. Spallek in *Ripper Notes*, July 2005, and by A. Morris in the *Journal of the Whitechapel Society*, April 2007. See also A. Wood & K. Skinner (*Ripperologist* 128 [2012], pp. 3–58).

6. A. Spallek, 'The "West of England MP" Identified', on www.casebook.org.

7. P. Begg, *Jack the Ripper: The Facts* (London, 2004); R. House, *Jack the Ripper and the Case for Scotland Yard's Prime Suspect* (Hoboken NJ, 2011).

8. S. Evans & P. Gainey, *The Lodger* (London, 1995), p. 230.

9. S. Evans & P. Gainey, *The Lodger* (London, 1995).

10. T. B. Riordan, *Prince of Quacks* (Jefferson NC, 2009). See also the articles by J. Chetcuti (*Ripperologist* 59 [2005], pp. 12–18 and 60 [2005], pp. 17–21) and T. Marriott (*Ripperologist* 127 [2012], pp. 34–45). Tumblety attracted interest from a medical historian before he became a Ripper suspect: see M. McCulloch (*Canadian Bulletin of Medical History* 10 [1993], pp. 49–66).

11. E. Zinna (*Ripperologist* 33 [2001], pp. 7–12); J. L. Scarsi (*Ripperologist* 63 [2006], pp. 6–12).

12. T. Marriott, *Jack the Ripper: The 21st Century Investigation* (London, 2007); *Daily Mail* 2 Sept. 2011.

13. P. Sugden, *The Complete History of Jack the Ripper* (London, 1994), pp. 441–66; S. P. Evans & K. Skinner, *The Ultimate Jack the Ripper Sourcebook* (London, 2000), 645–51.

14. R. M. Gordon, *Alias Jack the Ripper* (Jefferson NC, 2001), *The Thames Torso Murders of Victorian London* (Jefferson NC, 2002), and *The Poison Murders of Jack the Ripper* (Jefferson NC, 2008).

About the Authors

GUY LOGAN was active as a journalist during the latter part of the hunt for Jack the Ripper. He later wrote seven important books of essays on true crime, including *Masters of Crime* (1928), a study of multiple murders.

JAN BONDESON is a senior lecturer at Cardiff University. His many critically acclaimed books include *Cabinet of Medical Curiosities*, *The London Monster* ('Gripping' *GUARDIAN*), the best-selling *Buried Alive: The Terrifying History of Our Most Primal Fear* ('A little masterpiece of social history' *MAIL ON SUNDAY*) and *Queen Victoria's Stalker* ('Amazing' *THE SUN*). His next book will be *Murder Houses of London*.

Coming Soon from Amberley Publishing

Jack the Ripper: The Definitive Casebook
Richard Whittington-Egan
978-1-4456-1768-8
£25

The case of Jack the Ripper and his savage serial killing and horrendous mutilation of five women in the East End of Victorian London is the greatest of all unsolved murder mysteries. For over 100 years the long line of candidates for the bloodstained laurels of Jack the Ripper has been paraded before us. Policemen and Ripperologists have tried in vain to put a name to the faceless silent killer.

Richard Whittington-Egan, one of the founding fathers of the search, published, in 1975, his *Casebook on Jack the Ripper*, now eagerly sought but long out of print and virtually unobtainable (except at mammoth prices), in which he documented the history, the crimes, the investigations and the investigators. He also included some fundamentally new discoveries and points, such as the real story of the kidney in Mr Lusk's renal post-bag, wrongly said to be that of Catherine Eddowes (Ripper Victim No. 4).

The endless nightmare of Jack the Ripper has rolled on, unstoppable, and now Richard Whittington-Egan, in a completely revised and very considerably enlarged edition of the 1975 *Casebook*, has taken a new look, from a longer perspective, at the theories and the personages who advanced them, from the time of the murders right up to the present day.

Praise for *Jack the Ripper: The Definitive Casebook*

Jack the Ripper: the Definitive Casebook is a masterly distillation of the facts and theories that have built up over the past half century. The public fascination with the Ripper shows no signs of abating and for anyone coming new to this subject or indeed, for the older Ripperologists who may have missed a theory or two, this book is an absolute must.'
Donald Rumbelow, author of *The Complete Jack the Ripper*

'In a field where there are many books constantly published this is a must-have and necessary volume ... This is not merely another Ripper volume – it is an investment for anyone with an interest, at whatever level, in the Whitechapel murders of 1888.'
Stewart P. Evans

Available soon from all good bookshops or to order direct
Please call **01453-847-800**
www.amberleybooks.com

Also available from Amberley Publishing

'One of the must-have Ripper books' *RIPPEROLOGIST*

The Man Who Hunted
Jack the Ripper

Nicholas Connell & Stewart P. Evans